OBSESSION

The murder of a child was news. It ran as the lead story at six o'clock. Dominique smiled, gratified.

She had ventured into new aesthetic territory. Death as theater. Murder as performance art. She was hungry for an audience.

The newscast cut to videotape. Detective Robert Card hurrying past the camera, caught in the glare of an arc light. Dominique leaned forward, studying his face.

This was the man who was hunting her. Her severest critic.

What would he do if he tracked her down? Would he shoot her? Put his gun to her head? In her mouth?

She hugged herself, twisting in her chair. A shudder moved through her and left her weak.

"Bang," Dominique whispered. "Bang. Bang. *Bang.*"

SHUDDER

SHUDDER

by

Brian Harper

A SIGNET BOOK

SIGNET
Published by the Penguin Group
Penguin Books USA Inc., 375 Hudson Street,
New York, New York 10014, U.S.A.
Penguin Books Ltd, 27 Wrights Lane,
London W8 5TZ, England
Penguin Books Australia Ltd, Ringwood,
Victoria, Australia
Penguin Books Canada Ltd, 10 Alcorn Avenue,
Toronto, Ontario, Canada M4V 3B2
Penguin Books (N.Z.) Ltd, 182–190 Wairau Road,
Auckland 10, New Zealand

Penguin Books Ltd, Registered Offices:
Harmondsworth, Middlesex, England

First published by Signet,
an imprint of Dutton Signet,
a division of Penguin Books USA Inc.

First Printing, January, 1994
10 9 8 7 6 5 4 3 2 1

PUBLISHER'S NOTE
This is a work of fiction. Names, characters, places, and incidents either
are the product of the author's imagination or are used fictitiously, and
any resemblance to actual persons, living or dead, events, or locales is
entirely coincidental.

Author's Note

I'd like to express my sincere gratitude and appreciation to everyone who helped me with this project, including:

Kevin Mulroy, whose sound editorial judgment was invaluable in shaping and developing the story;

Joe Pittman, who supervised the final stages of the book's editing and publication;

Jane Dystel, my agent, who looked after my interests and kept things running smoothly, as always;

and Spencer Marks of the Los Angeles Police Department, who reviewed sections of the manuscript and alerted me to errors, both large and small, in my depiction of police procedure. Of course, any remaining mistakes are solely my own.

Finally, special thanks to all my friends in L.A. for taking my mind off work from time to time; to my parents, for never failing to support and encourage me in my unorthodox vocation; and to the many readers whose purchases and, in some cases, word-of-mouth recommendations contributed to the success of my first novel, *Shiver*. I hope you like this one too.

—Brian Harper

1

Jamie Frisch was afraid of breaking his mother's back, so he kept his head down, carefully avoiding cracks in the sidewalk, as he walked home from school bouncing his blue rubber ball. The cracks probably held no danger, but you never knew. His mother already got back pains, sometimes so bad she had to lie down in the bedroom with the lights off and the door shut. Whenever he saw that closed door, Jamie thought guiltily of the miles of incautious steps behind him and resolved to do better.

The wide street was empty, the shouts from the schoolyard fading with distance. A whisper of wind teased the flower-whitened branches of the elm trees at the border of the park as he passed by. Houses with red-tile roofs and stucco walls lined the far side of the street, arched windows peeking out between palms and spiky yuccas. The April sky was washed clean with pale sunlight. His mother said the light in California was different from anywhere else. Jamie had never been anywhere else.

At the corner, near the entrance to the park, he stopped. He stared down at the sidewalk, looking not at a crack but at something infinitely more interesting.

A dinosaur.

It lay on the verge of the grass, a bright green *Tyrannosaurus rex,* ten inches long, with scarlet bands striping its humped and warty back. Yellow fangs like toothpicks studded a wide, grinning mouth.

"Cool," Jamie breathed.

He knelt and picked up the dinosaur, studying it intently. He wondered what little kid had left it here, and how anybody could have been careless enough to lose such a wonderful thing.

A car swished past, sun bursting on chrome and glass, a Mexican song wailing through the open windows. The music pained Jamie, reminding him of his father, who had filled the house with noisy *huapangos, rancheras,* and *corridos* until he moved down to San Diego last year. At Christmastime Jamie's grandfather had taken him to visit his dad, and the same records had been spinning on the turntable in a way that seemed vaguely disloyal.

Then the car and its music were gone, and in the contrasting silence Jamie became aware of a new sound, faint but insistent, coming from somewhere in the park. The sound of someone crying.

He tucked the dinosaur into the waistband of his pants, then stood up, listening.

At first he thought it was a kid who was crying, maybe the same kid who had lost the dinosaur. The idea of having to give back the toy disturbed him. He thought about running before the other kid saw him, but no; that wouldn't be honest.

Anyway, he had heard kids cry—in the playground, for instance, when they fell and skinned their knees—and this sound was different. This was a grown-up sound.

He was pretty sure it was a lady. Maybe she had fallen down and hurt herself, broken her leg, even. Or maybe she'd gotten her foot caught in a bear trap, or she was sinking in quicksand, or a tiger was about to eat her.

On TV, women were always in danger, and guys—like himself—would come to their rescue. Of course, TV was all bullshit. But even so, it would be neat to rush to an adult's aid and be a hero. He might even get to be on the news.

The trouble was, Jamie wasn't supposed to go in the park by himself. Children never played there alone. The park was small, with no sandlots and little open space; trees darkened its secret recesses. Sometimes bums lounged on the benches, though the police tried to keep them out.

His mom would be real ticked off at him if he went in there. But somebody ought to help that lady, who might be dying right now, for all he knew.

He looked up and down the street. No one was around.

Jamie hesitated, rocking slightly on his heels, then shrugged the strap of his book bag higher on his shoulder, wedged his blue ball under one arm, and entered the park. He ran lightly across the grass, following a trail of sobs like bread crumbs.

Rosebushes in red bloom brushed past him, stray thorns grabbing at his shirt sleeves. A squirrel skittered up a tree, frightened by his footfalls, and peered down from a high branch. The lid of a plastic container crunched like a shell under his sneakers.

The weeping was loud now, and close. It came from behind a green wall of hedges. Jamie crept up to a gap in the wall and looked through.

A fountain splashed there, an iron fish spitting a loop of water into a small circular pool littered with coins. Ringing the fountain were rusty benches backed by the tall green hedges that made this a private place. On one of the benches sat a woman, her legs folded under her, her face in her hands.

She didn't appear to be hurt, and, to Jamie's disappointment, there were no bear traps, tigers, or quicksand in evidence. But she was crying, all right. He watched as her shoulders jerked and her blond bangs swung. He had never seen an adult cry. The sight was fascinating and horrible. He wondered if his mom had cried like this after she and his dad had gotten divorced. If so, she had been quieter about it.

The woman slumped, groaning, and then as her head lolled in Jamie's direction, she saw him. He flinched and nearly ran.

"Hello," she said, her voice thick.

He guessed he had to answer. "Hi."

"What's your name?"

"Jamie Frisch."

"How old are you, Jamie?"

"Seven and a half."

"That's good. That's a good age to be."

"I'd like to be older."

"No, you shouldn't want that. As you get older,

you see more of the corruption in the world. Gradually it infects you. You lose your innocence."

"Did that happen to you?"

"It happens to all of us, Jamie. All of us."

"Is that why you're crying?"

"Yes."

Jamie frowned. He hadn't followed everything the lady had said, but he understood that she had been hurt somehow, after all, and he felt sorry for her.

"I wish you'd feel better," he said quietly. "I don't like to see you cry."

"That's sweet, Jamie. You're a good boy, aren't you?"

"I don't know."

"Of course you are. Your mother must be very proud of you."

"Yeah, I guess."

"Does she tell you how much she loves you? Does she hug you and call you her little man?"

"She does stuff like that, sure."

"And you love her too, don't you?"

"She's my mom."

"She bakes cookies in the afternoon, I'll bet. So you can smell them fresh out of the oven when you get home."

"No, she's at the office till five-thirty. She's an executive assistant."

"An executive assistant. I see. Mothers can't be just mothers anymore, can they?"

"What?"

"Nothing. I had a mother, too, you know."

"Everybody does."

"My mother never baked cookies for me either."

"You're old enough now to bake them yourself."

She laughed. Bleak, unhappy laughter. "That's true. I'm old enough to do lots of things by myself." She brushed a blond wisp from her face. "May I ask you a question?"

"Sure."

"Come here."

Jamie eased between the two hedges, then crossed the green spring carpet, grateful there were no cracks to worry about. He bounced the ball once, and it jumped back into his hand wet and sticky from the grass. The lady patted the bench with a white-gloved hand.

"Sit."

He sat, legs dangling, the ball in his lap. She smoothed his hair, and he squirmed, mildly embarrassed. When he looked up, he saw that her eyes were still damp, but her mouth was smiling. A nice smile made of clean white teeth and wide, thin lips. He thought she was younger than his mother, and probably prettier too.

"So what's the question?" he asked.

She turned her face from him, gazing at the water that leaped from the fish's mouth in a sparkling arc.

"Do you ever think about what it was like for you before you were born?"

"Huh?"

"You grew in your mother's tummy, you know."

"Yeah, my dad planted a seed there. I know about that stuff."

"A seed. That's right. That's how you started. And for nine months you were inside your mother, and she nourished you and kept you safe and warm. You were part of her. The two of you were like one person. Do you think about that, sometimes?"

"No," Jamie answered truthfully. It had never occurred to him to think about such weird stuff.

"Do you suppose you were happy that way? Inside her? Joined with her?"

"I don't know. I don't remember that far back."

"But you can imagine it. Wouldn't it be nice to be so close to your mother, with nothing between you and her, no barriers, no separateness?"

"Jeez, I don't *know*," he snapped, frightened by this strange talk, and then the lady was crying again, quietly this time, silent tears streaking her pretty face.

"All right," she whispered, "I was only asking. I wanted to know how you felt about it, that's all. Because it doesn't sound to me as if you're very close to your mother now—this executive assistant who *calls* herself your mother but never even bakes you any damn cookies—and I thought you might be a little sad about that. Sad and lonely. Like me."

Jamie looked at her, wariness and sympathy in conflict inside him. He wondered if this lady might be sort of crazy, like the women who pushed shopping carts along Ventura Boulevard and mumbled to themselves.

He wasn't sure. With those other women, it was easy to tell that their minds were all messed up; they tramped around in bedroom slippers and galoshes, stuffed their carts with yellow newspapers, slept on bus-stop benches. This lady was nicely dressed and polite and beautiful. She didn't match Jamie's idea of a crazy person at all, except for some of the things she said, which seemed pretty bizarre; but then, grown-ups were always saying stuff he didn't understand.

Caution receded as pity advanced. Hesitantly Jamie reached out and took the crying lady's hand. Her cotton glove was silky to his touch.

"I didn't mean to make you feel bad," he whispered. "I'm sorry."

"Oh, Jamie"—she sniffed wetly—"I'm sorry too."

Her fingers tightened on his. She pulled him close. Jamie saw pain in her eyes, and something more. Something like hunger.

"So very sorry," she breathed in a different voice, and then a cold wetness filled his world, and he thought of winter in the mountains, white snow bending the branches of fir trees, a crust of ice on the rain gutters, everything cold, so cold. His eyelids fluttered, then closed, and he was running, running through the deep drifted snow.

2

Arms laden with bulging grocery sacks, breath coming hard after a fast walk up the front steps, Laura Frisch fumbled her key into the keyhole and pushed open the front door. The living-room lights were on, activated at dusk by light-sensitive timers, but as she hustled the groceries into the kitchen she entered a corridor of darkness.

"Jamie?"

Sudden fear was jumping in her voice. The two brown bags thudded onto the kitchen table. She called her son's name again as she hurried through the house slapping wall switches. Batman frowned down at her from the wall of Jamie's room, his gaze accusatory.

The backyard smelled of star jasmine and emptiness. The garage, which had become a storage shed, was cluttered with the usual junk. Laura looked frantically for the basement door before remembering there was no basement. She kept repeating Jamie's name in a voice no longer audible.

The hand that gripped the plastic shell of the telephone receiver was shaking.

"Pam? Laura. Is Jamie there? I just got home from work, and . . . I see. Thanks."

He was not at the Gruders', or at the Neilmans', or at Lois Aguilar's.

She left the house without her coat, though the temperature had dropped with evening, and retraced the route Jamie must have taken after leaving school.

My fault, she thought as she first walked, then ran. My fault for letting him go home alone. Only two and a half blocks in daylight in a good neighborhood; I didn't think it was dangerous. Oh, God, Jamie.

She reached the school and circled it. A few older kids played basketball under a mercury-vapor lamp. She described her son and asked if they'd seen him. No. The basketball, bouncing brightly on the asphalt under one boy's lazy hand, made her think of Jamie's blue rubber ball.

She headed back to the house, forcing herself to go slowly, to peer down side streets and throw hoarse shouts at the night. There was no answer.

The park drew her into its shadows. Jamie might have stopped to play here, though he knew he shouldn't. She thought of the ragged derelicts who had been seen loitering among the roses and elms. Suppose one of them—

Don't think it.

Footfalls drummed the dirt path at her back. Raspy breathing chuffed closer. She spun, heart pounding, but it was only a jogger in gray sweats. He paused, running in place, while she asked the same senseless questions she'd tried at the school-yard, and got the same useless response.

Nobody had seen her son. He had dropped off the earth.

Dampness was soaking through her blouse when she returned home. The door was open, and for a wild moment of relief she was sure Jamie was inside; then she realized she'd forgotten to shut the door when she left.

The house felt cold and stuffy, a tomb. She tried to decide what to do. Call the police? She wasn't sure; on TV they always said you had to wait twenty-four hours. Call Ron? Yes, right; a lot of help he would be, in San Diego with his fiancée, drinking scotch and sodas at the marina and bitching about child support. Call the local hospitals, then. And ask—

She called. Asked. Nothing. No little boy matching Jamie's description. She didn't know whether or not to be relieved.

"Hello, Pam? Laura again. No, I still haven't found him, and I'm going out of my mind. Do you think we could get some of the neighbors together and go look for him? Look everywhere?"

Flashlights bobbing in the dark. Scuffing of shoes on sidewalks. Voices hushed in a way that made Laura think of funerals, and funerals were the one thing she didn't want to think about right now. Her heart was beating hard in her throat, and her body ached with what might have been a fever coming on.

They had been searching for nearly an hour, she and a dozen friends and vague acquaintances. At first the search had been more or less random, but then Tom Reynolds had taken charge, organizing the volunteers into two-person teams and assigning each team to a separate block. Tom was en-

joying himself, you could see that. He liked to read
military books.

Laura wanted to help out with the search, but
she was too frantic to be useful. Every few minutes
she found herself wondering if Jamie had come
home on his own; each time, the hope became a
certainty, and she raced for the house, heels clacking madly on the pavement, only to find the rooms
still empty, the lights burning in the windows like
beacons to a traveler whose arrival is long delayed.
Then, thinking that perhaps Jamie had been found
somewhere outside, she would hurry back to Tom
Reynolds for the latest report.

Shortly after seven-thirty Tom, looking more
worried than before, advised her to call the police.
Not long afterward a patrol car cruised by, a great
silver shark, beaming its spotlight into bushes and
alleys while the radio crackled like wet power
lines. The two officers assured Laura that, contrary
to the impression left by TV dramas, there was no
twenty-four-hour waiting period in a case like this.
Other units were already on their way; a command
post would be set up at her house; Jamie would be
found.

The park pulled Laura back again and again. The
park with its feathery shadows and chittering
leaves. Children could never resist a place of grass
and trees. She had told Jamie not to go in there,
she had *told* him, but what if he hadn't listened?

There was a man who rooted in trash Dumpsters
in the alley behind the building where Laura
worked. She had seen him up close once—his filthy
hands, his whiskered face, his filmy, staring eyes.
He wore a wool hat, and under it a skullcap of tin

foil. The crazy ones wore foil things like that to keep the alien mind-control rays from warping their brains; she had read about it in the paper. The mentally ill were everywhere today. Not all of them were harmless. And parks attracted them. Parks like this one.

"Any sign of him?" she asked Lois Aguilar and Paul Crowe as they hailed her from the darkness of the trees.

"Not yet," Lois said. She was kind to say it that way, as if finding Jamie were merely a matter of time.

"He'll turn up," Paul added.

Laura didn't answer. The two patrol officers had promised much the same thing. Such words came easily when the lost child wasn't your own.

She wandered along the perimeter of the park, eyes hot, vision blurring. Stupid thoughts occurred to her. It was late now, past eight o'clock; Jamie would be getting hungry. On her way home from work she'd picked up the fixings for chicken burritos, one of his favorites. She liked to cook for him. Cooking for Ron had been only a chore. Ron—God, she would have to call him, tell him. He would yell at her for not looking after Jamie, and she would scream a furious rebuttal. It would be ugly, and would get worse still when Ron was up here, waiting with her for—

"Laura!"

Lois Aguilar's voice, tinny and tremulous.

Laura ran. She stumbled through the park, her mind flashing on images of Jamie alive, Jamie dead, Jamie unconscious.

She found Paul standing near a fountain, Lois on

hands and knees shining her flashlight into a drift of shrubbery.

"What . . . what is it?" Gasping, shaking, stomach twisting. "Did you find him?"

Paul looked at her. His face, lit from below by the lantern in his hand, was eerie, corpselike, a detail out of a dream. A moth buzzed the lantern, its glittery body tracing curlicues against the darkness.

"No," he said gently. "But we did find this."

He extended a hand in unreal slow motion.

Laura stared at the hand and at the object it held, the small blue ball crusted with dirt.

"That's his." She reached for it, took it, clutched it. "That's his, he was here, he was in the park." Sobs were tearing at her voice. "Jamie? Jamie, are you hiding? Come out this minute! This isn't funny! *Jamie!*"

"Oh, Lord," Lois whispered, staring deeper into the shrubbery.

Laura dropped the ball and fell on her knees at Lois's side, wresting the flashlight from her hands. She beamed it into the leaves.

A blue mound. Jamie's book bag.

She hauled it out and spilled the books onto the grass, then opened them one at a time, aiming the flashlight at the name JAMIE FRISCH printed on the inside covers in large capitals. "Jamie Frisch," she said as she read each inscription. "Jamie Frisch. Jamie Frisch. Jamie Frisch."

Lois was patting her shoulder, and Paul was shouting for help. Laura paid no attention to any of it. She let go of the flashlight and ran her hands blindly over the smooth pages, then lifted the books to her face, smelling ink and glue. She was crying.

3

"This is a bad one."

Card nodded. He pressed the steering-wheel wand, squirting wiper fluid onto the windshield. The blades ticked briefly.

"Seven years old," Lindstrom said.

"Yes."

"Kid would be in, what, second grade?"

"First."

The catch in his voice made Lindstrom remember. "Shit, Bobby, I'm sorry."

She always called him Bobby. He didn't hate it as much as he once had.

"It's all right. Mike's safe at home. Anyway"— he tried to sound like a tough L.A. cop—"kids disappear every day."

"Great world, huh?" Lindstrom smiled. Laugh lines cut her cheeks. She was sexy when she looked like that. Card wondered if she knew it.

Probably not, he mused as he guided the unmarked Chevy Caprice down Burbank Boulevard in Woodland Hills. *Sexy* was not a word ordinarily applied to a woman like Ellen Lindstrom, an eighteen-year veteran of the LAPD, rumpled, fidgety, and frazzled, addicted to adrenaline and nico-

tine, her eyes socketed in dark rings, her skin too
pale, her nails ragged from nervous chewing. A
woman as tough and durable and abrasive as a
steel-wool scouring pad. Card could almost hear
the harsh bark of laughter from her mouth if he
were to suggest that she had an attractive smile.
He could hear her voice, froggy from too many cigarettes, chiding him for his bad joke: _Or your bad
taste, Bobby. Whichever it was._

Yet lately he had been noticing small things
about his partner: that smile; her restless, finely
shaped hands; the crinkles at the edges of her eyes;
the shifting color of those eyes, gray at certain
times, green at others; the brown waves of her hair,
threaded here and there with silver, a detail he
found unaccountably alluring.

Sexy. Yes, in her own way, she was. Or maybe
he was only feeling lonely. Three years was a long
time. He would be forty soon. Forty and a widower
with child.

Card shook off these thoughts and spun the
wheel. The Chevy hooked south onto a residential
side street. An elementary school swam past in a
mist of purple incandescence. He glimpsed a flicker
of lights behind a webwork of branches in a pocket
park, a strand of crime-scene ribbon strung between two trees.

Two blocks ahead, dome lights threw pulsing
stripes of red and blue on a Mediterranean-style
ranch house. The stucco walls had been recently
repainted in the sandstone hue made fashionable
by the Southwestern craze. Blue trim on the windows, ersatz Navajo art on the front door. Card
wondered how people could afford such indul-

gences when he had to dig deep for two tickets to
Disneyland.

A white van was parked in the driveway. Card
nodded at it as he pulled up to the curb behind
one of the patrol cars. "Scientific Investigation got
here fast."

"Hope they can do some good."

The spacious living room had become a command
post. An electronics technician was rigging one of
the telephones with a tape recorder in case a ransom demand was made. The phone rang constantly
as anxious friends called to ask if there was any
news; a tired patrol sergeant kept telling the callers to please hang up and leave the line clear.
Other uniforms drifted among the low-backed
chairs and floor-hugging sofas, trailing streams of
static from the radios clipped to their Sam
Brownes.

Lindstrom nudged Card. "Look who's here."

Card saw Captain Edward Jacobs, commanding
officer of the LAPD's West Valley Division, talking
with Martin Payton, the officer in charge of evidence collection for Scientific Investigation Division's Valley Section.

"What made him decide to crash this party?"
Lindstrom asked with a nod at Jacobs. It was unusual for a captain to show up at the scene before
any media had arrived.

Card shrugged. "Let's find out."

He and Lindstrom crossed the room. Payton,
Card noted, had been on the job tonight. Grass
stains smeared his pants; crumbs of dirt ringed his
shirt collar. Had he been looking in the yard? No,
the SID Valley Section van would not have been

left in the driveway if evidence techs were working anywhere on the property.

Then Card remembered the park down the street, the glimmer of light from within the trees, the yellow ribbon. That was where Payton and his team were working. The kid must have been nabbed there. In the park. Mike played in parks sometimes, but Consuelo watched him closely. At least Card hoped she did.

Jacobs noticed the two detectives and smiled, his mouth curving downward at the corners. "Looks like I beat you to it this time." He sounded pleased with himself, a state of mind that was not unusual for him.

"Looks like," Lindstrom agreed. "Pretty rare for you to make a house call. This kid the heir to a royal throne or something?"

"Not exactly, but you're on the right track. Seems his father, who lives down in San Diego, is a friend of Sam MacLean." MacLean was a member of the L.A. City Council. "Apparently the kid's mother called her ex to tell him the news, and about five minutes later MacLean gets a long-distance call from San Diego. The honorable councilman gets on the horn with the chief, who pulls me away from a TV dinner and the Dodgers game. And here I am."

He rocked on his heels, smiling faintly, as if wanting to be congratulated. It was Card's observation that rocking on one's heels was a mannerism typical of small men. Ed Jacobs, however, was not a small man; he stood six-two, three inches taller than Card himself, a tower of meat and muscle, beefy and thick-waisted. His broad flat face, startlingly handsome on television and slightly disappointing in real life, was framed by white hair swept back from his tanned, age-spotted forehead and deftly moussed into little hornlike projections over the ears. The effect was oddly reminiscent of Michelangelo's "Moses," but Card doubted that Jacobs knew it.

"GTE monitoring the calls?" Card asked.

Jacobs nodded. "Obtained a warrant in two minutes. The central office will trace every incoming call."

"The boy's parents here?"

"Only his mother. You'll need to talk to her. When you do, don't mention the fact that you're detailed to Homicide."

"Good point," Lindstrom said. Like many Homicide detectives, she and Card occasionally worked cases of other kinds: spousal battery, armed robbery, hate crimes. Their presence at the scene did not automatically mean murder, but a civilian wouldn't know that. "Is his mother the one who called it in?"

This time Payton answered. He spoke rapidly in a businesslike tone empty of emotion. Card thought of a corporate board member reading the minutes of the last meeting.

"Yes, but not right away. First she and the neighbors organized a search party. Couple minutes after the first black-and-white responded, one of the searchers found the boy's book bag and a rubber ball stashed under some ground cover in that park over on the next block." He paused to nudge his steel-rimmed glasses onto the bridge of his nose. "Definitely his stuff; he'd printed his name in his books. Dick-and-Jane stories. I didn't think they still published those."

Card knew they still published them. Sometimes, at night, he and Mike read from storybooks together. Dick and Jane, and the Grinch, and Horton the elephant. Mike would move his small index finger over the page, spelling out the words.

"And there was something else in those bushes," Payton added, "something I found. A dishcloth soaked with chloroform."

"Damn," Card said. His gut tightened.

"Whoever did this," Jacobs said, "planned it out nice and neat. Lured or coerced the kid into the park, then slapped that rag on his face. Hid the things we found, and took Jamie away."

"It was a mistake to leave the cloth behind," Lindstrom said. "An experienced kidnapper wouldn't let us have that kind of evidence."

"Maybe." Jacobs moved his big shoulders. "Or maybe not. The asshole might want us to know it's a snatch. To prepare the mother for a ransom call, if there is one. Or just to scare the bejeezus out of her."

"My guys are still crawling around in the bushes, bagging and tagging," Payton said, "but I don't hold out much hope of finding anything else that's useful. Whole crime scene is contaminated." His voice was bitter. "Those good-Samaritan neighbors went through there like a buffalo herd. Any evidence probably got stepped on at least twice." He snorted. "Bunch of amateurs."

Card doubted he would have been any more careful under the circumstances. "So where do we stand?"

"Knee-deep in shit," Jacobs answered. "But I guess you're looking for a more specific response."

"If possible."

"All right, here goes." Jacobs consulted his notes. "The kid's name is Jamie Frisch, seven years old, blond and brown, no distinguishing marks, three feet eleven inches, fifty-one pounds. There's one piece of luck: Jamie was printed in a child-safety program at school. We've got the fingerprint card and his dental charts. His mother provided a recent snapshot. This one."

Card looked at a boy with sandy hair and big ears and brown eyes. He was relieved to see that Jamie looked nothing like Mike.

"The mother is Laura Frisch, thirty-one, divorced. Her ex is Ron Frisch. An attorney. They split up a year ago, and he moved to San Diego and bought a boat. He's driving up here right now."

"Any chance the father snatched him?" Lindstrom asked.

"Always a chance. But Laura says there's never been any custody dispute. Frisch was confirmed in San Diego tonight; she reached him at his apartment there. So he would have needed an accomplice. And it seems to me that chloroform would be a damn funny way to grab your own kid."

"No witnesses?" Card asked.

"Not so far. A-cars and plainclothes officers are canvassing the neighborhood. We're hoping somebody saw a vehicle; not likely the guy would carry off an unconscious kid on foot. We've got bulletins going out on the Teletype and fax machines to every police department and sheriff's substation in the state. We gave out the story to TV; live-remote vans will be here any minute."

"Airports? Union Station?"

"Way ahead of you, Detective Card. Security guards at LAX and all other airports in the vicinity have been notified. Ditto the bus and train stations. And we've sent word to the hospitals and morgues."

"How about the Feds?" Lindstrom asked. "Why aren't they in on this?"

"No ransom demand yet. If there is one, the FBI will jump in with both feet. Otherwise they normally wait twenty-four hours before getting involved in a missing-person case. After that, they're entitled to presume Jamie may have been transported across state lines."

"They could be doing something, for Christ's sake," Lindstrom grumbled.

"Well," Payton said brusquely, a bureaucrat defending his faceless counterparts, "they did enter the kid's descriptors into the NCIC computer in Washington." NCIC was the National Crime Information Center, a vast federal data base.

Lindstrom was not appeased. "Hell of a lot of good that does us."

"What was a seven-year-old doing in the park by himself anyway?" Card asked. He would never let Mike wander off on his own.

"He's a latchkey kid," Jacobs said. "Walks home from school every day at three o'clock. Right past the park."

"Do we know for certain that Jamie left school at three today?" Lindstrom asked.

"Yes. His mother called some of the other parents and had them ask their children about it. All the kids said Jamie went home right after the last bell. He would have passed by the park at about five or ten minutes after three. Neighbors say the park is usually deserted on weekdays."

"Good place for a snatch," Payton said. "Nobody around, lots of bushes to provide cover, and a school nearby."

"Okay." Card snapped his notepad shut. "Where's Mrs. Frisch now?"

Jacobs cocked his thumb. "In the kitchen."

Payton leaned close, as if sharing a confidence. "She's in real bad shape. Sort of hysterical. You know how they get."

Card thought of Mike catching a football on Will Rogers Beach, then flinging it back in a ragged, dying arc, his laughter blending with the cries of sea birds.

"Yeah," Card said, the words acid in his mouth. "I guess I do."

4

Laura Frisch did not remind Card of Jessica, and that was good. She was tall and angular like a wire sculpture, melted by trauma into a shapeless heap in one of the kitchen chairs. She spoke of pain in the language of her body—white fingers squeezing the seat cushion, one knee drawn up in self-defense, bare toes curled. She had kicked off her shoes. That much was like Jessie. Card remembered their nights together in the house in Canoga Park, Jessie sitting on the floor and sinking her toes into the pile carpet. When he and Mike moved to the apartment in Studio City, Card had cut a square of that carpet, not knowing why he wanted it. Funny, the things that mattered.

"Mrs. Frisch, I'm Detective Robert Card. This is my partner, Detective Ellen Lindstrom."

Laura glanced at them, then let her head fall back as she expelled a ragged breath. "I didn't know they had women detectives. Except on TV."

Lindstrom smiled. "Life imitates art."

"Please be seated, won't you?" Mrs. Frisch was a good hostess. Even now, she saw to the comfort of her guests with reflexive courtesy.

Card and Lindstrom sat at the kitchen table, separated from Laura Frisch by two paper bags of groceries in a spreading pool of water. Something frozen had thawed and soaked through the bottom of one bag.

Automatically Card scanned the room. Spice rack. Microwave. Overhead fluorescents. His gaze came to rest on a litter of crayon drawings taped to the refrigerator door. Grass and sun and sky, green and orange and blue. A child's world. Did any adult see the world that way? The colors faded, the sky shrank. And there were shadows. You never saw shadows in kids' drawings.

He wondered if Jamie was learning about shadows right now, or if it was already too late for that.

"We know how difficult this is for you," Lindstrom said. "But we need to ask some more questions."

Card watched his partner lean forward in her chair, pad in hand, and he knew that she intended to handle the interview. That was fine with him. He was taking this one too personally. He needed to get a grip.

"There's nothing more I can tell you people," Laura said. "He's gone, someone took him, that's all I know."

"We just want to get a few things straight. Jamie goes to the school down the street?"

"Woodland Hills Elementary. Yes."

"And he walks home every day?"

"Yes. At three o'clock. Sometimes he stays a little later. Three-fifteen or three-thirty. He plays kickball with his friends in the playground. Or catch. Sometimes he plays catch."

"But not today?"

"No. Today he left at three."

"And every day he walks the same route? Past the park?"

"It's the most direct way."

"And he walks alone?"

"His other friends don't live right around here."

"I see."

Mrs. Frisch heard a judgment in those words. "I didn't think it was dangerous. Nobody did. It's only two blocks. Two and a half. This is a safe neighborhood. Never any trouble."

"This is one of the best neighborhoods in L.A.," Lindstrom said, her voice soothing.

"Yes."

"Lots of kids walk home from school alone."

"Sure."

"Anyway, you work all day, don't you?"

"Yes, I've had to, since the divorce. I get alimony and child support, but that's not nearly enough if I want to hold on to the house. Jamie loves this house, loves the backyard." A spurt of tears. "Oh, Christ."

"Please, Laura," Lindstrom said softly. "It'll be all right."

Card wondered what those words meant and why people said them. He had said the same thing to Jessie many times during the last weeks of her life, both of them knowing the promise was a lie.

"I'm sorry to be like this," Laura whispered. "It's just that I'm afraid." She looked first at Lindstrom, then at Card, and spread her hands. "He's my only child," she said as if an explanation were required. "And he's such a good boy. Polite and helpful around the house; well, he tries to help anyway.

And he's smart too. Good in school. Talented. He wrote a poem about the sky. The teacher said it was excellent. They were going to print it in the school newspaper. Do you think they'll print it now?"

Lindstrom reached across the table and took Laura's hand. "Of course they will."

"I want them to print it. Maybe if whoever's got him reads that poem and . . . and sees how special he is . . ."

She was crying again. Lindstrom looked helplessly at Card, and Card looked helplessly back. Even false words would be good to say now, but he could think of none. He just sat there while the two women held hands and somewhere a clock ticked. After a few minutes he excused himself and left the kitchen.

Card pushed his way through the milling crowd in the living room, out the front door, down the slate steps. The night air was cool on his face. He walked to the unmarked Chevrolet.

Inside the car he'd stashed a transportable cellular phone, the kind that could be plugged into a cigarette lighter or operated via battery pack. He gave the ignition key a quarter-turn to start the car battery, plugged in the phone jack, and extended the antenna. He used the memory feature to dial his own number.

"Consuelo? I'll be late tonight. Is Mike in bed yet? Okay, I guess he can stay up another fifteen minutes." Seven years old, and already a night owl. "What's he doing? No, I don't need to talk to him. Just tell me what's he's up to."

He closed his eyes and saw his son, snug in his

p.j.'s, curled in the easy chair petting Willy, his small fingers scratching the dachshund's tummy, while TV images danced like candle flames, the colors green and orange and blue, and bright, so bright. Card felt himself smiling.

"Good, Connie. That's fine. I just wanted to know."

He was walking back to the house when Jacobs signaled him from the doorway.

"Ransom call," he said tensely. "Or a crank."

Card's heart was pumping harder as the patrol sergeant handed him the living-room extension.

". . . is it you want?" Laura Frisch asked in the kitchen, panic chewing at her words.

A muffled voice, barely audible: "You'll know our demands in due time."

"Is Jamie all right? Please tell me."

"In due time," the voice repeated.

Click. Dial tone. Mrs. Frisch gasping into the mouthpiece: "Hello? Hello?"

Card handed back the phone.

"Sergeant Rand took the call," Jacobs said. "Identified himself as the answering service; that's the routine. When he tumbled to who was calling, he got Laura on the line. The son of a bitch talked for only about thirty seconds, didn't say a damn thing except that he had the boy and was taking care of him. He was in a sweat to hang up."

Card nodded. "Must have figured the call couldn't be traced if he kept it short."

"He watches too many old movies. These new phone company computers do an instantaneous trace."

"GTE got the phone number and address of the

calling party," reported the SID technician who'd hooked up the tape recorder. "Not a pay phone. Private residence."

Card looked at the scribbled address. "That's only a few blocks from here. Near Fallbrook and Burbank. Upscale area, single-family homes. Funny neighborhood for a kidnapper."

"Think it's for real?" Jacobs asked.

Card thought of the whispery voice, the melodramatic wording, the call so easily traced. "If it is, this guy's strictly amateur hour."

"Well, we're taking no chances. You and Lindstrom are going in with full backup and SWAT on standby, ready to roll if anything goes down."

"I'm guessing it's a stunt. Prank call. Some nut."

"Yeah," Jacobs said. "But is it *our* nut?"

5

The house was what Card had expected, another stucco Mediterranean. Lights burned in the front windows, washing the close-cropped lawn with a coppery sheen. He and Lindstrom sat in the unmarked car, the engine ticking as it cooled, while behind them three black-and-whites, headlights off and sirens silent, glided up to the curb.

"Think he's in there?" Lindstrom asked. "Jamie, I mean."

"No."

"Neither do I." She fingered the slight bulge under her jacket where a 9mm Beretta semiautomatic was snugged in an armpit holster. "But hell, what do we know?"

They got out of the car. Around them the six uniforms were taking their positions behind the parked cruisers. Moonlight glanced off the barrels of their own Berettas, cocked and locked, loaded with fifteen-round magazines. The LAPD had switched to semiautomatic pistols back in 1986, when it became clear that the drug trade and the gang wars had rendered six-shooters obsolete. Card, however, was stubbornly old-fashioned; the gun pancaked under his right arm was a K-frame Smith & Wesson .38.

He had his reasons for using it. Automatics had been known to jam; and anyway, he liked the stopping power of the .38 Special + P rounds the revolver packed. As insurance, he carried an ankle gun under his trouser leg, another Smith .38, the snub-nosed J-frame model. A sweet little gun, kept in excellent condition, the front sight filed down slightly to prevent it from snagging on the holster in a draw.

Ordinarily such matters were academic to him, as they were to most cops; in Card's eighteen years on the force, first in uniform, then in the detective division, he had seldom drawn a gun and never fired one except on the shooting range. Shoot-outs in the line of duty were rarer than people thought.

Tonight might be a different story, though—if Jamie Frisch was inside this house.

Card looked down the street and saw Jacobs's car parked well back from the others. The captain would observe what happened in the next few minutes, staying close to his radio, ready to call for additional backup or the SWAT team. The five SWAT commandos, Card knew, had already donned their hardshell armor and web gear and were standing by at Parker Center, the police headquarters downtown. One of the Bell Jet Rangers stationed on the rooftop helipad could chopper them here in eight minutes if a hostage situation developed.

Maybe none of that would be necessary. Maybe Jamie was miles from here, the call a sick joke. Card wasn't sure whether he hoped it turned out that way or not.

"Ready?" he asked Lindstrom.

"Shit, yes."

Squaring his shoulders, Card headed up the front walk, Lindstrom at his side. They made two sweet targets for anyone watching from the windows. Card was grateful for the heavy stiffness of the Kevlar vest. He and Lindstrom had both been outfitted with ballistic armor before leaving Laura Frisch's house. Still, a vest wouldn't offer much protection if the guy had Card's head in his sights.

Card tried not to think about that. His hand was nearly steady as he rang the bell.

It took a long moment for the door to open, and both he and Lindstrom tensed when it did. A man stood in the doorway, dressed in a cardigan and baggy pants. Plenty of room in either article of clothing to stash a gun.

He frowned at them. "May I help you?"

Card did not think his voice was the one on the phone.

"Mr. Sinclair?" Card asked. That name was listed for this address in the reverse directory.

"Yes."

"I'm Detective Robert Card, LAPD." He showed his badge. "This is my partner, Detective Lindstrom." Card's gaze was fixed on Sinclair's face, but his peripheral vision was alert for any hint of movement by the man's hands—the right hand resting on the doorknob, the left hanging, fingers splayed, at his side.

The hands did nothing. "This is about the Frisch boy, isn't it?" Sinclair asked.

Card blinked. "Yes."

"Awful thing. I don't know what I can tell you.

Karen spoke to Laura Frisch earlier. Maybe you should talk to her."

"Karen?"

"My wife."

"May we come in, Mr. Sinclair?" Lindstrom asked.

The living room was full of overstuffed armchairs and plush sofas and deep pile carpet. Card knew as soon as he entered it that this was a home, not a dungeon of horrors. The glance he traded with Lindstrom told him she knew it too. It was hardly even necessary to meet Karen Sinclair or hear her breathlessly genuine concern for little Jamie.

"Mrs. Frisch called you sometime tonight?" Lindstrom asked her.

"Yes, around eight-fifteen. After she found Jamie's things in the park. She wanted me to ask Kimberly if she'd seen Jamie leave school today, and if so, at what time."

"Kimberly is your daughter?"

"Yes, I'm sorry, I should have explained that. Anyway, Kimberly *did* see Jamie leave, and it was at three o'clock on the dot. She was sure of it. I think she was watching him go. She has sort of a crush on him. Lots of the girls in the first grade do. You should see them spin like little coquettes when he's around. Oh, my, I hope he's all right."

Card was fairly sure he knew who had made the call. A simple question would confirm it.

"Do you have any other children?"

"Yes, two boys."

"Older than Kimberly?"

"They're twelve and thirteen." A frown creased her forehead. "Why?"

"May we speak with them, please?"

After some consternation on the Sinclairs' part, and some calming words from Detective Lindstrom, Card found himself knocking on the closed door of an upstairs bedroom. He opened the door without waiting for an answer.

The wide, fearful eyes of the two boys inside were proof that they had overheard the conversation. That was good. It saved time.

"Not very funny, what you guys did," Card said quietly once the door was shut again. Lindstrom was silent, but Card could feel the heat of her gaze on the kids.

"We didn't do anything," one of them said.

"The call was traced to this house. And it was tape-recorded. Want us to generate a voice print of the tape and compare it with your own voice prints? They're like fingerprints; no two people's are identical. In this case, I'm willing to bet there'd be a match."

That shut them up.

While Lindstrom used her radio handset to tell the officers outside that it was a false alarm, Card sat on the bed and gave the kids a lecture. He told them how bad Mrs. Frisch was feeling, how scared she was for her little boy—as scared as their own mother would be if one of them was missing—and how the phantom phone call had only made things worse. The speech elicited two mumbled apologies that sounded sincere.

"Do we have to go to jail?" the younger boy asked.

Card did not smile. "No."

"You gonna tell our parents?" A greater fear, it seemed.

Card looked at Lindstrom. She shook her head.

"Not this time," Card said. "We'll say we just wanted to ask if you'd been near the park today. Routine questioning, that's all. But if you try a stunt like this again . . ."

"We won't."

"We promise."

Card believed them.

Going down the stairs, Lindstrom whispered in Card's ear: "You're good with kids. I envy you."

"Thanks. But so are you. Good with Mike, anyway."

"Not me. I'm a tough broad. I scare children. They think I'm the witch who tried to make muffins out of Hansel and Gretel."

"Mike doesn't think you're a witch. He likes you. He told Consuelo he hopes you and I get married."

"Did he? That's . . . that's cute."

A smile flickered at the corners of Lindstrom's mouth. A secret smile, which Card could not decipher.

He thought about that smile as he and Lindstrom drove back to the Frisch house. But he stopped thinking about it when he saw Jacobs talking with Laura Frisch in the front yard. The captain had obviously told her that the call was a prank, crushing her desperate hopes. Now Mrs. Frisch just stood there shaking her head in grief or helplessness or denial, while Jacobs said to her what Card had said to Jessie, what Lindstrom had said in the kitchen, what all human beings seem compelled to say at such moments—that there was no reason to be afraid, because everything, of course, would be all right.

6

The buzz of the alarm clock jerked Card out of sleep.

He swatted the clock into silence, then blinked at the digital display. Six A.M. Too early. He and Lindstrom didn't start work till nine. He must have set the alarm wrong.

Then he remembered Jamie Frisch.

He came awake instantly. Rose in one rapid motion. Stretched, feeling small pops in his shoulders. Ran the shower hot, stepped under the steaming spray. Dressed swiftly. Brown jacket and pants. Handcuffs in one pocket. Ankle gun strapped to his right leg with a Velcro fastener. Shoulder holster snug under his arm.

Consuelo was fixing breakfast when he entered the kitchen. Last night he had told her not to bother; no reason for her to get up so early; he could pour himself a bowl of cereal or grab a take-out sausage sandwich on the way to the station. She hadn't answered, had merely smiled as she padded off to the den, where a foldout bed and a Spanish-language Bible awaited her. She liked to read the Psalms at bedtime.

"Good morning, Mr. Card," she said, keeping her voice low so as not to wake Mike.

Card had fought and lost a long battle to persuade his housekeeper to address him by his first name. " 'Morning, Connie. Smells good."

"Pancakes."

"I'm supposed to be watching my weight."

She dismissed this statement with a laugh. Consuelo believed in eating well. Her own considerable girth proved it.

Card watched the swift darting movements of the spatula in her hand as she transferred the pancakes from the griddle to a plate. He was always mildly saddened by the sight of Consuelo making breakfast for him, though he would never have told her so. Jessica used to like fixing breakfast. She had been so inexplicably cheerful in the morning. She would hum to herself and tell silly jokes, and he, half awake, would respond grouchily, vaguely annoyed. Now he regretted not having shared in her happiness when he'd had the chance.

The pancakes were excellent, made not from a packaged mix but from scratch, and garnished with sliced strawberries. Consuelo treated him well. She had never forgotten the nights and weekends he'd spent tutoring her for the citizenship test. She had passed on her first attempt. He and Mike had attended the swearing-in ceremony, Mike still so small then, dressed in the tiny tweed suit that no longer fit but which Card couldn't bring himself to give up.

He remembered Consuelo's solemn expression as she stood to recite the oath, a stout middle-aged peasant woman in her best dress. From a slum village in southern Mexico to that moment in a judge's chambers—it must have been a long journey, and hard, pitilessly hard. Card had suffered through Jessie's death less than a year earlier, and as he listened to the judge recite the words, he had found himself thinking that his own journey had not been any easier.

He was finishing breakfast when Mike shuffled into the kitchen, sleepy-eyed, Willy in frantic pursuit. The dachshund's toenails clicked madly on the linoleum tiles.

"Hey, pal," Card said through a plume of steam from his coffee cup, "what are you doing up so early?"

"Heard you in here."

He climbed into a chair at the kitchen table. Consuelo poured him a glass of orange juice.

"You ought to go back to bed," Card said, ruffling his hair. The brown strands were spiked and corkscrewed.

"Nah, I'm awake."

He wasn't, though. Not really. He merely felt that he should see his father off to work. His loyalty touched Card in a tender place.

The two of them talked about school, which was going okay, and work, which was going okay too. Allergy season was here, and Mike, who reacted badly to ragweed pollen, was scheduled for a shot this afternoon. He tried, for the third time, to convince his father that the shot was really not necessary this year, but a series of wet sneezes undercut his argument.

Card brushed his teeth and gargled with mouthwash. The face in the bathroom mirror was unquestionably that of Michael Card's father; there had never been any doubt as to the boy's paternity.

Card saw the same short brown hair, the same vivid blue eyes, the same sharp nose and slightly too-prominent chin.

Mike will look like this when he's thirty-nine, he thought, then added: I'll be seventy-one then . . . if I'm still alive.

He wondered what the world would be like in three decades. Once, he would have visualized spaceships like ocean liners ferrying passengers to and from resort colonies on the moon. Now he imagined only a slow and uncontested decline. Rust and weeds in the smaller towns, frenzy and violence in the cities. The rough beast slouching towards Bethlehem—where had he read that? Some poem from his college days. He had not believed in the poet's dark vision then, but after Jessie's death and seventeen years as a cop, seventeen years that had bled the innocence out of him, he did not know what he believed anymore.

Yes, he did. Jamie Frisch was missing and had to be found. That was what he believed.

He gave Mike a hug at the doorway, told him to get some more sleep or he'd doze off in class, told him not to worry about the allergy shot, told him to be good and to look out for Consuelo.

"I will, Dad."

"I know you will. Thanks for getting up to have breakfast with me."

The memory of Mike in his arms lingered as he rode the elevator to the lobby. He wondered if Jamie had felt like that in his parents' embrace. Of course he had.

7

Card and Lindstrom had put in five hours of over-time on the Jamie Frisch case the night before, but even so, they were back in the same neighborhood at seven A.M. They rang doorbells and asked questions, interviewing many of the local residents for the second or third time, still hoping someone would remember seeing a suspicious individual or vehicle near the park yesterday afternoon. No one did.

In early afternoon they visited Jamie's school. The kids were panicky, the danger of abduction having been impressed on them by parents and teachers throughout the day. Several of them had seen Jamie leave school, bouncing his rubber ball. None knew more than that.

After leaving the school, Card and Lindstrom dropped by Laura Frisch's house. A day-watch patrol sergeant was taking occasional calls, mostly from psychics and private investigators angling for a piece of the action. Two patrol officers from the night tour and a pair of detectives from Juvenile Division were there on their own time, helping with household chores and mapping strategies. That was a nice gesture, the kind of thing that happened all the time but never made the papers.

Laura and her ex-husband Ron, who had arrived from San Diego shortly before midnight, wore the dazed faces of people who had not slept in too long. Both had spent the last eighteen hours doing everything possible to find their son.

They had phoned the Adam Walsh Child Resource Center in Fort Lauderdale and the National Center for Missing and Exploited Children in Washington, D.C. On the advice of both organizations, they had consented to countless interviews with TV, radio, and print reporters, and had printed thousands of posters featuring Jamie's photo, along with the phone number of the West Valley police station. The posters offered a $50,000 reward for information leading to Jamie's return. Friends, neighbors, and relatives were distributing the posters citywide. The publicity had generated dozens of alleged sightings of Jamie Frisch. Uniformed and plainclothes officers resolutely followed up on every plausible tip.

Nearly a hundred volunteers, prompted to action by the media reports, were searching every park, alley, vacant lot, construction site, and dead-end street within a five-mile radius. The searches had begun at daybreak and were expected to continue through the night, aided by flashlights and night-vision equipment supplied by the LAPD.

Unmarked police sedans were staking out Laura's house in the hope that the kidnapper would cruise past. Half a dozen slow-moving cars had already been stopped, but the drivers had no criminal records and were apparently just gawking.

The phone company was monitoring Laura's phone line at work and Ron's home and work phones in San Diego. No suspicious calls had been received.

The West Valley station house in Reseda had been visited by two individuals anxious to admit to the kidnapping. One was an elderly drunk, the other a bum who apparently wanted to take shelter in the county jail. Neither knew about the use of chloroform in the abduction; the discovery of the dishrag had been kept out of media reports.

So far the LAPD was handling the case without federal assistance. The FBI had stated that agents from its Los Angeles field office would enter the investigation at three P.M., twenty-four hours after Jamie's disappearance, or sooner in the event of a ransom demand.

Card and Lindstrom spoke with Mr. and Mrs. Frisch for a while, filling in a few details and providing whatever comfort was possible. Ron Frisch was wired, his lean aerobicized body trembling with a restless need for action, but Laura looked half dead, her eyes bruised with dark circles, her lips bloodless and cracked. She had brushed her hair and put on fresh clothes for the cameras, but she had not showered or washed her hands; the pads of her fingers were still smudged with ink from the fingerprinting Payton had done last night. Card recalled her asking "Am I a suspect?" in a voice thin with hysteria, and Payton's reassurances that he needed her prints only to distinguish them from others that might be found on Jamie's belongings.

The thought of Payton prompted Card to call the crime lab at Parker Center. The day-watch commander informed him that the SID team had recovered a variety of items from the park—the heel of a shoe, a rain-swollen magazine, a condom in a sealed packet, other trash—but nothing that could be linked to Jamie's disappearance. The ball and the tote bag bore Laura's and Jamie's prints, as well as a few partials left by smooth gloves. That was all.

"So what do you think?" Lindstrom asked Card when they were back in the unmarked car.

His fingers drummed the steering wheel. "Not a custody dispute," he said quietly. A glance at Ron Frisch's face had ruled out that faint possibility.

"No." Lindstrom chomped hard on a wad of Nicorette. She was trying to kick the cancer-stick habit. Again.

"No shakedown for ransom so far."

"Uh-uh."

"No known vendettas against the family."

Lindstrom grunted. "No motive. That's what you're saying."

"There's always a motive."

"But this is the kind we don't want to think about."

Card didn't answer right away. He looked sideways at his partner. "You're not supposed to chew that stuff, you know."

"Huh?"

"Nicorette. You're supposed to just let it dissolve in your mouth."

"I'm nervous. When I'm nervous, I chew."

"Does it help?"

"A little."

"Got any extra?"

"Yeah, Bobby, I got extra."

She handed him a piece. Card tried it. Working his jaws was better than grinding them.

"You're right," he said. "It does help."

"That gum's expensive. You owe me."

"I'll remember."

They ran out of words then, so they just sat and chewed and thought about Jamie Frisch.

8

The bike path that ran along the bank of the Los Angeles River was not meant for pedestrians, as stern signs pointed out. Howard Kellogg, a law-abiding citizen, kept off the path as best he could, walking instead on the uneven ground beside it. Occasional bicyclists rushed past, their T-shirts beating against their bodies like windblown sails, sunglasses flashing in the glow of twilight.

Kellogg smiled. He loved this time of the day more than any other. Nearly every evening, after leaving work at five-thirty or six, he drove to the park and walked along the river and smiled up at the big golden sky. He found such walks to be the perfect recipe for relaxation after a day spent inside the four walls of his real-estate office in Encino.

Most locals thought of the L.A. River only as a concrete arroyo, bare and unlovely, a crude slash in the naked earth. It had been dug by man and banked in concrete, created as one link in the chain of waterways and aqueducts, dams and reservoirs, that irrigated the city of Los Angeles with water bought or swindled from other parts of the state, or from other states entirely. In the summer, the

river was empty of water for most of its length—
dry and white as a bone.

But the area near Sepulveda Dam was different.
Here the water was reassuringly deep all year long,
and as a result, huge drifts of vegetation had grown
up on the riverbanks, ferns and cypress and im-
mense growths of weeds that marched down into
the muddy water itself. The plants were mirrored
in the water, their reflection shimmering with
small circles made by the tiny fish that surfaced
intermittently for some purpose Kellogg could not
guess.

The spot was so pleasant that a park had grown
up around it, the Sepulveda Dam Recreation Area,
acres of flat green land ringed by distant mountains. Kids played soccer and softball, joggers
chuffed and dogs strained on taut leashes, people
bought hot dogs and sodas at refreshment stands.
The park was an anomaly in the Valley, where hectic development had sown tract housing and strip
malls and little else. Kellogg supposed he couldn't
complain about that. He was in real estate, after
all. But he was glad to have a place like this, where
he could see no houses, no shopping centers—a
place where he could catch his breath.

He walked slowly along the side of the bike path,
past the wire-mesh fence screening the river. A
group of bicyclists raced by with a whir of tires
and a clatter of changing gears. A few yards away,
the river and the path passed under a bridge; overhead, rush-hour traffic on Balboa Boulevard
hummed and roared, the busy sounds of people
hurrying to get someplace.

Kellogg reached the bridge and paused, enjoying

the shade and the stillness. Through the wire mesh
he studied the gentle ripples of the water. The
bridge was supported by rows of cement pylons
mounted on horizontal blocks; they made an interesting pattern to the eye, like rows of Doric columns. He wondered if some future archaeologist,
coming upon the ruins of this bridge and this cement river, would ponder the mystery of the people who had made it—people who, like the
Romans, had built aqueducts and roads, casting
nets of stone over their cities.

He was still considering that question when he
noticed something bobbing against one of the
pylons.

At first he thought it was only a cast-off shirt—
a blue-and-white-striped shirt, soggy and limp.
Then, looking closer, he made out a pair of pants
and sneakers at one end of the shirt and, at the
other, a small blondish head.

"Oh," Kellogg said, the word registering no more
than mild surprise.

He stared at the child in the water. The dead
child. Well, of course it was dead. The body was
floating facedown—no, not floating, exactly—the
slow current had nudged it partway up onto one of
the cement blocks that supported the pylons, like
a bit of driftwood urged by the tide onto a beach.
There was no sign of struggling, no hint of life.

Kellogg threaded his fingers through the mesh-
work of the fence. He gripped the wire and heard
the fence shiver in his grasp.

How long had the body been here? Why hadn't
anyone seen it? But of course no one would see it.
He was the only one who walked here. The racing

bicyclists would not notice such a small thing, half hidden in the shadows under the bridge. The body might have been here for hours, even for days.

Was it a boy or girl? He couldn't tell. Must have drowned. Fallen into the water somehow—off the bridge, maybe—kids were always playing where they weren't supposed to . . .

No. Wrong. The child had not fallen in. Had not died by accident at all. Not when its small pale wrists were lashed together behind its back with what looked like white rope or string. Not when its head was wrapped in sheer plastic, soggy and crinkled, like leftovers in cellophane.

Kellogg drew a deep breath, then regretted it. He had caught a bad smell, the smell of foul water and decay.

The fish got to it, he thought. The fish—the ones who make the ripples—they've been feeding. . . .

His stomach clenched. He turned away, feeling ill, then regained his composure. He considered what to do. A phone. He needed a phone. There must be one somewhere in the parking lot. He would go there, call 911, tell them what he'd found. Fine. Do that.

Kellogg walked slowly away from the child, refusing to run, to let panic seize him. He knew that his evening visits to the park were over. He could not return to this place; he could not look at the river again.

9

The sun was gone, the bruised sky fading to black, when Card and Lindstrom arrived at the Sepulveda Dam Recreation Area.

LAPD cruisers clogged the parking lot. Card saw no live-remote vans; the TV people had not yet made an appearance. Good. Ron and Laura Frisch shouldn't have to hear about this on the news.

Detective Roger Adams, commanding officer of the West Valley Detective Division, was waiting for them near his car, a cigarette glowing like a leisurely firefly as it made the circuit from his hand to his mouth. He was a small, neat man, a shade too pretty for a law officer, but with a certain squinty toughness around the eyes.

"I guess you know the basics," Adams said as he led Card and Lindstrom away from the parking lot, shining a flashlight to guide their footsteps. "Guy named Kellogg was taking a stroll here at about six-thirty when he found the kid in the water under the bridge. An A-car showed up ninety seconds after Kellogg's phone call; pretty good response time, wouldn't you say? The patrol cops got close enough to determine that the child was deceased and that it was a little boy."

"Jamie?" Lindstrom asked.

"Can't tell. Body is facedown, and we haven't moved it. Also, there's some plastic covering the victim's head, making identification that much more difficult."

"Plastic," Card whispered as his heart chilled. "God Almighty."

He and Lindstrom followed Adams along a bike path to a gap in the wire-mesh fence, then blundered down the steep embankment to the river's edge. They hurried toward the bridge.

"Is SID here yet?" Lindstrom asked.

"Got here two minutes before you did. Payton's in charge, just like last time."

The three of them passed under the bridge into the glare of battery-powered lanterns. The crime-scene photographer was snapping flash pictures. Martin Payton, tugging on cotton gloves, nodded a brief hello to Card and Lindstrom, then got to work. Adams stood with them, watching from a distance, as Payton stepped gingerly onto the cement block where the body had washed up. The technician knelt and gently placed plastic bags over the small bound hands, then secured the bags with wire tabs. After that, he measured the body with tape. He nodded slowly.

"Forty-seven inches," Payton said without looking up. He continued his work. The only sounds were the dull slapping of water on cement and the rumble of traffic overhead.

Lindstrom turned to Card. "The right height," she said quietly.

"Outfit's right too." Card sighed. "White Keds.

White tube socks. Beltless blue denim pants with elastic waistband. Blue-and-white-striped T-shirt."

"The hair looks blond from here. How did Jamie's mother describe his hair? Sandy blond?"

"Sandy, uh-huh. That was what she said."

"It's him, Bobby."

"I know."

"Somebody snatched him, tied him up, put a bag over his head."

"Yes."

"Asphyxiated the goddamn kid. Oh, Jesus, that's a bad way to die."

"Maybe he was still unconscious from the chloroform," Adams said.

"Then why the ligatures on the wrists?" Lindstrom asked.

Adams pursed his lips. "Could have been a precaution. In case he came to at the last minute or went into spasms."

Card looked away. "You don't believe that."

"No." The other man drew a quick shaky breath. "I guess I don't."

"It happened the way we said," Lindstrom whispered. "The guy did it while Jamie was alert. Clear plastic bag, you notice that?"

Card nodded. "So the motherfucker could see his face, watch him die."

"I've seen some nasty ones. But not like this. He's so . . . so *little*." Lindstrom's voice was steady, but her left eyelid was fluttering.

Finished, Payton got up, stepped back onto the gravel at the edge of the river, and joined the others. "Horrible," he said softly. His usual business-like air had evaporated.

None of them said anything for a moment. They stood in uneasy silence, awed by the enormity of the evil before them.

"Indications of a struggle?" Card asked finally.

"Cadaveric spasms in the hands. And one sneaker is partially off, the laces loose. Could have been worked free in the water, but I think he was kicking." Some of Payton's professional assurance returned as he spoke.

"What's binding his wrists anyway?" Adams asked. "Rope? Twine?"

"Braided nylon cord, an eighth of an inch in diameter, used for hanging draperies and indoor clotheslines. Standard overhand knot, good and strong, but not fancy. There's more cord around his neck, knotted the same way, to hold the bag in place."

Card looked at his feet. "Poor little guy." He felt sick.

"Whoever did this . . ." Adams's words started off bravely, then trailed away. "I don't know what I want to say."

Lindstrom touched Card's arm. "Let's take a closer look."

The two of them walked to the water's edge, then stepped onto the cement island. The boy still lay facedown, his position unaltered by the evidence technician's work. Card crouched down and shone his flashlight at the face in the water. Dimly he made out one eye, opened wide, glazed with death. Blue lips parted, swollen tongue protruding.

For a bad moment it was Mike's face. Card blinked back the vivid image. He concentrated on what was there, what was real. Jamie, not Mike. Jamie.

"You okay, Bobby?" Lindstrom whispered.

"I'm fine." He tried to find something to talk about. "Look at his neck. I can see a deep ligature mark on the nape, below the hairline."

"Killer tied it tight."

"Maybe Jamie strangled instead of suffocating."

"Postmortem will tell us that. At least I hope it will."

They studied the body a little longer without touching it, then returned to the spot where Adams and Payton were standing.

"He was snatched in Woodland Hills," Lindstrom said thoughtfully. "Could have been dumped anywhere along the length of the river channel. Anyplace that's deserted at night."

"Maybe right here," Payton said. "Asshole could have dropped the body off the bridge."

Adams shook his head. "Doubtful. Too much traffic. Even in the middle of the night, cars would be passing by."

"And a fall from that height probably would have ripped the bag free," Lindstrom added.

"Do you suppose the guy knew the current would carry the body here?" Card asked softly. "Once it washed up, someone was bound to find it."

Adams shrugged. "I don't know if that was even a consideration. The killer could have kept the body submerged indefinitely by tying on weights, if he'd wanted to."

"Maybe he did," Lindstrom said, "and the weights didn't hold."

"Or maybe," Adams returned, "he just doesn't give a damn if it's found."

Card sighed. "Well, when we catch him, we'll ask."

The coroner's investigator showed up not long

afterward. While he did his job, Card and Lindstrom interviewed the two patrol cops who had been first on the scene.

"Where's this man Kellogg?" Card asked.

"At the station. Giving a statement."

"He'll need an alibi for yesterday afternoon."

"He's got one," Adams said from a few yards away. "Worked in his real-estate office in Encino till six o'clock. Witnesses can verify."

Lindstrom spread her hands. "It would have been too easy."

A few minutes later the examination of the body was finished.

"Cause of death, asphyxiation," the pathologist reported. He was a big-shouldered, heavyset man who looked more like a cop than most cops. Vince Neal was his name. "Faint petechial hemorrhages. Cyanosis clearly evident. Strangulation is an outside possibility, with the plastic bag just a gimmick to throw us off. If the hyoid bone or the cricoid cartilages are fractured, we'll know it's a strangle, but for now I'm guessing it played out just the way it looks."

"Lividity patterns?" Card asked.

"Nothing clear-cut. He was probably tossed in the water soon after death, and then the current would have pushed him around for a while before washing him up. That didn't happen too long ago; I found maggot eggs on him that haven't hatched yet. In an environment like this, those eggs would have been deposited immediately, and it takes them less than twenty-four hours to mature."

"Defense cuts? Anything to indicate a struggle before he was bound?"

"Nothing I could see. But, you know, the hands and the other exposed parts of the body are in bad shape. It'll complicate the autopsy."

"Can you estimate how long he's been dead?"

"Well, assuming we know when he ate his last meal, we can make a decent guess after we've opened his stomach. The body's ice-cold, and rigor has already passed; there's plenty of give to the eyeballs. It's definitely been more than twenty-four hours."

"He could have been killed right after he was taken," Lindstrom said.

"I hope so," Card answered. "At least then it would have been quick."

The morgue wagon arrived. Neal and the driver wrapped Jamie's small body in plastic, bundled it into brown sheets, and strapped it to a gurney. Somewhere a cicada conversed irritably with the night, then fell silent.

As the driver wheeled the gurney toward the parking lot, Card asked Neal another question. "We've got his fingerprint card and dental charts. Do you think his fingers are too badly damaged to be printed?"

"Always tricky with a floater. But I think Prints can get enough points to do a comparison."

"We'll have them do it fast," Card told Lindstrom. "There shouldn't be any need for the parents to make a visual identification."

She nodded. "Right."

"Once SID gets the results, they can call Laura Frisch's house."

"You going over there now?" Neal asked.

"Yes."

Lindstrom hugged herself as she and Card

walked away from the river. "We'll get him, Bobby. The man who did this."

"The man," Card said quietly. He turned to her. "What makes us so certain it was a man?"

"Any reason to think it wasn't?"

"No. Except . . . a kid might be more likely to be lured into a park by a woman. A female stranger would be less threatening to him."

Lindstrom frowned. "Maybe. But a violent snuff job like this—hard to figure a woman doing it. I mean, the percentages argue for a male suspect in any brutal homicide."

"Can't always trust the percentages."

"What else do we have to go by?"

Card nodded, conceding the point. "Nothing," he said softly. "Nothing at all. No leads, no physical evidence, no eyewitnesses, no apparent motive."

"We'll break the case anyway. Somehow."

"Sure we will."

"You don't sound like you believe it."

He didn't believe it, but he knew that his partner wanted—needed—reassurance. He took her arm in a good firm grip.

"I'm just tired, that's all," he lied. "We'll hunt down this miserable sack of shit and put him out of business. Unless he's been kind enough to do our job for us. It's possible, you know. He might have killed himself already. Hell, he could be the next one to wash up in the river."

Lindstrom studied his face. Slowly she smiled.

"Nice try, Bobby. But I stopped believing in Santa Claus a long time ago." Then her smile died as she added, "I wonder if Jamie ever did."

10

Two men were talking with Ron and Laura Frisch when Card and Lindstrom arrived at the house. Both wore conservative brown suits carefully tailored to conceal speedloaders and underarm holsters.

"Haskell, FBI," one of them said with a firm handshake.

His partner repeated the gesture. "Dan Robertson."

The twenty-four-hour deadline had passed, and the Feds were finally on the case. But much too late.

Card and Lindstrom introduced themselves, then sat opposite the sofa where Mr. and Mrs. Frisch were huddled.

"I'm afraid we've got some bad news," Card said quietly.

A low quavering moan escaped Laura's pursed lips.

"How bad?" Ron asked in a voice like paste.

Lindstrom cleared her throat. "Someone found a little boy's remains in the L.A. River."

"Jamie?" Laura whispered.

"We're not sure. The body has to be finger-printed. Then we'll know."

"Did you see the body?" Ron asked. His hands flexed in his lap.

"Yes," Card said. "We just came from the scene."

"Well, then you must have been able to tell. I mean, you've seen Jamie's photo, and you've seen the boy in the river—"

"It looked like him." Card spoke slowly, evenly. "And the clothes match. But until the results of the fingerprinting come in, we won't know with absolute certainty."

"Oh, no," Laura muttered. "No, it can't be. It's got to be some other boy. Jamie—he was kidnapped—kidnappers ask for ransom, don't they? They don't just kill somebody for no reason. They call you up and tell you they want money. That's why the phones were tapped, isn't it? Isn't it?"

She was glancing wildly from the FBI men to Card and Lindstrom, then to the patrol sergeant waiting by the silent telephone, her eyes pleading for reassurance.

"Take it easy, Laura," Ron said, patting her hand.

"They've got to ask for money! It doesn't make sense if they don't. Doesn't make sense . . ."

She gripped her face with both hands, the fingertips squeezed white against her temples and jaw. She rocked on the sofa, moaning.

Ron looked at Agent Haskell. "In the medicine cabinet—sleeping pills—prescription stuff."

Haskell nodded. "I'll get it."

Card poured a glass of water in the kitchen. He returned to the living room just as Haskell brought in a small white-labeled jar. Ron Frisch spun the cap off the jar and shook two pills into his palm. He fed them to Laura, then handed her the glass. She drank clumsily, spilling water down her blouse, and coughed.

"What do we do now?" Ron asked Card.

"Wait for the phone call."

Ron swallowed the rest of the water in the glass. "Think they'll call soon?"

"They should."

"How long?"

"An hour, maybe. They're giving this case top priority."

They all sat waiting. Lindstrom chewed her nicotine gum. Card watched the dark sky out the window. The two FBI agents talked quietly, their voices whisper-soft. Ron Frisch bit his knuckles. Laura fought back tears. The patrol sergeant got up once in a while, balanced briefly on the balls of his feet to improve the circulation in his legs, and sat down again.

The phone rang. The sergeant answered, still using the answering-service ruse. A buzz of words on the other end of the line. "No, they aren't," the sergeant snapped, "and stop calling this goddamn number!" He hung up and glanced at the others. "One of those private dicks again, hustling work. Christ, I hate them."

Silence stretched, taut as rope. Card thought about Mike, how his visit to the allergist might have gone, what he'd had for dinner, whether he'd brushed his teeth at bedtime. He tried to picture Mike rolling on the carpet with Willy, the dachshund bicycling his stubby legs and Mike giggling and calling him "Silly-Willy," but he couldn't quite see it; freeze-frame images of the boy in the water kept flashing before his imagination's eye like flashcube bursts. He remembered Lindstrom's voice: "He's so . . . so *little*." As little as Mike was, he thought; as small and helpless.

The sudden shrilling of the phone stabbed him like an ice pick. The sergeant picked up the handset halfway through the first ring.

"Hello. You've reached the answering service of Mrs. Laura Frisch—oh. Yeah, they're here." He looked at Card and Lindstrom. "SID."

Card took it. "This is Detective Card."

"We printed the boy." Card recognized the voice: the crime lab's night-watch commander. "Farris from Prints compared points with Jamie Frisch's fingerprint card. It's a match."

"You're sure?"

"No doubt about it. We also checked the deceased's dental work against the Frisch boy's charts. Again, a match. It's Jamie, all right."

"I see."

Card cradled the phone. He took his time turning to face Mr. and Mrs. Frisch.

"I'm sorry," he said softly.

Laura screamed.

It was a high warbling scream torn out of her throat as she half rose from the sofa, hands clawing air. Ron tried automatically to restrain her, and then the meaning of Card's words struck him like a fist, and he twisted away from his ex-wife and hammered at the arm of the sofa, saying the word "No" again and again in a strangled voice. Laura fell back on the couch, then began to rise a second time. Haskell and Robertson held her down, their strong hands gentle on her shoulders, their faces averted from her flailing blows.

"Let go of me!" she shrieked. *"I have to see Jamie, have to see him!"*

"Please, Laura, calm down, now, calm down—"

"Baby, I'm coming, *Mommy's coming!*"

Ron Frisch was on his feet, breaking things. He kicked over an end table, hurled a metal wastebasket at the fireplace, wiped a row of knickknacks off the mantle with a sweep of his hand. Then the patrol sergeant was all over him, and Card came up fast to help.

"Motherfuckers killed my son," Ron raged, his face blood-mottled, nostrils flaring. "Fucking cocksucking sons of bitches *killed my little boy!*"

Lindstrom was talking to Laura, trying to be heard over the screams—"You can't help him this way, please, Laura, you'll only hurt yourself!"— and Laura was wild on the couch, thrashing and writhing, a blur of stabbing fingers and flying hair.

The phone rang again.

Everyone froze, listening.

"They made a mistake," Ron croaked. "They're calling back to say they made a mistake."

"Answer it, *answer it!*" Laura was sobbing.

Lindstrom snatched the phone. "Hello? . . . No, god-fucking-dammit, they don't need a fucking private eye!"

The handset slammed down like a gunshot.

Silence. Stillness.

Laura wept into her hands.

Ron found a chair and sat down slowly.

Card drew a deep breath. Sweat pasted his shirt to his chest. He ran a shaky hand through his hair.

"We'll stay with them," Haskell said softly.

Robertson nodded. "All night."

Card looked from one to the other. Tough Feds. Two of Quantico's best; had to be, or they wouldn't have rated assignments to the L.A. office. Men trained to take on drug lords and serial killers.

Tears sparkled in their eyes.

"You have kids?" Card asked them.

"I do," Robertson said. "Little girl. She's four."

"Me, I'm a bachelor," Haskell said. "I like kids, though. This one—we saw the pictures—he was a cute little guy." His voice snagged on the words.

"Yeah," Card said. Some species of emotion, he couldn't tell if it was grief or fury, rose in him like a cresting wave; he swallowed it down. "We'll leave you two to handle it, then."

Lindstrom stood glaring at the phone. Card had the feeling that if it rang once more, she would whip out her gun and shoot it.

He touched the sleeve of her jacket. "Let's go."

"I want to stay with them."

"Bad idea. We've been on the job since seven A.M. And the, uh"—he lowered his voice—"the autopsy is tomorrow, early. We need to be fresh."

She nodded. She let him steer her to the door.

"I'm going to start smoking again," she said abruptly.

"Why?"

"Because this fucking gum tastes like shit."

"Everything tastes that way right now."

Neither Ron nor Laura looked up as they left.

11

At eleven o'clock, at the end of a sixteen-hour day, Card pulled into the parking lot behind the West Valley station house. He and Lindstrom went upstairs to drop off their keys, then emerged into the cool night again. They crossed the lot to the rear section where their own cars were parked.

Lindstrom stopped by her Mazda. Card looked at her. In the wan light of the mercury-vapor lamp overhead, her face looked sallow and unhealthy, older than forty-one.

"I hate this job," he said.

Abruptly she smiled, and the sexy laugh lines were back, teasing him. "You'd have to be crazy not to hate it sometimes."

"You'd have to be crazy to do it at all." Card heard self-pity in the joke. He switched subjects. "What do you suppose his motive was?"

Lindstrom sighed. "Does it matter?"

Card thought it did. "I say it's something sexual. He gets his kicks offing little boys. A pervert."

Lindstrom studied her hands.

"Sometimes," Card said softly, "I wish we weren't so damn tolerant in California. I wish we'd be a little more redneck. Maybe they all wouldn't migrate here—"

"Who?"

"The creeps. The weirdos. The leather punks and their boyfriends wearing dog dollars, and the dykes with their shaved skulls and their swastika earrings. Goddamn, I wish they would go somewhere else."

"We don't know he was one of them. The man who did this."

"He was."

"We don't *know*." Lindstrom sniffed. "Sorry. But I don't like to hear you talking like the fundamentalist preachers on the Orange County channels. 'Lord, save us from the Communists and the homosexuals,' all that tripe."

Card fingered his car keys. "It's late, that's all. I don't mean it."

But he did. They both knew that. It had been different before he had Mike to worry about. He could afford to be a good liberal then. Now he saw things like the ligature marks and scavenger bites scarring Jamie Frisch, and he thought of Mike in the tub all soapy and shiny, his skin smooth and pink. Fear made him intolerant, made him want to lash out in defense of his son. Ellen was different. She could take care of herself, and she had no one else to fear for.

"Don't let it get to you," she told him. Her hand brushed his shoulder. "Too much."

"You too."

"Oh, nothing ever gets to me. I'm a tough bitch. 'Night."

She climbed behind the wheel of the Mazda and tipped him a wave. He walked to his own car, a gray Mercury Sable with sixty thousand miles on the odometer and a dent in the side, and got in. He put the cellular phone and battery pack in the backseat.

As he turned the key in the ignition, he thought about what Lindstrom had said. A tough bitch—the words had been a joke, yet there was a core of truth in them. She was tough. Tougher than he was, in many ways. It was a source of amusement to them both that she invariably took the villain's role in the good cop–bad cop routine.

Card drove home, remembering the touch of Ellen Lindstrom's hand on his shoulder, wondering what she would feel like in the dark. She was two years older than he, her looks going, her face showing lines and puffiness. She lived on adrenaline and caffeine, chomping Nicorette and swilling coffee, constantly wired. But they had been partners for three years, and he thought they understood each other. And she was good with Mike.

That smile too. Hell of a sexy smile.

Consuelo greeted him in the foyer. They spoke in whispers, a precaution that was hardly necessary; Mike was a sound sleeper. Card shrugged off his coat and asked Connie to microwave something edible. He heard her fussing in the kitchen, going to more trouble than she should, as he eased open the door of his son's bedroom and looked in.

Mike was curled under a tasseled spread printed with the images of the Incredible Hulk and the Fantastic Four. Willy lay alongside him, burring steadily. Card smiled. The two had shared this bed since Willy was a pup.

He adjusted the bedspread and blankets unnecessarily. Mike's thumb was plugged in his mouth; he still did that when he slept. Card knew he ought to break the boy of that habit, but he didn't have the heart.

Jessie, I wish you could be here. He's growing up. He's growing up just fine.

He was not really speaking to his wife or her ghost. He did not commune with the dead. He'd lost his religion years ago. But when he looked at his son, he felt his nearest approach to prayer.

Keep him safe, Card asked the universe. Protect him. Please.

But he knew the universe did not hear.

12

Smoke and laughter weaving like snakes in the dark. Clink of glasses, murmur of speech. Spotlights swept slowly through a gauze of mist, picking out tables and chairs of rough-hewn wood and, in the center of the big room, a few dancers swaying in languid slow motion like underwater creatures. Faint music, atonal, discordant, played in the background like distant traffic noise.

At the rear of the room, fringed by silhouetted heads, burned the blue glare of the stage. Bands had played there back when this place had been just a regular bar. Now there was no band, only a stool and, on the stool, a woman seated cross-legged, hugging herself, her face a painted skull. The microphone at her mouth carried her hushed verses to a mixing board, where they were blended with the music and sent to the speakers mounted on the walls.

She wore a black spandex body stocking that stressed the perfect roundness of her breasts, the elegant lines of her long sculptured legs. Her hair, tied back in a tight chignon, shimmered in the blue spotlight. It was possible to imagine how that hair, unclipped, would fall over her shoulders like some magical coalescence of smoke and silk.

She was unconscious of her appearance and of her audience. For her, the people at the tables were hidden behind a scrim of intensely blue light, leaving her alone with pain and poetry. That was as it should be. She did not write or recite her verses for *them*—the witless crowd, the graspers and pretenders. She addressed only the timeless part of herself.

"Blood contaminates," she whispered. "Blood washes clean. The child reborn becomes the child redeemed."

Finished, she lowered her head to a patter of hands. Weariness stole over her and left her limp. She escaped the spotlight and found Gregory at the bar.

"That was brilliant," he told her.

The compliment was annoying, as was the stupid sincerity in his eyes. She brushed both aside. "Let me have that." She took his drink and gulped it down, not noticing what it was.

"You're a genius, Dominique."

Without answering, she turned away. Her gaze swept the long mahogany bar. Near it was a lighted fish tank. Exotic fish drifted among ropy strands of bubbles, fish with strangely human faces. Their mouths were bordered with black markings, their eyes set off by black rings. They looked a great deal like Gregory, she thought—Gregory with his black lipstick and deep sockets of mascara in the hollows of his eyes. She imagined Gregory drifting in the water; the image reminded her of Jamie Frisch. A dark and pleasing warmth stole over her like a shadow on a sultry day.

"Beautiful poem, Dominique."

Jonathan's voice. She turned to look at him. He stood behind the bar polishing a glass. A tall, big-shouldered man with one ear. He had lost the other in prison. Someone had bitten it off. The guards had made the inmate spit it out and give it back. Jonathan claimed to still have it in a jar at home.

She chose to acknowledge his offering, because she respected Jonathan, as much as it was possible for her to respect anyone who lacked her gifts. "Thank you."

Gregory's jealousy burned on his face. She found his pettiness amusing.

Jonathan leaned close. Lowered his voice. A conspirator. "None of the others can hold a candle to you."

She disliked his stale metaphor, but decided it would be ungracious to say so. Still, she could not pretend to be delighted at such an obvious truism.

"I know," she said quietly, as a simple statement of fact.

Jonathan smiled, his teeth very white against the port-wine stain that covered half his face. The stain was not a birthmark. It was a tattoo. He had gotten it, he'd once told her, because handsomeness was dull and ordinary. Stockbrokers were handsome. His father had been handsome. She found his deliberate disfigurement exciting in a way that Gregory's makeup could never be.

Another performer had taken the stage, trilling about masturbation and despair. Cheap sentiments. Jonathan was right. She had no competition in this place or anywhere else. Let the others try to best her; none could. Yesterday's accomplishment had only sharpened her vision, extended her range.

The warmth inside her became a painful heat. She looked at Gregory again.

"I want to fuck," she said.

Gregory frowned, batting his spangled lashes. "I just got here. It's not even midnight yet."

She ignored that. Pivoted away from him. Tossed a bored question over her shoulder.

"You coming, or do I find a dog to hump?"

"I'm coming."

She left the bar, Gregory tailing her like a pale shadow. Unclothed mannequins passed by, lit by stationary spotlights, posed in acts of violent eroticism. Here and there television sets and videotape players were mounted on glass pedestals. The volume was off, the tapes running silently. A pastyfaced cowboy rode through a sagebrush desert in shades of gray, lariat twirling. Soap-opera actors caressed each other in a shadowed bedroom. A mushroom cloud bloomed on a blue horizon.

Dominique looked around at the couples scattered in the smoke. Men powdered like whores, women waxed like corpses. Leather and spandex, Velcro and Mylar. Jackboots and spiked bracelets, youth's homage to death camp and dungeon. Fingernails curving like talons, sparkling in the dim light. Mouths filled with humorless laughter and rows of teeth filed down to fangs; vampire chic. Thick circles of eyeliner making raccoon faces. Hair was a statement; both sexes displayed crewcuts and bald scalps and heads half shaved. Such children, all wishing to be what she was. They put on their masks and costumes, and played Halloween games.

What she had done to Jamie Frisch was no game.

She was better than all of them. They dreamed. She *dared*.

The headlights of Gregory's Mustang brightened the interior of her car as she wound her way home. Wordlessly she led him into her apartment. The living room was dark. He fumbled for the wall switch. She swatted his hand away.

"Afraid of the dark, little boy?"

"Yeth, Mommy." The lisp in his voice was automatic by now. He knew what Dominique liked. "Yeth, I'm thcared."

"There are no boogeymen here."

"Gregowy'th thcared." He was six years old again.

"Mommy will protect you. Mommy loves her little boy."

He hugged her, his hands squeezing her buttocks. Her breasts rubbed lazily against his chest like nuzzling kittens.

"Do you love Mommy?"

"Love you. Love you vewy, vewy much."

He kissed her as she drew him into the bedroom.

They did the usual things. Afterward she slipped out of bed without loosening the leather strap. It might cut off the circulation in his wrists; she didn't care. She had given up worrying about Gregory's delicacy, his tendency to bruise and bleed.

Dominique knew her apartment better in darkness than in light. Soundless steps carried her into the kitchen. She opened the refrigerator door; light fanned across the peeling linoleum. She poured a glass of chilled water from a bottle and drank it down.

Gregory's petulance floated down the hall, asking

Mommy to untie him, please. Dominique paid no
attention. She stood in the half-light of the refrigerator, a slender young woman with long showgirl
legs, her breasts heaving, thin shoulders drawn
tight, arms folded against her sides like the blades
of a utility knife. She swayed, swinging her head
and unbound hair, her face briefly catching the
light. Despite the frenzy of their lovemaking, her
makeup was still largely intact. She had applied
the white greasepaint first, then had gone to work
with the pencil, enlarging her nostrils to triangular
sockets, shading batwing triangles under her high
cheekbones. Her eyes had been quickly lost in black
hollows. Last had come the bloody lipstick and the
febrile splotches of rouge on cheeks and forehead.
She had looked in the vanity mirror and smiled,
seeing death's face.

She wished Jamie could have seen her this way,
not scrubbed and wholesome in the blond wig she
had discarded in a trash dumpster after the killing.
She wished he could have seen her painted mouth
leering like a red sickle against the impossible pallor of her skin. The plastic bag had been transpar-
ent; she had made sure of that, knowing she would
want to watch his face. His eyes, so wide, had seen
her clearly in his last moments as he squirmed beneath her, the bag expanding and contracting with
each desperate breath, the tissuey plastic finally
pasted to his nose and mouth like a caul.

Yes, a missed opportunity. If only she'd had her
makeup kit, she could have transformed herself
while Jamie lay chloroformed.

Still, she was pleased with her work. She was

venturing into new aesthetic territory: death as theater, murder as performance art.

The toy dinosaur had been a clever touch. Boys of that age were drawn to dinosaurs like mice to cheese. And she had never doubted that Jamie would see the small plastic prize lying there on the sidewalk. On three previous afternoons she had waited in the park, watching as he passed by, alone, on his way home from school. On each occasion he had kept his eyes on the pavement. He seemed to be wary of stepping on cracks.

She had chosen the boy the very first day she saw him, because he was so small and beautiful and innocent. She had known nothing about him, not even his name. But she had sensed that he was meant for her.

After that, she had spent several nights devising a plan of elegant simplicity, a means of luring him into the park's leafy recesses. A faultless plan, expertly executed.

Admittedly her noisy sobbing had been overdone, a shade too histrionic for her taste. Nevertheless it had worked; the boy had heard the sounds and approached to investigate, as she had hoped he would. And she had handled the rest of their encounter to perfection.

Gaining his trust. Drawing him to the bench. Then clapping the chloroform-soaked cloth over his nose and mouth. She ditched his rubber ball and book bag in the bushes, along with the wet rag, death's calling card. Then she lifted Jamie in her arms. He was surprisingly heavy, and she was panting as she carried him through the trees to her parked car and swiftly pushed him into the backseat.

Nobody was in sight. No witnesses. She was certain of it.

After that, the drive to the alley, where the car was hidden from strangers' eyes. Her gloved hands fumbled as she hurriedly bound the boy's wrists behind his back. Already he was coming to, eyelids fluttering, small mouth forming soundless words. She turned him faceup, tugged the bag over his head, lashed it tight.

Sudden terror shocked him alert. He squirmed and wriggled under her as she straddled him, pinning him on the car seat, watching his face through the sheer plastic.

His dying took only a minute or two. His little lungs hadn't room for much stored air, she supposed.

For some period of time she hugged the limp body, rocking it gently, singing lullabies. She cried for the child, sick with love for him.

After a while she recovered her composure. She left the alley and drove aimlessly, trying to decide where to dispose of the body. Rush hour was under way; her car became one more pair of headlights in a glittering daisy chain of commuters. Jamie lay on the floor of the backseat where she had left him, uncovered even by a blanket, sure to be seen by any cop if she were pulled over. The danger made the adventure real, lighting up her senses like a busy switchboard. She almost hoped to hear a siren, see a sparkle of dome lights in her rearview mirror.

Sometime during her drive, she stopped in another alley and disposed of the blond wig in a trash Dumpster. Even if the wig were found there, it would never be connected with the abduction that had taken place miles away.

At midnight she pulled off White Oak Avenue onto a lightless turnout at the edge of the Los Angeles River. She got out and surveyed the area. A vacant lot spread around her on three sides, a blank expanse of dust and scruffy dry weeds. On the fourth side was a wire fence; beyond it was the river. Water glinted in the starlight.

She hauled Jamie out of the car, lifted him over the fence, and let him go. He hit the steep embankment and tumbled swiftly down into the black water. She did not know if he would float or sink. He sank. She imagined he would stay down for a while, till gases from his rupturing organs inflated his body and brought him puffy to the surface.

She blew Jamie a kiss before climbing back into her car. Tears stood in her eyes, burning like drops of acid. She was filled with hot blind love for the boy, a mother's love, instinctive and unconditional.

You're mine, Jamie. You're Mommy's little baby. You've come home to your mother at last.

She continued driving for hours, singing tunelessly to herself in the rushing darkness. She could feel Jamie inside her, almost as if he were growing in her belly, nourished by her blood. She loved him, loved all the motherless children, loved them so very much.

"Blood contaminates," Dominique recited now, as she stood swaying in the kitchen. "Blood washes clean. The child reborn becomes the child redeemed."

13

Lindstrom's hands on the steering wheel were tense, the nails well bitten. She asked Card if he thought Estoban was their man, and Card said he didn't know, and Lindstrom told him to take a shot at it, hell, she wasn't keeping score. So Card said yeah, he thought maybe. Lindstrom was grumpily satisfied.

Engine hum replaced conversation. Card thought about Luis Estoban, who had lured ten-year-old Jorge Morro into a park in North Hollywood and fellated the boy while holding a knife to his throat. Jorge's memory had proved good enough for the IdentiKit artist; one of Estoban's neighbors had recognized his face on the six o'clock news. Eighteen months at Chino had made Luis a reformed man. He had never missed an appointment with his parole officer, had in fact tried to bring the officer closer to Christ, whom Luis had met in prison.

The parallel with the Jamie Frisch case was not perfect; Jorge Morro had not been kidnapped or killed. But there were similarities—a park, a child victim—common elements sufficiently intriguing to catch the attention of the CCAP computer jockeys. CCAP was the Career Criminal Apprehension Program, the LAPD's latest antirecidivism project.

Data on recent felonies were fed into a computer, which then compared the crimes with the MOs of parolees. In this instance, a match was made, and Luis Estoban's name was promptly spit out.

Card and Lindstrom had learned of this development after a grim morning spent observing Jamie's autopsy. At least one of the detectives working the case was required to be there, in order to preserve the chain of evidence necessary in the event of a trial; since neither of them had wanted to stick the other with the unpleasant detail, they ended up doing it together. Card had tried not to think too much about Mike as Vince Neal cut open Jamie's small body and removed the vital organs, placing each in a jar, sometimes drawing off fluid for separate analysis. The body had been in the water for roughly twenty-four hours, Neal believed, and its condition was not good. He confirmed that the cause of death was asphyxiation; the hyoid bone at the root of the tongue was unbroken, ruling out strangulation. Other than that, he had little to say.

Medical evidence was not going to catch Jamie's killer. Maybe CCAP would.

Luis Estoban, now a good Christian, had a job at a shelter for the homeless in East L.A. The shelter had been a church named St. Matthew's once. Gothic spires rose above cinquefoils and double lancet windows, architectural conceits incongruous in the barrio.

Lindstrom parked the unmarked Chevy in a curbside space near the front steps. She and Card got out, looking around. Except for the church, the street was typical of this neighborhood. Stunted brick buildings, the windows broken and boarded up. Graffiti everywhere, the twisted black markings crawling over walls and curbs like some fantastically abundant species of jungle plant. Trash in the gutters. Fragments of beer bottles and safety glass on the pavement, evidence of drunkenness and auto thefts.

A crowd of Hispanic kids loitered at a corner, one of them slapping a paddleball around. They watched Card and Lindstrom with slitted eyes, their faces expressionless yet somehow hostile. Card found himself thinking that they ought to be in school.

Big double doors opened onto what had been the narthex of St. Matthew's. A second doorway, the doors wedged open, led into the nave. Noon sun slanted through a rose window, filling the vast echoing room with a dusty haze of light. The two detectives advanced into the bowels of the church with the edgy wariness of sinners.

The pews were gone, replaced with sagging, creaking cots arrayed in rows. Most were empty now, a few occupied by men too tired to rise. The rest of the derelicts were on their feet, shuffling aimlessly around the room, some crouching alone in corners, others clumped together in conspiratorial gatherings. Card saw mostly men, a few women, several children. The buzz of droning voices competed with coughs and wet sneezes and the mingled music and static of tinny radios. Rising over it all was the brief, heart-twisting cry of a baby, shrieking lustily, then dissolving into hiccuping sobs.

"Makes you glad you've got a roof over your head," Lindstrom said.

"And over Mike's head," Card answered.

They walked through the shifting crowd in search of someone in authority. Bad smells invaded Card's nostrils. The smells of people who had gone too long without washing, who carried the odors of the street in their greasy, matted hair and ragged clothes.

"They won't let me see my daughter," muttered a bearded figure outstretched on a cot as Card and Lindstrom passed by. "She's got the head of a goat. Head of a goat. They won't let me see her because she's got the head of a goat."

Card felt his shoulders hunch reflexively. Insanity had never scared him until he saw Jessie start to rave in her last days. Then he had experienced a terror he hadn't known since childhood nightmares—the terror of seeing a loved one become a shrieking stranger.

"Head of a goat!" the man moaned loudly, his voice a restless spirit's wail.

He and Lindstrom reached the chancel, where the altar had been. Now it served as a dining area. Long wooden tables were butted together, flanked by folding chairs. No one was sitting there yet, but the aroma of beef stew drifting in from the rear of the building promised that lunch would begin soon. A hot meal, then a long afternoon spent blinking at memories, then dinner and, after that, restless sleep in a shadowed hall alive with dark mutterings. And all the while the crucified Christ, still mounted on the rear wall above the altar platform, would gaze down sorrowfully on the scene.

A man was setting out picnic plates on the tables, Styrofoam plates with wreaths of flowers printed on them. Card looked him over and decided he did not resemble the photo in Estoban's file.

"Excuse me." Card showed his badge. "Can you tell us where to find Luis Estoban?"

The man, looking suspicious, mumbled that he didn't know.

"All right, then, whoever runs this place, whoever's in charge—where would we find him?"

The man frowned. "Not a him. Mrs. Martinez is in the storeroom."

He gave inept directions. Card and Lindstrom went through the north transept and down a musty hallway to what must have been the rectory. In a room no bigger than a walk-in closet they found Mrs. Martinez, clipboard in hand, preparing an inventory of canned goods.

She was a small, brown, wrinkled woman determined to speak no ill of Luis Estoban. He was an excellent employee, she told them stiffly after they explained their reason for being there. He worked for the minimum wage with no complaints. He had a sincere and touching faith in the Lord. Whatever his past sins—and she didn't want to know about them—he was a new man now.

"You may be right, Mrs. Martinez," Lindstrom said, "but we need to talk with him anyway."

She sighed. "In the kitchen."

Lindstrom started to go. Card stopped her. "Mrs. Martinez, what are Luis's hours?"

"Eight to two, six days a week. On Sundays we use only volunteers. Luis has, in fact, volunteered several times, but those duties are not part of his job."

"Does he leave promptly at two every day?"

"I would say so, for the most part."

"Do you remember when he left on Tuesday? The day before yesterday, I mean."

A yellow fingernail scratched a brown cheek. "Day before yesterday, let's see . . . I believe he

stayed a few minutes late. Yes. One of the men had
cut his hand on a bottle in a trash can and needed
a bandage. He'd been looking for beer, you see. It
happens all the time. Luis helped me fix him up.
A generous gesture typical of him."

"Could you estimate the time when he left?"

"Quarter after two."

"Does he have a car?"

"I'm sure I don't know. It's none of my business
how he gets to and from his work." And none of
yours either, her frowning mouth seemed to add.

"Two-fifteen," Lindstrom muttered as she and
Card walked down the short hallway to the
kitchen, following the smell of cooking stew.
"Think he could have made it all the way from
here to Woodland Hills by three?"

"Yes, if the freeway traffic cooperated. And if he
has a car."

She nodded. "The killer's got to have wheels anyway. No way he could've gotten Jamie to the Sepulveda Dam area otherwise. You don't carry a dead
body with you on the bus."

"I'll bet it's been tried," Card said sourly as he
pushed open the kitchen door.

Luis Estoban was alone in the narrow window-
less room. He had gained weight and lost hair
since the mug shots in his file were taken. He
looked older than his age, thirty. The crucifix
around his neck glinted through billows of steam.

"Mr. Estoban?" Card was handling this one.
Lower-class Hispanics were often scornful of lady
cops. "Detective Lindstrom and I would like to ask
you a few questions."

Estoban turned away from the four huge pots

boiling on the stove. He spread his hands, palms up. "Hey, man, I ain't done nothing."

"We'd just like to talk with you."

"I'm working."

"Take a five-minute break. We'll make it square with the management."

"Shit."

"You a religious man, Luis?"

He crossed himself. "Jesus is my Savior. He could save you too."

"Later. Luis, where were you on Tuesday afternoon between the hours of three and four?"

Suddenly his eyes were darting. "Here, man. I got a job here."

A lie. Card felt a punch of adrenaline.

"You left work no later than two-fifteen. Mrs. Martinez told us so a minute ago."

"Oh, right. You said three o'clock, huh?"

"Yeah."

"Tuesday? Day before yesterday?"

"You got it."

"I guess I was home then." Brown eyes flicking like marbles.

"Bullshit."

"Truth, man." Stubby fingers on the silver crucifix, leaving green pea stains. "I swear."

"Cut the crap."

"Hey, listen, you got no business talking to me like that. I did my time, you know? I'm, like, reformed."

"Sure you are. You're an honest, taxpaying citizen. Only, you don't want to tell us where you were on Tuesday. Maybe because you were doing something you don't like to talk about?"

"No. Uh-uh."

"Something nasty? Something Jesus wouldn't approve of?"

He was squirming now, fear flashing in his eyes. "I don't know what the fuck you're talking about."

"I think you do." Card disliked being lied to. He decided to push hard. "You're into a real ugly game this time, aren't you, Luis? You're doing bad things? Things even worse than what you did to Jorge Morro?"

"No, man, I don't do that shit no more. I swear. The Bible set me straight, you know? I read it every night."

"Do you ask forgiveness every night? For the things you do?"

"I'm not doing it no more!"

Tears threatened. His fleshy face was screwed into a wincing mask.

"Come clean with us, Luis." Card gentled his voice. "Tell us what you've been up to. Maybe it's not your fault, what you've done. Maybe somebody can help you, make you stop."

Estoban wasn't listening. "You're not sending me back," he whispered in a hopeless monotone. *"La cárcel . . . la cárcel . . ."*

The jail, he was saying. He didn't want to be sent back to jail. And why would he worry about that, unless he'd done something on Tuesday afternoon at three, something sure to put him away again?

Goddamn computer came through, Card thought in rising excitement. What the hell do you know.

"Talk to us, Luis. Come on. You'll feel better. You know you will."

Estoban shook his head once, with the stubborn, tearful defiance of a child.

Card looked at Lindstrom. Silent agreement passed between them.

"Okay, Luis. I'm afraid we've got to take you in for questioning—"

Estoban tore the crucifix from his neck, whipped it at Card's face, and bolted.

Card ducked. The steel cross nicked his cheek. There might have been blood. He barely noticed. He was running.

The rear door of the kitchen opened onto a narrow hallway lit by unshaded ceiling bulbs. Card fingered the .38 Detective Special in the armpit holster under his jacket as he sprinted down the hall. No need to draw his piece yet; just nice to know it was there.

Luis was running fast but sloppily, caroming off the walls like a pinball. Chuffs of breath and piggish grunts rose over his slapping footsteps.

Card glanced behind him and caught a glimpse of Lindstrom's face in the sweep of light from a bare bulb. Flushed and wild-eyed, hair bouncing everywhere. He flashed on the thought that this was how she must look during sex.

The hallway veered to the left. A wall shot out of darkness funhouse-fast. Card skidded and banged his shoulder, driving his arm into his gun and the gun into his ribs. The pancake holster softened the blow, but he was wincing as he and Lindstrom pounded out of the hall into the transept.

Estoban was just ahead, running through the nave, zigzagging among the cots and the dazed men who hovered near them. Card pursued. Pallid faces snapped past him, the faces of corpses not yet made up for display. He thudded into a man in a heavy coat and saw dust rise like a powder of chalk from a blackboard eraser. Then he was past the man, vaulting empty cots, ducking under a clothesline strung between two columns and draped with drying underwear. Somewhere the baby was screaming again.

At the doorway of the narthex Card grabbed for Estoban; his hand caught a flapping shirttail that tore free.

One of the double doors swung wide. An aureole of sun flared around Estoban's silhouetted figure as he vanished down the front steps. Card followed, shouting at him to stop. The sunlight was shockingly bright, a splash of acid on his retinas.

Estoban ran to a parked hatchback, tugged open the door. A Plymouth Horizon. Card was running for the hatchback when the tailpipe coughed smoke. Estoban pulled away, and Card staggered to a stop, clutching his stomach and gulping air. He memorized the license number, then turned to Lindstrom, but she wasn't there.

"Ellen?"

The unmarked Chevy screamed away from the curb, fishtailed, straightened out, and arrowed itself at the fleeing Plymouth.

My partner, Card thought proudly.

Lindstrom wished she were a TV cop with a portable siren she could clamp on the window frame. Unmarked LAPD cars had no such niceties, so she leaned on the horn. Estoban's car swung toward a side street. Lindstrom swore. Grungy little Jesus freak seemed to think he could escape. She jammed her foot on the gas pedal. The driver's seat bucked as the Chevy shot forward.

She thought of Jamie Frisch, his small nude body laid out on the stainless-steel table under the fluorescent chill. Anger made her reckless. She arrowed the Chevy at the Estoban's car, rammed his rear bumper with a crunch of buckling metal, and bulldozed him into a utility pole.

The impact tossed her onto the steering wheel, then flung her backward against the headrest. She fumbled for the door handle, and then the windshield starred in time with a handgun's report.

Shit. Asshole's armed.

She ducked under the dash and jerked her Beretta out of its shoulder holster. Another shot, and a shower of glass as the windshield imploded.

Bobby, get me out of this.

Card, breathless after chasing both cars, took aim at Luis Estoban from behind the fender of a parked van. The man was leaning out the driver's-side window, twisted in his seat to fire behind him at Lindstrom hunched down in the Chevy. Card squeezed off a round that dimpled the hatchback's door. Luis fired back. A bullet pinged off the van's hubcap. Card raised his head again and tried another trigger-pull. He had no time to aim, it was just point-and-shoot, and he didn't know he'd hit his target until he saw Estoban slammed backward in his seat.

Bullets are unpredictable, their paths like snowflakes, no two alike. Card's semijacketed hollowpoint shattered Luis Estoban's clavicle and flattened instantly. Deflected south, the bullet tumbled through soft tissue, chewing a wide wound channel. It ripped up the left atrium of the heart, punctured both lobes of the right lung, fractured the seventh rib, and exited via the man's back, lodging in the floor of the car.

Estoban's beating heart flooded his chest cavity with blood. His mind was a buzzing hive. He did not think about Jesus as he died. Slumped in the driver's seat, numb fingers curled around the handle of his .32, he remembered a cat he had shot to pieces for target practice on a summer day of his childhood. He'd found it funny, the way the cat jumped like a kicked can as he blew off first one leg, then another. Death took him before he grasped the point of his reminiscence.

Card couldn't see Estoban, couldn't determine his condition. Caution competed with the urgent need to check on Lindstrom. He emerged from behind the van and approached the hatchback in a half crouch, his finger exerting two pounds of pull on the trigger. Looking inside the car would be the most dangerous moment. If the man was lying in wait for him, poised to squeeze off a head shot at close range . . .

Card sucked a quick breath, then raised his head fast over the doorframe, into the open window, and saw Luis Estoban sprawled across the gearshift, his knees drawn up in a fetal pose, a thread of spit dangling from his mouth.

Dead.

Not wounded. Not unconscious. Dead.

I killed him, Card thought, the words numbing like Novocain.

The door of the Chevy creaked open, and Lindstrom climbed out, pushing her hair into place. "You get him?"

"Yes."

"Killed the bastard?"

"Yes."

"Good."

Card closed his eyes. "Shut up."

His body shook. He thought about the shooting range. Paper silhouettes. Nothing like this.

A swell of nausea rose in him. He turned away from the car, hands gripping his knees, and poured a wet splatter on the pavement. He went on retching long after his stomach was empty.

Lindstrom's grip was tight on his shoulder. "The motherfucker deserved it, Bobby. He wasted the Frisch kid."

"Yes." Card wiped his mouth with the back of his hand. The hand passed close to his nose, bringing a bad smell with it. "He did. He must have."

"Kidnapped him, and tied him up, and bagged his head, and watched him suffocate."

"Yes."

Card straightened up slowly. Drew a shallow breath, then a deeper one.

"And after the kid was dead," Lindstrom said, "he dumped the body in the river, like a sack of garbage."

"I know."

"So it's all right. He goddamn asked for it."

"Sure he did. Still, I wish ... I wish ..." The sentence groped for completion, found none. He didn't know what he wished.

"Don't grieve for him," Lindstrom said, walking away. "Don't waste your tears."

But there were no tears. That was the thing. Nausea, yes, and shock and horror. But no tears.

Card's eyes were dry as he listened to Lindstrom call it in.

14

Paramedics arrived at the scene eight minutes later. Card and Lindstrom watched them cut away Luis Estoban's shirt and attach electrodes from a Lifepak 5 monitor to his chest. A strip of tape slid out of the monitor, etched with a perfectly flat line.

"Zero electrical activity," one paramedic said.

"He's gone," his partner agreed.

Radio cars and unmarked sedans arrived, clogging the street. Yellow evidence tape was strung around the scene to hold back the slowly gathering crowd. Murmured Spanish drifted through the air like lazy smoke. There were many children watching, their faces pale and large-eyed. Children always gathered at crime scenes in the barrio. Presumably they had nothing better to do.

The pathologist and the shooting-team investigator showed up almost simultaneously. While the coroner's man worked on Luis Estoban, taking a temperature reading in the liver, the investigator, a gray-haired Robbery-Homicide detective named Spanner, separated Card and Lindstrom and had them transported to Hollenbech, the divisional station.

While Lindstrom waited outside, Card sat with

Spanner in the older detective's office. A portable
tape recorder rested on the desk, but Spanner
didn't turn it on right away. First he fixed Card
with his fatherly gaze and asked him to summarize
the circumstances that had led to the death of Luis
Estoban. Card briefly recounted what had happened, slipping self-consciously into cop jargon at
times; words like *deployed* and *utilized* peppered his
speech like grit in a sandwich, tasting sour in his
mouth.

Then Spanner had him go over it again, more
slowly. "Okay," he said when Card was finished.
"Ready to give a formal statement?" Card said yes.
Spanner switched on the tape recorder, and the
interview proceeded for the third time.

Spanner let Card go with a polite thank-you. He
then interviewed Lindstrom privately.

After that, a squad car took Card and Lindstrom
back to the scene of the shooting. Spanner and two
other Robbery-Homicide detectives followed. At
the scene, Card and Lindstrom did a complete
walk-through of the incident. Estoban's body had
been taken away, but the two vehicles were still in
place.

Before returning to Hollenbech with his colleagues, Spanner took Card aside and told him, off
the record, that his actions appeared to constitute
a justifiable use of his service revolver.

Card didn't expect any trouble from the shooting
team. Still, Jacobs would have to put him on desk
duty till the investigation was completed. This
would be his last chance for a while to do any work
in the field.

"Let's check out his apartment," he told Lindstrom.

She frowned. "You're supposed to go back to Hollenbech and talk to the ballistics guys."

"They can wait."

"Procedure—"

"Screw procedure." Card used the edge of his voice. "I want to make Luis on the Jamie Frisch case. I want to nail the bastard." Maybe then the sick, irrational feelings of guilt would pass.

Slowly Lindstrom nodded. "Okay, Bobby. We'll take a detour to his apartment on the way to the station. Assuming Estoban gave his parole officer a valid address."

"He probably did. No point in raising the P.O.'s suspicions unnecessarily."

The squad car rattled along barrio streets, past brick walls cobwebbed with graffiti. In the backseat Card and Lindstrom were silent, thinking. They had no idea what they would find in Estoban's apartment. The remains of other little boys, perhaps. That nut in Chicago, John Wayne Gacy, had kept his dead victims in a crawlspace. There had been a serial killer in L.A. not long ago who pickled the heads of his female victims in jars of formaldehyde, like medical specimens. Anything was possible.

Lindstrom broke the silence once. "Hey, Bobby, you remember that gum you bummed off me yesterday? I said you owed me."

"I remember."

"Yeah, well, seeing as how you saved my butt and all—let's call it even."

Estoban's building was a ratty tenement vivid

with strange smells. Astonishingly, the landlord not only lived on the premises but was in when Card knocked.

"Never trusted that *campesino*," the man said after the two detectives explained why they were there. "Knew he was bad news. Knew it." Card had the impression he would have said the same about any of his tenants, perhaps with good reason.

The landlord led them up three flights of stairs, pausing on each landing to wheeze theatrically and hawk up a huge gob of phlegm. The two uniformed cops from the patrol car trailed Card and Lindstrom, intermittent static from their radios sizzling like grilled meat.

The group marched down a long dark hallway past rows of closed doors that looked as thin as balsa wood. Card heard the nearby flushing of toilets; some of the tenants had heard the police radios and were frantically disposing of drugs in expectation of a raid.

"That one there," the landlord said, pointing.

Lindstrom rapped on the apartment door, Card behind her, the two uniforms backing them up. When there was no answer, Card signaled to the landlord, who handed over a master key.

The door eased open on a narrow hole striped with wan daylight filtering through venetian blinds. One room and a bath; no kitchen; garage-sale furnishings.

Lindstrom entered first, Card following. They crept across a carpet that smelled like mange. Card scanned the room: unmade bed, compact fridge, hot plate, velvet painting of a haloed Jesus. He looked at the painting for a long time.

"Bobby. Take a look."

Lindstrom was peering into a closet. Draped on the wire hangers were nightgowns, bras, panties, nylons.

"Think he had a girlfriend?" she asked.

"I don't know. Maybe he liked to play dress-up."

One of the patrol officers murmured, "Fucking queer."

Card reached past Lindstrom and slid the hangers to one end of the closet, exposing a cache of electronic gear heaped against the rear wall. Boomboxes, microwave ovens, portable TVs.

Lindstrom frowned. "He was in business."

"I have a funny feeling," Card said. His stomach had tightened. "I think we screwed up. I think . . ."

The .38 bucking in his hand. Bloom of blood on Estoban's chest.

Lindstrom read his mind. "It was self-defense, Bobby. Your fellow officer was under fire and so were you. You took him out, and that was playing it by the book."

"We wouldn't have been under fire if I hadn't come on so strong in the kitchen. I spooked him. That's why he ran."

"You're way ahead of yourself. So what if he was doing some four-five-nine on the side? He still might have cooled the Frisch kid."

"Might have. But didn't." Card touched the frilled hem of a nightgown. "This is what he was into. He burgled houses. Took TVs and stereos for money, ladies' wear for his fantasy life."

"He was into little boys too. That's what put him in the can, remember?"

Card nodded at her, but he knew she was wrong.

The picture of Jesus proved it. Luis really had gotten religion at Chino. He couldn't help sinning, but he had limited himself to lesser sins. Card looked around the room and saw Luis squatting on the bed, handling bras and panties, his shadow huge on the closed blinds. After he relieved his secret urges, did he kneel before the velvet Christ and beg forgiveness? Hear him whisper in his peasant Spanish: *Please, Savior, I hurt no little ones this time, I only took a few pretty things no one will miss.*

"He was a killer, Bobby." Lindstrom's voice was low and insistent in his ear like the muttering of conscience.

"I don't think so."

"Well, he sure as shit tried to waste me. There's a slug in the Chevy's passenger seat to prove it."

"He panicked. He was afraid we'd send him back to jail. *La cárcel.* He was weak. You know what they do to the weak ones in there."

"Goddammit, you're making him out to be Snow fucking White. He had a loaded piece stashed in his car."

"Protection. He was selling stolen goods to rough customers. That's all."

"You honestly don't think he bagged Jamie?"

"No."

"Hell." Lindstrom sighed. "Then I guess I don't either. But I still say nobody can question your handling of the situation."

Card wasn't looking at her. "You didn't pull the trigger."

15

The emptiness of his apartment disturbed Robert Card, triggering too many associations: the empty rooms in the Canoga Park house on moving day, the empty place beside him in his bed, the hollow center of his heart. Three years should have been time enough to heal, but the deadness remained. He had not cried over Luis Estoban; all right, that was understandable. But his own wife, for God's sake, his *wife*. No tears at her funeral, no tears since. When she died, she took part of him with her. His capacity for grief had been cut out of him like a tumorous organ. No, wrong; what had been excised was something healthy, while the malignancy remained. And spread.

He started thinking about the corpse in the car again, then spent some time in the bathroom leaning over the toilet, expecting to be sick. The feeling passed. He swore he could still smell Estoban's blood. He dabbed at his nose with a damp cloth to rub the clinging scent from his nostrils, before deciding the smell was only in his mind.

The man had been a loser, what Captain Jacobs would call "a knucklehead" in that half-contemptuous, half-sympathetic tone of voice he reserved for the dregs of the dregs. Still, he had been a man. Card did not want to get sloppy with sentiment, but any human being was irreplaceable, unique; never again would there be another just like him. He thought about Luis Estoban, alive this morning and dead this afternoon, purely because of a bullet fired by the gun pulled from Card's armpit holster. Julius Caesar was dead, as were the men who built Ur and Babylon; now Luis had joined them. Card felt queasy at the idea that the small flabby ex-con with the crucifix at his throat was now as distant from this world as any man buried a thousand years ago, or ten thousand.

Yet at his center there was a place these musings could not reach. A place nothing could touch, a bundle of deadened nerves, a white lump of scar tissue. Even the first spadeful of dirt on Jessica's casket had not touched him there. Nothing would, ever again.

After a while he saw that he was thinking about Luis Estoban in order to squeeze some few drops of grief out of himself, and that those drops were to be his compensation for not having mourned Jessie as he should have, an expiation for old sins. The realization made him feel cheap, an exploiter of the dead. That was when he put the shooting out of his mind, leaving no thoughts there, only a wordless calm.

He played with Willy, TV chatter crowding out unwelcome silence. The long brown dog rolled happily on the floor, thrusting his belly up at Card to demand a tummy-tickling, then squirming away before Card could comply. Finally Card hoisted

Willy onto the sofa, where he wasn't supposed to be, and cuddled the dachshund in his lap.

At three-fifteen Mike exploded into the foyer, followed by Consuelo.

"Dad!"

"Hey, it's the Mikester. Come here, guy."

Mike bounced onto the couch. Willy's dry tongue lapped eagerly at father and son as they hugged.

"Mr. Card, what are you doing home?" Consuelo was worried.

"Took some personal time. Rough day at the office."

"Can I fix you a drink?"

"Already made one." He lifted his glass with a tinkle of ice. "You could refresh me, though. Scotch. The bottle's on the counter."

She took the glass and bustled into the kitchen.

"Catch any crooks today?" Mike asked.

Killed one, Card answered silently. "Sort of."

"The guys in school, they don't believe me when I say my dad's a cop."

"Not even after I went there?" Card and two other fathers with glamorous jobs, a firefighter and a stuntman, had spoken to Mike's class last fall. The stuntman had taken the most questions.

"The new guys, I mean. Todd and Kyle and Lindsay. They're transfers."

Didn't kids have names like John and Joe anymore? "Well, you tell them to ask some of the kids who were there. They can corroborate your story."

"Co-robbery-ate." Testing the word.

"Corroborate." Card said it slowly. "It means— uh, let's see. If one person says he saw something, and another person says he saw it too, then the second person has corroborated the story."

"Crobberate."

"Close enough."

They played Chinese checkers, Card making occasional bad moves to keep the game close. He watched his son bent over the board, frowning in concentration, and he knew there was one part of his heart that was not hollow. He reached out and smoothed Mike's hair.

"You're a good kid, you know that?"

"Quit it, Dad." He jumped one of Card's marbles and captured it. "You're dead meat now."

The TV was still on when the four o'clock news invaded the living room with its Teletype music. Card stiffened, hearing the top story.

". . . possible resolution of the shocking case we first reported at the eleven o'clock hour last night. Seven-year-old Jamie Frisch was brutally murdered, his body dumped in the waters of the L.A. River. Now police believe a suspect killed in a gun battle today may have been little Jamie's murderer. Patti Castillo is here with the latest. Patti?"

"Judy, police are saying nothing official as of yet. But unofficially, a high-ranking member of the LAPD has made it clear that the man shot a few hours ago by homicide detectives in East Los Angeles was—"

"Dad, it's your move."

"In a second."

"—name reported to be Luis Estoban, a parolee with a history of violent assaults against children. The two detectives investigating Jamie's murder, seen here at the Sepulveda Dam Recreation Area last night—"

Videotape rolling on the screen. Card and Lindstrom on their way out of the parking lot, hurrying past lights and cameras. The media, monitoring police-band cross talk, had arrived just as the two of them were leaving for Woodland Hills.

"Hey, Dad," Mike said, looking up, "that's you and Ellen. You're on TV. Cool."

"—tried to flee, then opened fire on the detectives, who returned the shots. Estoban was pronounced dead at the scene."

"You wasted him? All *right!*"

"Quiet, Mike. Quiet."

Consuelo was in the doorway. "Mike, please help me in the kitchen, will you?"

"Did you hear about Dad?"

"I heard. Give me a hand in here."

"Okay, okay."

Mike scampered out, the dog chasing him and yapping. Card stared at the game board. He picked up a marble and rolled it between thumb and forefinger.

A high-ranking member of the LAPD. Christ.

There was heat on the Frisch case; the story had headlined the late local news and received first-page coverage, above the fold, in the Metro section of today's *Times*. Somebody downtown had seen the initial report on Estoban and had been too eager to score P.R. points. By now the stolen goods in Estoban's apartment would be changing some minds, but the story was already leaked. The department would look bad tomorrow, when the truth came out.

The phone rang. Consuelo answered, then leaned into the living room. "Miss Lindstrom."

Card took it on the extension.

"Bobby, have you seen the local news yet?"

He heard the sounds of the station house behind her voice. "I saw it."

"Not so great, huh?"

"A disaster. Right now I really do hate my job, no joke."

"You're entitled. This was a pretty stupid move on someone's part. But it'll blow over."

"Yeah, like a cyclone. They blow over too."

"What I can't figure out is who'd be dumb enough to flap his gums on something this sensitive. Can't be the chief—he didn't get where he is by being a total bonehead, only a partial bonehead. Warner, maybe—that asswipe loves to brown-nose with the pressies. Or Fitzpatrick . . ."

Lindstrom kept talking. Card shut his eyes, not quite listening, and an image flickered like heat lightning in his brain: his partner's hair flying, her face flushed, as she ran hard down the hallway behind him. His fingertips tingled with the sudden need to touch that hair, that skin. He hadn't known until that moment how lonely he was.

He waited till she finished saying whatever it was she had to say.

"Hey, look, Ellen"—keep it casual—"you, uh, doing anything tonight? You want to meet me later for"—dinner? No—"coffee or something?"

"I guess I could squeeze it into my crowded schedule. Where?"

"Ventura Café? Eight o'clock?"

"Deal. Hey, you're not expecting me to pick up the tab, are you?"

"Why would I?"

"Well, considering that you recently saved my life, you might think it was the least I could do."

"I didn't save your life."

"Mr. Modesty."

"I was protecting myself as much as you."

"You weren't the one he was shooting at. Not initially anyhow. I was the prime target. Did you see where that round landed? If I hadn't ducked, old Luis would have plugged me right in the noggin."

"But you did duck. Your reflexes saved you. Not me."

"My reflexes take half the credit. You take the rest."

"I don't want to hear about it, Ellen."

"Okay, pardner. Then I won't say another word. But you'll know what I'm thinking."

She hung up before he could reply.

Card looked at the humming phone in his hand and noticed that he was smiling. That was the thing about Lindstrom—not the best-looking woman in the world, maybe, but she could ease his mind when it needed easing. She could make him smile.

16

Dominique ate dinner with the TV on, the six o'clock news upcoming. Before tonight she had paid no attention to news reports, even though Jamie's disappearance would have been among them. Now she was intrigued.

Jamie was the lead story. Dominique smiled, her teeth red with spaghetti sauce. Her project was garnering great publicity, and she was pleased. Every artist wants an audience.

She gathered that the boy's body had been found last night. Surprising that it would surface so soon. Apparently it had washed up underneath a bridge not far from the dam.

But a more interesting development had occurred today, when a man suspected of the crime had been killed by two detectives investigating the murder.

Killed.

Dominique leaned forward in her chair as the detectives were shown in blurry videotape. A man and a woman. They passed by the camera, their faces caught in the harsh glare of an arc light. The woman was rumpled and harried and angry. The man was . . . interesting. Dominique liked his face. She saw death in it, or the memory of death.

She wondered which of the two had fired the fatal shot. She hoped it had been the man. Women should not carry guns. Terribly unfeminine. But a man with a gun was a different matter. Exciting, somehow. Arousing.

In a sense, the bullet that ended the suspect's life had been meant for her.

Her hands crept inside her jeans. She touched herself in her private place.

Would that policeman shoot her if he tracked her down? Would he put his gun to her head? In her mouth? Would he let her lick the blued barrel as he jerked the trigger?

The thought racked her with delicious shudders.

She pictured the dead man, whose name was Luis Estoban, laid out on a tray in a locker, a tag wired to his toe. The image flickered, her own body now superimposed on his. Her breasts pulped by the bloody bullet track. Eyes shiny like buttons.

The newscast proceeded to other subjects. Dominique paid no attention. She shut her eyes, twisting in her chair, dinner forgotten, everything forgotten as she imagined the gun in that policeman's hand. The gun that would rip out her throat in a bloody Niagara, blast a spume of brains out the back of her skull.

"Bang," she whispered. "Bang. Bang."

Pleasure groaned in her. She slid bonelessly onto the floor and curled up like a shrimp, her mouth tasting the skin of her forearms. She hugged her knees and rocked herself for a long time.

17

"You sounded kind of shook up on the phone."

"I was playing checkers with Mike. Then that damn thing came on the news. I wasn't expecting the media to get in on this so soon."

"It won't last. Reporters have a short attention span."

"Not short enough. Tomorrow the department will have to retract the story they leaked. Unless it turns out Luis really was the killer after all."

Lindstrom fingered the crumbs on her plate, the remains of a slice of cheesecake. "Doesn't look like he was. Some of the stuff in his closet was linked to a burglary on Tuesday afternoon in West Hollywood. The break-in occurred while the lady of the house was out shopping; time frame approximately one to four."

Card thought it over, stirring nondairy creamer into his second cup of coffee and watching clouds form. "Luis left the shelter at two-fifteen, if Mrs. Martinez can be trusted."

"She can. We got confirmation of his time of departure from two other employees."

"All right. The drive from East L.A. to West Hollywood takes at least twenty minutes, and that's assuming no traffic. Then he would have needed another ten or fifteen minutes to case the house, jimmy the window, and snatch the goods."

Lindstrom nodded. "Which means he didn't leave West Hollywood before two-forty-five at the earliest."

"And Jamie was grabbed all the way across town, in Woodland Hills, a few minutes after three." Card sighed. "Unless Luis had a helicopter at his disposal—or one of those teleportation things in *Star Trek*—there's no way he could have covered that much distance in so little time."

"Unfortunately, I think you're right."

Card sipped his coffee. He stared out the window at the red streaks of taillights smearing Ventura Boulevard like brush strokes of watercolor.

"You know," he said quietly, "I'll bet Luis didn't pull the job in West Hollywood till after three anyway. He probably drove around looking for a house to hit for a half hour or so. Maybe apologizing to Jesus the whole time."

"What makes you think it was later?"

"Remember how nervous he got when I asked him where he was between the hours of three and four?"

Lindstrom nodded. "Right. He thought we had him made on the burglary. And we didn't even know about it."

"Good one on him, huh?" Card regretted the bitterness in his voice.

"Cut it, Bobby. You made a mistake about Estoban being Jamie's killer. Okay, so did I. But you didn't make any mistake taking out a guy who was throwing lead at your partner."

"Throwing lead?"

"It's the Clint Eastwood in me."

"That explains the resemblance."

"Sweet."

They sat without speaking for a while, a cloud of strangers' conversations drifting around them. Card tapped his spoon thoughtfully on the rim of his plate. Lindstrom repeated the action with her own spoon. They tapped out meaningless messages to each other until people started staring. Then they went back to drinking their coffee like grown-ups.

Put some moves on her, Robert. Come on, have you forgotten how?

He hadn't forgotten, but the situation was tricky. The embarrassment potential for both of them was disconcertingly high.

He studied the place where her slender neck met her collarbone. Something pleasing about the angles there. The skin of her neck was looser than it had been a few years ago. She was forty-one and single. Never talked about any men in her life. What was the worst that could happen? Even if she turned him down, she would be flattered, right?

Go for it.

"Ellen, you know what I've been thinking? We ought to have dinner sometime."

"Dinner? We have dinner all the time. We had dinner last Thursday, or was it Wednesday, when we were setting up the Sarbello bust."

"That was fast food. I mean a real dinner. At a decent restaurant."

"Sure, we can do that."

She wasn't getting it. He wanted her to understand. "I mean we should get to know each other better."

"Better than we do now?"

"Well, yeah. Look, we spend a lot of time together, but how much do I really know about you? Your interests, your likes and dislikes. Personal things."

"I guess I don't get too personal on the job."

"This wouldn't be on the job."

"I'm not real good at opening up like that."

"Neither am I. But we ought to learn. I mean, I'm thirty-nine."

"And I'm forty-one. What's that got to do with it?"

"It's just that I'm not getting any younger." He didn't bite back the cliché in time.

Lindstrom studied him, her coffee cup raised to her face, masking her expression. "Nobody is," she said cautiously.

"What I'm saying is"—Card pressed ahead—"I think it's time for me to start being more open, start connecting with people a little more. I'd like it to be with you." His voice sounded an octave higher than normal, and there was a funny quaver in it. "I, well, I respect you, Ellen. And I trust you. Right now, the way things are with me, you're the only woman I can say that about."

Her eyes flickered. "You're asking me out, aren't you? Like, on a date?"

"Yes."

"The two of us? An item?"

The skepticism in her voice pricked him. "Crazier things have happened."

"Have they?"

"Damn right they have. Hey, look, we could both do worse. And as far as I know, neither of us got swamped with Valentines last February fourteenth." Anger made him harsh.

Lindstrom shook her head. "It's not a good idea, people who work together."

"I don't know too many people I don't work with, except the snitches we shake down for leads. And Consuelo. She'd marry me out of gratitude for helping her get citizenship, but I'm not sure we'd have much to talk about in the dark."

"And you think we would?"

His fist struck the table, rattling the silverware. "Christ."

"Sorry, Bobby. But I just don't see it."

His heart was beating hard, and he could feel the red heat in his face. He wanted this to be over.

"All right," he said softly, "forget it, then. It was a thought, that's all. A stupid thought. I'm all mixed up after what happened today."

"I'm sorry."

"Stop saying that. You don't have to apologize." His chair scraped back from the table. "I've got to be going. Promised Mike a bedtime story."

Something glittered at the corners of Lindstrom's eyes. "Be sure it has a happy ending."

"They always do." Card managed a smile. "I screwed this up. Don't hold it against me."

"I won't. You didn't. I mean . . ."

"I know what you mean. Good night, Ellen. Take care."

Lindstrom watched him go, her hands gripping the coffee cup. She wished Bobby had stayed. She wished he'd promised her a bedtime story. Happily

ever after. That was how life should be. Happily
ever after, and no pain.

She lingered at the table a few moments longer,
still holding the cup but not drinking from it.
Abruptly she rose and tossed a tip on the table;
the handful of coins jangled crisply. At the cash
register she fumbled in her purse for her wallet till
the cashier told her not to bother; her friend had
covered the tab on his way out. Thoughtful of
Bobby to remember.

The cafe was part of a mini-mall, all concrete
and glass and unimaginative functionalism. In a
corner of the mall she found a telephone kiosk. She
punched in seven digits from memory.

"Hey, it's me. Doing anything tonight?"

"Not really. You feeling okay, Ellen?"

"Sure, I'm fine. Why wouldn't I be?"

"You sound a little shaky."

"Well, you'd be shaky too if you'd just consumed
your sixty-ninth cup of coffee for the day. So what
do you say we meet someplace?"

"All right, but I get to pick the spot. And you
know what that means."

Lindstrom closed her eyes. "Shit."

"You guessed it."

"You don't really want to go there again?"

"Come on, Ellen, don't be such a pill. Loosen up.
Learn to live a little."

"Spare me the clichés. I'll go, but under protest.
Half an hour?"

"No problem. See you."

The dial tone buzzed.

Lindstrom replaced the handset on its hook, then
walked to her parked car. A tall pale man loitering

near a vacant store checked her over as she passed by, his gaze moving brazenly over her body. She didn't know what, if anything, he intended: a come-on, a mugging, a rape. She met his eyes with a deadly stare. He looked away, shoulders slumping, and she knew he would give her no trouble.

Creeps were easy to deal with, she thought as she unlocked her car and slid inside. You just had to be tough.

"Yeah, that's me, all right." Her voice was low over the cough of the engine. "One tough bitch."

She dabbed her eyes with a tissue before starting to drive.

18

"All Van Nuys units, Code Thirty, Miguel's Budget Fashion, eighty-five thirty-nine Sepulveda Boulevard. Incident five-four-two-one."

"We can take that," Lawton said over the crackle of the RTO's voice on the squad-car radio.

Tillis unhooked the microphone and pressed the transmit button. "Nine-A-fourteen will handle the Code Thirty." He replaced the mike on the dashboard hook. "All right, partner, let's check it out."

A Code Thirty referred to the activation of a security alarm. It was a low-priority call; false alarms were common. Lawton drove fast but not recklessly. He did not flip the toggle switches that turned on the siren and dome lights; unlike movie cops, real patrol units went Code Three only in emergencies.

Traffic on Sherman Way was thin at twenty minutes to midnight. The rare cars pulled over to let the black-and-white whip past. In less than ninety seconds Lawton was turning onto Sepulveda. He cut his speed and scanned the street.

The stretch of Sepulveda between Sherman Way and Parthenia was a strip of liquor stores, used-car lots, and cheap motels. Years ago it had been a

decent middle-class neighborhood, until the poly-
glot Third Word tide washed in. Lawton and
Tillis—both white, both raised in affluent suburbs,
both chafing at Affirmative Action policies that,
they felt sure, had restricted their opportunities
for promotion—saw little good in such neighborhoods or in what they implied for the future.

Lawton guided the cruiser down the street while
Tillis studied the dark storefronts.

"Hey. Look what we got here."

Lawton followed his partner's gaze. The sound
he made was half grunt, half chuckle. "Asshole
must think he's Willie fucking Mays."

Up ahead a solitary figure was swinging a base-
ball bat in brisk, vicious sweeps, clobbering imaginary fastballs that had just nicked the sweet spot
over the plate.

Tillis's startled laughter died when, on his next
swing, the guy punched the bat smack through a
shop window.

"Oh, Christ."

Glass showered the sidewalk, glittering prettily
in the funnel of light from a street lamp. Lawton
was reminded of plastic snowflakes shimmering in
one of those glass paperweights.

"No wonder the frigging alarm went off," Tillis
said, disgust thick in his voice.

"Let's take him."

The radio car skidded up to the curb. Instantly
both officers were out, service pistols drawn. They
were taking no chances. Neither Lawton nor Tillis
had forgotten the female rookie who stopped to
issue a routine citation to an El Salvadoran for

drinking in public and got a round in the face at point-blank range from one of his friends.

"Sir, you are under arrest!" Lawton said, making his voice big and dangerous.

The man spun to face them. Hispanic, teens or twenties, dark loose hair and scruffy beard, sweat-blotched T-shirt and thrift-shop dungarees. A stream of slurred Spanish exploded from his mouth.

Lawton tried again. "Drop the bat!"

The man lurched forward, then stood there, rocking on the balls of his feet, eyes wide and rheumy.

"Suelte la arma!" Tillis said, repeating Lawton's order in Spanish. The command was taught to all trainees at the academy.

An unintelligible reply. Grimy fingers gripped the bat, drew it back slowly. Lawton estimated the radius of a swing. He was out of range; his partner was not. The drunk's lurching step had brought him close to Tillis, too damn close, and Tillis, either out of machismo or stupidity, had not retreated.

These thoughts flashed in Lawton's mind as Tillis tried reasoning with the man before him, speaking slowly in his clumsy Spanish. *"No estas estudipo, sí? Quebrar ventanas es nada. Resistir arresto es un crimen mayor."*

The drunk shifted his gaze from one cop to the other. Lawton thought of a mean dog getting ready to fight.

If he swings, I'll have to shoot him. Have to.

Lawton had never shot anybody. He had heard stories, though. Stories from the veteran patrol sergeants at Van Nuys Division, who claimed to have fired four rounds or more into men jacked up with liquor and adrenaline, with no immediate effect. He knew that even a perfectly placed shot might not stop the swing that would open Tillis's skull.

His two hands tightened their hold on his Beretta's black plastic grip. He was aware of the hard steady pounding of his heart, the night heat, the swish of tires on the street behind him as passing cars slowed down, drivers gawking.

Tillis was still speaking. *"Somos ambos razonable. Queremos evitar molestia—"*

From the drunk, a shouted curse. Blur of motion—the bat circled forward, flew free of the man's hands. The drunk had flung it wildly, not at Tillis, at *him*. Lawton saw it coming, tumbling end over end like a bola. He ducked. Crack of glass. The squad-car windshield starred, crumbling. Racing footsteps as the drunk took off, trailing idiot laughter.

"You all right?" That was Tillis.

"Yeah, let's go, let's *go!*"

Lawton switched on his rover radio as he ran. "Nine-A-fourteen, we're in foot pursuit of ADW-on-PO suspect, running south on Sepulveda near Parthenia, request backup. Suspect is a male Hispanic, eighteen to twenty-two, dark hair and beard, T-shirt, dungarees, intoxicated."

The man was fast, for a drunk. He sprinted down the sidewalk, then darted into the street. Blare of horns, screech of rubber. A hard thump as he bounced off a sedan's grillwork. Lawton thought the impact would slow him down for sure, but he simply staggered, steadied himself, and ran on.

He had just reached the curb on the opposite side of the street when a bus rumbled by, obscuring him momentarily. When it had passed, the man was gone.

Lawton and Tillis came to a halt in the middle of the sidewalk, looking up and down the street.

"Where the fuck did he go?" Tillis was flustered.

"Someplace close. We only lost him for a second."

"Ducked down an alley."

"What alley?"

"I don't know, Christ, maybe he dropped into a manhole, a storm drain—"

"The bar."

It was a few doors down, unlighted, easy to miss.

"Yeah." Tillis nodded. "That freak-show place."

"Come on."

They were running again, toward a squat brick-faced building with a dark marquee above a darker doorway.

Lawton and Tillis knew the history of that building, just as they knew nearly everything about the neighborhoods they worked. The place had started off as a legitimate movie theater in the fifties, turned porno in the sixties, then metamorphosed into a bar around the time Jimmy Carter was reciting his oath of office. A disco bar at first, later a punk hangout. Now—well, now it was hard to say just what kind of bar it was.

The black capitals on the unilluminated marquee spelled out the words MERE ANARCHY.

Although the two cops had heard about the bar, they'd never been inside. There had been no disturbances here during any of the night tours they'd worked, no problems of any kind. Either the bar's clientele were remarkably well behaved, or the management took pains to avoid visits from the police. Lawton suspected the latter; in places like this, troublemakers were disciplined with brass knuckles and sent home with a warning to keep their mouths shut.

Warily he and Tillis stepped into an empty room that once had been the theater lobby. Nobody stood at the doorway taking money; no cover charge, apparently. No checkroom clerk either, just a roomy closet with shelves and coat racks where jackets and coats could be stored and picked up on the honor system.

Lawton pushed aside a heavy black velour curtain, then entered the bar itself, a cavernous high-ceilinged room crawling with slithery smoke that turned weird colors as it passed through the pencil-fine beams of moving spotlights. Nude mannequins in obscene poses were mounted here and there, grotesque statues gazing on the scene with pupilless eyes. TV sets on glass pedestals displayed silent images of other worlds. Tables, jammed uncomfortably close together, filled most of the room, but a central space had been cleared to form a dance floor, where a few somnambulistic couples undulated slowly like waving strands of kelp. On the stage at the rear of the bar, a woman sat on a stool, garishly lit in blue, reciting lines of disjointed poetry into a microphone.

Both cops scanned the room and caught glimpses of the customers in the spotlights' pendulum arcs. Masklike faces floating in the smoke like nightmares. The men more elaborately sequined and painted than the women, Tattooed arms, legs, breasts. Ringlets looped through noses and nipples. A woman with shaved eyebrows and a bowl hair-cut, a meerschaum pipe in her mouth. A man in a sleeveless shirt flexing his huge biceps to make a tattooed lady dance. Another man with his shirt unbuttoned, carrying on a conversation while his girlfriend plucked hairs from his chest and ate them, giggling.

"Christ," Tillis muttered, "it's Disneyland for weirdos."

"Yeah, but where's *our* weirdo?"

"I don't see him. Maybe he didn't come in here after all."

Lawton figured his partner was looking for an excuse to get out of this pit. Couldn't blame him. But there was a job to do.

"Let's find out," he said brusquely.

A mahogany bar ran along one wall, the good wood painted black and sloppily shellacked. Lawton approached it, Tillis following. At each table they passed, conversation died like the buzz of insects stilled by a moving cloud of bug spray.

The bartender was a big man with a blue-stained face. He studied the two cops, his eyes flat like bottle tops, registering no fondness for men in uniform. "Yeah?"

Lawton told him they were looking for a Hispanic male who had run in here a few seconds ago. Probably frightened, out of breath, inebriated.

"Haven't seen him."

"We saw him enter this place," Lawton bluffed.

"I don't eyeball everyone who comes in." The bartender kept his voice low, and it was hard to hear him over the amplified poetry and background music.

"Christ." Lawton looked around in frustration. He saw a young man with black lipstick and a ponytail a few stools away, watching the stage raptly, mesmerized by the female poet or whatever the hell she was. Lawton tapped his shoulder. "Hey. You see a guy run into this place just before we came in?"

The man blinked as if emerging from a trance. He swiveled on his stool, looked up at Lawton, and batted his spangled lashes. "Why, no, officer. I'm sorry to say I didn't." Immediately he returned his attention to the stage.

Lawton heard sarcasm in the man's exaggerated politeness. A wise-ass. He was momentarily tempted to run the guy in, but he couldn't think of a charge.

His circling gaze settled on two women at the other end of the bar. In contrast to most of the other patrons, they were dressed like normal human beings.

He nudged Tillis. "Ask them."

Tillis complied. One woman looked away as he spoke, refusing to meet his eyes. The other one listened respectfully.

"A small man?" she asked. "T-shirt? Dungarees?"

"Yeah," Tillis said, surprised. "That's the guy."

"He went out the back door. Over there."

Lawton and Tillis both turned their heads, following the line of her pointing finger. Blurrily visible through the haze, a glowing exit sign hovered near the stage. One of the movie theater's original exits, Lawton guessed; kids probably used to sneak in that way after the feature started. The thought made him sad.

He motioned to Tillis. "Let's go."

They hurried toward the exit. As they reached the door, sudden silence froze the room. The poetry recital had stopped in midverse. Lawton glanced up and saw the performer staring at them, her eyes big and fearful. He frowned. Another freak, her face painted bone white, her lips smeared bright red, creating the overall effect of a bloody-mouthed skull. Disgusting. That creep at the bar seemed to go for her, though. Maybe he was her boyfriend. If so, they deserved each other.

He opened the door. Together he and Tillis stepped cautiously into an alley. A low choking sound came from a few feet away.

"Look at this shit," Tillis said with a mixture of humor, contempt, and pity.

The drunk stood doubled over, hands on knees. The exertion of running had brought up the liquor and whatever else was in his stomach.

They let him finish as the backup units squealed into the alley, dome lights flashing. It was not a Code Three call, but cops got serious when one of their own had been assaulted.

Lawton and Tillis read the guy his Miranda rights in both English and Spanish as they led him to the nearest car. He put up no resistance; all the fight had left him now, and he was just a stupid kid who'd gone a little crazy on a summer night.

"Let's hitch a ride to our vehicle," Tillis suggested.

Lawton nodded. To walk back would mean going

through the bar, and neither of them wanted to enter Mere Anarchy again. It wasn't just the freaks. It was something more, something beyond ugliness, beyond perversion.

He'd felt—hell—he'd felt something evil in there.

Gregory studied Dominique as she continued her recital in a voice that was almost steady. Though his gaze was fixed on her, he was no longer listening to the words she spoke. He was remembering the terror that had flashed in her eyes when she saw the two blue uniforms advancing on her out of the smoke.

Interesting how she had reacted. He'd never seen fear in Dominique's face until that moment. He hadn't known fear was even possible to her. The sudden perception of a human weakness in her character was disturbing, like the first glimpse of a crack in the wall of a fortress thought to be invulnerable; yet at the same time he found himself strangely, almost erotically intrigued.

How she loved to dominate him—and he let her; oh, yes, there was no question of that. He enjoyed surrendering to her, playing the helpless child in her bed.

Yet it would be sweet to switch roles with her, wouldn't it? To be the one in control. The one with power.

Why do you fear the police, darling? he asked her in his thoughts. What have you done, what guilty secrets do you harbor?

The answer might be nothing at all. Perhaps she feared all authority figures. Or perhaps he had misinterpreted her reaction as fear, when actually it had been hostility or mere surprise.

Perhaps.

But he didn't think so.

He could ask her directly, of course. But he knew she wouldn't tell him. She never told him anything that mattered. She treated him with airy contempt, a goddess smiling down at her kneeling sycophant, pleased to let him worship her, but giving him nothing of herself.

Yet she had given him something tonight, without meaning to. A clue.

Gregory smiled. He ran the palm of his hand along the polished surface of the bar, imagining the smooth skin of Dominique's legs, her back, her neck.

He knew he was not her equal. He could not match her brilliance or her boldness or her strength. He could never be what she was.

But once, just once, he wanted to see her outstretched before him like this slab of wood. Just once he wanted her to lie prostrate beneath his body, to submit to his desires, to surrender to his will. Just once he wished to command her and to see that sparkle of fear in her eyes as she obeyed.

His lips were drawn back tight against his teeth. He pressed his fingers against the wood, squeezing the tips bloodless.

Just once.

19

"God, you're really wound up tight about this, aren't you?"

"Damn right I am."

"Come on, Ellen, it's no big deal."

"You're sure they didn't see my face?"

"Positive."

"I don't know. They were right there. They might have gotten a glimpse. . . ."

"For Christ's sake, they weren't paying any attention to you. It was that guy they were looking for, that grungy little Mexican runt. Anyway, you don't know them, do you?"

"No, they must be with Van Nuys Division. The bar's in their territory."

"So you're okay, then, no matter what."

"Not necessarily. Bobby and I deal with beat cops from other divisions all the time. If we meet these guys, and they recognize me—"

"They won't. They can't. So forget about it."

Ellen Lindstrom drew a deep drag on her cigarette, the burning end bright against the darkness of her bedroom. She no longer chain-smoked—the nicotine gum had succeeded to that extent—but when under stress she still needed a hit of the real thing.

She let her head fall back on the pile of pillows bunched up against the headboard, drew her knees up close in a defensive posture, smoothed her rumpled nightgown. Beside her, Christine lay sprawled facedown on the bed in her underwear, one lazy hand idly fingering Ellen's bare toes. Low music played from the clock-radio on the nightstand. Lacy J. Dalton singing about trains.

"I wish we hadn't gone to that place," Ellen said grimly after releasing a breath of smoke.

"You never want to go *any*place."

"Not anyplace weird."

"The weirdness is what makes it interesting. Like that poet tonight. She's pretty bizarre."

"I'll say."

"She does a lot of recitals there. Writes all her own stuff."

"Terrific." Ellen tried blowing a smoke ring, failed. "She reminded me of the Phantom of the Opera."

"Michael Crawford?"

"Lon Chaney."

"Yeah, that freaky skull makeup." Chris treated herself to a pleasurable shiver. "I thought it was rather becoming."

"You would."

"It's all part of the atmosphere."

"An atmosphere I could have done without. Aren't there any normal places you like to go?"

"Hey, come on, Ellen. You don't like hanging out at the gay bars—"

"Because there might be Vice people working undercover. I've explained that."

"All right. Well, Mere Anarchy may be a lot of

things, all of them plenty strange, but one thing it is not, is a gay bar. *Chiaro?*"

Ellen sighed, giving in. *"Capisco."*

She knew there was no point in arguing. Barhopping at underground hangouts was Chris's idea of fun, not her own. Ellen was always nervous in such places, certain she would be spotted by someone she knew. Yet she went anyway, choosing risk over loneliness. She had spent too much of her life alone. Alone and afraid and empty inside.

She remembered the nightmare of high school— her female classmates gossiping excitedly about boys, sharing whispered stories of their first sexual experiences, while she loitered at the fringes of the group, feigning interest, conscious only of a frightening indifference to the heated encounters they described. For years she had believed she was frigid, neutered, some kind of sexless freak. Until that night in her junior year of college when she and her best friend, Rachel Woodward, were cramming for an impossibly difficult economics midterm the next day.

Her memory of it was vivid even now, twenty years later, a nostalgic remembrance, precious and sweetly painful. The two of them alone together in Rachel's room. Heads close, bent over pages of notes. Ellen breathing in the smell of Rachel's skin. Then a sudden tingle on the back of her hand— Rachel's fingertips resting on her knuckles, making gentle contact, tentative, exploratory. Her voice soft over the buzz of the electric heater: "You didn't know it, did you? About me ... or you." A smile in the words, and a certainty.

Didn't know what? Ellen wanted to ask, but

didn't. She couldn't pretend not to understand. Not when the tingle in her hand had traveled up her arm, to her neck, her spine, her breasts. Not when she felt her nipples stiffening slowly, magically, in a response she hadn't thought possible to her, ever.

Rachel lifted her hand, touched her cheek, brushed her hair. "Don't be afraid, Ellen."

But she was afraid. Fear and shame competed with the secret thrill of pleasure. She wanted to pull away. Or was that only what she thought she should want? No, come on, this was wrong. Wasn't it? Why? How could it be, when her body was coming alive for the first time in her life?

And then Rachel was kissing her lightly on the mouth, and there were no more questions, no resistance, no fear, only a sweet sharing and an end, finally, to her alienation from others and herself. She was a sexual being. She was a whole person. And in the bright afterglow of her discovery, she had been young enough to think that she would never be alone again.

Chris's voice, drifting in the dark like the trail of smoke from the cigarette, tugged her back to this moment. "You know, honey, I think you're making way too big a thing out of all this. I mean, it's the nineties. At least it was, the last time I looked."

"So?"

"So even if your fellow cops did find out, would it really matter that much?"

Ellen grunted.

"That's not a very informative reply."

"Yeah, it would really matter. That much."

"All my friends at work know about me."

"Oh, hell, that's different. I mean, a print shop is one thing. The LAPD is something else."

"They can't fire you. If they tried, you could sue the hell out of them. Sic the good old ACLU on the homophobic bastards."

"It's not being fired I'm worried about."

"Well, then—what?"

"Being . . . ostracized." She thought of the years she had spent on patrol, her male partners' cruel jokes at the expense of her femininity simply because she wore a uniform and a gun. "You don't know how cops are."

She felt Chris's shrug, the lift of her shoulders rocking the mattress slightly. "Like any other bunch of people, I assume. There are good ones and bad ones. Take Bobby Card. He wouldn't turn against you."

"Don't be so sure." She hesitated, then decided to say it. "You know what he said to me after we found Jamie Frisch? He said he wished Californians weren't so tolerant. Wished we'd keep out the, uh, how did he put it? The creeps, the weirdos, the leather punks, and the . . . the dykes." She heard the tremor in her own voice. "That's what Detective Robert Card told me."

"Shit." Chris was silent.

Ellen felt vaguely guilty at having presented Bobby so negatively. Suddenly she wanted to soften her words.

"The thing is, this case has put him in a bad way. Pushed all his buttons. That little boy reminded him of his own kid."

"Still no excuse." Chris sounded angry, wounded. "Pretty damn insensitive."

"Yeah, well, he doesn't have a corner on that market. I wasn't too smooth with him tonight."

"What happened?"

"He asked me out."

"You're kidding."

"Don't sound so shocked. I get the occasional offer."

"I'm not shocked." Chris ran an index finger along the sole of Ellen's foot, tickling gently. "Not that way. As you ought to know."

"Okay, sorry. Wrong thing to say."

"So what did you tell him?"

"What do you think? I told him no."

"Did you give a reason?"

"I said it wouldn't work out. Or some equally meaningless words to that effect." She shut her eyes, enclosing herself in a deeper darkness. "You should have seen how much it cost him to ask me. And how much it hurt him when I turned him down."

"Even so, there was nothing else you could do."

"I could have handled it better. If I'd been prepared. And I should have been. Should have seen it coming. I mean, we're together constantly, and ever since his wife died, he's had nobody else." She inhaled smoke, blew it out slowly. "You know, for a minute there, I really wanted to tell him the truth. Reveal everything."

"What the hell for?"

"Because that way he wouldn't think he was being rejected. He would know it had nothing to do with him." She rolled the cigarette thoughtfully between thumb and forefinger. "Then I remembered what he'd said about the weirdos and the dykes. And I decided it wasn't such a good idea. So to protect myself, I let him walk away limping."

"Ellen, you've got to quit being so hard on yourself. It's not healthy."

"Neither are these fucking things." She mashed the cigarette in the ashtray on her nightstand. A gesture, really; she had smoked it nearly down to the filter.

The music on the radio faded out, replaced by a deejay's chatter, then the one o'clock news update. Ellen remembered what the lead story would be. She fumbled for the on-off switch but couldn't find it in the dark. Then the news reader was talking about the most recent development in the Jamie Frisch case, and it was too late.

". . . two LAPD Homicide detectives investigating the murder of seven-year-old Jamie Frisch . . . under fire from a suspect . . . Luis Estoban, a paroled child molester . . . shot and killed . . ."

Chris rolled onto her side and propped herself up on one elbow, listening. Ellen waited, feeling tired.

"That was you, wasn't it?" Chris asked in a small, querulous voice once the report was over. "You and Bobby?"

"Yeah."

"You were in a shoot-out? *Today?*"

"Technically, yesterday. It's after midnight, you know."

"Somebody tried to *kill* you?"

"They're making it out to be a bigger thing than it was."

"Jesus. Oh, Jesus."

Ellen blinked. "Chris? You all right?"

"Jesus Christ."

Her voice was thick, and Ellen realized with a small painful shock that Chris was struggling to hold back tears.

"Hey, hey," she said, alarmed. Crying always frightened her. She was uncomfortable with displays of emotion.

"I'm sorry." A sniffle. "It just . . . hit me kind of hard."

Ellen switched on the light, silenced the radio. Chris was rubbing her eyes with the heel of her hand, an incongruous smile pasted on her face like a grimace.

"Why didn't you tell me?" she asked petulantly. "You know I never listen to the news."

"I was sort of counting on that. I didn't want to talk about it. I wanted to get away from it for a while."

"You should have said something anyway. Oh, fuck. I hate it that you're a cop. I just hate it."

"I won't be a cop much longer. I'm two years away from retirement on full pension."

"In two years you could be dead."

"This sort of thing doesn't happen very often. In fact, it's never happened to me before. Today—yesterday—was the first time I've ever been shot at."

"Great. That's immensely reassuring."

A thought struck Ellen and made her laugh. "You sound like my wife."

"Oh, shut up."

Humor, apparently, was not what was called for here. What was called for was tenderness—an embrace, a shared cry. But Ellen was no good at any of that. She just sat there holding Chris's hand and wishing she knew what to say.

"No wonder you're so jumpy tonight," Chris said after a long silence. "You weren't hurt, were you?"

"Do I look hurt?"

"How many times did he shoot at you?"

"Two or three."

"Did you shoot back?"

"Me? I was too busy hiding under the dashboard. Bobby nailed the guy."

"Oh."

"Yeah. Now you see why I felt so bad about throwing cold water on him when he asked me out? All he'd done was save my life a few hours earlier."

"Don't change the subject. I'm still trying to deal with the fact that you were nearly killed."

"It wouldn't have been a total tragedy. You would have gotten my tape collection. My dirty magazines too—"

"Don't joke about it!"

"Okay, okay, I'm sorry." Ellen kept her voice low and soothing. It was the voice she had once used to talk a jumper off a rooftop. "I guess the jokes are just my way of staying halfway sane."

Chris didn't answer. She pulled her legs under her in the lotus position and lowered her head. Her dark brown hair fell across her face and hung there, swinging slowly back and forth. Ellen studied her thin pale shoulders, her smooth skin. She looked vulnerable and delicate and young. Well, she *was* young, only thirty, and she was vulnerable too.

Not a tough bitch like me, she thought. Just a scared little girl.

"Next time," Chris said finally, lifting her head

and brushing back her hair, "you'd better tell me. No excuses. You tell me or else."

"There won't be a next time."

"If there is."

"Okay. I'll tell you."

"Promise?"

"Promise."

Chris nodded, satisfied, the issue resolved. She looked past Ellen at the clock-radio's digital display.

"God, it's late. Guess I ought to mosey on home, huh?"

Ellen smiled. "You don't have to. In fact, I wish you wouldn't."

Her smile faltered as she thought of the bullets blowing out the Ford's windshield, the ugly scene in the coffee shop, her fear of exposure in the bar. Suddenly she needed another cigarette or . . . or something.

She saw Chris watching her and tried to shrug. The movement of her shoulder became a tremor that set her lower lip quivering.

"Wish you wouldn't," she repeated senselessly. "Tonight I . . ." She wasn't certain of the words she wanted. "I don't . . ."

Slowly Chris reached out to her, stroked her hair, ran a fingertip lightly along the line of her jaw. The touch of that gentle hand reminded Ellen of Rachel's first caress so many years ago, the caress that had ended her long loneliness. She thought of that, and then she knew what she meant to say.

"I guess tonight I just don't want to be alone."

Chris kissed her cheek. "Well, who does, honey?" she asked in a voice that was whisper-soft. "Honestly . . . who ever does?"

20

Card survived the Officer-Involved Shooting review.

He had been worried at first. A dozen local residents had witnessed part or all of the incident from street corners or apartment windows. Among them were the kids who had studied him and Lindstrom with dark, suspicious eyes. If they were gangbangers, hostile to the police, they could report what had happened in a damaging way, make a complaint, force an Internal Affairs investigation. But astonishingly they told the story straight.

The news coverage continued on and off for three weeks, gradually falling in intensity. Card's identity was made public on the day after the shooting. That evening, reporters ambushed him outside the station, sticking cameras and microphones in his face. They tried to tail him home; he shook them loose with some fancy moves that pleased him.

His private phone number was unlisted, but cranks got hold of it anyway. The callers usually sounded drunk or high; often they spoke with a Spanish accent. Threats were made. He wondered if he should make Mike stay with Jessie's mother in Oakland. But school was still in session—the

L.A. schools went year-round now—and Mike wouldn't be able to finish first grade with the rest of his class. Card decided against it. Finally he had his number changed, and the calls stopped.

The worst of the ordeal, however, was not the hate messages or the press reports or even the investigation itself. The worst was having Mike approach him with worried eyes and ask if it was true what the kids were saying in school. "They say you're in trouble 'cause you shot that guy. They say you might go to jail. I don't get it. Hunter shoots people all the time, and he never goes to jail."

"I won't, either. Don't you worry about it, Mike."

He had never missed Jessica so badly. At night, in bed, he found himself hugging his pillow to his chest as if it were a woman. He had not done that since high school.

The other cops were on his side. He received a lot of slaps on the back, friendly grins, and thumbs-up signals. The support was nice, but he had the uneasy feeling that his colleagues would have rallied around him even if he'd shot an unarmed man. The merits of his case seemed less important than the fact that he was a member of the force, one of their own.

The final report on the shooting of Luis Estoban was nine pages long. Its last sentence was the only one that mattered. "Inasmuch as both Detective Card and Detective Lindstrom have stated that Luis Estoban's use of his firearm placed them in immediate peril, and inasmuch as twelve witnesses have corroborated the officers' accounts of the incident, the investigation hereby concludes that Detective Card was justified in the use of deadly force."

The ruling relieved Card and ended the public's

interest in the matter. Mike heard no more gossip in school. Everything was fine.

Except that for weeks afterward Card woke in the night with the afterimages of vivid dreams swimming before him in the dark, dreams of a pale dead man stretched across the gear selector of a Plymouth Horizon. Indigestion bothered him more than usual, and at times he still felt sure he smelled Estoban's blood.

He and Lindstrom never spoke of his awkward proposition and her chilly rebuff. The incident shaded their friendship but did not darken it too much. Anyway, they were both professionals, and there was work to do.

Throughout the OIS inquiry, Card had been assigned to desk work, but Lindstrom, assisted by other officers, had continued to investigate the Jamie Frisch case. From the sidelines Card followed the progress—or lack of it—as closely as possible.

Jamie was buried at Forest Lawn in a mahogany casket, heartbreakingly small. Family members were recruited to serve as spotters at the funeral; they scanned the crowd for unfamiliar faces, but the few individuals they pointed out were easily alibied.

Mr. and Mrs. Frisch advertised a large reward for information leading to the conviction of Jamie's killer. The offer produced a slew of worthless tips methodically investigated by uniformed cops. Lindstrom and the two detectives working with her concentrated on developing other leads.

They again canvassed Jamie's neighborhood in search of witnesses to the abduction. They set up a roadblock near the park, stopping drivers in the hope that one of them had passed through on Tuesday afternoon and seen something. They made discreet inquiries into the backgrounds of Jamie's neighbors and relatives, on the chance that the boy had been killed by someone he knew, perhaps as retaliation against his parents for some past grievance. They checked out the people who had volunteered for the search parties also; it was not unknown for a killer to take part in the hunt for his own victim. They sent bulletins to the FBI, the state police, the sheriff's department, and out-of-state P.D.s, asking for word of any similar crime committed in another jurisdiction.

Nothing panned out.

The CCAP computer scanned its data base for paroled child murderers living in the L.A. area. The names of three possible suspects surfaced, but subsequent investigations cleared them all.

Evidence technicians determined that the nylon cord and the plastic bag found on Jamie's body were common commercial brands that could have been purchased anywhere. The same analysts compared bits of junk and threads of fiber collected at the Woodland Hills park with items picked up along the perimeter of the L.A. River. Nothing matched. The corpse itself had been washed clean of any possible evidence as it drifted through the murky water.

The FBI withdrew from the investigation; nothing in a standard homicide required federal participation. If the murderer struck again, showing a serial-killer pattern, agents Haskell and Robertson would be brought back into the case.

Mrs. Frisch called either Card or Lindstrom daily, but there was nothing they could tell her.

Mr. Frisch, who returned to San Diego shortly after Jamie's funeral, phoned less often. When he did, his voice was often slurred.

By the time Card was reassigned to field duty, the Jamie Frisch case had reached a dead end. Other matters had come up, cases that touched him less deeply but offered more hope of a successful resolution. Naturally these took priority.

The Caldera case was typical.

Walter Caldera was a first-generation American of Guatemalan descent. Relentless, punishing work had earned him an enviable life in Woodland Hills: a two-bedroom apartment in the Warner Center, a new BMW, season tickets to Universal Amphitheatre and the Hollywood Bowl. On weekends he liked to shed his tailored suits in favor of faded jeans and a paint-spotted plaid shirt. In these clothes he did not look like a successful businessman.

Caldera was wearing this outfit on a Saturday night in mid-May when he walked to a convenience store to pick up a newspaper. As he returned home, a man began walking alongside him, harassing him with comments to the effect that wetbacks and greasers were not welcome in this neighborhood. Caldera challenged the man, who became violent. There was a scuffle. The stranger overpowered Caldera, threw him to the sidewalk, and kicked and pummeled him, fracturing Caldera's skull and three ribs. Sometime later a passerby found Caldera lying unconscious at the curb and called an ambulance.

Card and Lindstrom were assigned the detail; normally a felony battery would fall under the purview of the Crimes Against Persons squad, but the obvious racial motivation made this a hate crime, which was considered a special case.

They found they had little to go on. Caldera's description of his assailant was vague. The purpose of the beating had not been robbery—nothing was stolen—so talking to the usual informants would be useless.

The two detectives interviewed everyone who lived in the vicinity of the crime scene. Few had been home on a Saturday night. Those few had seen nothing. One man, however, supplied a lead without knowing it. He mentioned having ordered a pizza, which had been delivered around the time Caldera said he'd been attacked. Card and Lindstrom tracked down the delivery boy. He recalled that, as he arrived at the address, he'd seen a man running along the street to a parked car. A station wagon; he couldn't say what color. The wagon pulled away so quickly that it banged the rear bumper of the car parked in front of it.

Further inquiries identified the owner of the dented car. She had not yet had the damage repaired. The extent of the damage and the angle of impact indicated that the station wagon had crunched its front quarter panel pretty badly.

Card and Lindstrom called out an evidence technician, who found flecks of green paint on the crumpled bumper. The paint was analyzed in the mass spectrometer at the downtown crime lab; it was identified as a factory paint used on several G.M. cars, but only one station wagon, the Buick LeSabre, the 1987 and '88 models.

Caldera's assailant had told him to stay out of the neighborhood. Presumably he lived in the vicinity. If so, he might get his car patched up at a local garage. Card and Lindstrom made the rounds of service stations and auto-body shops, asking about a green '87 or '88 LeSabre with a crushed fender. No one had seen it, but at each place they left their number in case the car showed up. A week later Lindstrom's desk phone rang. A car matching that description had just been dropped off for service.

Card and Lindstrom obtained the owner's name and address, which he had thoughtfully provided when he filled out the receipt. He was Frank Richardson, and he lived in an apartment in Canoga Park, just north of Woodland Hills.

They found him at home in midafternoon, watching game shows with the volume cranked up. He denied everything. He had never beaten up any Hispanic guy. He liked Hispanics. Friendly people, though the women tended to run to fat as they got older. He said all this while his eyes darted, reminding Card of Luis Estoban.

They brought him in for questioning, took his picture, then showed a photo six-pack to Caldera at the hospital. He studied half a dozen snapshots of different men, displayed in a specially modified manila envelope with cut-out windows, and identified Frank Richardson at once.

"That's him," he muttered. "That's the son of a bitch."

Richardson was held on suspicion of battery in commission of a hate crime, a felony offense, while paint scrapings from his LeSabre were compared with those found on the dented bumper. A match. Card and Lindstrom obtained a warrant, searched

Richardson's apartment, and found a pair of sharp-toed boots at the back of his closet, the oiled leather spotted with dried blood. Confronted with this evidence and Caldera's testimony, Richardson took the advice of his attorney and admitted guilt.

"I don't like spics," he explained matter-of-factly. "They just tick me off, you know?"

Another case cleared. Card and Lindstrom toasted each other with vanilla shakes at McDonald's to celebrate.

That was one of many cases they handled in the month of June, with varying degrees of success. They clocked a lot of overtime, and Card saw Mike less often than he wanted to. He did, however, witness the boy's dramatic debut. Michael R. Card played the role of an eraser in a theatrical production entitled *School Supplies on Parade*. Card thought Mike was very good as an eraser, bringing depth and understated realism to the part. He wished Jessica could have seen it.

In the first week of July, three months after the killing of Jamie Frisch, Jacobs ushered Card into his office and told him that he needed a volunteer to deliver a lecture to some local residents who were interested in forming a neighborhood-watch group. Topic: the invaluable contributions of concerned citizens in the fight against crime.

"Oh, Christ." Card rubbed his forehead. "Why me? I've had enough public exposure as it is."

"But not the right kind of exposure." Jacobs leaned back in his swivel chair and steepled his hands behind his head. "You've been dragged through the mud. This is a chance to show how clean you are."

"The OIS report already showed that."

"In an abstract way. But I want you out there where people can see you. I want to show you're not hiding. Your name has been cleared. Totally and completely. Therefore, why shouldn't you appear in public as a spokesman for the LAPD?"

"I don't see how talking to thirty or forty people in a room somewhere will have much effect on my image one way or the other."

"It won't. But the newspaper stories announcing the event will be read by a lot more people than the few who attend. We're getting this in the *Times,* the *Daily News,* the neighborhood papers, the works."

"Suppose all this publicity prompts some of these civil-rights activists to show up and start heckling. How does that help my rehabilitation in the public eye?"

"Forget about it. They won't show. They're already manning the barricades on that Downey P.D. thing—you know, the black guy who got zapped with a Taser and who's supposedly been brain-damaged." A grunted chuckle indicated Jacobs's assessment of that claim. "These creeps can only handle one controversy at a time. You're old news."

"I still wish you'd find someone else."

"If wishes were horses, Detective, we'd have to shovel our way to work. Right?"

Card sighed, defeated by the captain's eloquence. "Right."

He told Lindstrom about his newly discovered passion for public-relations work. She declined to accompany him to the lecture. "I'm clipping my toenails that night," she said soberly.

21

Deliverance.

Dominique lowered the newspaper slowly. She stared at a few paragraphs of text buried below the fold on an inside page of the Metro section. The brief article, which read like a press release, announced that Detective Robert Card of West Valley Division would deliver a talk on neighborhood-watch groups at a Winnetka high school tomorrow night.

"Yes," she whispered. "Oh, yes."

She had been intrigued with Card, obsessed by him, ever since she'd seen the first TV report of the death of Luis Estoban. Subsequent news stories had given details of the shooting-team investigation; she'd learned Card's name, his rank, a few fragments of his background.

The image of the gun in his hand had clung to her dreams and fantasies. She wrote poetry about it, secret poems she did not recite in public, poems littered with imaginings of her own death like corpses on a battlefield. Tangled in the sheets with Gregory, she saw herself in Card's arms, taking his gun into her mouth, licking the blued steel as he squeezed the trigger.

Soon Gregory began to bore her. He posed no threat, held no danger; he was nothing, only a womanish boy, her acolyte, worshipful of her genius, fascinated by her body, eager to play the games she liked. Too eager, puppy-eager. Her interest in him deteriorated to tolerance and finally to disgust. She spent fewer nights at the bar; for the last two weeks she had not been there at all. She supposed Gregory might be upset about that; she didn't care.

Card was the man she desired. Card, who was hunting her with his deadly gun.

She wanted to see him in the flesh, watch him from a distance, get as close to him as she dared. She conceived a dozen strategies for tracking him down, discarded each. He was not listed in the phone book; she supposed cops never were. She drove past the police station on Vanowen Street in Reseda every day, hoping for a glimpse of him as he hurried in or out, never spotting him; she could not risk lingering at the scene for fear of calling attention to herself.

Now she had a chance to see him at last. Perhaps even to follow him home, learn where he lived. Or even . . .

She drew a sharp breath.

Suppose she were to approach him after his lecture. Smile and say hello. Ask him out for coffee, come on strong, seduce him. . . . Was he married? She didn't know, but it made no difference. Married men fooled around all the time.

He would fuck her and she would think of Luis Estoban. She would think of Jamie Frisch.

She floated on the cloud of this pleasant daydream a moment longer, then slowly shook her head.

It was no good. It wouldn't work.

She wanted Card, but she knew he would never be drawn to a woman like her. No matter what sort of act she put on, he would see through it. He would see that she was not normal, not safely conventional. She could not hide her gifts.

I'll tell him, then, she thought wildly. I'll tell everything—he may understand—if I explain it well enough, he'll see—

Nonsense. Card could never comprehend her genius, her talents. He would look at the murder of Jamie Frisch as a crime to be solved, an injustice to be avenged. He could not grasp that by killing Jamie she had gifted him with a new and more exalted life. It was only the boy's body she had murdered, his physical being, the ugly, evil part of any child, the part that would keep him in contact with the world and corrupt him, poison his spirit. To murder a child's body was to liberate his soul and to guarantee that it would remain pure forever.

She sighed. The pinnacle on which she stood was lonely at times. She would have liked to share her insights with someone who could understand, someone worthy of her trust. She would have liked to describe the wondrous moment when death passed over the boy's face and glazed his eyes, when she felt the electrifying frisson of contact with his soul, when she thrilled to his spirit's entry into her body, the rush of a ghostly presence between her legs, into her belly, a reverse-birth, a child returning to the womb.

Card was incapable of grasping such sublime truths. He would never want her, never love her.

Her mouth tightened. Her eyes sparkled with a chilly feral light.

All right, then. She could not have him. But she could hurt him. She could draw blood, inflict pain, and achieve a different kind of intimacy, the special intimacy known to torturer and victim, killer and prey.

She did not know how, not yet. But she would consider the problem. There had to be a way.

22

On Tuesday night Card drove to a high school in Winnetka, where a small, earnest crowd was assembled on folding chairs in the auditorium. He was grouchily pleased to see no TV or radio people around.

Taking the stage, he delivered his prepared remarks, glancing occasionally at the small stack of note cards in his hand. He began with a general discussion of steps that people could take to minimize the risk of burglary: target-hardening their homes, trimming shrubbery, installing window-sill flower boxes, engraving social security numbers on valuables.

"But no family wants to be held prisoner in their own home," he said, segueing into the next part of his presentation, "and fortunately, there are things we can do to fight fear as well as crime. One of those things is the resident-organized block-watch program."

The key to the block-watch approach was community involvement. Every night a team of unarmed volunteers would patrol the neighborhood, wearing brightly colored jackets and carrying shriek alarms, using walkie-talkies to stay in con-

tact with a base station in somebody's house. If a
suspicious individual was sighted, the radio operator at the base station would summon the police.
Ancillary programs could combat graffiti and assist
in peacefully resolving conflicts between neighbors.

He concluded by quoting statistics showing the
effectiveness of neighborhood crime-prevention
groups, then opened a question-and-answer period.
As he called on people shyly raising their hands,
he felt a little bit like Mike's homeroom teacher.

"We like greenery around the house, but you said
it provides cover for criminals. Is there anything
safe to plant?"

Card recommended rosebushes and cacti.

"Our car has been stolen three times. Do you
know of an alarm system that really works?"

Card thought most automobile alarm systems
were a waste of money; any halfway competent
thief could defeat them. He suggested disabling the
car by removing the rotor from the distributor shaft
whenever it was to be left unattended.

"How do we get started organizing a block-watch
group?"

Card advised collecting the names, addresses,
and phone numbers of all those who were interested, then sending out fliers to publicize the effort. If enough people signed up, the LAPD would
provide training and assistance.

He was thinking of wrapping up the evening
when he saw an eager hand flapping for attention
at the back of the room.

"Yes?"

"Detective Card"—the speaker was a young man,
his cheeks dusted with a stubble of beard—"what

you've said is all very informative, but I think many people may be more interested in the shooting of Luis Estoban."

Shit.

"That is not the subject of tonight's gathering," Card said stiffly.

"But wouldn't you like to go on record with your side of the story?"

"On record?"

"Yes, sir. I represent the *Daily News.*" A woman beside him stood up and started snapping flash photos. "Don't you owe the public a full explanation, Detective?"

Card blinked at the bursts of white light. He hoped these two were only stringers, and that the *News* wouldn't use the story. "I've already said everything I have to say about that, uh, regrettable incident."

"Is that all it is to you? A regrettable incident?"

Murmurs of annoyance from the Winnetka homeowners, who were shifting in their seats and tossing angry glances at the troublemakers in the back row.

"It was a tragedy," Card said as another flashcube popped, "but under the circumstances, it could not have been handled differently. I want to thank you all for coming, and good night."

"But, sir—"

"Good *night.*"

Card escaped from the room, pursued by the reporter and his camera-toting friend. He fumbled open the door of his car and got in. The reporter was still shouting questions at him through the closed window as he gunned the engine and sped off.

He drove fast for a few miles, then checked his speed and forced himself to cool down. The evening had turned out to be a disaster. Well, so what? At least he wouldn't get stuck with any more P.R. assignments after this.

He drew a breath, let it out slowly. As he drove past a supermarket, he thought how good it would be to have a cold beer when he got home. Probably no beer in the fridge, though. Consuelo rarely remembered to buy it for him, a memory lapse possibly connected with her stern disapproval of alcohol. "*Cerveza* is no good for you, Mr. Card," she would tell him with a waggling finger. "*Cerveza* puts a cloud over your brain."

She was right, of course. But a cloud over his brain was exactly what was called for tonight.

He turned the car around, executing an illegal U-turn and not giving a damn, and pulled into the parking lot.

Dominique's heart was beating fast as she followed Robert Card into the supermarket.

She was close to him now. So intoxicatingly close.

The evening had gone beautifully. She had arrived at the high school shortly after Card began his talk. She had not joined the audience; she would not be part of any crowd. But as he'd delivered his remarks, she had peeked into the auditorium through a crack in the door. She had experienced a curious sense of unreality when she'd seen him in person for the first time, a man in a gray jacket and blue tie, a man like any other, except for the gun he must be carrying, the gun that had killed Luis Estoban and could kill her too.

When he'd left the school, she had shadowed his car. A cop ought to be alert to surveillance, but he had appeared to notice nothing.

Now she was trailing him on foot. Stalking him. Yes.

The supermarket was largely empty. A stockroom clerk lethargically swept out the wide aisles. Somewhere a lone cart rattled like a ghost's chains. From a distance, partially concealed behind a pyramid of breakfast cereals, Dominique watched Card pick out a six-pack of beer.

She wanted to shout his name, kiss his mouth, go down on her knees on the tile floor and do him right here, under the cold fluorescent lights. Her body trembled.

Control. She needed control. And patience. Patience was the essential characteristic of artists and predators.

She wasn't sure which of the two she was tonight.

23

Card found the liquor section, grabbed a six-pack of Coors, and brought it to the front of the store. Only one register was open; a short line had formed. He stood there, the cans of beer cold against his side, reading the nonsensical headlines of tabloid magazines.

CANNIBAL MOTHER EATS HER YOUNG. SPACE PROBE REVEALS NAZI DEATH CAMP ON MOON. AMAZING HAMBURGER DIET CURES CANCER. "I HAD BIGFOOT'S BABY": EXCLUSIVE DETAILS INSIDE.

He shook his head slowly. People would believe anything. All it took to convince them were a few words set in type or uttered with authority over the air. The power of the press. The power to distort, to manipulate, to insinuate, to mislead.

He thought of Mike telling him about the rumors at school, his own voice explaining that none of it was true. Then why are they saying all that stuff about you? I don't know, Mike, I don't know. . . .

"You look tired."

He blinked. At first he wasn't sure if the words had been addressed to him. He looked inquiringly at the woman standing behind him in line.

"You look tired," she repeated.

"Oh. Yes. I am."

"Hard day at the office?"

"You could say so." His answer struck him as unnecessarily mysterious. "I just gave a speech," he elaborated. "Well, not a speech exactly. A talk." He moved his hand vaguely. "I'm lousy at talks."

"Oh, I'll bet you're not."

That surprised him. Sounded friendly, complimentary, almost like a come-on.

No, couldn't be. This woman was young, midtwenties at most—too young to be interested in Robert Card, thirty-nine, widower with child. And she was attractive, even beautiful in a fresh-faced, toothpaste-commercial way: clear skin, bright eyes, a wash of brown hair falling loose over her shoulders.

Lindstrom was more his speed. But Lindstrom had turned him down.

"What makes you think I wouldn't be lousy at talks?" he asked. The line inched forward, and he found himself hoping the cashier was slow.

The woman's eyes moved over him appraisingly. Her gaze made him self-conscious in a good way. Conscious of his size; he was a head taller than she. Conscious of the width of his shoulders, the hard muscles of his arms, his flat stomach.

"The way you carry yourself," she said at last. "Your body language. It suggests confidence. Strength."

"Does it?"

"I think so." Her expression was intense, serious. "You seem like a man who can rely on himself. The sort of person who'd be good in a crisis."

"I'm not so sure about that." He was thinking of Luis Estoban.

She smiled at him. "Yes, you are. You just don't want to admit it. You're afraid of your own competence."

Card blinked. Was that true?

He had killed Estoban to save himself and his partner. Then, for weeks, he had flogged himself with the memory of the shooting. He was still beating himself up. He refused to let it go. And why? Was it because secretly he was proud of what he'd done? Proud of how fast he'd reacted, how expertly he'd neutralized the threat? Did pride scare him because it was too close to happiness, and happiness was something he ran from now?

His thoughts were racing. The floor was suddenly unsteady, and he found himself gripping the edge of the counter.

He looked at the woman, staring past her surface beauty into the depths of her intelligent gray eyes.

"What's your name?" his voice asked. The question surprised him; he had not intended to ask it. Not quite yet anyway.

"Angela Westmore."

"I'm Robert Card."

He felt himself tense up, worried that she might recognize his name from the news reports. But she didn't seem to.

"Nice to meet you, Robert Card," she said easily. "Come here often, as they say in the singles bars?"

"No. You?"

"Now and then." She lifted a bag of celery stalks and a jug of nonfat milk. "You caught me in one of my healthy moods."

"Did I—catch you?" Card's own words shocked him with their boldness.

Angela laughed. "Well, let's say you've made a good start."

Card had reached the front of the line. As he handed the six-pack to the cashier, the ring on the third finger of his left hand flashed in the light of the overhead fluorescents.

"Are you married, Robert Card?" Angela asked.

The woman missed nothing. She should be a detective. Card smiled at the thought.

"I was," he answered. "Not anymore. I still wear the ring for . . . sentimental reasons."

"Five-sixty," the cashier said.

Card fumbled a ten-dollar bill out of his wallet. He collected his change, then waited while Angela paid for her purchases.

Wordlessly they walked to the exit. The door slid open automatically, and they emerged into the cool, dry night. A half-moon cast a misty nimbus of light over a cold scatter of stars.

"So," Angela said, "are you going to let me give you my number?"

Card nodded, relieved that she had spared him the effort of asking. "Yes. I'm definitely going to let you do that."

She recited seven digits. He repeated them.

"I'll be expecting you to call," she told him sternly.

"I will."

"You'll disappoint me if you don't."

"I won't disappoint you."

"Okay, then." She nodded toward the far end of the lot. "My car's that way."

"Mine's over there." The other direction.

"Well . . . I'll be seeing you. Good night, Robert Card."

She moved away from him.

"Angela."

She stopped. Turned.

"I'm a cop."

He had to say it. A lot of women were turned off—scared off—by cops. They moved in circles where drugs were used, or where hostility to the law was fashionable. No point in pursuing this one if she was like that.

"Are you?" she said.

"Detective. West Valley Division."

Now she might connect him with the news reports. Might start asking questions about Luis Estoban. Might ruin everything.

She didn't. She merely smiled.

"A detective. Well. That's very intriguing." She swung her grocery bag lightly in one hand. "I like you better all the time."

The intensity of Card's relief astonished him.

"Take care of yourself, Detective. Don't get shot or anything."

"I'll try not to."

She blew him a kiss as she walked away.

Card wrote down her number as soon as he climbed into his car. He was terrified of forgetting it. His fear did not vanish until he had carefully folded the slip of paper and placed it in his wallet.

He shut the door and turned the key in the ignition. He was starting to back up when he remembered the six-pack, which he'd left on the pavement outside the driver's-side door. Grinning at himself, he retrieved the beer and put it on the passenger seat.

The grin remained fixed on his face during the drive home. Suddenly Ellen Lindstrom didn't seem so important, did she? In fact, she was downright irrelevant.

He thought about Angela Westmore. A woman like that, young, beautiful, intelligent, perceptive—a woman like that, interested in him.

Card sighed, a schoolboy sound.

"You had your chance, Ellen," he said aloud in the car. "And you blew it. Too late now."

24

The bitch.

Dominique fumed. She had watched the entire exchange. She had seen the eager interest in Card's eyes as he traded smiles with that giggly little tart.

Oh, it was hardly surprising that he would find such a woman attractive. She was the kind he would be drawn to—not a genius, not a poet—merely a smiling schoolgirl, pretty and pleasant and conventional. She was one of *them*, the ordinary ones, the ones who lived dull, stupid lives and died in spiritual poverty, their minds closed to the secrets of the universe that only a questing, thirsty spirit could drink in.

Dominique hated her. No, hate was not what she felt. The *ordinaries* were not worthy of her hatred. Contempt, disgust, revulsion, every species of abhorrence—that was the only proper response to the subanimal creatures that called themselves human, creatures like that grinning slut.

And yet . . .

The girl might be useful. Yes. She just might.

Dominique had meant to tail Card home in order to learn his address; instead she stayed in the parking lot after he left. She studied the sweet young thing Card had met, observing her with predatory fascination, the malign interest of a spider appraising a fly.

She had wanted to hurt Card, to destroy him if possible. Yet she dared not attack him directly. It was one thing to kill a child; to go after an armed man, a police officer trained in self-defense, would be something else entirely.

No, what she needed was a point of vulnerability she could exploit, a way to wreck his life, to reduce him to shock and tears.

The girl he'd met tonight could be the key. The silly, laughing little cunt with her celery stalks and her jug of milk.

Card had seemed happy as he walked away, pleased to have made the acquaintance of such a charming young lady. His happiness might not last.

He might find himself investigating a new homicide very soon.

25

Angela Westmore woke at dawn. Sleep had been good to her, gifting her with dreams of the man she had met at the supermarket last night, the man named Robert Card.

Lying in bed, gazing up at the sun rays slanting through the open window, she warned herself not to move too fast this time. Hell, she knew nothing about Card except that he was a police detective and he'd been married once. And she knew the risks of falling for a guy at first sight. She'd had only a few affairs since moving to L.A. from Tucson four years ago, but those few had been disastrous. She had learned not to trust her instincts, which unfailingly directed her to the worst possible partner.

Still, Card seemed different. His face intrigued her. It was not the kind of face she associated with her previous boyfriends—the mask of smiling blandness that concealed power lust and a neurotic need for control. She had seen those masks slip in intimate moments, had seen what those men were like when inflamed by sexual heat. They were brutal, violent, destructive; they would take her like an animal, finding pleasure in her protests and her degradation.

Card, on the other hand, struck her as honest, unaffected, old-fashioned, even shy. A stolid, slightly boring man who was nervous around women and sentimental about his failed marriage. Not threatening, not crazed, not a lunatic on a power trip. Just someone who would be safe and pleasant to be with. How refreshing.

She sighed, rising from bed. Oh, well, he probably wouldn't call; the good ones never did. And if he did date her, he would likely turn out to be weird in his own way. He was a cop; he might be into kinky sex with handcuffs or some damn thing. Even so, the experience could at least provide material for a couple of interesting sessions with Dr. Reiss.

A hot shower yanked her firmly into the reality of her daily routine. She dressed quickly in casual clothes. She ate no breakfast, never did. By six-thirty she was behind the wheel of her ancient, rattling Pinto. The car delivered her to the Happy Childhood Daycare Center at six-forty-five.

Marjorie, the supervising provider, was already there. " 'Morning, Angie."

Angela hated being called Angie, but she endured it with a smile. "Hi, Marge." She suspected that Marjorie disliked that name, as well. As the kids would say: Even-Steven.

"You look bright-eyed and bushy-tailed today," Marjorie remarked. Like many daycare providers, she had picked up the habit of addressing adults as if they were children.

"Met an interesting guy last night."

"Oh?"

"A cop. Detective."

"Really?" A sly smile. "Did he show you his nightstick?"

Angela blushed. "Jesus, I just met him."

"When I was your age, I was a fast operator."

"We talked, that's all. I don't know, he might call me."

"He will if he's got any sense." Marjorie looked out the front window and frowned. "Uh-oh, there's Mr. Lachman. Early as usual." A sedan parked at the curb, and a man got out, leading a small boy by the hand. "Bet you a dollar Timothy loses his lunch again."

"I won't take that bet," Angela said, laughing. "Last time he threw up on *me*."

The other two assistant providers on the morning shift, Rachel and Laurie, showed up a few minutes later. Shortly after seven, the rest of the children began to arrive. The center served preschoolers aged four and five, caring for them from seven in the morning to seven at night. Few kids stayed the full twelve hours, but the long day was necessary to accommodate the varied schedules of their parents.

Angela worked the seven-to-one shift. Her afternoons were free, giving her time to shop, see a movie matinee, or just relax and read. For the last two months, every Wednesday and Thursday, she had seen Dr. Reiss at three P.M.

The morning progressed smoothly, following the schedule Marjorie had laid out. An hour of Free Play. Breakfast at eight. Next, Outdoor Play and Circle Time. After that came Work Time, Small Group Activity, and the blissful interlude of Quiet Time.

Throughout the morning small voices tugged at Angela like anxious hands on the hem of her dress.

"Angela, will you help me make a picture at the art table?"

"Angela, Cindy's hogging the horsey again!"

"Angela, do you think I'm pretty? As pretty as you?"

"Angela—*owww!*—make him stop it!"

"Angela, my dollie likes you. She says you're her best friend."

The best part of the job was being with kids all day. She thought of all the children as her friends; she knew their names, their talents, their vulnerabilities. Bobby Reynolds, who was allergic to everything on earth, and who played the toy piano like a virtuoso. Samantha Pozarski, boisterous and high-spirited, prone to ordering the other kids around. Hector Alvarez, master of the art table, his restless ambitions driving him to ever greater aesthetic accomplishments in his chosen medium of construction paper and glue. Little Timmy Lachman, whose nervous stomach had been the cause of so many emergency clean-up operations that the staff really did take bets on when, where, and how he would blow his cookies on any given day.

It was fascinating to see each child's personality already largely formed, even at the age of four or five. Her small charges were miniature people, startlingly mature in some ways, amusingly naive in others, with a fresh perspective on life that no grown-up could share. She often thought the world was not only a bigger place to the very young, but a more richly textured place, where every scent, sight, and sound was somehow sharper, more immediate, more vivid, where every emotion was more intense—and that childhood was a time when life itself was more fully lived than it ever would be again.

Angela enjoyed her job and was good at it. She worked well with kids, and she had learned the skills her profession required. She knew the formula for making bubbles at the water table—three-quarters of a cup of liquid soap, one-quarter cup of glycerine, eight cups of water. She knew how to prepare a homemade version of Silly Putty by mixing Elmer's Glue and liquid starch, with food coloring blended in for extra fun. She could build bendable figures out of L'eggs cartons and pipe cleaners. She excelled at finger painting. When called upon to exercise her literary and dramatic talents at Story Time, she always held her audience's close attention. And nobody could match her proficiency with the Etch-A-Sketch tablet.

She often felt that she had the best job possible, a job so good it hardly seemed like work at all.

Lunchtime arrived. Angela spread creamy peanut butter onto slices of Wonder Bread, then opened the small milk cartons and inserted a flexible straw in each. Kids liked flexible straws.

The warm July day made it unthinkable to eat lunch indoors. She set out the plates on the picnic tables in the front yard. A dry breeze stirred the branches of the eucalyptus tree near the swing set. The paper plates slid around, threatening to blow away, and the children squealed with laughter. Angela smiled.

She ate her own sandwich—tuna fish, not peanut butter—at a table with Rachel and Laurie. The other two women chattered about a party they'd attended last night. Angela had been invited but had declined; she wasn't real big on parties. Lately, she hadn't gone in much for any kind of socializing. She spent her nights alone, thumbing listlessly through the pages of a magazine or watching TV till she fell asleep. She ought to get out more, meet new people, start dating again; but after the last few relationships she'd had, she just couldn't seem to make the effort.

Thoughts of her social life reminded her that this afternoon she would have a session with Dr. Reiss. She wondered what he would say about Robert Card. Nothing, probably; he would just watch her with his heavy-lidded eyes while she sat in the big easy chair, nervously drumming the armrests.

At first she'd felt self-conscious about seeing a shrink. Finally she had confided in Marjorie, who had reassured her that regular therapy sessions were an essential part of the L.A. life-style. "Though I don't know what you've got to worry about," she'd added with a trace of envy. "With your looks and your brains, you shouldn't need help in any department."

But looks and brains hadn't prevented her from plunging into a series of destructive affairs. She needed to know why she kept screwing up her love life so badly. Maybe Dr. Reiss could help her find out.

Then again, maybe, just maybe, she wouldn't require his assistance after all. Maybe Robert Card would turn out to be a man who didn't wear a mask.

She realized she was smiling. She felt light and

free, optimistic about love for the first time in years.

Then her smile faded as she became aware of being watched.

She looked around slowly, the skin of her forearms prickling. Her gaze drifted past the white picket fence to the tree-shaded street beyond.

No one was in sight. Of course, somebody might be watching her from some concealed location—inside one of the houses across the street, perhaps, or in one of the parked cars lining the curb.

She shook her head. Ridiculous. Paranoid.

A chorus of shrieks erupted from the nearest table. Angela turned to see Timmy Lachman barf up his sandwich on the lawn.

"There he goes again," Rachel said cheerfully.

Laurie sighed, rising from her seat. "I'll get it."

"No," Angela said quickly. "Let me."

She felt the sudden need for activity. Briskly she cleaned up the mess, then went into the kitchen to discard the soiled sponges and paper towels.

When she stepped outside again, she no longer had any sense of being watched. Yet she couldn't shake the certainty that someone had been observing her, studying her; and though she knew the feeling was irrational, she was afraid.

26

Card waited till the weekend before calling Angela Westmore.

His hand was damp as he picked up the phone and punched in seven digits. He knew the number by heart; several times during the week he had removed the folded slip of paper from his wallet and studied it, simply to reassure himself that the ink had not faded to invisibility. Once, Lindstrom had caught him looking, her face an unasked question. He'd told her nothing.

The phone at the other end of the line was ringing. Card wished he had a glass of water. He found some spit and moistened his tongue.

It was crazy to be so scared. He was thirty-nine years old, for Christ's sake. He had asked women out before.

But not for a long time. That was the thing. He had been thirty-one when he married Jessica, and he'd been involved with no women since her death. Eight years had passed since his last date as an unmarried man.

Four rings. Five.

She wasn't home. Well, of course not. Who would be home on a Saturday afternoon in July? Relief competed with disappointment as he began to lower the phone.

Click. "Hello?"

Hastily he raised the mouthpiece to his lips. "Angela?"

"Yes." He heard a smile in her voice. "Is that you, Robert Card?"

She remembered him, thank God. "It's me."

"You took your time about calling." Reproachful now. "Four days."

"I'm sorry." No, wrong to apologize; it sounded weak. "I've been busy." Lame, very lame.

"Catching criminals?"

"Trying to."

"I want to hear all about it. I want to know about the cases you're involved in, and the bad guys you're after. You told me you're a detective."

"Yes."

"What kind of detective? Vice? Narcotics?"

"Homicide."

"Really?"

"Well, we work other cases too. Spousal battery, hate crimes. The West Valley has a fairly low homicide rate, at least by L.A. standards, so there's some additional work that comes our way."

He felt stupidly pleased to be able to talk about these things. Even Jessie had never shown much interest in his work, had never wanted him to bring the job home. . . . Guilt lanced him as he realized what he was thinking.

"But there are *some* murders in that part of town, I'm sure," Angela said. "And you hunt the killers."

"Yes."

"Sounds . . . dangerous."

The purr in her voice made him a little dizzy.

"It can be," he answered evenly. Part of him wanted to brag about the close scrapes he'd had, while another part wanted to hold back, not embarrass himself by preening like a teenager. Self-restraint won. "But usually it's just routine. A lot of paperwork. Filling out requisition forms for other requisition forms. You know."

"Well, it's glamorous enough for me." Her voice stroked him. "So aren't you going to ask me out?"

"That was the plan." He hesitated. "I guess you're probably busy tonight."

"Why do you guess that?"

"Saturday night. I just thought . . ."

"Aren't detectives trained not to make unwarranted assumptions?"

"Does that mean you're not busy?"

"Of course I'm busy. I'm going out with you."

"Right." He gripped the phone tighter.

"That's okay, isn't it?"

Something seemed to be caught in Card's throat. "Definitely okay."

Then she laughed. A rich throaty laugh he liked.

"You're funny, Robert Card. Not at all what I'd imagined a detective to be."

"How so?"

"You're shy."

He felt the need to deny it. "Out of practice, that's all. Ever since my wife died . . ." Christ, shut up. "Well, I don't want to get into that."

A beat of thoughtful silence on the line. Angela sounded serious when she said softly, "I understand." Another pause. Then, tentatively: "I didn't mean it as an insult when I said you were funny."

"I didn't take it as one."

"Good. So what time are you picking me up?"

He thought about it. There were a few things he needed to do at the station house. "How about . . . uh . . . seven-thirty?"

"Sound more positive."

"Seven-thirty."

"I haven't given you my address, have I? Do you have a pencil?"

He didn't, dammit. "Hold on." He searched frantically through a desk drawer, snatched a black marker and an envelope. "Okay, go ahead."

She told him an address in North Hollywood. He knew the neighborhood vaguely. Low-income area.

"My place is a mess," she said. "Why don't you pick me up out front?"

"That's fine."

"I'll be waiting, Inspector."

She hung up. He cradled the phone gently.

Could have handled that one a little smoother, Bobby, said a critic in his mind. It took him a moment to identify the critic as Lindstrom.

Card smiled. Shut up, Ellen, he replied silently. And what the hell have *you* got planned for tonight anyway?

Detective Lindstrom had no answer to that.

27

Angela was sitting on the steps of her apartment building in the fading daylight when Card's sedan pulled up to the curb. She rose to her feet as he got out of the car. He looked nervous and harried.

"Sorry I'm late."

"That's all right. Beautiful evening, isn't it?"

He was looking at her. "Beautiful," he echoed.

She walked to the car. He watched her appreciatively. The dress had been a good choice, she decided. It was a neat little dark blue number, low-cut and short-hemmed, the silky fabric clinging to her body.

He opened the passenger-side door for her, and she slipped into the car as if into a warm bath.

They said a few meaningless things as he chauffeured her to a restaurant in Sherman Oaks. Their route took them due west, into the glare of the swollen sun. Angela half shut her eyes, and the sun became a stellate blur, an orange smear projecting needles of light in all directions, like a child's depiction of a star.

A valet parked the car behind a nicely landscaped restaurant in the Tudor style. The maître d' led them through a maze of stained oak tables and leatherette banquettes, seated them in a corner booth, and lit the candles that flanked the floral centerpiece. Dusky flickering light danced on Card's face and her own, coloring them in the varnished-wood tones of the Dutch masters.

Card ordered wine, then smiled at Angela across the table. "So tell me about yourself," he said, straining to assume the role of a casual conversationalist.

"I'm sure you're much more interesting."

"I doubt that."

"Well, here goes, then. I'm twenty-four. Single. Live alone. College degree. From the University of Arizona, if that matters."

"Are you from Arizona originally?"

"Yes. A town called Oro Valley, adjacent to Tucson."

"I've never been to Tucson. Phoenix I've seen."

"Phoenix is much different, more like L.A., actually. Tucson is smaller, and the mountains are closer, and the desert more lush on account of the higher altitude. Saguaro cacti everywhere, forests of them. Quite scenic. On overcast days the low-lying clouds are speared by jagged rocks, like hors d'ouevres on toothpicks."

"So you liked it there?"

"Hated it. Heat and dust. Cowboys in pickup trucks and ten-gallon hats. I grabbed my degree and ran."

A waiter arrived with wine and menus. She was pleased to see that Card did not make a show of tasting the wine.

"What did you get your degree in?" he asked when the waiter was gone.

"English." She smiled. "My diploma didn't turn out to be much of a meal ticket."

"Are you a writer?"

"No. I tried it for a while, but I couldn't make any money at it, and the work was too solitary, too depressing. Now I work at a daycare center."

"Really?" Obvious interest lit up his face. "You like kids?"

"I love them."

"I've got a little boy, you know."

"You do?"

She wondered why it hadn't occurred to her that he might have a child. Of course, she had assumed that his marriage had ended in divorce, in which case the mother would most likely have gotten custody of any children. She hadn't learned he was a widower until he'd told her so on the phone a few hours ago.

"What's your boy's name?" she asked.

"Mike."

"How old is he?"

"Seven."

"He's starting second grade, then."

"As soon as the summer break is over. How old are the children you work with?"

"Four and five. They're so cute at that age."

"Yes." She saw fatherly fondness in his eyes as he perhaps remembered his own son as a four-year-old. "What kinds of activities do you supervise at the daycare center?"

"Oh, artistic things—you know, finger paints and modeling clay—and games, projects, a little bit of educational instruction. And storytelling. We sit in a circle and make up stories."

Card grinned. "Your literary background must come in handy for that."

She caught his smile and returned it. "Uh-huh. I guess those four years weren't wasted after all. Now, enough about me. You're the one with the intriguing job. Police detective. Have you solved a lot of cases?"

"A fair number. Homicide squads generally have the highest solve rates in any department. It's not like in the movies, though. Mostly we just pay off informers for tips, or canvass a neighborhood for witnesses. Sometimes there are stakeouts, but those are pretty boring."

"Oh, yes, I'm sure it's terribly dull. Not at all like the glamorous life of a daycare provider." She sipped her wine. "I suppose you've gotten into some dangerous situations."

"A few."

"Life and death?"

"Only once."

"What happened?"

"A guy was shooting at my partner. She was hunkered down in the car, and he was firing through the windshield."

"A woman for a partner? I guess we really have come a long way."

"Female detectives are still pretty rare. But things are changing."

"So what did you do? About the man with the gun?"

"I . . . shot him."

"Oh."

"Dead."

"I see."

"It happened recently." He spoke quickly now, the words coming out in a tumbled rush. "You might have heard about it. Luis Estoban."

The name meant nothing to her. "I'm afraid I don't follow the news very closely. Too depressing. And frightening."

"It's a frightening world."

"Funny you should say that. Being a cop, I mean."

"Why?"

"Aren't cops supposed to be fearless?"

"Only the stupid ones. The others know enough to be scared."

"Were you scared when you shot that man?" she asked, then regretted it. Tactless thing to say.

"Yes," Card said. "Well, no. I'm not sure. It happened very fast. I had no time to think, even to aim. I just squeezed off two rounds. Afterward I was sick to my stomach. I was sort of scared then, I guess. Or maybe just guilt-ridden."

"I don't see where guilt would enter into it. After all, you had no choice. You can't blame yourself."

Card shook his head, frowning in bitter wisdom. "You don't know how it feels to kill someone."

Silence settled between them, heavy and uncomfortable. Angela wished she'd been intelligent enough not to press him on that subject.

She picked up her menu and studied it. Card did the same.

"Roast beef for me," she said finally. "How about you?"

"Filet mignon." The words were flat. He seemed distant and morose.

"Robert? You okay?"

"Fine. I'm fine."

"I'm sorry I asked you about . . . your work. You probably want to get away from all that."

"No, I don't mind." He closed his menu, and his mouth formed the shape of a smile. "In fact, when we talked on the phone, I found myself thinking how nice it was for somebody to be interested in what I do."

The waiter came back to take their orders, then vanished again. Their conversation resumed, focusing this time on safe, familiar topics. Life in the Valley, the unhip part of town. The movie business and what those Hollywood assholes were like. The high cost of rent and car insurance. The color of the sky on smoggy days.

Dinner arrived, two plates smelling of beef and blood. Angela dug in hungrily.

"Delicious," she said. "You know, I'm having a good time, Robert. For a man who's supposed to be out of practice at this sort of thing, you're doing just fine."

He looked embarrassed. "Thanks."

"You're not really all that much out of practice, though, are you?"

"I'm afraid I am. This is the first time I . . ."

"What?"

His drifting gaze locked on hers. "The first time I've been on a date since Jessica died."

"When did you lose her?"

"Three years ago. Three years this August."

She didn't ask the obvious question. He answered it anyway.

"Cancer," he said.

Angela heard raw pain in his voice. "I'm sorry," she whispered.

He brushed away her sympathy. "I should have gotten over it by now, I guess. Maybe if Jessie had died suddenly, in a car crash or something, I could have dealt with it better. But this was different. It was . . . drawn out."

"How long?"

"Nearly two years."

"Mike must have been quite young when she got sick."

"He was two. Had just turned two. Jessie was diagnosed right after his second birthday. I remember we had cake and ice cream. He slopped it all over himself, and Jessie laughed and said something about welcome to the terrible twos. That's what they call it, you know, that age. We didn't know how terrible—for us."

He wasn't looking at her, and she knew he was far away, lost in memories. She said nothing.

"Have you ever lost anyone to cancer?" he asked after a long moment.

"No."

"It's not fun." He chuckled, a hollow sound. "Not fun at all."

"Do you want to talk about it?"

He blinked. She had the impression that he'd abruptly remembered where he was. "Uh . . . no. It's not an appropriate topic for dinner conversation."

"You can tell me, if you want to. I'm a good listener."

"Actually, there's not a whole lot to tell. I mean, it pretty much followed its usual course."

She had the feeling that he wanted to say more, but she didn't prod him. If he wanted to go on, he would.

"She'd been feeling tired," Card said quietly, "and she had a funny rash. She saw her doctor, had a blood test; a couple of days later he said he wanted to do a bone marrow biopsy. We waited two more days. A long wait. Then we went to his office to hear the diagnosis." He took a breath. "Acute myelocytic leukemia."

She swallowed. "How awful."

"She started chemo the next day. They pumped her full of, Christ, antibiotics and, uh, antimetabolites and antiviral agents. Anti-everything. She was on megadoses for six weeks."

"I've heard about the side effects of chemo."

"It's bad as they say. She didn't lose her hair, though. She'd been concerned about that, so she wore an ice pack around her head during the treatments. She'd read somewhere that it was supposed to help." He played with his fork, the silver tines coruscating prettily in the candlelight. "The initial treatment was successful. The cancer went into remission. Temporarily, at least."

"She got to go home then, I suppose."

"Uh-huh. For a while she was living an almost-normal life. I used to watch her and Mike together, him so small in her arms, and I told myself nothing could take her away. But we both knew the odds. She would probably have a relapse, and the chemo wasn't likely to be as effective the second time. Then the best hope, last hope, would be a bone marrow transplant."

"I see."

"Jessie's relatives were tested, but none of them was a suitable donor. Still, there's such a thing as an autologous transplant."

"I've heard of that. It's where the patient serves as both donor and recipient."

"Right. The idea is to donate your own marrow during remission, then use it if a relapse occurs. Jessie banked her marrow, and then we just waited to find out what would happen. Fourteen months went by, and she was still in remission. We started to talk about driving across the Southwest, seeing the national parks in Utah and New Mexico. Jessie bought a road atlas; we mapped out the route we would take. Then she got sick again."

Angela wanted to say she was sorry, but the words seemed inadequate, meaningless.

"She went back on the full chemo program. They kept trying different combinations of drugs, but nothing worked. She got weaker every day. The ice packs did no good anymore, if they ever had. Her hair turned brittle and started falling out. One day I found her looking into a hand mirror, crying. She saw me, got embarrassed. Apologized for being a baby. Said a little hair didn't mean anything, and besides, it would all grow back as soon as this was over. And I said uh-huh, sure it would. Then we started laughing. Both of us, such bad liars . . ."

"Couldn't they try the transplant?"

"They did. That was her—our—last option. To prep her for surgery, the doctors put her on the highest chemo doses she could stand. The chemicals wrecked her immune system, so she had to be kept free of infection. She went into a restricted room. I could watch her through the glass or on a

TV monitor, but to go in I had to be suited up in a sterile mask and gown and gloves. I couldn't touch her."

He put his hand to his cheek, then slowly dragged it down, his fingertips leaving brief white trails in his skin.

"The day of the operation, they irradiated her with a thousand rads, enough to kill off every bone-marrow cell in her body. They call it a blitzkrieg. When she was half dead, they wheeled her into the operating room and injected the marrow she'd donated. Then she went back to the isolation room." He coughed into his fist. "And after all that, she died anyway."

Angela's voice was very soft: "How?"

"Another relapse, shortly after the operation. Because, see, the marrow she'd donated during her remission hadn't been totally free of cancer cells."

"Didn't the doctors know that?"

"There was no way to tell for sure. They had told us it was a possibility. Always is, in that kind of procedure. But we'd gone ahead, because we'd had no choice." Card looked away. "It was quick at the end, anyway. She was too weak to take much more chemo, so the cancer spread fast. Spread everywhere. Into her central nervous system." He made a throat-clearing sound, a man's substitute for a sob. "Into her brain."

"Oh, Robert . . ."

"She had periods of irrationality. She would rave at the doctors till they sedated her. I couldn't take Mike to see her anymore. I could barely stand to see her myself. Finally she died. I wasn't with her. There was no warning. Her body just gave out. The nurse on duty told me Jessie was lying there, and she stopped breathing, that was all."

Card looked directly at Angela, his gaze meeting hers. His eyes were bright in the candles' flickering glow, wide and unblinking and intense.

"I loved her," he whispered. "I really did. But I didn't cry at her funeral. And I haven't cried since. Seeing her waste away like that—it ripped something out of me. My tear ducts, maybe, I don't know. There's an . . . an emptiness where she was."

He said nothing more. Angela watched him, thinking of men who wore masks, men who were not what they seemed, men who liked to inflict pain, the kind of men she had always been drawn to. Then slowly she reached across the table and took his hand. Her voice was a whisper, tender as a caress.

"You don't seem empty to me, Robert Card."

28

Card was quiet as he drove Angela home. He felt secretly humiliated as he thought of the things he'd said in the restaurant, the unhealed anguish he'd exposed to this woman's eyes. She had asked him to talk about it, true, but looking back, he was sure he had misinterpreted the situation; her gentle prompting must have been mere politeness. There was no way she could have wanted to hear the horror story he'd told.

He imagined her chatting on the phone tomorrow with some girlfriend of hers: "Then the guy starts telling me all about how his wife died of cancer, every last detail, can you believe it?" His gut clenched like a fist.

He parked, then wordlessly walked Angela to the door of her building. A fragrance of perfume sweetened the air around her.

"Well, good night," he said as they stood together at the top of the steps.

"I had a good time, Robert."

The sound he made was not quite a laugh. "Oh, yeah. I've been a riot."

"I wasn't looking for a riot. I wanted someone I could talk to."

"You're a nice girl, Angela. But let's face it. Hearing about Jessie's leukemia is not exactly the kind of evening you had in mind."

"There'll be other evenings."

"Will there?"

"Damn right there will."

She raised herself on tiptoe, and her mouth brushed his cheek in a momentary contact more provocative than a lingering kiss.

"Call me," she breathed.

She stepped into the lobby, the door swinging shut behind her. Card stood speechless, blinking.

Slowly he returned to his car and got in.

He had been sure he'd blown it, certain she had written him off as a melancholy loser. But apparently not. She still wanted to see him. She had even *kissed* him, for God's sake.

He fingered his cheek, remembering the whisper of her lips against his skin, the sultry, breathless quality of her voice as she told him to call. And suddenly he knew he could have her as a lover. He could take her to bed. Not on a second date, perhaps. But soon.

She's got to meet Mike, he thought, then chided himself: What is this, an audition for the role of stepmother? Still, he wanted to see how the two of them got along together. Maybe the next time he took her out, he could arrange for her to meet him at his apartment, when Mike was there.

She worked with kids. She would love Mike. She'd probably—

A flicker of motion from across the street.

He looked out the window, squinting into the darkness, studying the windbreak of fir trees directly opposite Angela's apartment building. Dimly he made out a pale shape, a human figure, crouching in the shadows.

Someone was hiding there. Watching him. Someone who perhaps had been watching when he escorted Angela to the door and kissed her.

Card's heartbeat accelerated. He reached down, folded up his pants leg, and removed the J-frame Smith from its ankle holster.

He eased open the car door. The ceiling light snapped on, washing him in its yellow glow; he cursed under his breath. He got out fast, shut the door softly, and looked toward the trees again. It took a moment for his eyes to readjust to the dark.

The stranger was gone.

Cautiously he approached the row of fir trees, holding the .38 tightly in one hand. Time took on the peculiar slowness known only in dreams or in moments of acute stress. He reached the trees and crept among the wind-sculpted branches, his breathing quick and shallow, all his senses alert.

Behind him, a rustle of shrubbery. He turned. A grove of bushes lay a few yards away, near the entrance to a passageway between two apartment buildings. Footsteps receded down the passage; a fleeing shadow bobbed on the stucco walls.

Card ran in pursuit. The stranger glanced back once; Card glimpsed a pale face framed by dark hair, tied back. Man or woman? Couldn't tell.

His quarry darted into an intersecting alley. Card stopped at the end of the passageway, wary of an ambush. He released the Smith's safety, hugged the wall, and peered cautiously around the corner.

Twenty yards away, taillights flared in time with the cough of an engine.

"Shit," Card hissed.

Tires squealed. The car bulleted down the alley, veered onto a side street, and was gone.

Card stared into the darkness, seeing the blue contrails printed on his vision by the streak of taillights. He hadn't seen the vehicle clearly enough to observe any details: make, model, color, license number. He had nothing to go on. No leads at all.

He wondered who would want to spy on him— or on Angela. A mugger, maybe, or a burglar casing the neighborhood.

Frowning, Card retraced his steps to the street. He climbed into his Mercury Sable, turned the ignition key, and pulled away from the curb.

As he drove home, his thoughts ticked like a pendulum from the pleasure of Angela's kiss to the mystery of the watcher in the trees.

29

Dominique entered her apartment flushed and panting, her heart racing, her body on fire with a fever of excitement.

She had taken a risk tonight, and it had paid off. She had him now. She had Robert Card.

Only one celebration was possible. She knew what she must do. She sat before her makeup mirror and put on her skull face, trembling fingers smearing the design.

As she worked, she thought about Card and the young fool, Angela Westmore, whom he had met at the supermarket. They had gone out on a date tonight. Before parting, they had kissed like shy children.

It seemed Card had found the sort of woman that suited him. Safely normal, girlish, saccharine sweet. She even worked in a daycare center, for Christ's sake. Dominique had watched dear Angela smiling at the little ones and tousling their hair. The dim-witted little bitch was like something out of a 1950s television show, the perky prom queen, the happy homemaker, some loathsome hybrid of Gidget and Donna Reed.

Yes, the ideal woman for Robert Card. And the ideal chance to wound him, cut him, savage him. The chance, finally, to make him bleed.

Her makeup was finished. Dominique studied her reflection, pleased by the image of death in the silvered glass. She stripped off her clothes, kicked them aside.

Naked, she danced.

The bathroom was her dancing place, because there she could watch herself in the full-length mirror on the door. She performed a spastic ballet, the snap and jerk of her arms like the flutter of insect appendages. Her head bobbed, loose on her shoulders. Sitar music thrummed in her brain. She was Kali, goddess of death, the mother who feasts on her young. See her necklace of heads, her girdle of limbs. See her tongue lap blood.

She danced faster, her gyrating body oiled with sweat. Danced and trilled unmelodic sounds, sounds that might have been orgasmic gasps or stifled screams. Danced till breathlessness carried her to the floor in a mound of flapping arms and kicking legs.

Then she lay still, drifting toward dreams.

Card must be happy tonight. Happy and in love. It was all very sweet. A tender romance.

What a shame if the romance were to end in a funeral.

Dominique smiled. She felt the tingling warmth in the muscles of her cheeks as her lips curved upward. She imagined the hard, steely whiteness of her teeth.

She had discovered someone Card cared for. Someone he did not want to lose. Someone whose death would twist a knife between his ribs and jerk a gasp of agony out of his throat.

There remained only the question of how to do it. And when.

30

At ten-thirty on Monday morning half a dozen teenage boys were standing around idly on a street corner in Northridge when a passing car sprayed them with a flurry of rounds from an automatic rifle. One boy was killed; two others were seriously wounded and required hospitalization.

Initially the case was assigned to the West Bureau CRASH section—Community Resources Against Street Hoodlums—which handled all gang-related incidents. But interviews with survivors and witnesses quickly established that no gang slogans had been shouted, and the teens who'd been fired on, although gangbangers themselves, were not at war with any rival gangs. At that point CRASH lost interest in the case, which was transferred to Lindstrom and Card.

The investigation occupied most of their attention throughout Monday and Tuesday. The three boys who escaped injury were able to identify the shooting car only as a dark-colored Chevrolet Monte Carlo, the vehicle of choice for nearly all L.A. gang members. Gang Information Section of Headquarters Bureau had hundreds of Monte Carlos on file; without more information, there was no way to narrow the search.

On Wednesday morning one of the two hospital-ized victims recovered sufficient strength to an-swer questions. He had glimpsed the license plate and recalled part of it: 2GH . . . 4.

GIS listed no Monte Carlo with that plate. Trying another strategy, Card entered the partial number into the Ticket Information System, which came up with several hits. But a series of phone calls estab-lished that all the Monte Carlos were owned and driven by people who in no way fit the suspect pro-file, and none of the cars had ever been stolen.

"Back to square one," Lindstrom said in disgust as she set down the receiver after the last call.

Card didn't answer. He was thinking about An-gela. He'd held off calling her on Sunday or Mon-day—not good to look too anxious. Yesterday evening he'd phoned her place, but an answering machine had taken the call. He'd asked her to call him back and left both his home and work numbers. So far there had been no answer, and he was beginning to worry that he really had blown it, after all.

Had to be the worst first date in history, he told himself morosely. No matter what kind of spin any-one tries to put on it, I still screwed up. Dammit to hell.

"Bobby?" Lindstrom was looking at him from across the desk they shared. "You awake over there?"

"Huh? Oh. Yeah."

"You seem a little distracted today."

"Just tired."

"Something on your mind?"

"No, I said."

She grunted in a way that registered disbelief and went back to the file.

Twenty minutes later the phone rang. Card reached for it impulsively, then stopped himself when he saw Lindstrom watching him.

"You're in an awful hurry to answer that thing," she said with a lift of her eyebrows.

The phone rang a second time. Card's hand hovered near the handset. "Just reflex. You know."

"You expecting a call?"

A third ring. "Of course not."

"Mind if I answer it, then?" Lindstrom asked.

He shrugged and withdrew his hand. "Be my guest."

She lifted the handset, her eyes still locked on his, her mouth forming a wry half smile.

"Homicide, Lindstrom."

A pause. The corners of her mouth eased higher into her cheeks, cutting those laugh lines Card liked.

"Oh, you'd like to speak with Detective Card? Detective Robert Card?"

Another pause. Card waited helplessly.

"Yes, he's my partner. I'm Detective Lindstrom; we share this desk. Who may I say is calling?"

Card uttered a mock snarl and lunged for the phone, but Lindstrom was too quick for him; she kicked her swivel chair away from the desk, pulling the handset out of his reach.

"Angela Westmore?" she said. "I see."

"Give me the fucking phone," Card whispered.

"Hold on, Angela. I'll see if he's here." She muffled the receiver with her hand. "Somebody named Westmore wants to talk to you. I think she's a civilian."

"For Christ's sake, stop playing around and hand it over."

"She sounds pretty, Bobby."

He swiped at the phone again, missed. "Give me that!"

"But of course you probably don't know her." Lindstrom was laughing soundlessly. "I mean, you said you weren't expecting a call."

"I wasn't," he lied lamely.

"Oh. Probably a crank, then. Guess I'd better hang up."

She lowered the handset toward the cradle. Card snatched it away, shot her an exaggerated glare, and spun his swivel chair to turn his back on his partner.

"Hi, Angela." He hoped his voice sounded unstressed.

"Robert. I got your message. I was so glad to hear from you."

Card was uncomfortably aware of Lindstrom eavesdropping on his half of the conversation. He chose his words carefully. "I was hoping we could get together again."

"Of course we can. Anytime you like."

"Tonight?"

Damn. Instantly he regretted saying that. He didn't want to go too fast, push too hard.

But Angela didn't seem to mind. "Tonight's fine."

"You know, I was thinking . . ." He hesitated, still concerned about what Lindstrom might hear, then dismissed his fears. "It might be nice if you had dinner at my place. I've got a housekeeper,

Consuelo—she's an excellent cook—do you like Mexican food?"

Angela laughed. "You can't grow up in Tucson and not like it. And I'd love to see your place."

"That would be great. Just great."

"Will Mike be there?"

"Sure."

"I look forward to meeting him."

"You two will get along fine. I'm sure you will. He's a great kid. Look, is eight o'clock too late? See, it looks like I'll be working overtime every night this week. . . ."

"Eight is perfect. We'll dine fashionably late, European-style. Can I bring anything? Wine or appetizers?"

"No, Consuelo will take care of all that. Let me give you my address."

He recited his address, and she repeated it.

"Okay, Robert. I'll see you at eight. 'Bye."

" 'Bye."

The line went dead, but he kept the phone pressed to his ear for a few moments longer, lost in thought.

Dinner at home on only the second date—Christ, it was too soon. He hadn't meant to invite Angela to his apartment at all, but the words had tumbled out before he could stop them. He supposed he simply couldn't feel comfortable with her until she had met Mike and seen how the two of them lived.

Then he remembered Ellen Lindstrom, watching him from the other side of the gunmetal-gray desk. Slowly he swiveled around to face her and cradled the phone.

"Wrong number," he said soberly.

"Uh-huh." Her ballpoint pen was ticking against the edge of the desk. "Come on, Bobby, spill it."

"Well . . . I've got sort of a date tonight."

"So I gathered. Who is she?"

"Angela Westmore."

"I know her name, for God's sake. I mean what's she like?"

"She's smart. Easy to talk to. Works at a daycare center. Lives in North Hollywood. From Arizona originally."

"How'd you meet her?"

"I was at the supermarket. On the checkout line."

"You make the first move?"

"Yeah," Card lied.

"Congratulations. Tonight the first time you're taking her out?"

"No, we had dinner once before. I took her to the Carriage House over on Moorpark, you know, near where the Ritano bust went down. That was a piece-of-shit case."

"Don't change the subject. How'd it go?"

"We had a good time, I guess. I don't know. I started talking about Jessie. Shouldn't have done that. I felt stupid afterward, but she didn't seem to mind." He shrugged. "I'm pretty rusty at this dating business."

"You like her, though, huh?"

"She's nice, yeah. Maybe a little young for me."

"How young?"

"Twenty-four."

"Jesus. You're robbing the cradle."

"Okay, okay, it's not that bad."

"Seriously, Bobby, I think this is real good for you. You need something like this."

"Yes," Card said softly. "I think so too."

31

The nervous tension fluttering in his stomach annoyed Card. Stupid to be nervous for a second date. A first date, sure, but not the second one. Had he been nervous about dating Jessie? He must have been, but oddly, he couldn't remember.

He fussed in front of the bathroom mirror, combing and recombing his hair till he was finally satisfied. Then he put down the comb, swished a swig of Listerine around in his mouth, spit it into the sink, and sponged the sink clean. Standing back from the mirror, he studied himself. He'd decided not to wear a jacket and tie—too formal. Instead he'd put on a blue shirt, first rolling up the sleeves, then pulling them down again. He wasn't sure if he'd made the right choice. There might still be time to change.

The intercom buzzed.

Too late.

He left the bathroom and walked swiftly through the apartment, past the kitchen where Consuelo was chopping boneless chicken breasts into bite-sized cubes, past the dining table arranged with three place settings, past Mike lounging on the sofa and tickling Willy on the floor with his outstretched hand.

"That her?" Mike asked.

"I think so." Tension clipped his speech. He thumbed the button on the intercom. "Hello?"

Her voice crackled: "It's me."

"Come on in. Third floor, number three-oh-five."

He buzzed her in, then opened the front door and waited in the hall till she emerged from the elevator a minute later. She walked swiftly toward him, ravishing in a blue skirt and white blouse and waves of silken hair like tumbled smoke. Card felt mildly dizzy.

"Hello, Robert."

"Angela. Hi." Words deserted him momentarily.

"Tell her to come in, Dad."

Card turned and saw Mike leaning out the door.

Angela laughed. "Excellent suggestion." She was already brushing past Card, bending eagerly to shake Mike's hand. "You must be Michael."

"Mike. Nobody calls me Michael."

"Except his grandfather," Card added pointlessly as they went into the apartment.

Angela beamed at the boy. "Your father tells me you're seven."

"Almost eight."

"He'll be eight in September," Card said.

"You're starting second grade, aren't you?"

"Next month. Gotta go back to school then." Mike frowned. "Dad says in the old days the kids got the whole summer off, not just a month and a half."

"That's true," Angela said. "But we didn't get six weeks off at Christmas, the way you do now. So it balances out."

"I guess." He didn't seem too sure.

"What do you study in school?"

"All kinds of stuff. We did lizards and snakes in June. They're pretty cool."

"I saw lots of lizards and snakes where I grew up, in Arizona. And one morning, when I was twelve years old, I opened my eyes and you know what I found right beside me in bed? A scorpion."

"Jesus," Card breathed.

"Neat!"

"It was only a few inches from my face. It just lay there, motionless, waiting."

"Did you smash it?" Mike squashed an imaginary scorpion with his fist.

"No. I just stared. I was too frightened to move. I still remember the scorpion clearly, every detail. It was less than four inches long, copper-colored, shiny. In its own way, it was beautiful, I suppose. Beautiful and deadly."

"How come the damn thing didn't sting you?" Card asked.

A tremor danced lightly over her shoulders like a shrug. "I can't say. Maybe it wasn't my time to go." She smiled. "Maybe there was some purpose for me in life, something I was meant to do."

"I'm glad you didn't get stung," Mike said.

Angela reached down and brushed his hair affectionately. "Thank you, Mike. I'm glad too. If I had, I never would have met your father . . . or you."

Dinner was a success. Consuelo had prepared a huge tostada, the flaky shell nearly overflowing with chicken, shredded lettuce, and black beans. Mike dug in hungrily, taking extra helpings.

Toward the end of the meal he belched twice and, Card noted gratefully, excused himself each time.

A cheap chandelier hung over the table, its glass globes fitted with forty-watt bulbs like flickerless candle flames. In the three years Card had lived in this apartment, he could not recall ever having used the chandelier. He was not sure he had even noticed that it was there.

He found it strangely unreal to sit in the straight-backed chair directly across from Angela, talking quietly, refilling her wineglass, watching her trade smiles and winks with Mike. It felt like . . . like having a family again.

If Jessie had lived—

He cut the thought short. She had not lived. He felt that it was time for him to face that fact. Time for him to get on with his own life and put away the past.

The conversation kept returning to Mike, and Angela was the one nudging it there. At first Card thought she was merely being polite, but eventually he decided she honestly enjoyed hearing about the boy. Once, when Mike left the table to use the bathroom, Angela turned to Card and flashed a dreamy smile.

"He's wonderful."

"You two seem to get along very well."

"Oh, I love children. I told you that. Wish I had a kid like Mike for my own."

Who knows? he thought. Maybe you will.

After dessert, Card asked Mike to get ready for bed, and Mike pleaded to stay up longer, as usual. "No, but I'll read you a bedtime story when you're in your jammies." Mike relented, and soon water was hissing through the bathroom pipes as he brushed his teeth.

"Do you read to him every night?" Angela asked.

Card shook his head, pricked by guilt. "I ought to, but I don't get home before his bedtime often enough."

"That's too bad. It's so nice, reading to a child. Like singing lullabies. Did you ever sing to Mike when he was a baby?'

"Jessie did. Not me."

Card heard tightness in his voice and realized he was thinking of the house in Canoga Park, the smell of star jasmine in the garden on summer evenings, Jessie swaying on the porch swing with Mike in her arms, humming softly.

Stop it. Stop it right now.

"You know," Angela was saying, "I'm pretty good with stories." Her fingers picked idly at the table-cloth. "I don't suppose . . ."

He understood. "You want to read something to Mike?"

A shy smile. "Wouldn't mind." The smile flickered, a frown tugging at the corners of her mouth. "But he'd probably rather hear a story from you."

"Let me ask him," Card said quickly. He scraped his chair away from the table. "I'll be right back," he added as he left the table. Stupid thing to say. But he was afraid to come back and find her gone, the evening a fantasy or an evil joke.

He found Mike in the bedroom, pulling down the covers. The windows were open to the July night; a moth batted witlessly against one of the screens. Somewhere down the block, a dog split the night with big throaty barks like coughs of gunfire.

Card explained Angela's request.

"Yeah, okay," Mike said immediately. "She's nice. I like her."

"Me too."

"You going to marry her, Dad?"

Card didn't answer right away. He sat on the edge of the bed, pulled Mike near. "I just met her. We hardly know each other. And she's a lot younger than I am."

Wide blue eyes gazed up at him. The lashes fluttered once, in time with a rustle of moth wings. "So you're not?"

"Well . . . I can't say. Don't count on it."

Mike nodded. He kicked his legs, a child on a fishing pier. The mattress springs creaked.

"Is Angela like Mom?" he asked.

"Not much, no."

"Was Mom nicer?"

"Different."

"How?"

"She wasn't as . . . outgoing. That's not quite the right word. What I mean is, Angela is more of a big-city girl. Take the way we met. She just started talking to me at the grocery store. I don't think your mom would have done that."

"How did you meet Mom?"

Card ran a hand through Mike's hair. Soft.

"I was working Robbery Division back then," he said slowly. "Mom had come out of a store at night, and somebody had held her up and taken her purse. My partner and I interviewed her. She had just moved to L.A., and she didn't know anybody. I asked her out."

They had made love the very first night they

were together. The memory of it was both sweet and stabbing now.

"Did you know right away you were gonna marry her?"

"Yes."

"Did she know?"

Card felt a smile brush his face like a ghost's hand. "I think so."

"Was she as pretty as Angela?"

"She was beautiful, Mike. You've seen pictures."

"Yeah, but . . ."

"I know. It's hard to tell from just snapshots. But she was. Don't you remember her at all?"

"A little. At the hospital."

"I wish you could remember the way she was before that. Toward the end . . . that wasn't really her. She was very tired, and she hurt a lot."

"I think about her sometimes."

"So do I. I think about her every day. She loved us both. She would be so proud of you."

There was a burning in Card's eyes, but it was not tears, only the need for them.

Mike yawned and rubbed his face with his small fists. "Can Angela come tell me a story now?"

"Sure. But first you get into bed."

He climbed under the covers. Card tucked him in, then kissed the boy's forehead, held him gently, breathed in the clean soapy smell of his pajamas, the sweet fragrance of his skin.

"I love you," Card whispered into a delicate ear.

"I love you too, Dad."

Consuelo was clearing the dishes from the table. She gave Card a knowing look as he passed by, her eyes telling him she approved of his date for the evening. Card smiled, and Consuelo mouthed two words: *Muy hermosa.* Very beautiful.

He found Angela in the living room, sitting on the floor, her long legs folded under her. She was rubbing Willy's tummy while the dog thumped his tail and quivered happily.

"Sorry I took so long," he said.

"That's all right. I've made friends with this little guy."

"You've made friends with Mike too. He'd love for you to read him a story."

"Really?" She glowed.

"No lie. There's a bookshelf near the bed. He can tell you which books are his favorites."

"This will be fun, Robert. Thanks."

He watched her go, then petted the dachshund lazily while Consuelo cleaned up the kitchen. After a few minutes he made an unnecessary trip to the bathroom, passing Mike's room on the way.

Angela sat on a corner of the bed, a thin illustrated book in her hands, reading quietly to Mike, her gentle voice lulling him to sleep.

32

"Look at us, cruising like teenagers. You'd think we'd act our age."

"Hey, speak for yourself, Detective. It wasn't so long ago that I couldn't buy a legal beer in this town. I still get carded sometimes."

Ellen smiled. "That's right, rub it in."

She leaned back in the passenger seat of Christine's Volkswagen and watched the neon scenery of Ventura Boulevard streak past. Warm night air rushed through the open windows with a hissing roar. As always, Chris drove fast and recklessly, stitching seams through the traffic, changing lanes and gunning the engine to power around slower cars.

"I'm aggressive behind the wheel," she had explained after Ellen's first nerve-shredding experience as her passenger. "Sue me."

Ellen didn't want to sue her, but she did wish Chris would cut her speed just a little. Suppose they got pulled over for a moving violation and the patrol officer saw her face. . . .

"So whaddya wanna do tonight, Marty?" Chris asked, quoting the old Ernest Borgnine flick, as the bug idled at a stoplight. Her voice was raised over the burr of the motor and the rattle of the dash.

"I don't know. We could get a drink somewhere. Not any place too kinky, though, okay?"

"Kinky? *Moi?*" The traffic light cycled to green, and the Volkswagen shot forward, the slam of acceleration knocking Ellen backward in her seat. "So give me an update on your fascinating life. How are things going?"

"Same as usual. We've been working this drive-by."

"Any luck?"

"Not yet, but gangbangers always get nabbed eventually."

"Then how come they keep killing people?"

"Because they get out of the joint too soon, and because no matter how many of them we catch, there are always more."

Chris burned rubber as she veered north onto Van Nuys Boulevard. "Legalize drugs, and all these dirtbags will be out of business pronto. No more profit in it."

"They'd still kill one another, though." Ellen sighed. "Some kind of macho thing."

A yellow light glared at them as they shot through an intersection. "Gets you down, huh?" Chris said sympathetically.

"Yeah. But I've had worse cases. Jamie Frisch—now, that was bad."

"Hard on Bobby too."

"Uh-huh."

"How is your venerable, albeit homophobic, partner?"

"Doing great. He's got himself a girlfriend."

Chris hooked left on Oxnard Street. "Since when?"

"Last weekend. He picked her up at a supermarket."

"Personally I prefer bookstores."

Ellen smiled at that. She and Chris had met at a bookstore specializing in gay literature. "So do I," she said quietly.

"Hey, watch it, don't get all sentimental on me. Tell me more about Bobby's sweetheart. She a dish?"

"I haven't met her yet. But this afternoon I talked to her on the phone for a second. She seemed nice enough."

"Yeah?" Squeal of tires as the bug veered onto Sepulveda. "Well, good for Bobby. Maybe love will help him loosen up a little."

"Maybe. So what bar are we going to hang out at tonight?"

Chris favored her with a sly smile. "There's an interesting place right in the neighborhood. Few blocks north of here."

North of here. What was north of here? Vanowen Street, Saticoy, Parthenia . . .

"Oh, no," Ellen said. "No way."

"Come on, El, we haven't been there since the night when the cops came in chasing that drunk."

"That's why we haven't been there."

"It was a fluke."

"Maybe so, but it spooked me. Anyway, I never liked that place. Damn decor gives me the creeps."

"Give it another chance, will you?"

Ellen sighed, resistance hissing out of her like air from a punctured balloon. "I guess I can stand it if I have to."

"Yahoo. The detective lets down her hair for once."

A few blocks later, the dark marquee above the entrance to the bar floated out of the night like a manta ray gliding through the murk.

Chris parked the VW at the curb. "You'll get to like Mere Anarchy eventually," she assured Ellen as they walked to the front doors. "It grows on you."

"Like fungus."

"Yeah. Well, kind of."

The interior of the bar was unchanged since their last visit: smoke and roving spotlights, androgynous waiters and freakish clientele, a performer on stage wailing into the mike.

Chris led her to a pair of bar stools, then ordered two gin and tonics. The bartender poured and served. Ellen remembered him: a big ugly man with a port-wine stain across half his face like the shadow of the moon. One of his ears was badly mangled. His big arms and slitted eyes spoke of time in the joint.

She didn't like to look at him. Turning, she watched the stage instead. The singer was a skeletal female with a shaved head; her shoulders twitched. She wore no makeup.

Ellen was fairly sure she hadn't seen that particular sideshow attraction before. Last time the featured performer had been a poet—some creepy Vampirella type, her face made up to resemble a skull, who had recited her obscure verses in a whispery voice.

"Place is really jumping tonight," Chris said over the rim of her glass.

Ellen nodded. "Uh-huh."

Her response was automatic. She was still thinking about that poet. A blue spotlight, a painted face. A breathless whisper from the speakers.

"Earth to Ellen," Chris said. "Come in, Ellen."

Twisted, ugly poetry, spoken in a soft, seductive voice. A voice that teased like a gentle stroking of fingers, a voice that was both sultry and faintly amused, passionate and weary. A voice . . .

She blinked. Slowly her hand reached out for the edge of the bar and gripped it tight.

"No," she muttered. "Not possible."

Chris was staring at her. "Hey, you zoning out or something?"

Ellen ignored her. She listened to the hard, steady beating of her heart against her eardrums.

The idea was crazy. Of course it was. Totally insane. No rational person would even consider it.

And yet . . .

She could almost swear that the voice on the phone this afternoon, the voice of Card's new girlfriend, was the same voice she had heard over the speakers in this bar.

33

At ten o'clock, Consuelo retired to the converted den that served as her bedroom. Card and Angela took Willy for a walk, strolling down the empty sidewalk, then pausing at a telephone pole to let the dog take care of business.

"I never walk at night," Angela said as she looked around at the big sky rusted by city lights, the distant towers of office buildings along Ventura. "Too dangerous. But I feel safe with you."

"Because I'm a cop."

"Just because. Period."

The words warmed him. He moved closer to her, studying her face in the shadowless glow of a street lamp. Her eyes held secrets.

"I'm glad I make you feel safe." His voice was unexpectedly husky.

"How do I make you feel?" She teased him with a flickering half smile.

"At first, nervous as hell. But now ... well, still nervous as hell, I guess. But for a different reason."

"What reason?"

The dog, having relieved himself, was tugging at his leash. Card ignored him.

"I'm worried that I'll screw up somehow," he

said quietly. "It matters to me that I don't. It matters more than I thought it would."

"How could you screw up?"

"By moving too fast. Or not fast enough. Or misinterpreting the situation. I'm not good at this." He jerked the leash irritably. "Cut it out, Willy."

"He wants to go home."

"Yeah. He's ready for bed. He sleeps with Mike. They're cute, lying there together."

"I'd like to see that."

"Would you? Well, let's go, then."

They walked back to the apartment building in silence, then rode the elevator to the third floor. Card fumbled his keys out of his pants pocket and opened the door. In the foyer he restrained the dog with one hand while unclipping the leash from his collar. Willy scampered off in the direction of Mike's room, and a moment later they heard a bounce of mattress springs.

"Doesn't he wake up Mike, jumping on the bed like that?" Angela asked, her voice low.

"No. The kid sleeps like a stone."

Card led her to the doorway of the bedroom. Angela looked in. She stared at the bed for a long time before turning.

"Precious," she whispered. "Norman Rockwell couldn't have pictured it better."

Card nodded. "Sometimes that's all I see of him after work. I get home so late, and he's been asleep for hours. I just stand there and watch, and the dog's belly goes up and down with each breath, and Mike is smiling."

They went back to the living room, Card debating what to do next, whether to make a move or hold off. The evening had been perfect; he didn't want to spoil it with a clumsy, failed seduction. But his need for the woman beside him was achingly strong.

"Want some coffee?" he asked. "I'm almost capable of making some without Consuelo's help."

His phony jocularity annoyed him. He wondered why he was talking about coffee anyway, why people always talked about coffee and other meaningless things at the crucial moments of their lives.

"No, thanks." Angela circled the room, her steps elegant like a dancer's. "I don't care much for coffee."

"Neither do I." Card tried leaning against a doorway, felt awkward, gave it up, and then just stood there trying to decide what to do with his hands. "My partner lives on the stuff. She thinks it's one of the essential food groups, along with nicotine."

Angela stopped near the gas-fueled fireplace, one hand on the mantle, her head cocked inquisitively. "She's the one I talked to on the phone? Linwood?"

"Lindstrom. Ellen Lindstrom."

"Is she pretty?"

Card wasn't sure why he'd invited Lindstrom into this room, and now he wanted her to leave. "She's a good cop," he said brusquely, hoping to change the subject.

Angela took a step forward, away from the fireplace. "That hardly answers my question."

"She's all right, I guess. Not like you."

Another step. "So I'm *not* all right?" Teasing.

"You know what I mean."

She closed the distance between them. Lifted her

head. Looked up at him from under the hooded lids of her eyes.

"A woman likes to hear what a man means, Robert Card."

He met her gaze, and he knew. There was no doubt at all. None.

Fear left him. He had never been so calm. His arms encircled her waist as he drew her to him.

"I mean that you are the most beautiful"—he was stroking her back, feeling the strap of her bra through the cotton blouse—"the sexiest"—her long fingers moved over his rib cage, his hips—"the most exciting . . ."

Then he was kissing her hard, she responding, sudden heat racing like a brush fire through his body, his erection coming so fast it startled him, her eager hands slipping inside his waistband, caressing him, while her mouth formed whispered words in his ear: "The bedroom."

Moving down the hall in a succession of kisses. Groping for the doorknob with his face buried in her hair. Shutting the door behind them with a soft, secret click.

She was already unbuttoning her blouse. He stopped her. "Let me do that." He undid the buttons, then the bra, and stared at her breasts, small and firm, her erect nipples casting curved shadows on the smooth rounded skin. Flawless breasts, an airbrushed fantasy in a glossy magazine.

"You like?" she asked.

"I like."

"My turn now." She helped him remove his shirt. He wished he were younger, his muscles harder, skin tighter. Then she made a sound that was part purr, part groan, and nuzzled his chest hair, and after that he didn't wish for anything more.

They kicked off their shoes, shed the last of their clothes. Card reached for the J-frame Smith strapped to his ankle.

"You're armed," she whispered.

"It's a good idea for a cop to carry a weapon at all times."

"Even at home?"

"Well, actually, I put it on before we walked the dog."

"Really. How . . . interesting."

Something peculiar about the tone of her voice. He looked at her. Oddly, he seemed to detect a subtle difference in her face, some shade of expression he hadn't seen before, a dancing fire in her eyes, a hungry look in the set of her mouth. Her hands were shaking slightly, and her breasts heaved.

"Leave it on." She growled the words.

"You serious?"

"Yes. Leave it on."

He shrugged. "Okay."

"Hold me."

They swayed together, moving toward the bed in slow side steps, and then they were squirming among the lumpy sheets.

"I'll do you first," she said. "I'll do you the way men like it."

She lowered her head, brown hair shiny in the dim light of the bedside lamp. He leaned back against the headboard, stomach muscles fluttering, as she took him into her mouth. Her tongue, nimble, wicked, teased him to bursting fullness. He rolled his head, pressing his cheek to the pillows, wanting to contain himself, knowing it was impossible.

"I'm coming," he whispered, then louder: "I'm coming."

He thought she might pull away, but she didn't. His sudden spurting release burned him; he hissed through gritted teeth as painful pleasure radiated from his groin, hot and cold at once. He saw her swallow, hunger in her eyes, and the furtive thought sneaked through his mind that even on their honeymoon Jessica had never been like this.

"You taste good, Robert."

"Angela . . ."

"Now it's your turn." She lay supine, spreading her legs, touching herself. "Dinner's served. Come and get it."

He kissed her breasts, her belly, then tucked his head between her thighs, licking, sucking, lost in her warmth and moisture.

"Bite me," she breathed. He hesitated, afraid of hurting her. *"Bite me!"*

He nibbled gently, heard her shivery moan.

"Harder, please, oh, Jesus, harder!"

"I don't want to hurt you," he whispered.

"Do it." The words were a demand. "For Christ's sake, *do it!*"

His teeth tugged at the lips of her sex. She squirmed under him, her legs thrashing, back arching, and he knew she liked this, liked being chewed, torn. He didn't understand it and almost withdrew, but she was pleading with him to continue.

"Let me feel it," she gasped. "God, let me *feel* it—harder, please, bite me, rip me up!"

He moistened his mouth with her wetness, inhaled the smell of it, burrowed deep. He bit her, gouging the tender flesh, feeling pleasure shudder through her body. He wouldn't judge her for what she liked. He had seen enough of the streets to know that sexual needs could take any form. If this was what she wanted, he would give it to her, and more and more and more.

Finally, with racking gasps, she came. Multiple orgasms shook her till she was limp and loose-jointed like a rag doll, her skin slick with sweat, glistening in the lamplight.

He pulled free of her legs and crawled up to place his head beside hers.

For a long time there were no words, only hard breathing, two bodies spent. They lay together like panting dogs. Trivial thoughts appeared and vanished in Card's mind, details of unsolved cases, minutiae of the endless forms he was required to fill out. He had to think about something, but he could not focus on what had just happened, it was too real, too immediate, too powerful; it would wipe him out.

Her hand squeezing his. "You're wonderful, Robert."

"Angela . . . I hope I wasn't too rough. I mean . . ."

"That's the way I wanted it. Rough."

He touched the inside of her thigh and his fingers came away pink and tacky. "Jesus, you're bleeding."

"I told you, it's what I wanted. What I haven't

had in so long." She rolled over to watch his face. "Did you find me overly . . . experimental?"

"No." The truth was, he didn't know how he felt.

"I like to try new things."

"Sure."

"You didn't mind, then?"

"I didn't mind." He caught his breath. "But I have to admit that you, uh, kind of took me by surprise. You're a very different person in bed."

"Aren't I, though?" She snuggled closer. "Rest now. Sleep."

Card switched off the bedside lamp. He shut his eyes, relaxed his body, let sleep take him. In a few moments the only sound in the room was his deep breathing, low and regular.

Beside him, in the darkness, Dominique lay awake, her lips skinned back from her teeth in a cold white smile.

34

Mr. Howard Elbaum had been peddling a stationary bicycle in a health spa on Tuesday night, working up a pretty good sweat, when something squeezed his heart like a fist. The pain was the worst he'd ever felt, a terrible crushing agony that made him think idiotically of a hippopotamus sitting on his chest. The image of the hippo, wiggling its comical ears as its enormous hindquarters bore down, was the last clear picture in his mind as he slid off the bike onto the floor.

After that, a confusion of activity. Paramedics massaging his heart, clapping an oxygen mask over his face, lifting him onto a stretcher. A syringe in his arm. The doors of an ambulance springing open. The hiccuping wail of a siren. Voices: "Lidocaine, seventy-five milligrams. Bicarb, two amps." "Lidocaine going in. Bicarb in." "Vitals?" "Blood pressure falling. Look out—V-fib." "Prep for defib. Stat, stat!" "Prepped." "Get back!" His heart slammed. More terse instructions and brusque replies. Another jolt. Another. "BP rising. EKG shows sinus rhythm." "It's holding." "He's okay. Jesus, we did it."

Now, at ten-thirty on Wednesday night, slightly

more than twenty-four hours after he had nearly died, Mr. Elbaum lay in the Cardiac Care Unit of Westside General Hospital, having his temperature taken by a very nice young orderly.

"You're doing just super," the orderly said after studying the column of mercury. He did not lisp, but his manner of speaking was rather, well, feminine. He had long lashes and delicate features, and he wore his hair tied in a ponytail. Mr. Elbaum thought he might be gay. Well, that was all right. Mr. Elbaum had lived in L.A. all his life, fifty-five years, and he had no prejudices.

"Must get pretty dull, reading thermometers all the time," Mr. Elbaum said. He was determined to be cheerful and pleasant. He had no patience for whiners.

The orderly smiled. An attractive smile, despite the pallor of his skin, the thinness of his face.

"Not at all," he said politely. "I enjoy my job."

"And you're good at it too. At least, you've certainly treated me well—better than some of these wooden-Indian nurses they have around here. What's your name anyway?"

"Gregory."

"Good to know you, Greg." The IV line was attached to Mr. Elbaum's right hand, so he shook hands with his left. "I hope you'll call me Howard."

"I'll do that, Howard. You go back to sleep now. Can I get you something to drink before I go?"

"Scotch and water would be nice."

"Water is all I can do for you."

"Skip it, then."

Gregory Almont smiled again. He dimmed the

lights in Mr. Elbaum's cubicle and stepped out into the hall. The ward was hushed, most of the patients sleeping. The faint beeps of cardiographs competed with raspy snores.

As he continued with his last round of activities on tonight's shift, emptying wastebaskets and wiping up spilled nondairy creamer near the coffee machine, he challenged himself with the difficult problem of how best to kill Howard Elbaum.

Only yesterday the man had suffered a ventricular tachycardia; he was still very weak. Right now his heart monitor was displaying a healthy pattern. But suppose, just suppose, Gregory were to slip into Elbaum's cubicle while he slept and disconnect the monitor's transducer dome. Easy enough— simply reach behind the console and unscrew it.

Suddenly the screen would show a confused pattern. An alarm would sound. Mrs. Lynwood, the charge nurse, would glance at her station monitor and see graphic evidence of a coronary arrest. She would call a Code Blue. The crash cart would be wheeled in as the Code Team assembled. Elbaum would be shot up with drugs, which naturally would have no effect on the monitor's display. In desperation the defibrillator would be used, first at low wattage, then in increasingly powerful jolts.

Gregory flashed on a vivid image of Elbaum's face reddening in panic as the Code Team crowded around him. The startling *whump!* of the defibrillator. His back arching under the jolt. His weak heart pounding faster, harder.

Would the excitement, combined with the stress of repeated precordial shocks, be enough to stop his heart for good? Gregory didn't know. He was no doctor.

But it would be interesting to find out.

He felt a pleasant warmth in his groin and realized that the fantasy had given him an erection. That was a common problem on the job. It was not unusual for him to have a dozen or more hard-ons during his eight-hour shift. He typically wore three pairs of underpants to keep the bulge from showing.

Lately such daydreams provided the only sexual relief available to him. Dominique had stopped coming to Mere Anarchy. She had found something better to do. Gregory gritted his teeth.

Irritably he distanced himself from those thoughts, escaping into his favorite fantasy again. Killing patients. Killing them with great skill and subtlety, so his work would never be detected. Over the years he had devised hundreds of plans to carry out a murder in this ward. The trouble was, he had never found the nerve to put any of them into practice. He lacked courage, and at times he hated himself for it.

Dominique wouldn't be afraid, he thought wistfully. She would do it, then compose a poem about it afterward, a work of genius.

At eleven P.M., his shift over, Gregory drove home to his apartment in Van Nuys. The apartment was small and bleak and largely bare. The bedroom smelled of too many nights alone. A magazine was tented on the pillow; the glossy cover showed a naked woman, blindfolded, hands manacled behind her back, fellating a Doberman with a pistol to her head.

Quickly he stripped off his hospital whites, then changed into black boots and leather. He still went to the bar every night, hoping she would be there. He would forgive her for abandoning him, of course. She was Dominique, an artist, a genius. Whatever she was doing, she was sure to have a good reason. He didn't even care what the reason was. He just wanted her to take him back. He wanted to share her bed again.

The thought of their lovemaking agitated him, and his heart was pumping fast as he sat before his makeup mirror, adding lipstick—purple tonight—and eyelash glitter.

Before leaving, he pulled a folded scrap of paper from his wallet, then got out his scrapbook.

The scrapbook was a photo album, really, the kind with spiral-bound cardboard pages covered with acetate sheets that could be peeled back to insert snapshots of Aunt Edna and the dog. Gregory had no Aunt Edna, no dog; his album contained no snapshots. Pressed under the thin plastic were clippings from magazines and newspapers dating back four years to his arrival in Los Angeles.

He turned to a blank page, loosened the acetate, and slipped his latest find underneath. He had discovered it in a back issue of *Time* that he'd dug out of one of the wastebaskets at the start of his shift. Its presence in his wallet throughout the rest of his workday had been exciting, sexually arousing, like the gentle pressure of Dominique's fingers on the inside of his thigh.

The article concerned a particularly gory political assassination in Colombia. A minister of the government and his young wife had been machine-gunned in their home. The story contained a photo of the couple, laughing on a beach, as well as a lovely shot of the interior of their house after the crime. Tracks of blood on the off-white walls. Expended shell casings glittering in the deep pile carpet like gemstones.

Gregory smoothed out the acetate. He studied the article intently, paying particular attention to the photo of the couple at the seashore. Such clarity, such detail, such vivid colors. The wife had been pretty, her body slender and athletic, her suntanned face wonderfully expressive. He pictured her mouth stretched in a scream as the assassins opened fire, the twitches and jerks of her limbs, the spumes of blood, the spastic staggers that carried her backward a few steps before her final groaning collapse. Lovely.

The clipping made an excellent addition to his collection. It was not the best of his pieces, but it was quite good.

Smiling, he flipped through the scrapbook, watching headlines and AP photos strobe past.

FAMILY'S BRUTAL MURDER STUNS NEIGHBORS. GREEN RIVER KILLER CLAIMS NEW VICTIM. DEATH TOLL RISES IN CIVIL WAR. MASS GRAVE TIED TO RITUAL SLAYINGS. TORTURE, EXECUTIONS OF DISSIDENTS ALLEGED. PREMEDITATION CHARGED IN RAPE-MURDER CASE.

Sheeted corpses. Mug shots. IdentiKit sketches. Maps of city neighborhoods, the crime scenes marked like burial sites in a killing field.

What he liked best were the faces of the victims. A yearbook photo of a smiling girl, smug in her happiness. She had not smiled when a rapist's

straight razor ended her life six weeks after gradu-
ation. A family portrait, all self-conscious grins and
joined hands; husband, wife, two children, sorrow-
ful basset hound—every one of them, the dog in-
cluded, shot to death by a methodical burglar. A
Polaroid taken at an office party, one man's face
circled in white. He wore glasses, the lenses
blanked by the flashcube's burst, his eyes invisible.
Police had found him stripped nude, bound,
gagged, wedged inside his refrigerator, the door
sealed with strapping tape. He had kicked wildly
at the unyielding door until he finally suffocated
in the dark, amid the bagged leftovers and slightly
sour milk. His lover, an older man who wrongly
believed his victim had given him AIDS, was ar-
rested the next day.

The faces were fascinating. Gregory could stare
at them for hours, memorizing every feature, imagining those eyes and mouths widened in terror.

But not tonight. He had to get to the bar. Dominique might be there. God, he hoped so.

As he was closing the book, one particular photo
caught his eye.

He spread the book open on his lap again and
bent his head to the page. The acetate, rippling
with reflected light, made the details of the picture
hard to see. He folded back the plastic and stared
at the photo directly.

It was a shot taken at nighttime in the parking
lot of the Sepulveda Dam Recreation Area. He remembered the accompanying story vividly. Little
Jamie Frisch, kidnapped, murdered, dumped in the
river. How very sad.

Uniformed cops and plainclothes personnel

swirled in the background of the photo. In the foreground were two people frozen in midstride as they walked past the camera. One was a woman, perhaps forty, frowzy and harried. The other . . .

Gregory blinked.

Him.

It was *him*.

He read the caption of the photo. The pair were identified only as LAPD Homicide detectives; no names. But in the text of the article he found references to the two investigators working the Jamie Frisch case. Ellen Lindstrom and Robert Card.

That was his name, then. Card. And he was a police detective.

But it made no sense.

Or maybe it did. Dominique shared his own fascination with death. This man Card worked homicide cases; he was a connoisseur of murder and violence. And the case described in the scrapbook clipping would be particularly appealing to Dominique, wouldn't it? As Gregory knew well enough from their bedroom games, she liked to fantasize about hurting little boys. . . .

Hurting little boys.

The thought touched him first as a tingle in his fingertips, then as a roaring in his ears.

He remembered the night when the two patrol officers had come blundering through the bar. Dominique's face in the blue spotlight—the glaze of fear in her eyes—her stare fixed on the uniforms moving toward her out of smoke and darkness.

He had wondered why she would be so afraid of the police.

Now he knew.

Gregory looked at Robert Card, at the inset photo of Jamie Frisch. He thought of Dominique with her skull face and bloody mouth. He smiled. He was still smiling, the grin fixed on his face like the humorless smirk of a paralytic, as his hand slid under the waistband of his pants and closed over his penis. He stroked himself slowly, slowly, feeling heat in his face, the heat of an inner fire raging wildly, fire that was power. Power.

"I've got you, Dominique," he breathed. "Darling. Sweetheart. Mommy. Oh, yes. I've got you now."

35

Eyes shut, breath hushed, Dominique listened to the night.

Somewhere beyond the walls and curtained windows of Card's bedroom, there was a rush of traffic even at this postmidnight hour. Engines droned. Tires hissed on smooth macadam. In her mind she pictured the cars as humming insects flitting here and there like pollinating bees, their concerns remote from her own, the motives of their frantic activity alien and strange.

Her thoughts drifted to the people in the apartments nearby, asleep by now or reading late into the night or making love in the sweat-misted dark. They, too, seemed foreign to her, members of another species. There were times when she would gaze at the lighted windows of other apartment buildings in her neighborhood, studying the figures framed in the glass as they did their household chores, made dinner, watched television. Creatures in glass cages; zoo exhibits; specimens on display.

In department stores and shopping centers, customers sometimes brushed against her, their casual touch chilling, like the caress of a jellyfish against her bare leg. People were a bizarre phenomenon to her, as inexplicable and revolting as the world it-self, a world eaten by corruption like a corpse by maggots.

She had never been part of any group, gathering, or tribe. Art and poetry and solipsistic explorations of her own mysterious depths were her manner of living, of feeling alive. On stage at the bar, wrapped in the spotlight's blue mist, performing for the witless crowd, she was free. Here in the darkness she knew freedom also, freedom and the delicious, sensual pleasure of communion with her-self. And in the park with Jamie, as she had deliv-ered her scripted lines and lured him closer, closer—oh, yes, she had felt free then, free and powerful and unquenchably creative, on fire with the flaming purity of her art.

Angela would have understood none of that. She was weak, stupid, conventional, a silly little bitch, easily manipulated, ignorant even of Dominique's existence. Poor witless Angela had no idea that her body played host to two minds, two personalities. She knew nothing of Mere Anarchy, nothing of the sex games with Gregory, nothing of the poetry her own hand wrote or the makeup that transformed her face into a bleached skull.

But Dominique knew everything about Angela. She observed the poor fool constantly, studying her with contemptuous curiosity. She was aware of An-gela at all times, though Angela remained uncon-scious of Dominique's scrutiny. Sometimes Dominique did more than merely observe; she would speak to Angela in a muted whisper that passed for the voice of the subconscious, planting suggestions in her mind, impelling her to actions she would never have considered taking on her own.

Angela wondered why she was so often drawn to brutal men, men who indulged in sadism and violence; lately she had been seeing a shrink twice a week to discuss the problem. She could never have guessed that it was Dominique who drew her to those men, Dominique who took pleasure in seeing Angela beaten and humiliated again and again, Dominique who savored Angela's bewilderment and pointless self-reproach.

Those instances of manipulation had been mere games, diversions, amusing but inconsequential. But the seduction of Robert Card had been serious business. Dominique had known that Card would have no interest in her; he could not grasp her genius or appreciate her gifts. Angela, however, was his type. Sweet, sensitive Angela, who would never break a law or harm a child.

It was Dominique who had spied on Card while he delivered his lecture on neighborhood-watch groups, and it was she who had followed him to the supermarket afterward. But it was Angela who had found herself on the checkout line, with a clear memory of having driven directly from her apartment to the store, moved by a peculiar urge to buy celery and milk. Such illusory memories were easy to manufacture. Angela was never troubled by gaps in her recollection; on every morning after Dominique had recited poetry at the bar and romped in bed with Gregory, Angela would remember having spent the night alone in her apartment, reading or watching TV.

Angela had been honestly attracted to Card. He

was the sort of man she would have dated more often, if not for Dominique's playful interference. It had been almost unnecessary for Dominique to urge her on, whispering in her ear that she ought to smile at him, start a conversation, make herself available. Angela, of course, had suspected nothing. As far as she was concerned, her encounter with Card was the result of pure chance.

Card had responded at once. Irrationally Dominique had found herself resentful of Angela's success at beguiling him. She had known that Card would be drawn to the bitch, had arranged and prompted the meeting between them, had stage-managed the encounter with expert proficiency; and yet, when the ruse succeeded, she had been jealous of her alter ego, angry that such a stupidly ordinary female should win the favor of the man she wanted. It made no difference that Angela's body was her own; Angela was another person. A lesser person.

Despite her smoldering envy, Dominique had allowed Angela to handle her first date with Card, as well as tonight's dinner. Even the seduction had been Angela's doing; the girl was not frigid, at least. But in the bedroom, Dominique had taken over. She had seen the gun strapped to Card's leg, and in a fever of lust she had *emerged;* Angela had been pushed down into darkness, her consciousness swallowed in a blackout.

Angela would not have taken Card's cock in her mouth or demanded that his teeth tear her sex. Even Dominique had not wanted or permitted any man to do that to her, not Gregory or any lover she'd had before him ... with one exception, of course. The one precious, unforgettable exception.

She smiled. It was in tribute to that other man that she had made Card take her so savagely tonight. She stretched her legs and felt pain in her crotch, a sharp pain that would linger as an ache, a familiar ache she had not felt in years.

Angela would feel the ache also, but she would not recall the passion that had birthed it. When the bitch awoke tomorrow morning, she would relive hazy memories of gentle lovemaking, phantom memories that Dominique would generously supply.

One day—perhaps very soon—Angela would not awake ever again. Dominique would submerge the little fool into blackness forever and take permanent control of the body they shared. Angela had been a useful tool, a convenient cover, but Dominique was tired of her; she had no doubt that she could snuff out her alter ego whenever she chose.

But first she would bring her relationship with Robert Card to its proper finish. She would make him suffer. She would watch him bleed.

On their first date, in the restaurant, Card had told Angela he had a little boy. Dominique had danced that night, danced in celebration. She had promised herself that Card's romance with Angela would end in a funeral. As she had drifted toward sleep, the last image in her thoughts had been a small casket and, inside, a doll-like body, hands folded on its chest.

Tonight Dominique had watched, fascinated, as Angela met the boy, talked with him, read him a bedtime story. The child was perfect. Seven years old—the same age Jamie had been. Small and warm, skin smooth, eyes bright, spirit still unsoiled.

Michael Card. Dear little Mike. Poor motherless thing.

Somehow she would have that boy. She would absorb his soul. With his innocence she would purge and purify herself; and Angela would comfort Robert Card as he grieved.

Dominique rolled her head on the pillow. The clock on the nightstand glowed green in the dark. One-fifteen.

She wondered if Angela should be here in the morning, when Card woke. Perhaps not. It would be better to leave him wanting more.

She rose, careful not to disturb the man beside her. She found Angela's discarded clothes and dressed swiftly.

With her hand on the knob of the bedroom door, she paused, frozen by a thought.

Card and his housekeeper were asleep. And in the room down the hall, Mike lay in bed.

The doorknob rattled. Dominique stared at it, surprised that it should jump around for no reason. Then she realized that her hand was shaking.

She released the knob. Breath shuddered out of her. Weird sounds like hiccups bumped up against her clenched teeth.

She wanted him. Oh, God, she wanted him so badly.

And he was close, only a few yards away, asleep, unsuspecting, unprotected.

She could take him tonight.

She hadn't planned to make her move this soon.

But the opportunity—it was ideal. Why wait? Why delay the delicious thrill of their union?

How sweet it would be to hold him in her arms and hum lullabies.

She hugged herself. She could feel his body close to hers. Her lips puckered; she thought of his smooth forehead, ripe for kisses.

Couldn't wait. Couldn't. Couldn't.

She had to do it *now*.

Dominique removed her shoes for silence. Carrying them in one hand, she opened the door and peered into the dark hallway.

A clock ticked. From the kitchen, refrigerator hum. Nothing else. No movement. No activity. No one awake to stop her.

She went down the hall, her steps as soundless as a shadow's tread, her breath hushed. The door to Mike's room was just ahead. She pushed it open with care, wary of squeaky hinges. Then she was inside, joining him and the dog in the dark. Two small shapes sighing, the dachshund's belly pumping, Mike with a thumb corked in his mouth.

She watched them. Debated how to carry out her plan. The dog was an obstacle. If not for him, she could have used the pillow. Suffocation, quick and clean and nearly noiseless if handled properly. But the dog would bark and bite. She wrinkled her nose. Filthy animals, dogs. Flea carriers, tick magnets, stool sniffers. She had never killed one, but she imagined that the job would be tricky. A knife ought to work. There must be knives in the kitchen drawers.

That was the way, then. Kill the dog with one quick thrust, then the child a moment later.

Still holding her shoes, she left Mike's room and crept down the hall into the kitchen. She opened the refrigerator door for a little light, then searched the drawers till she found a butcher knife. Her fist closed over the fat handle. Gingerly she ran the tip of the blade along her forearm and felt a small welt rise where the skin was gently nicked. Perfect.

Card would have a nice surprise when he woke up. Some fine new scars would be engraved on his soul. He—

Her hand started shaking again, more violently this time. The knife nearly fell. With effort she lowered it to the open drawer, replaced it, slid the drawer shut.

"Oh, Christ, Dominique," she whispered aloud. "What were you doing? What were you thinking of?"

She felt sick. She leaned over the sink, quivering with nausea.

She had meant to kill the boy. Kill him, even though there could be no way for her to cover up the crime, no way to escape arrest, trial, conviction. Card would have gotten her for both murders, Mike's and Jamie's. Would have locked her away for life.

"What were you thinking of?" she asked again.

But that was the worst part, the terrifying part. She had not been thinking at all. She had been driven by the wordless need to make that child her own, breathe in his lovely soul, hold his small life-less body tight to her bosom.

Love. That was what she'd felt. Surging, soaring, blinding love. A mother's love. It had overwhelmed her, wiping out all awareness of context and consequences.

Her loss of control was inexplicable, horrible. She remembered how carefully she planned Jamie's murder, how expertly she carried it out. Even in the delirium of her love, the hot rush of blood roaring in her ears, she had remained alert to the requirements of her survival. She had made no stupid mistakes.

But tonight . . .

Terror groaned in her. Terror and the first self-doubt she had ever known.

She became aware of the shoes still clutched in her left hand. Quickly she slipped them on, then found her purse in the living room where she had left it.

She was crying as she escaped from the apartment and ran blindly down the hall.

36

Dominique was still shaking as she guided the Pinto into the underground parking garage of her apartment building. The automatic gate slid slowly shut behind her. She wheeled into her assigned space, her headlights splashing the cinder-block wall, then killed the engine and sat in the abrupt silence, gripping the wheel with both hands.

You're all right now, she told herself. You're fine, just fine. Whatever happened was a momentary aberration, nothing more. Lapse of judgment. Failure of—

A rap of knuckles on her window.

She spun in her seat, swallowing a gasp, and saw Gregory standing there in his club makeup.

"Jesus," she hissed.

Unsteadily she climbed out of the car. Shut the door with a hollow echoing thud. Faced Gregory under the orange globe of an overhead light.

"What the hell are you doing here?" She spat the words.

"Waiting for you."

"How did you get into the garage?"

"I loitered outside all night. Walked in here a second ago, right after you drove in, while the gate was still open. You didn't even see me." He leaned closer. "I had the impression you might be preoccupied, darling. Upset about something."

"I'm just tired. Why were you waiting for me?"

"You weren't at the bar tonight."

"I haven't been at the bar for some time."

"Suppose I was anxious to see you."

"Suppose I don't give a fuck." She started walking through the garage, her heels clacking on the concrete floor and bouncing echoes off the walls. "Get out of here. Go home and scrub your face and get some sleep."

"Is that what I should do?" He made no move to follow her.

"Or slash your wrists. Or cut off your dick and stuff it down your throat. Do anything you want. Just leave me alone."

"Is he good in bed?"

She stopped. Standing motionless, her back to him, she drew a breath and released it slowly. Without turning, she asked, "Who?"

"Robert Card."

Dominique swallowed once. She made no reply.

"We have some things to talk about," Gregory said softly, impertinence implied in the exaggerated politeness of his tone. "Important things."

She pivoted to face him. The garage canted dangerously. Blood throbbed behind her eyes. There was a frightening, explosive pressure in her head. She pictured her brain bursting, her skull rupturing into fragments of gleaming bone.

"All right." Her voice was nearly steady. "Talk."

"In your place." Gregory studied his long fingernails. "Where it's private."

"Come on."

They rode the elevator like strangers, both watching the numbers change.

Yards of black-velvet night pressed against the windows of her living room. She flipped up the light switch, locked her door, gestured to a beanbag chair.

"Sit."

He sat. She sank onto a futon. Watched him.

"Well?" she asked finally.

"You never answered my question. Is he a good lover?"

"I don't have much to go by."

"Don't you?"

She bristled at the sardonic lilt in his voice. "Tonight was our first time."

"Oh, come on."

"It was."

Gregory let his head fall back, exposing his pale throat, his prominent Adam's apple. Dominique thought of the knife she had taken from the drawer in Card's kitchen, the sharp blade that would slice flesh like wax. Her palms itched.

"Did you seduce him? Make the first move?"

"Yes."

In truth, Angela had carried out the seduction; but Gregory had no knowledge of her. He knew the woman who sat facing him only as Dominique.

"You didn't play our games with him," Gregory asked, "did you?"

"Naturally not."

"Naturally not," he echoed mincingly. "He might not play along. And if he did, he might learn too much."

"What are you talking about?"

"Why, Jamie Frisch, of course. What else?"

Fear iced her belly. It took an effort to remain slumped casually on the futon, to keep her facial muscles slack.

She invested a moment's thought in her reply. Complete ignorance of the murder would be implausible under the circumstances. Best to reveal part of the truth. A small part, no more than a sliver. Careful, careful.

"Jamie Frisch?" she said with elaborate casualness. "So you figured that out, did you?"

His head jerked up, surprise registering on his face.

"Yes," he said slowly, "I figured it out."

She waved her hand in languid slow motion, brushing away an imaginary insect. "I read about Jamie in the paper, just as you did, I presume. The case fascinated me. Card was one of the detectives in charge of the investigation. I became, well, rather obsessed with him, I suppose. Eventually I contrived a way for us to meet, seemingly by chance."

Gregory locked his hands behind his head, studying her. "And what was it about that particular crime that piqued your interest?"

"The brutishness of it. You should understand about *that*, dear."

Gregory smiled. "Oh, I do understand, Dominique. I understand completely."

The pressure in her head was building. She felt her brain expanding like a balloon, gray matter pressing against bone. A headache was coming on, and with it, a sense of suffocation as her sinuses closed up.

She couldn't stay seated. Had to move about. As fluidly as possible she rose, walked to the kitchen, filled a glass with water. The hand holding the glass did not tremble too badly.

"I'd appreciate it if you would get to the point," she said through the doorway to the living room. "It's late, and I have to go to work tomorrow." Or rather, Angela does, she added silently.

She tilted the glass to her lips. The water was lukewarm with a chemical taste, disgusting. Her stomach rolled.

"Work," Gregory said. "Well, of course. The dear little tots will be expecting you."

She set down the glass on the counter with a hard thump.

"Yes, darling." Gregory's voice wafted into the kitchen, carrying the image of his smile. "I know where you work. I've seen you there."

She stepped into the kitchen doorway and stared at him across the living room. "Seen me?"

"I followed you one morning. You hadn't made an appearance at the bar in some time. I wanted to know what you were up to. And I always had been curious about what you did with yourself during the day."

"You should have had better things to worry about."

He ignored that. "So I followed your car to the, uh, Happy Childhood Daycare Center, as I believe it's called. Did you have a happy childhood, Dominique?"

"I had a perfect childhood," she answered truthfully. "Keep talking."

"I parked a block away, then concealed myself behind somebody's van and watched you feed lunch to the children. Laughing, teasing their hair. What an actress you are, darling."

It had been no act, of course. It had been Angela.

"Anyway, I continued to spy on you from time to time. I suspected that you were seeing someone else. And I was jealous; I admit it."

"As if you had any special claim on me," she snapped, but the words were empty, weightless.

Gregory smiled, unperturbed. "Last Saturday night I watched this building for hours, hidden behind some trees across the street. I saw a man pick you up and, later, return you to your door. You kissed him. When he got back in his car, I saw his face clearly. Unfortunately, he saw me too. Nearly caught me when I ran away."

"I wish he had."

"I doubt that. I would have told him some interesting things."

Threats now. Threats from Gregory. Anger flared in her, wiping out fear.

"Enough of this," she said curtly. "If you have something to say, I'm willing to listen. But not for long."

"All right, then." He twisted to his feet. Approached her. His eyes locked on hers. "Why are you dating Robert Card?"

"I already explained that."

"Because you wanted to hear about Jamie?"

"Yes."

"Hasn't Card satisfied your curiosity on that subject by now?"

"We've only gone out twice."

"You could have made him tell everything he knows on the first night."

"Perhaps." She took a step backward, out of the kitchen doorway, hating to retreat from Gregory but unable to withstand his gaze any longer. "But there are other murders he's looking into. He likes to talk about them. The subject appeals to me. If you understand my art, you'll know why."

"I think you've taken your interest in that particular subject well beyond the realm of art."

"Meaning?"

"How did you do it, Dominique?"

"Do what?"

"The paper said he was asphyxiated, but the story was short on details. What was it, a strangulation? A smothering?"

She forced laughter out of her throat. A light airy laugh like a tinkle of wind chimes. "You're not serious."

"I want to hear how you did it."

"Time for you to go, Gregory. Home to bed. You'll sleep well, I'm sure. You're dreaming already."

With a last attempt at cool indifference, she brushed past him, laughing soundlessly, and then hard fingers, surprisingly strong, clamped on her arm and shoved her up against the wall. His face was inches from hers, filling her field of vision like a gigantic close-up on a movie screen.

"I know you did it," he breathed. "I saw your eyes. I saw your goddamned *eyes.*"

"What are you babbling about?" She tried to put irony in her voice, heard panic instead.

"In the bar. That night. When the cops came in, chasing that drunk. You saw them. You froze. Rigid with fear."

"Policemen scare me."

"Then why are you fucking one?"

"I like danger—"

"You like little boys. You like to play Mommy. Mommy with a whip. Games weren't good enough anymore, where they? So you tried something that wasn't a game. You killed Jamie Frisch. Seven years old, and you wasted him like a bug. And you know what I think about that?"

His panting breath fanned her face. He smelled of sweat, a stale, sour odor that made her think of kennels. His eyes flashed with a febrile light.

"You know what I think?" he asked again, insistently. "Do you? *Do you?*"

His mouth was hot as he mashed his lips against hers, kissing hard, smearing her chin with purple lipstick, his hands frantic as they groped her body. She broke away, gasping.

"That's what I think," he whispered.

"Gregory . . . what . . . ?" Confusion left her helpless, unable to voice a question.

"I've always known you were a genius." He was kissing her neck, her cleavage. "And brave. Of course you're brave. It takes courage to be an artist, to hunt truth. But I never knew just how much courage you had. You've gone beyond poetry. You've taken your work to a new level, a new height."

She was numb, blank, empty of feeling and

thought. She stared down at the silky teardrop of his ponytail as he pressed his face to her breasts.

"You have to tell me all about it. How did it feel to kill him? Did you watch him die? Did you see his face?"

An emotion tingled in her like a phantom limb. She needed a moment to identify it. Pride. Pride in her brilliant accomplishment, her perfect crime. She had wanted to share her secret with someone who would understand. Now she had the opportunity. She could not pass it up.

"Did you see his face?" he demanded, still kissing her, nuzzling her with his cheek and leaving white powder on her skin.

"Yes, Gregory," she said quietly, and as she spoke the words she felt a sudden shocking sense of calm. "Yes," she repeated more firmly. "I saw . . . everything."

"Describe it to me. All of it."

"I chloroformed him, carried him to my car, drove to an isolated location. While he was still unconscious, I bound him, then tied a plastic bag over his head. At the last moment he came to, and I had to pin him down to keep him from tearing free of the bag. His death throes were wonderful. He writhed like a belly dancer, his small arms and legs marvelously supple."

Gregory lifted his face to her. His lips were shiny, not with gloss. "Did he turn blue?"

"A little, yes. Tinge of aqua in the cheeks."

"His eyes—were they open wide?"

"Round as marbles. You could see the terror in them, and the stupid incomprehension, and finally the shocked recognition of mortality."

"Did it feel good? Was it as special as you'd hoped?"

"It was better. Better than anything I've ever known. And the best part was the moment of his death. Because he entered me. His spirit, I mean. His pure and uncontaminated essence. He slid between my legs and passed into my belly, reversing birth, returning to the womb. We were joined in holy union. We became one." She felt herself smiling, her face warm. "He's with me still."

"Tell me what you did with the body."

Dominique sighed. Gregory was such a hopeless materialist. "I tossed it in the L.A. River. It made a soft splash in the dark."

"You drove there with the boy in your car?"

"Not right away. First I drove aimlessly for hours. With the windows open and the night air blowing in."

"If you had been stopped, pulled over—"

Her chin lifted. "I knew I wouldn't be."

"You're fearless, Dominique. An artist and a daredevil. So infinitely superior to . . . all of them."

"All of whom?" she asked, knowing what he meant but wanting to hear him say it.

"The people in the bar, and everyone else—everyone who isn't you, who could never be you—the drones, the ordinary ones. They commute to work and shuffle papers in their air conditioning, then go home and pop the tab of a beer can and root for the home team on TV. And they call themselves normal and healthy and alive. They disgust me. They've got no right even to stand in your shadow. What you've done, this masterpiece of yours, it will outlast all of them. Put it in your poetry, and you'll have touched a truth the rest of them are blind to."

"I know, Gregory. I know." Dominique surfed the cresting wave of his admiration. "But my latest achievement is greater still."

"Tell me."

"This man Card—he doesn't suspect. He's hunting me, hunting Jamie's killer, and meanwhile I've got him seduced, enthralled."

Gregory giggled. "It does make for an interesting situation, doesn't it?"

"I knew you'd understand."

"Then why did you hide it from me?"

"I shouldn't have. I'm sorry." He started to speak again, but she silenced him with a touch of her finger to his lips. "Wait. I haven't told you the best part. Robert Card—he's a widower—he has a son. Mike. Seven years old."

"Jamie's age."

"Yes."

"Magical number, seven," Gregory whispered. "Magical age. They believe in magic when they're seven."

"Mike does. I'm sure of it. He's so innocent and uncorrupted."

"He tempts you."

"I nearly slashed his throat tonight, while he lay sleeping."

"You would have been caught."

"That's why I didn't do it."

"Still . . ." Gregory stepped back, his narrowed eyes glinting. "There might be another way."

Her blank look was a question.

"If he dies while you're with him," he said

slowly, "you'll be the obvious suspect. Even if you were to make his death look like an accident, there would be inquiries. The kind of inquiries you can't afford."

"I know all that."

"So the answer is simple. You can't be with him. In fact, you have to be with Card. Out on a date. The perfect alibi."

"The perfect . . ." A slow smile crept across her face. "Gregory. You're a genius."

He blushed. Actually blushed. "You're the genius, Dominique. Not me."

"We both are—tonight." Thoughtfully she twisted a stray strand of her hair around her index finger. "But I've got to be the one who does the actual killing. I've got to make him mine."

"That can be arranged. I'll get hold of the boy for you, and you can finish him." He licked his lips. "As long as I get to watch."

Dominique clapped her hands like a delighted child. "Darling, I believe I've underestimated you rather badly."

"You'll get a chance to make up for it."

"I'm sure I will." She frowned. "The kidnapping will pose difficulties."

"Does Card hire a baby-sitter?"

"No, he has a live-in housekeeper, a large Hispanic woman named Consuelo who cooks well and smiles too much. You'll have to take care of her to get the boy."

"Kill her, you mean?"

She could not tell if the sudden twitching of his eyelids signaled fear or excitement. Both, possibly. She considered the problem.

"Yes," she said finally. "I think it would be best if you killed her."

"All right. All right." Gregory cupped his hands and blew into them as if trying to warm himself. "All right," he said again.

"Can you . . . do it?" she asked tentatively.

He smiled. A wide white smile that shocked her.

"Dearest," he said, "of course I can. All my life I've been waiting for just this opportunity."

Dominique returned his smile, buoyed by his confidence. "She won't be easy to dispatch. She's big and looks strong."

"With the right weapon, I can handle her."

"A gun will make too much noise."

"I wasn't thinking of a gun."

"Perhaps a knife would work. But there's a chance she could fight you off. A woman of her size—"

"I wasn't thinking of a knife either."

"What, then?"

"Just leave it to me. I know a method that won't fail." He hugged himself, his eyes dancing. "Believe me, I've given a great deal of thought to such matters."

There were depths to him that Dominique had never seen or sensed before this moment. The dark passions that moved her were alive in him, as well. Her recognition of their kinship, the abrupt acknowledgment of a relationship with another human being, left her stunned and a little giddy.

"This will be wonderful, Gregory. Magnificent. A triumph." She was babbling. She seemed unable to control her speech. "You'll be my co-author, my ally, my fellow fighter in the war against the ordinary." She could not stop thinking of Mike Card dead in her arms, his limp body swaying as she rocked him and sang. "We'll plan every move, leave nothing to chance. And we'll strike soon. Very soon."

He threw a sharp look at her. "When?"

A beat of silence ticked in the room as she thought it over.

"Friday night," she said firmly. "If Card can be persuaded to ask me out, as I'm sure he can."

"That's only two days from now."

"I can't wait any longer. I simply can't."

Gregory did not argue. He approached her, his face serious, lips pursed.

"You want him," he breathed, "don't you?"

Her reply a gasp: "I want him."

"And how about me?" His thin arms looped around her. His hands crawled over her back like spiders. "Do you want me too?"

Her eyes met his. She saw some part of her soul reflected in him, some splintered fragment of her own most urgent needs.

"You know I do," she said, meaning it, knowing for the first time that she and Gregory were right for each other, that he gave her something no other man could give.

Smiling, teeth bared, Dominique pulled his mouth down to hers.

37

Card woke at dawn, alone. For a heartbeat of time he wondered if last night had been only a beautiful dream. Then he became aware of the ache in his thighs and back. It was a good ache, a pleasant kind of pain.

He thought he might find Angela in the bathroom or somewhere else in the apartment; but she was gone. Must have slipped away in the night. He was sorry she'd left. It would have been nice to wake up with a woman beside him in his bed. Three years had passed since he'd done that.

A hot shower shocked him fully awake. As he toweled off, he heard Consuelo rousing Mike, the madcap clatter of Willy's toenails on the kitchen floor, the murmur of the *Today* show. Morning sounds. He wished Angela had stayed to hear them, to be part of the beginning of this day.

Mike was quiet at breakfast, picking at his corn flakes. Card asked him what was wrong.

"I had a bad dream," Mike said.

"What happened in the dream?"

He frowned, his small face pinched in concentration. "I don't remember too much about it, except I was someplace dark, and there was somebody with me. Somebody scary."

"A man or a woman?"

Mike shrugged his thin shoulders. "Don't know. Couldn't see. They didn't say anything. They just stood there looking at me. And, uh, breathing. In, out. In, out."

Card smiled. "Like Darth Vader?"

Mike shook his head, irritated. "No, Dad. This was a real person." He looked at his bowl of cereal. "A bad person."

"What made you think so?"

"I could tell, that's all. I could tell they wanted to hurt me."

Card was mildly disturbed. His son rarely had nightmares. Well, perhaps the excitement of meeting Angela had rattled him a little.

It sure rattled me, he thought wryly. A lot.

Card worked at home for an hour, reviewing paperwork he'd neglected last night. At ten he said good-bye to Mike and drove to the station. The day was hot, the Valley heating up in mid-July. A gray paste of smog clung to the humps of distant mountains, browning the horizon.

Card parked in the lot behind the station, then went inside. Daylight yielded to the chill of fluorescence. He hurried down a narrow corridor, past the focused breeze of desktop fans and the sour smell of bad coffee percolating in ancient machines. Bulletin boards glided by, their corkboard surfaces almost totally obscured by masses of thumbtacked memos and circulars.

He entered a large functional room partitioned into smaller work spaces by rows of file cabinets. In each work area several cheap metal desks were butted up against one another. Men with their jackets off and their neckties loosened sat at the desks talking on the phone or leafing through reports or exchanging noisy opinions. Most of them nodded to Card or waved at him as he passed.

Lindstrom was already at her desk, adjacent to his own.

" 'Morning, Ellen."

She looked up from a half-eaten cruller and a mug of steaming coffee. "Hi, Bobby. Jesus, you look happy. Have a good time last night?"

"Pretty good."

Lindstrom studied him, her face unreadable. "You're crazy about her, aren't you?"

"I like her. 'Crazy' might be a little strong."

His partner nodded. She said nothing.

They were still working the Northridge drive-by. One of the teenage victims had been released from the hospital and was well enough to look at mug shots. Card and Lindstrom picked him up and drove him to the station, and then Card commandeered a vacant office and sat with the kid as he flipped through sheets of photos.

At quarter to twelve he left the kid briefly to search for a file in one of the gray cabinets in the detective squad room. His desk phone rang while he was pawing through manila envelopes. He answered it.

"Card, Homicide."

"Robert?"

"Angela." He sat on the edge of the desk, smiling. "Hello."

"It's good to hear your voice," she said.

"Yours too."

"I'm sorry I ran out on you last night. I had to

get up early for work. The center opens at seven A.M., you know. And besides, I . . . Well, I wasn't sure if you wanted me to be there in the morning."

"Why wouldn't I?"

"I thought it might be a problem for Mike. You know. Seeing that I'd spent the night."

"It would have been okay," Card said glibly, then frowned. Was he sure of that? Had he considered Mike's feelings at all? He was uncomfortable with the idea that Angela had shown more sensitivity to his son's reaction than he had. Brusquely he dismissed those thoughts. "I want to see you again."

"Of course."

"How about tonight?" He was pushing, he knew; shouldn't seem too possessive; couldn't help it.

"Uh, no. Tonight isn't good. Anyway, I need time to recover."

"You're young and strong. You'll bounce back faster than I will."

"Oh, yes, I forgot. You're an old man." Soft laughter. "Didn't act like one last night, though."

"You inspired me." Damn, he wanted to be with her again. "If not tonight, how about tomorrow?"

"Well . . ."

"Come on, nobody wants to be alone on a Friday night. Maybe we can take in a movie or a show or something."

"Now that you mention it," Angela said slowly, "I did notice an ad in the *L.A. Times* for a concert at the Hollywood Bowl. *Rhapsody in Blue* and some other Gershwin pieces, performed by the Hollywood Bowl Orchestra. John Mauceri is conducting. Does that appeal to you?"

Card had little interest in music, but the answer

he gave was truthful anyway. "It does if you want to go."

"Let's do it, then. I'll get the tickets. There's a TicketMaster outlet not far from where I work."

"Okay, but I'll reimburse you."

"Robert," she chided, "don't be sexist."

"Suppose we go dutch. Is that okay?"

"Fair enough. The show starts at eight-thirty, just after sunset. I know you sometimes work late. Do you think we'll have time to eat?"

He frowned. On a Friday night the drive from his place to Hollywood would take a good forty minutes. "It could be tight."

"I've got an idea. There are picnic tables on the grounds of the amphitheater. Suppose I get there early and grab a table. You arrive when you can, and I'll have dinner waiting."

"Sounds great—if it's not too much trouble."

"No trouble at all. I'll stop at the market and pick up a few cold cuts, wine, cheese."

"Can I bring anything?"

"Just yourself."

"All right. I'll try to make it there by seven forty-five. Or, uh, maybe eight."

"I'm looking forward to this, Robert. Well, I have to get back to work now. See you tomorrow."

Buzz of a dial tone. Card was smiling as he cradled the handset. He rose from the desk and saw Lindstrom standing a few yards away, riffling through a stapled collection of departmental advisories with a businesslike preoccupation that was not altogether convincing.

"Eavesdropping," he said, not bothering to make it a question.

"Obviously. I gather you're seeing her again."

"Tomorrow night. Gershwin concert at the Bowl."

"Gershwin?" Lindstrom chuckled. "Her idea, I assume."

"Yeah. But it might not be so bad."

"I didn't say it would. So she's classy, huh? Highbrow?"

"English major."

"Really? She's a writer?"

"No, I told you, she works at a daycare center."

"Job like that can't pay too well."

"She definitely lives low-rent. But she likes the work."

"Do you suppose she does anything to supplement her income? You know, maybe write on the side? A lot of these English Lit types are frustrated writers."

"She said she tried it but didn't like it."

"What did she try? Short stories? Or maybe ... poetry?"

"I don't know. What makes you ask?"

"Just wondered."

"You've got a funny look on your face."

"Indigestion."

"Come on, Ellen, what's that matter?"

"I'm just a little concerned, that's all."

"Concerned?"

"How well do you know her, Bobby?"

"Not too well, not yet. Friday's only our third date."

"But she's got you hooked already. I can see it."

"Cut it out."

"No joke. You're in love. And the thing is, it

could be dangerous. I mean, you don't really know what you're getting into."

"Nobody ever knows. That's what relationships are all about. Finding out. Learning." He shrugged. "I was still learning new things about Jessie almost up to the day she died."

"Sure, but . . ."

"But what?"

"Never mind."

"You're suspicious of her, aren't you? You think she's hiding something?"

"Anything's possible."

"You have any grounds for suspicion?"

A pause. Then a firm shake of her head. "No."

"Then what prompted this inquisitorial attitude?"

"Excess of caffeine in my system. Makes me paranoid. Don't worry about it."

Lindstrom walked away, toward the coffee room. Card stared after her for a long moment, then returned to the office he'd taken over, where the shooting victim was still patiently flipping through mug shots. He took a seat and gazed thoughtfully at the wall.

Weird behavior on Lindstrom's part. She seemed almost resentful of Angela. Could she be jealous? No, impossible. Hell, he'd asked her out and she'd given him the brush-off. Ridiculous to think she'd be interested in him now. Anyway, it was far too late for that.

Maybe she was just worried about him in a maternal way. Card smiled. The idea of Lindstrom feeling maternal toward anybody struck him as faintly amusing. Or maybe the congenital suspi-

ciousness of all detectives, the hypervigilance culti-
vated by the demands of the job, had gotten to her.

Whatever it was, it didn't matter. Lindstrom
wasn't going to turn him against Angela. He loved
her, for God's sake. He—

Loved her.

Did he? Did he really? Was he that serious about
her after only two dates?

Well, of course he was. What had last night been,
anyway, if not a rehearsal for living together? It
had been more than a date. It had been a simulation
of marriage.

Marriage. A new family. The three of them having dinner every night, he and Angela trading small
talk about their jobs and asking Mike about school.
Then, later, Angela sitting on the corner of the bed
reading stories from children's books. Mike with a
mother again.

Abruptly Card realized he was fingering the ring
on his left hand, tugging gently at it, picking at the
small gold band like a scab. He froze, lanced by
guilt.

No.

He had never taken off that ring. He would not
do it now. What it symbolized was too precious to
be surrendered.

The flipping of pages went on. The teenager
gazed at the endless photos.

What it symbolized, he repeated to himself.

Sure, that sounded good. But what exactly did it
mean?

He had read somewhere that nuns wore wedding
rings to symbolically affirm their marriage to

Christ. The idea had struck him as creepy, unhealthy. Marriage to a ghost.

He looked at the ring. Slowly he began to twist it, trying to work it loose.

A ghost, yes—that was what Jessie was. Not even that. She was a corpse, that was all. A green, moldering corpse. He had seen long-buried bodies exhumed. He had watched them autopsied on the stainless steel tables of the morgue's Decomposed Room. He knew what lay in his wife's casket. That was what he was married to.

He was pulling harder at the ring now, pulling with sudden, desperate urgency. Briefly he worried that it might not come off at all, that it might have bonded with his skin somehow, or even with bone, becoming part of him forever. Then it loosened, and a moment later, it slid free, leaving only a narrow indentation and a faint discoloration between his knuckles.

Card held the ring between thumb and forefinger, watching it flash in the light of the overhead fluorescents.

Good-bye, Jessie.

He stared at the ring for another long moment, then palmed it like a magician doing a coin trick, making it disappear.

The ring went into his pocket. He would put it away when he got home. Put it away with the square of carpet he had saved from the Canoga Park house, the photo albums, Jessie's diary, which he had found after her death but had never read, and all the other mementos of their marriage that would be meaningless to anyone but him.

He would put it away, and then he would get on with his life.

38

There was only one Angela Westmore of Studio City in the White Pages. Her address was listed, saving Lindstrom the trouble of looking it up in the reverse directory.

She waited till Bobby was out of the room, then used a computer terminal to call up the DMV files and obtain the make, model, and license number of Angela's car. By the time Bobby returned, she was back at her desk. No way she was going to let him in on her suspicions, not yet.

Already she was losing her hold on the certainty of the connection she'd made. The voice on the phone couldn't possibly have belonged to the poet in the bar. A woman like that, a post-punk avant-garde angst-worshiping freak, would never be interested in suit-jacketed, straight-arrow, widowed-with-child Bobby Card.

Unless Angela was setting him up somehow. For blackmail or scandal or something worse. Maybe she had a boyfriend Card had nailed, and she was manipulating him in order to lead him into a trap. Paranoid, crazy—sure it was—but such things had happened. Cops made enemies every day.

A simple tail job might resolve the matter. Lindstrom could stake out the apartment building tonight, follow Angela whenever she went out. If she drove to Mere Anarchy, climbed into the blue spotlight, and started another recital, then Lindstrom would have no further excuse for keeping her mouth shut.

After that, she would face only the question of how to tell Bobby.

It would break his heart, of course. His fling with Angela was his first love affair since Jessie had died. He needed companionship so badly; he was more vulnerable than he knew. But for his own protection, he would have to be told.

Card would want to know how Lindstrom had recognized Angela in the first place. What the hell she'd been doing in an underground bar that catered to a bizarre clientele. She could lie, say she'd been dating a guy who'd brought her there once or twice, but that tactic wouldn't work for long. To confirm her story, Bobby would check out the bar personally, interrogating the patrons, the performers, the bartender. Chris was a regular, known to many of the people he would talk to; and Lindstrom had been seen with Chris often enough that their relationship had undoubtedly been surmised.

Should she tell him the truth, then? Spill everything right up front? "And while we're on the subject, Bobby, maybe you'd like to meet Christine; she's heard so much about you."

Lindstrom shook her head. She didn't want to reveal all that. She cherished her privacy, guarded her secrets, preserved her false front with a fierce sense of self-protection.

But realistically she had to concede that the details of her private life were likely to be exposed. What would happen then? A lot would depend on how Bobby reacted to the news. She remembered what he'd said about the leather punks and the dykes. If he really felt that way, their partnership would be poisoned, unworkable. She would request a reassignment. The other detectives in the office, all of them male, would take their lead from Card. No matter whom she was paired with, she would have a rough time. There would be askance looks, whispered jokes, subtle ostracism.

Well, she could retire in less than two years on full pension. Hadn't planned to, but life was full of surprises.

God, she wished she had a cigarette. She needed one.

For just one moment she considered dropping the whole thing. Bobby was a big boy; he could look after himself.

Coward.

She knew she wouldn't drop it. Couldn't. Bobby had saved her life when Luis Estoban was popping caps at her. She still owed him for it. Besides, however he felt about her life-style, whatever blind spots he might have, he was fundamentally a good guy. They were friends, and she wouldn't run out on him. She would do what was necessary, and later . . .

She would face that nightmare when she had to.

Right now the woman in the bar—that creature of smoke and shadows, who recited lunatic poetry and dressed like death—was nightmare enough.

39

Angela finished her shift at the daycare center at one o'clock. She said good-bye to the kids, then got in her Pinto and drove to Ventura Boulevard, where she spent more than an hour window-shopping and people-watching, a pleasant diversion on a summer afternoon. At a Häagen-Dazs shop she bought an ice-cream cone. The cold vanilla made her teeth tingle.

She felt fine. Last night had been wonderful. Robert had been so kind in bed, so loving. She remembered few details of their intimacy; what lingered in her mind was an impression of tenderness and joy.

The only shadow on her happiness was the dull, nagging ache between her legs. Her sex was sore and raw. She had fingered it in the shower this morning and had winced, surprised to discover that her vulva was painfully torn. How had that happened? She didn't know, but the pain seemed oddly familiar to her, as if she had awoken with it on other mornings.

It was because she wanted time to heal that she had put off seeing Card tonight. Better not to rush things anyway. Tomorrow would be soon enough, and the Gershwin concert would make a wonderful centerpiece for their date. As soon as she'd spotted the ad in the *Times,* she'd known that she and Card had to see that performance, simply had to. Funny how strong the feeling had been. She hadn't realized she liked Gershwin quite that much.

At two-thirty she got back in her car and drove to Dr. Reiss's office on Van Nuys Boulevard. She sat in the waiting room, looking at a magazine, till the door to the inner office opened precisely at three.

Dr. Reiss smiled at her. "Hi, Angela."

He was a tall stoop-shouldered man, balding, with large ears. He wore a blue sports jacket over an open-collared shirt. Angela had been seeing him twice a week, every Wednesday and Thursday, for two months, and he had worn that same jacket in every one of their sessions.

He led her down a short hallway, past a kitchenette. "Would you like anything to drink? Coffee, tea?"

"Nothing, thanks."

They settled in his office, Angela in a plush armchair, Dr. Reiss on the couch.

"Well," she said.

He nodded. "Well."

She had expected today's session to be easy. She would talk about Robert Card, about their date last night, about how she had reversed her pattern of destructive relationships. Now she found that the words would not come. Her mouth was all gummed up, her mind empty.

"Have you given any more thought to what we discussed yesterday?" Dr. Reiss asked.

Yesterday. What had they talked about yesterday? Oh, yes. Her childhood. A favorite subject of any psychologist. Dr. Reiss was convinced that the key to her attraction to unstable men lay in her past. He had explored the subject persistently for much of their two months together. But she could recall nothing particularly unpleasant about her experiences as a child.

"Not really," she answered. "I mean, I've already told you everything I remember. I had a good time growing up. I did well in school, and I had friends, and later I dated a little." She shrugged. "I've probably said all that a hundred times."

"That's true. You always say your childhood was a happy time. But you never seem to be able to give me many specifics."

"I guess my memory isn't very good."

Silence.

"Do you keep in touch with your parents?" he asked after a long moment.

"Well, sure. I mean, maybe not as much as I should. Ever since moving to L.A., I've been so busy."

"Do you talk on the phone with them?"

"Once in a while."

"When was the last time you spoke?"

She frowned. The question disturbed her for some reason; she felt a little flustered. And the ache in her crotch was worse.

"I don't know." She sketched a vague motion with her hand. "It couldn't have been very long ago."

"Weeks? Months?"

"I really can't say."

"Have you gone home for the holidays?"

"No."

"Not even once, in four years?"

"No, I said."

"Have they come out here to visit you?"

"No, they haven't. But they live in Tucson. They're not exactly right next door."

"Tucson isn't that far from L.A." She said nothing. "Do you exchange cards? Send letters?"

"I'm not much of a letter writer."

"So you never hear from them, and they never hear from you?"

"Well, Christ, I said I've been busy."

She heard inexplicable anger in her voice. Dr. Reiss watched her, his pale face expressionless.

"Do you think that's the reason?" he asked.

"I don't know. Look, what's the point of all this?"

"The point is that, although you claim to keep in touch with your mother and father, you don't really seem to be in contact with them at all. And by the same token, while you say that your childhood was fine, you obviously don't recall much about it."

"So?"

"I'm wondering if perhaps there was something in your childhood that you've wanted to avoid facing. Something that prevents you from remembering your past and from dealing with your parents today."

The pain between her legs was intense now, burning, a splash of acid. She shifted in her seat.

Dr. Reiss studied her. "Are you all right?"

"Yes, fine."

"You seem a little uncomfortable."

"I'm just tired. Look, as I've told you before, I

had a very pleasant childhood. I loved my parents, and they loved me."

"Do you think you were close to them?"

"Yes, very."

"Were you closer to your mother or your father?"

"My father, I guess." She crossed her legs. "No, that's not right. I don't know why I said that."

"What's not right about it?"

"Well, he worked all day, so I got to see him only at night." Suddenly her mouth was dry. She was finding it hard to swallow. "You know, I think I might like something to drink after all."

"Okay." Reiss got to his feet. "Tea?"

"Just water."

"I'll be right back."

He left the office. The door clicked shut behind him. Angela sat gripping the armrests, heart pounding, black and red specks shuttling across her field of vision. It was hard to breathe, hard to think. She didn't know what was going on. Some kind of anxiety attack, maybe. A delayed reaction to the excitement of her date last night. Her date . . .

Card loving her in the dark. Tangled sheets— rough hands—scent of sweat and semen—

The door swung open with a squeal of hinges. Her head jerked up. A man entered the room, a tall man moving toward her out of the doorway, and she heard herself moan.

Not again, not *again*.

She twisted sideways in her chair, head hanging down, arms outstretched, fingers gnarled like claws. Pain racked her body, sudden stabbing pain that radiated from her groin.

"Angela? Angela?"

Pain as he bit her, bit her, and then she was going away, hiding inside herself—

"*Angela!*"

She slumped in the chair. Gazed up at him helplessly. Then blinked, mind and vision clearing.

Dr. Reiss. It was only Dr. Reiss.

He held a Pyrex mug half filled with water. She took the mug in a trembling hand. Drops spilled on the carpet, on her blouse. She tipped the mug to her mouth and swallowed what she could.

"Are you okay?" His voice was low and soothing.

"I think so."

"Tell me what happened."

She shut her eyes. "I thought . . . I thought you were him."

"Who?"

"My father."

"Go on."

"He loved me."

"Yes."

"He loved me at night."

"Tell me."

"He came into my bedroom. Came in and did things. Undressed me. Kissed me. Put his head between my legs and . . . bit me there. It hurt. It hurt."

"Is this the first time you've remembered what he did?"

She nodded shakily. "How could I have forgotten something like that?"

"Because it was too painful to think about."

"Then why did I remember now?"

"You tell me."

Because I hurt the same way, she thought. I hurt

down there, the same way I used to hurt every morning after he loved me.

But she couldn't say that. Couldn't. She shook her head mutely.

"What else do you remember?" Dr. Reiss asked.

"Well ... there's my mother. She knows about it. She lets him do it. She doesn't stop him." Vaguely she was aware that she was speaking in the present tense, as if she were still a child in a dark bedroom, a child sprawled on floral-print sheets smeared with blood. "And ... and after my father is done, my mother comes into my room and sits on the edge of the bed. She talks to me, and I lie there shivering."

"What does she say?"

"That my daddy loves me. That he's a very special daddy to show his love for me in such a special way. And that I must never, ever tell anybody about the secret, special things my daddy does for me, because the ordinaries wouldn't understand."

"The ordinaries?"

"That's what she calls other people. People who live ordinary lives and think ordinary thoughts and don't know what love is. We're different, she says. We're better than all of them. We've seen truths that none of the ordinaries could ever understand."

"Do you believe her?"

"I don't know. Part of me does. Part of me thinks she's right. Part of me even ... even ..."

She hitched in a breath.

"Even what, Angela?"

Sudden tears burned in her eyes. Her voice was a whisper.

"Part of me even likes what my daddy does. Part of me *wants* him to do it."

"And the other part of you?"

"That part wants to hide from him and from my mother. Wants to get away. Sometimes I find a place to hide when my father is with me. A place inside myself, where it's dark and quiet. I go in there and curl up, and I let him do what he wants with the rest of me."

"Who's with him, when you go away?"

"I don't know."

"Is it still you? Or is it someone else?"

She shook her head, said nothing.

"How long has your father done this with you?"

"Years."

"How old were you when it started?"

"Eight. I had just turned eight."

"And how long will it continue?"

"Till I'm thirteen."

"Why will it stop?"

"Because I—" She choked off her answer. "I don't know."

"What were you going to say, Angela?"

"I'm not sure."

"What happened when you were thirteen?"

She honestly could not remember. The memory had teased her, then vanished, elusive as a dream.

"I don't know. Can't we quit now?"

"Of course we can. I'm sorry. I shouldn't have pushed so hard. But this is important, Angela. It's a breakthrough. You see that, don't you?"

"I see it."

"The relationships you've been having, your

problems with men—it's all beginning to make sense, isn't it?"

"Yes."

"For years you've repressed the memory of your parents' abuse. Now it's out in the open, and you can start to deal with it."

"I hope so. I hope I can deal with it."

"You can. I know you can."

She wanted to believe him. But she wasn't sure.

Because the tender place between her legs was still raw and painful, and now she had to know why.

40

At five P.M., two hours after the start of his shift, Gregory took a break, ostensibly to use the rest room. He waited till Mrs. Lynwood, the charge nurse, was distracted by a complaining patient, then ducked into the stairwell. Quickly he descended two flights, emerging on the third floor.

Inconspicuous in his hospital whites, he moved swiftly through the net of intersecting corridors till he found the supply room. He tested the door. Unlocked. He had counted on that.

There was a chance he could take what he needed and escape without being noticed, but he preferred to improve the odds by creating a diversion.

A nurse bustled past, and Gregory veered into a side corridor. When she was gone, he hurried down the hall to an alcove where a coffeemaker perked and gurgled industriously. A smoke detector had been installed in the ceiling almost directly overhead.

He fished a wire stripper out of the pocket of his white cotton jacket, then unplugged the machine, quickly removed an inch of rubber insulation from the cord, and anchored the plug in its socket again. The exposed wire lay in contact with a paper doily.

From another pocket Gregory took out a cigarette lighter. He thumbed the wheel, sparked a flame, and set fire to the doily, a stack of paper napkins, and a tower of paper cups.

Smoke was curling toward the ceiling as he slipped into a vacant semiprivate room just down the hall. He huddled near the door, waiting. The smoke alarm went off a moment later with a whining buzz that reminded him of the tuneless singing of cicadas.

Footsteps and shouts from outside. Sounds of confusion. He wondered how bad the fire was. Probably a lot of smoke and little else. He had to move fast.

He left the room. Three nurses, a ward clerk, and a couple of orderlies were clustered around the alcove; one of the nurses was squirting chemical foam at gray wisps of smoke. Gregory walked fast in the opposite direction. Anybody looking at him would see only an anonymous orderly hurrying somewhere—to get help or another fire extinguisher, perhaps.

He glanced back. No one had seen him. He stepped into the supply room.

Hurry now.

He moved immediately to the refrigerator. Opened the door. Scanned the shelves arrayed with rows of vials. Saw what he needed. A 10-cc vial of succinycholine. The cap still unpopped, the membrane unpunctured. He pocketed it.

Turned to the drawers. Found a box of disposable plastic syringes. Stole one. It went in his pocket also.

When he looked out the door, he saw more people

gathered around the scene of the fire. The alarm was still screeching, but the flames had been put out. Nobody was paying any attention to this end of the corridor.

He exited the supply room, shutting the door softly, and hooked left at the nearest side corridor. Found the stairs. Returned to the fifth floor. He made it to the rest room in the cardiac ward without being seen, then emerged a moment later, making no effort to conceal himself any longer, and started industriously changing bed sheets.

Later he took another break. This time he really did use the toilet. Sitting in one of the stalls, he took out the syringe and vial. He turned them over and over in his hands.

He'd done it. No fantasy this time. The real thing.

He wondered if the theft would even be detected. The fire would be attributed to a frayed electrical cord—nothing suspicious about that. The syringe would not be missed; nobody kept inventory on throwaways. The absence of the vial would be noted eventually, but most likely someone would assume it had simply been misplaced. Succinylcholine was not codeine or Valium; no market for it on the street.

Even if theft was suspected, no one could possibly trace it to him. He didn't even work on that floor.

Gregory smiled. He ran his fingertip around the rim of the vial. Held its contents up to the overhead fluorescents. Stared at the clear liquid sloshing from side to side.

Succinylcholine was sometimes called synthetic

curare, and, like the natural substance, it brought on a temporary state of flaccid paralysis. Its chief medical use was as an aid to endotracheal intubation; by relaxing the muscles of the throat, a doctor could more easily guide the slender tube down a patient's windpipe. This procedure was nearly always followed in surgery, and was occasionally necessary in emergency situations in the intensive care wards, as well.

Curare, of course, was known to be deadly; and in a sufficiently large dose succinylcholine could prove fatal, as well. Ten cc's—the amount of the vial—would paralyze not only the limbs but the diaphragm, making it impossible for the victim to breathe. In normal medical practice this danger was circumvented by placing the patient on a respirator.

Gregory would not be using a respirator tomorrow night, when he injected Card's housekeeper with the drug.

He squirmed, fingering his penis and rubbing his buttocks against the toilet seat with slow, sensuous pleasure.

Dominique had warned him that Consuelo was big and strong, perhaps too strong to be overpowered even with the help of a chloroformed rag. A knife attack would be messy and uncertain; though he could probably inflict a lethal wound, she might not die instantly, and her screams would alert the neighborhood. And a gun was out of the question. Gregory had never fired or even handled a gun in his life. Firearms terrified him. Besides, a gunshot would be too noisy.

But poison was perfect for his needs. Silent, swift, certain. It guaranteed quick death.

A flawless plan. Dominique would be proud of him.

He wanted so much to please her, to prove himself worthy. Soon he would. He pictured the glitter in her eyes, the ravenous wolf's smile on her face, when she saw little Mike Card waiting for her, wrists tied and mouth gagged, his small heart beating rabbit-fast—when she tugged the plastic bag over his head and thrilled to the frantic jerking of his body—when she held the dead child in her arms and planted kisses on his warm forehead.

The boy was what she wanted. Very well. Gregory would give him to her; and she, in turn, would do what he asked. They would be partners, just as she had said. Allies, fellow fighters in the war against the ordinary. The abduction and murder of Michael Card would be their mutual achievement, their shared triumph over the mindless, mundane crowd. It would be a work of poetry, of art, and it would bear his signature as well as hers.

Gregory trembled, his penis hard in his hand.

He simply couldn't wait to add the clippings to his scrapbook.

41

Angela drove home fast, taking side streets to avoid the early rush-hour traffic. Her heart was pumping hard as she unlocked the door of her apartment. She shut the door, bolted it, and secured the chain, as if hoping to barricade herself against the wordless terror that pursued her.

Her bedroom windows were glazed with a white dimensionless glare. She drew the curtains, then flopped down in bed, fully dressed, and buried her face in the pillow. Her mind was a hive buzzing with frightened questions. Questions about her father and mother, about the loss of memory that had deleted the most crucial scenes from the filmstrip of her childhood, about the lingering soreness in her private parts and what it might mean.

Her thoughts returned obsessively to the nightly horrors in her bedroom—her father's sweating presence, his cruel mouth rooting in her like an animal's snout, his hands clamped on her buttocks, the bed rocking wildly, mattress springs creaking, soft moans warbling out of her young throat.

She ground her face into the pillow's soft foam. She didn't want to think about that, about any of it.

And yet she sensed that there was something worse. Something unspeakable.

The backseat of her parents' car. She was sitting there, curled in a corner, crying. Her father was behind the wheel, her mother beside him, both of them silent. The desert rushed past, saguaro forests and the blue humps of distant mountains. The car was speeding north to Phoenix, not on the freeway, but on Route 89, the old state highway.

Yes. She remembered that much. And no more.

She didn't know what the memory meant. She was too tired to look deeper. Too tired to think at all.

Eyes shut, she willed herself to relax. A pleasing numbness stole over her legs and arms. The bed began to spin, spin, and she spun with it, her body describing slow lazy circles like the blade of a ceiling fan.

Sleep took her. Calm, dreamless sleep.

The sun moved across the curtains, shifting the shadows in the room.

On the bed, among the jumbled sheets, Dominique stirred.

Her eyelids fluttered. She raised her head from the pillow. Yawned and stretched. Rolled languidly onto her back and kicked off Angela's sensible shoes.

The little bitch had learned a great deal today— too much—and yet she still understood nothing. Even after rediscovering the gift of love her parents had bestowed on her, she continued to think in stupidly conventional terms. She insisted on comparing her childhood with the upbringing of other girls, as if those others bore any relationship to her. She remained stubbornly, willfully blind.

And blind to other things, as well. Even now, she had not the faintest suspicion of Dominique's existence. Let the bitch search for answers, let her probe the shadowed corners of her mind: Dominique was invisible to her inward gaze.

Tingling warmth spread slowly through her body like nutrient through the roots and stems of a plant. She felt safe and wise and clever.

For some unmeasurable span of time Dominique lay in bed, hands steepled behind her head, puffing thoughts like smoke rings. She contemplated what she would do tomorrow night, the purification of her soul, the holy ritual that would unite her with Mike Card as she had been united with dear little Jamie.

After a while she felt the need to create. In the back of the bedroom closet she kept a carton filled with stacks of her poems and blank legal pads. The carton was concealed behind another box, and Angela had no idea it was there.

Dominique removed one of the pads, then uncapped a pen, stretched out on her belly on the bed, and began to compose a poem. A poem in honor of Mike.

As usual she wrote rapidly, in short bursts of inspiration, making no revisions. She was unconcerned with rhyme or meter, such petty, senseless restrictions, so typical of the hidebound society that made laws and morals to keep the cattle in their pens.

In a few hectic minutes she was done. She studied the jagged scratches of her penmanship overspilling the sensible ruled lines.

The poem was a lovely thing, her finest work so far. It humbled Dante, Milton, and Shakespeare. It exposed Keats and Shelley as foppish pretenders. It soared past Yeats and Eliot and the rest of the moderns. It was a masterpiece, a work of genius. It had to be. She was a genius; therefore all her works were works of genius. Airtight logic.

Angela had studied English in college and had briefly wanted to be a writer; but she had lacked talent and inspiration. It was Dominique who was the creative spirit, gifted with transcendent insights. Angela was one of the ordinaries. She was not special. She had rejected her parents' love.

Her creativity spent, Dominique rose from bed and watched the bloody sunset. She prepared dinner—something frozen and microwaved; she never noticed what she ate. Afterward she rested, reciting her new poem to herself, memorizing it for tonight's performance. Though she had not been to the bar in weeks, she had agreed to meet Gregory there at midnight in order to make their final preparations.

At ten-thirty she changed into black spandex, then sat before the makeup mirror putting on her face. As always she was fascinated to see the skull appear, death's visage superimposed over her living features, bone and eye sockets emerging from beneath the facade of flesh. She took care to do the job properly—the black hollows of the eyes, the red gash of her mouth, the painted pallor of her skin. In all things she was an artist.

Satisfied, she left her apartment and hurried

downstairs to the parking garage. She did not take the elevator, which was sometimes crowded; the back stairs, poorly lit and rarely used, were safer. She had always avoided contact with the other tenants while in costume. Their opinion of her was of no consequence, naturally, but she had not wanted Angela to face overt hostility from her neighbors. Seemingly causeless antagonism might raise questions in her mind.

Yes, she had taken great care to protect herself from Angela, wasting time and energy, squandering her resources. But such efforts need not continue much longer. Soon the bitch's usefulness would be ended, and she would be thrust down into darkness forever, her personality extinguished. Then this body would belong to Dominique alone, and Angela would be dead.

Yes. Soon.

Dominique climbed into Angela's Pinto, sparked the ignition, and pulled out of her parking space. She was singing a high tuneless song as she drove up the ramp into the dark street.

42

Lindstrom watched the white Pinto turn the corner, then eased away from the curb and followed, switching on her headlights halfway down the block. Feathery streamers of smoke issued from the cigarette in her mouth, her eighth. A stakeout was a strange kind of work, simultaneously boring and nerve-racking. She had brought along two packs, expecting to sit up all night.

But Angela Westmore was proving to be more cooperative than that.

After arriving at the building at eight o'clock, Lindstrom had risked a peek into the parking garage to confirm that the Pinto was there. The license number matched the one provided by DMV. When the car pulled out of the garage, she had caught a glimpse of a dark figure at the wheel, hair pulled back tightly from the forehead. The driver's face seemed unnaturally pale—the skull makeup? She couldn't be sure.

In her eighteen years on the force she had done a few tail jobs. The trick was to stay close to the quarry, but not too close. She timed her progress to ensure that she wouldn't get stuck at a red light while the Pinto cruised on down the street. Once or twice she let another vehicle slip in between her Mazda and Angela's car.

She was certain she had not revealed herself. Angela made no attempt to shake her pursuit, no sudden stops or unsignaled turns.

The Pinto hooked north onto Sepulveda. Lindstrom puffed faster on her cigarette. The bar was just ahead.

She was not even surprised when Angela guided her car into a curbside space across the street from Mere Anarchy.

Lindstrom passed her, risking a sidelong glance just as Angela was opening the car door. The glow of the reading lamp illuminated her face clearly. Her scarlet lips were hideous against the bleached pallor of her skin.

"Bobby, I'm sorry," Lindstrom whispered as she found a parking space down the street.

She watched Angela in the sideview mirror as she jaywalked across the busy street and disappeared inside the bar. Then she slumped in her seat and finished the cigarette, crushing it in the ashtray with unusual violence, her wrist flexing with the savage desire to mash and pulp the burning end.

What now? Home? A phone call to Bobby? No, this wasn't something that could be handled on the telephone. A visit to his place, then. Her vivid fantasy of the conversation that would follow sickened her.

Not tonight, she decided. Tomorrow. Let Bobby have one last night of being in love.

Anyway, she hadn't finished her assignment yet. She needed to see Angela on that stage, blue in the gelled light. Needed to hear her voice reciting lines of meaningless poetry, the words disturbing and amusing at the same time, like the posturings of a precocious but deeply troubled child.

She opened her door. Got out. Shut it, locked it. Touched the Beretta under her suit jacket, snug against her ribs in its shoulder holster.

Then crossed Sepulveda and entered the bar.

43

Dominique scanned the smoky bedlam, looking for Gregory. He wasn't there. She checked her watch. Eleven-fifteen. His shift ended at eleven; he rarely arrived before eleven-thirty.

Another performer had the spotlight at the moment. Dominique took a stool at the bar and nodded to Jonathan. He smiled at her.

"Dominique. Haven't seen you here in weeks."

"I felt the need to retreat for a time. Revive my energy and my creative powers."

"I've missed you. You're the only performer we've got who's worth a damn."

"Will you let me go next?"

"Of course."

"I have something very special for you tonight."

"Everything you have is special, Dominique."

Dominique smiled and drifted away to one of the tables up front. Jonathan, at least, appreciated her. Her gifts had not gone totally unacknowledged by the world.

She endured several minutes of inane, childish haiku compositions recited in a flat voice by a creature with spiked hair and taloned fingernails. She could not determine the creature's sex, if any.

The crowd bestowed a patter of listless applause, alms tossed to an unworthy beggar, as the haiku poet left the stage. Immediately Dominique claimed the spotlight. The stool was still warm from the sexless creature's buttocks. Her fingers curled lazily around the microphone stand. The metal cylinder made her think of gun barrels and erections, of Robert Card.

Her first selection was the poem she had written earlier today.

Art and love join hands in mystic union
My alchemy transmutes death into new life
Recital yields to theater
In the blue mist a dream is played out
To an audience of empty chairs
And mannequin eyes

She thought she might recite the poem to Mike before she killed him tomorrow night. He deserved to hear this tribute. After all, it was meant for him.

Now I take you in my trembling arms
Softly I smother you
Hear your unvoiced cries
Kiss your fear, lick your pain
Tasting salt and sadness
Then cry for you as you blush blue
Ashamed to lose the illusion of your life

The words were perfect, each one sparkling and flawless like a gem. The poem was a miracle of composition. She was making such fantastic progress. And soon, with Mike to cleanse her spirit of

its last impurities, there would be no limit to what
she could accomplish.

Moveless you embrace me
Lips like petals flower-soft on my breast
Your mother is here, small one
Her womb eager to receive you
Come to me
I rock you in the cradle of my arms
And whisper of my love

She was finished. She lowered her head, shaking
with emotion, with love and need.

I love you, Mike, Dominique added silently as a
private coda to the verse. Mommy loves you very
much.

44

Seated at a table near the doorway, an unlit cigarette drooping from her waxwork hand, Lindstrom listened to the poem.

The verse could not mean what she thought it did. Could not.

But if it did . . .

"Softly I smother you," she whispered, her voice dragging in her throat like tire chains on gravel. "Then cry for you as you blush blue."

Blush blue. Cyanosis.

Jamie must have turned blue as he asphyxiated in the plastic bag.

And his killer had watched.

No, it was too crazy.

But the poem referred to a child, didn't it? A child who died? Who was murdered?

Lindstrom remembered the Virginia Slims she was holding. Thumbed her lighter. It wavered badly, and she had trouble touching the flame to the cigarette.

The poem might not mean anything at all, she reminded herself. Might be only some obscure allegory.

Or it might be autobiographical, a memoir of a real crime. A crime as yet unsolved.

A waiter floated up to the table and asked for her order. Lindstrom heard herself say "Vodka, no ice" in a hollow voice, a voice that echoed inside her like a shout in a cave.

She sat rigid in her seat, staring at Angela in her death-mask makeup. Once, Angela turned her head and seemed to look right at her, and for a dizzy, disoriented instant Lindstrom was sure the woman knew her somehow, was on to her.

No, crazy. Keep it together, Ellen.

She focused her mind on what little she knew about Angela Westmore. According to Bobby, the woman claimed to work at a daycare center. Most people who worked with kids were genuinely affectionate toward them. But a few were sick, obsessed, malevolent. They were capable of molesting and abusing their young charges. In extreme cases they might be capable of murder.

She and Card had always assumed Jamie's killer was a man, because the percentages favored a male killer. But statistics never told the whole story. Anyway, it was possible that Angela hadn't committed the actual crime herself. She might have served merely as an accomplice.

Or she might not have had anything to do with the boy's death at all. The whole idea might be a fantasy spun out of a few obscure verses and a gut-level dislike of the woman on the stage.

Her drink arrived. Lindstrom dug a money clip out of her jacket pocket and paid, adding a tip.

The performance continued. More poems, all equally obsure, all featuring the recurring theme of motherhood. Motherhood and death.

Lindstrom took a long swallow of her drink.

All right. Suppose Angela was involved in the murder somehow. Why would she begin a relationship with one of the detectives handling the investigation?

But Ellen knew the answer to that one even before the question surfaced in her mind. Crazies liked to push the envelope. They got a kick out of seeing how far they could go, how bold they could be, how much they could get away with. Some killers sent taunting letters laced with subtle clues to the police department or the media, daring the authorities to catch them. Or take that serial killer, the one responsible for a string of grisly decapitations on the Westside last year—he'd mailed audiocassettes to the leader of the task force hunting him.

Sure. It happened all the time. And the same irrational impulse might drive Jamie's killer to seduce the cop who was working the case.

She remembered overhearing Card invite Angela to his place for dinner last night. Involuntarily she shivered, picturing the woman in skull makeup seated at the table with Bobby and Mike.

Mike . . .

"Oh, Jesus Christ."

The words came out too loud, and Lindstrom looked around nervously, afraid she had attracted the attention of the people near her; but the small crowd was still watching the stage, where Angela's recital continued.

Mike was Jamie's age. Was it possible . . . ? Could that bitch be thinking . . . ?

Jesus. Sweet Jesus.

Get hold of yourself, Ellen. You don't know that. You don't know anything for sure. Except that something weird and ugly is going down here. Something that's got to be stopped.

Lindstrom lifted her glass, gulped vodka. It burned.

45

Gregory was smiling as he entered the lobby of
Mere Anarchy. Parting the curtains, he stepped
into the familiar den of smoke and madness. A
chalk-white face floated in the blue spotlight at the
rear of the bar. Dominique, on stage, reciting.

Annoyance needled him. Normally she awaited
his arrival before beginning her performance.

He glided through the bar to a table near the
stage. Dominique saw him as he sat down. She nodded in recognition while continuing to recite. He
returned her silent greeting.

A waiter took his order and brought him a glass of
whiskey. Gregory sipped it, enjoying the smooth
sting of the alcohol as it went down. When the recital
was finished, he led the applause and went on clapping after the rest of the audience had stopped.

Dominique joined him at the table. "Is everything ready?" she asked immediately.

He kept his voice even, hoping to sound serenely
unconcerned. "Yes, dear. We're all set."

"You know how you're going to take care of the
housekeeper?"

"I've got it all worked out."

"Good." She grinned at him, flashing a sickle of

white teeth framed by the red wound of her mouth.
"Very good, Gregory. You're better at this than I'd
had any right to expect."

"Your inspiration is what makes it possible," he
answered truthfully.

The waiter took her order and returned moments
later with a glass of rum. She raised it in a toast.

"To Michael Card," she said, keeping her voice
low.

"To Mike," Gregory affirmed.

Two glasses clinked in celebration.

At one A.M. Lindstrom left Mere Anarchy. The
crowd was beginning to thin out, and she could stay
no longer without the risk of becoming conspicuous.

She returned to her Mazda but did not drive away.
Instead she waited, slumped behind the wheel. She
was curious about Angela Westmore's friend, the
young man who had entered at eleven-forty-five, and
who had sat with her, drinking and talking quietly.

The man was familiar. Lindstrom had seen him
in Mere Anarchy on the night when the Van Nuys
patrol cops came storming through. He'd been
seated at the bar, gazing raptly at Angela in the
blue spotlight; she seemed to recall that one of the
cops had asked him a question.

Was he Angela's boyfriend? Her real boyfriend,
as opposed to Robert Card? Was he perhaps her
accomplice in the murder of Jamie Frisch?

Stop thinking that, she ordered herself. You
don't know enough to make assumptions. Any assumptions. Not yet.

She sat behind the wheel for half an hour, smoking cigarettes and watching the entrance of the bar.

At one-thirty Angela and her friend emerged. They crossed the street to Angela's Pinto, parked about fifty feet behind Lindstrom's Mazda; both of them climbed inside. Lindstrom expected to hear the cough of the engine, then see the car pull away from the curb, but the Pinto just sat there.

Were they making out? Lindstrom studied the car in her rearview mirror. No. They were seated side by side, looking across the street, watching the entrance of the bar as she herself had been doing for the past thirty minutes.

Strange. Very strange.

Lindstrom lit another cigarette, careful to hide the flare of the lighter in her cupped hand, then waited for whatever would happen next.

Dominique and Gregory said nothing as they watched the last patrons of the bar depart alone or in couples.

It was two-fifteen when Jonathan shut the front doors and locked them from inside.

"He must go out the back way," Gregory said.

Dominique started the engine and drove around the corner. She parked near the alley behind the bar. Less than two minutes later Jonathan thundered out of the alley astride a big Harley, defiantly helmetless, a warrior on his steed. The bike sped off down the street, pursued by the angry buzz of the unmuffled motor.

Dominique pulled into the alley and eased the Pinto to a stop outside Mere Anarchy's back doors. She and Gregory got out.

Jonathan kept both doors unlocked while the bar was open for business, a procedure he had followed ever since the fire marshal had conducted an unannounced inspection that had resulted in a citation. After hours the doors were secured by large steel padlocks.

Gregory studied one of the padlocks in the funnel of light from Dominique's high beams. "Bolt cutter should do it," he said finally.

"Get one tomorrow."

"Right." He scratched his chin. "Are you sure he closes up at two every night? Even on a Friday?"

"I'm sure. And if he doesn't, you'll wait until he does close, however long it takes."

"There are other places we could do this."

She smiled, her bone-white face lit from below by the headlights, her black-socketed eyes lost in deep wells of shadow. "None as fitting."

He didn't argue. Because she was right.

Lindstrom drove slowly past the alley. The two of them were in there, all right. They'd gotten out of the Pinto and were standing near Mere Anarchy's back door.

"What the hell is going on?" she muttered. "You two charmers planning to pull a four-five-nine?"

She turned her Mazda around and parked on the side street, killing the headlights and engine. It occurred to her that she could enter the alley on foot, try getting close enough to them to eavesdrop on their conversation. She wasn't sure she felt brave enough or stealthy enough to do it. On the other hand, if they really were planning a break-in and she caught them in the act . . .

Before she could decide, the Pinto glided out of the alley, Angela driving. Lindstrom watched the car hook north onto Sepulveda; it executed an illegal U-turn and double-parked opposite a beat-up Mustang. The boyfriend got out of the Pinto and slipped behind the Mustang's steering wheel. Angela pulled away, heading south, and the boyfriend followed.

Lindstrom turned onto Sepulveda and dogged the Mustang, staying well behind it. She shadowed both cars back to Angela's apartment building, then observed from a safe distance as Angela parked her car in the garage and the boyfriend found a space on the street. He walked briskly up the front stairs and went inside.

Obviously they were spending the night together. Another thing Bobby wouldn't be happy about; but at this point, it hardly seemed to matter.

Leaving her car, Lindstrom examined the Mustang. She memorized the license number—DMV files would give her the owner's name and address—then inspected the interior of the vehicle in the purple light of a mercury-vapor street lamp. Piles of unidentifiable junk were strewn across the backseat. The two front seats were empty. Something white, like a large index card, sat on the dashboard.

She leaned over the windshield and stared at it. A parking permit for West Valley General Hospital in Tarzana. The permit was stamped with two words: JULY and EMPLOYEE.

"He works there," she whispers. "Shit, I hope he's not a doctor."

She had no intention of staking out Angela's apartment for the rest of the night. Returning to her car, she drove quickly away. As she headed home, the streets of the Valley seemed darker than usual, and her last cigarette carried the sour taste of fear.

46

Dominique led Gregory into the black cave of her bedroom.

"Scared of the dark, little boy?" she breathed.

"No, sweetheart. I'm not scared." He switched on a bedside lamp. "And I'm not going to be your little boy. Not yet."

She blinked at him in the sudden brightness.

"I'm going first this time," he said quietly.

"What do you mean, going first?"

"I mean we're partners now. It's time to indulge some of my fantasies along with yours."

He saw the heavy swallowing motion of her throat. He supposed she knew the kind of fantasies he meant. The kind that had kept him aroused throughout his long, monotonous evenings in the cardiac ward.

"All right," she breathed. "But . . . but don't get careless. If Robert sees bruises on me—"

"Shut up. Strip."

Her mouth opened in the beginning of an objection. He grasped her chin between thumb and forefinger. Her jaws clicked together.

"I told you to strip."

Mutely she studied him, flickers of expression

appearing and vanishing on her face. After a long moment, she shrugged.

He stood back, watching, as she wriggled out of the spandex body stocking to stand naked before him. Grafted onto the supple body of a young woman, the white skull face seemed unreal, hallucinatory, a vision out of Goya or Dali.

"Very nice," he said in a cool appraising tone. "Now unclip your hair."

Anger burned in her eyes as she complied. Her brown hair sprang free of the tight chignon and fell around her shoulders.

Gregory smiled. "Before we proceed, a little music might be in order."

Turning from her, he rummaged through a scattered assortment of audiocassettes. He selected a tape and loaded it in her cassette player, dialing the volume low. A minimalist composition dripped from the speakers, the notes monotonous and numbing like a patter of rain.

He turned to face her again.

"Aren't you going to get naked too?" she asked, watching him warily.

"No."

"What is it you want us to do?"

"Nothing too unusual." He put his hands on her shoulders. "Let's start with a kiss, shall we? A lovers' kiss."

He drew her close. Their lips met, then their tongues, and then he was pulling her down onto the bed, rolling her onto her back, straddling her with his hips, his hand kneading her breasts, his mouth leaving black lipstick on her neck and shoulders.

"You see?" he whispered. "This isn't so bad, is it—what I like to do?"

A feline purr: "Not bad at all."

Smiling, he kissed her again. As he did, his hands left her breasts and reached for a pillow.

"You're beautiful, Dominique. You're a genius. A goddess. I worship you."

"They'll all worship me someday."

"Of course they will. You—or your memory."

"Morbid thought."

"Death takes us all eventually. Even you, dearest."

A glimmer of understanding in her eyes. A sudden tensing of her body. Too late.

Gregory thrust the pillow onto her face.

"Even you!"

She kicked and writhed, her arms flailing, her squealing cries muffled. He bore down harder, till he could feel the outline of her head through the layers of foam stuffing.

"Even you." The words were magical. "Even you." Words of power, a sorcerer's incantation, promising death. "Even *you*."

Finally he lifted the pillow and let her breathe. She nearly choked on a huge gulp of air. Her makeup had been hopelessly smeared, the white greasepaint staining the dark blue pillowcase.

"Gregory—Jesus—what the hell—"

She tried to rise, but he held her down, her midsection wedged between his thighs. Slowly he unzipped his pants and withdrew his penis, stiffly erect.

"You thought I was going to kill you," Gregory said softly. "Didn't you?"

"You son of a bitch—"

He clapped a hand over her mouth. "Quiet now. Save your strength." He grinned at her. "Because you'll need it, darling. I'm not finished yet."

With his other hand he lifted the pillow again. Dominique squirmed, twisting her head from side to side, her hair flopping back and forth like the bushy tail of a struggling animal. Gregory heard ragged, giggling laughter and realized it was his own.

He yanked his hand away from her mouth. She tried to cry out. The pillow slammed down. His fingertips dug into the foam rubber, molding the pillow to her face. She fought wildly, crazed with terror, the cords of her neck standing out against her smooth pale flesh.

There was no doubt that she believed he might really do it this time, might smother her to death. And he could. He really could. All he had to do was maintain the suffocating pressure on her face till she was limp and lifeless. Starve her lungs. Stop her heart. Cheat the world of her genius, her art. Kill her. Asphyxiate her, as she had asphyxiated Jamie Frisch.

Yes. *Yes.*

He came. Semen spurted across her belly in a white spray.

The bedroom reeled. Gregory tore the pillow off her face, then rolled onto his side and lay there gasping.

"You *bastard*!" The words exploded from her mouth, followed by a series of thick rasping coughs. "Fucking bastard," she added in a weaker voice.

"Watch your language, dearest."

"What the hell kind of stunt was that, anyway?"

"You know perfectly well what it was."

"Don't you *ever* do anything like that again."

"Why not? Don't tell me you didn't enjoy it."

"Of course I didn't."

He reached between her legs. His fingers probed her sex, felt moisture there. "Liar."

She flushed. Said nothing.

"Don't fight it, Dominique. It's fun to play the victim sometimes. I ought to know."

She studied him. Slowly her expression changed, anger giving way to some unreadable emotion. "Yes. I guess you ought to. Which reminds me—it's your turn now."

"Fair enough."

He removed his clothes without needing to be told, then allowed her to strap his wrists to the headboard. The audiotape played on, fragments of melody endlessly repeated.

"You're my little boy," she breathed, "aren't you?"

He lisped for her. "Yeth, Mommy."

"And you're afraid."

"Yeth. I'm thcared of the dark."

But the room was not dark, and Dominique shook her head curtly. "No, that isn't the reason."

She picked up the pillow and shook it roughly till the pillowcase came free. A surreal impression of her face was imprinted on the blue fabric in greasepaint and rouge.

"You're afraid because you've been bad." She drew out the last word like a kiss. "You're a bad little boy."

She slipped the pillowcase over his head.

Gregory hitched in a breath. He was in darkness, breathing in the smells of her sweat and makeup.

Her feet padded on the carpet. The sound receded. She had left the room.

He waited, heart beating fast. She had never played this particular game before. He didn't know what to expect. Uneasily he wondered if he had pushed his newfound power over her too far.

Then she was back. Her hand caressing his chest. Something cool and smooth gliding along his left arm like a snake.

"Do you know what this is, little boy?"

"No, Mommy."

"This is your punishment for being so very, very bad."

A sharp jab. Red pain in his biceps. A knife. She had cut him with a *knife*.

"Christ, Dominique—"

"Stay in character or I'll make it worse for you."

"Mommy. Don't, Mommy." He tugged uselessly at the strap. The pillowcase stuck to his face in damp patches, making it difficult to breathe.

"And why not? Why shouldn't Mommy be rough with you, after the way you treated her? That nasty trick of yours?"

Another incision, this time in his forearm.

"Please—Mommy—please don't—"

"You'll be a good boy from now on?"

"Yes."

"Swear it?"

"I swear. I swear."

"I'm not sure I believe you."

The blade tested his genitals. He moaned. "No. Please. Don't cut me there. . . ."

"You have to learn your lesson. You have to learn not to misbehave."

Pain. Stabbing pain. Oh, Jesus, she was castrating him—

No. It was not the knife he felt. It was teeth, her teeth. She had bitten him, as she so often did in their bedroom games.

He expelled a ragged breath, then gasped in pleasurable pain as she attacked him again with her mouth.

"Do you like this, Gregory? Do you?"

He couldn't lie. "Yes."

"Of course you do."

"And you liked what I did for you," he said between gasps.

"You know I did."

"We belong together, Dominique."

"Always."

"No other man could appreciate you the way I do."

"No other."

She tugged off the pillowcase and tossed it aside, then released his wrists from the straps. He rubbed his injured arm, wincing. The cuts, he saw, were superficial, and the bleeding was not too bad.

"Let me fix that for you," she said kindly.

She went into the bathroom and returned with disinfectant and bandages. He lay still, savoring the burn of the ointment as she swabbed it on the wounds.

"You'll be fine by morning," she told him after applying the bandages and sealing each with a kiss, "except for a little ache."

"It will remind me of you." He sighed. "Should I leave now?"

"Not quite yet. Soon, though. You can't be here when I wake up at dawn."

"Of course."

Gregory was familiar with that condition of their relationship. No matter how intense their interludes, Dominique always made him leave during the night; she never allowed him to stay till morning. He had often wondered why he could not be present at the start of her day; and he had wondered, as well, why she would routinely scrub off her makeup as he left, sponging her face in the bathroom sink till no trace of greasepaint or rouge remained.

Once, he had come back, a few minutes after departing, to pick up his jacket, which he'd forgotten. She had met him at the door in satin pajamas and a blue terrycloth robe, boringly conventional clothes that were all wrong for her. Catching his unvoiced question, she'd smiled. "Just another costume," she had said.

The joke—if it had been a joke—remained obscure to him. The whole matter was a mystery. Simply another of her secrets, he supposed; she had so many of them. He would never plumb her depths.

Dominique clicked off the lamp. They snuggled together in darkness.

"You shouldn't have started your performance so early tonight," Gregory said after a long, thoughtful silence. "I missed most of it."

She sighed. "I'm sorry. I simply couldn't wait."

"Did you have anything new?"

"Oh, yes. A poem in honor of Mike."

"Let me hear it."

"Now?"

"Now."

She recited to him, her voice velvet-soft, and Gregory listened, thinking of the boy who was soon to die. And he knew that he'd been right—the two of them did belong together. They were moved by the same secret urges and unclean desires. They were soul mates. Dominique might call it spiritual bonding, but at root her need for Michael Card was the same need he had felt when he crushed the pillow against her face.

Their tryst was a ménage à trois, and their common lover was death.

47

Lindstrom showed up at work early the next morning. There were a few matters she wanted to take care of before her partner arrived.

Her first goal was to learn the name and address of the Mustang's owner. Thirty seconds on one of the computer terminals in the squad room gave her that information. The car was registered to Gregory Almont, who lived on Kittridge Street in Van Nuys.

Next she entered both Angela Westmore and Gregory Almont into the Personal History Index of the Justice Data System, a comprehensive data base of arrestees run by the sheriff's department. Neither name showed up in the files; Angela and Gregory had no priors in L.A. County. Which didn't mean they'd never done anything wrong, of course—only that they'd never been caught.

Then she decided to find out the details of Gregory Almont's employment. She could get the information easily enough by calling the hospital's personnel office and identifying herself as a cop, but she preferred not to use such a direct approach. An inquiry by an LAPD detective about a member of the hospital staff was likely to stimulate gossip, and it was entirely possible that the rumor and speculation could reach Gregory himself, tipping her hand. Better to pose as an innocuous caller on purely routine business, the sort of pro forma investigation that would invite no comment.

She phoned West Valley General Hospital and asked for the Personnel Department. The switchboard connected her with an officious woman who identified herself as Joan Price.

"Joan," Lindstrom said smoothly, "I'm calling from Metro Bank credit services. We have a credit card application here from a Mr. Gregory Almont, who lists your medical center as his place of employment. Is that correct?"

A tapping of keys at a computer terminal. "Yes, that's right."

"His application is a little unclear. What position exactly does he occupy?"

"Orderly."

"I see. How long has he held his current position?"

"Three years."

"He works a forty-hour week? Nine to five?"

"It's forty hours, but not nine to five. He's on the three-to-eleven P.M. shift, Monday through Friday."

Friday. He would be on duty tonight, then. Interesting.

Lindstrom asked a few more questions, then thanked Joan Price for her help and hung up.

As she made her way to the coffee machine, she tried to decide whether or not to pay a visit to West Valley General this evening. She could confront Gregory directly, ask him about Angela. But ask him what? She didn't know enough to do more than needle the man and maybe spook him into running away. And she didn't want him to run. She wanted him to stay put so that, if necessary, he and his girlfriend could be netted.

Still, it wouldn't be a bad idea to learn more about Mr. Gregory Almont. And to find out where he was on the afternoon when Jamie Frisch was kidnapped.

She decided to drop by the hospital after eleven P.M., when Gregory would be gone. She could talk with other staff members, maybe take a look at Gregory's time sheets and see if he'd been at his post when the abduction took place. Of course the credit-card dodge wouldn't work again; she'd have to reveal that she was a cop, and her appearance there was sure to start people talking. But Gregory wouldn't be back at work until Monday, so unless somebody contacted him at home he wouldn't know about her visit for more than forty-eight hours. By then she hoped to have enough to bring him or Angela in for questioning.

Card arrived shortly afterward. Together they visited the second victim of the drive-by shooting, who remained in Valley Park Medical Center in stable condition. They showed the kid an array of mug shots, among which was one that the first victim had selected yesterday as a possible suspect. This boy, however, identified none of the faces. Maybe he hadn't gotten a good look at the occupants of the Monte Carlo, or maybe he was just afraid to cooperate.

Even so, they took a trip to the suspect's home, a seedy apartment in Reseda. His mother answered the door and insisted that Hector wasn't home, that she hadn't seen him for two days. She seemed frightened; it was impossible to guess if she was shielding her son from the police or if she was honestly concerned that he had run away. She did permit Card and Lindstrom to enter the apartment without a warrant and conduct a brief search. Hector was nowhere to be found.

"So if she's hiding him," Card said as he drove the unmarked Chevy back to the station, "she's putting him up someplace else."

"Um." Lindstrom stared out the window. Scenery blurred past, tree-lined streets and rows of bungalows, steaming in the heat.

"Something on your mind?" Card asked.

She did not look at him. "I'm half asleep, I guess."

"Up late?"

"Yeah. But not dining and dancing. Just ..." Staking out your girlfriend, she wanted to say. "Just insomnia." She glanced at him and let the next words slip casually out of her mouth. "I don't have the active social life you've got."

"It hasn't been too active until recently."

"That's what I mean. You're seeing her tonight, aren't you?"

"Yeah, the Hollywood Bowl. Gershwin. Remember?"

"Uh-huh. Last time it was dinner at your place, right?"

"Consuelo fixed a terrific meal."

"So it worked out okay, huh?"

"It was perfect."

"How'd Mike get along with her?"

Card chuckled. "I was worried about that. But I shouldn't have bothered. They hit it off right away."

"Guess she's used to being around kids. What with the daycare center and all."

"Oh, yeah, she's a natural. She even read Mike a bedtime story."

"So she really liked him?" Lindstrom pressed.

Card nodded, smiling. "She said he was wonderful. Said she wished she had a boy of her own who was just like Mike."

"Wow."

"Hell, she's crazy about the kid."

Crazy, Lindstrom thought. Yeah. Maybe.

For one moment she was tempted to reveal everything, let it all out in a mad rush of words. But she resisted the impulse. If Angela or her boyfriend had showed up with a prior conviction, she would have felt no hesitation in speaking up. But neither had a record, and all she really had to go on was a weird encounter in a bar and a hunch.

Still, Card's words were hardly reassuring. That bitch wanted Mike. Wanted to mother him as she had mothered Jamie. Lindstrom was almost sure of it.

But Angela couldn't do anything tonight if she was going to be at the Bowl with Card. And Gregory would be at work. So there was still time to look into things a little more.

But not much time, she thought. By tomorrow or Sunday I'll have to break the news to Bobby. He has to know. Goddamn, he's going to hate my guts for telling him this. But he'll thank me eventually.

At least I hope he will.

48

Angela shut the door of her apartment and leaned against it, eyes shut.

Tired. She was so tired.

Work had dragged like chains. The children's squealing laughter had drilled holes in her concentration. Timmy Lachman had thrown up on schedule, and Angela, watching him, had felt the need to scream.

She was not herself today. Memories of her parents' abuse buzzed in her brain like wasps, stinging again and again.

Maybe she should cancel tonight's date. She considered it, then shook her head. Her past, concealed from her awareness, had distorted her behavior for years. Now that it had been exposed to her view, she would not allow it to continue spoiling every good thing in her life.

She wandered into the bedroom, thinking vaguely that she might take a nap. The bed was unmade; white sheets were piled like creaming waves around the wrinkled humps of pillows. It occurred to her that she had put blue sheets on the bed just two days ago. Funny. She must have changed the sheets and pillowcases yesterday, but she had no memory of doing so.

She checked the laundry hamper in the closet. Yes, the blue sheets were in it, stuffed on top of a pile of other clothes. A full load.

Do the laundry? What the hell. It might snap her out of the funk she was in.

The laundry room on the ground floor was empty, none of the machines in use. She stuffed the bed sheets into a washer, then removed a pillowcase from the hamper. Oddly, it had been turned inside-out. She reversed the pillowcase, then stared at it, frowning.

The blue fabric was stained with a white greasy substance and two kinds of red gook. The colors were smeared and blended, as if someone had rubbed at the fabric, trying to blot out the smudges but doing an incomplete job.

She looked closer and saw that two of the red stains were rouge, while a third blot, placed lower, was lipstick.

A face. That was what it was. A face printed on the fabric. A face made of clown-white skin, rouged cheeks, red mouth.

She swayed. Sudden suffocating pressure bore down on her. Strong hands were molding the pillow to her face, smothering her. Then the pillow was ripped free. She gulped air. A man giggled at her in the yellow lamplight, a thin pale man with spangled eyelashes. The blue slip of the pillow in his clutching fingers was greasy with makeup.

"What's going on?" Angela whispered to herself. "What the hell's happening?"

She dropped the pillowcase and stumbled out of the laundry room, leaving the hamper behind.

The elevator carried her back to her floor. She

ran to her apartment, fumbled open the door, and hid herself inside, shivering.

She was scared. Something was wrong with her, seriously wrong. The face on that pillowcase—it had been familiar, hadn't it? Hadn't it?

She paced the living room, trying to think. The first thing she had to know was when she had changed the sheets. It must have been sometime yesterday afternoon or evening. What had she done yesterday? There had been the session with Dr. Reiss, of course. She had driven home, frantic, then collapsed in bed and surrendered to sleep. Later, she had awakened, made dinner, read a magazine, watched TV. Sure. Her usual dull routine. Right?

She wasn't certain. Not anymore.

Her memories of the therapy session and her return to the apartment were vivid, immediate, the details defined with photographic sharpness. What had come after her nap was blurred, a hasty watercolor, the brush strokes bleeding together. It was an indistinct impression, oddly insubstantial, dreamy and diffuse, empty of specifics, like ... like her memories of the carefree childhood she'd believed she had lived.

Those memories had been a lie. Had last night been a lie also?

A shiver snaked through her. Her teeth chattered.

What had she made for dinner? Which magazine had she read? What TV shows had been on?

She didn't know. Dammit, she didn't *know*.

Her mind grasped for memories like a child snatching at sunbeams. Nothing came to her. Nothing but a misty suggestion that grew progressively less real, less persuasive, as she focused on it, like a dream examined in daylight, dissolving in tissuey strands, leaving a stretch of blankness in its place.

Her mouth was dry. Her tongue tasted like paste. She went into the bathroom for a drink of water. She turned the spigot, put the glass under the faucet. Her gaze drifted to the mirror.

The glass fell from her hand and shattered in the sink.

That face, that *face*.

It floated in the mirror where her reflection should be. Bleached skin, a red slash of lips, eyes hiding in black sockets. The face preserved on the pillowcase. The face of a skull. A painted skull.

"Hello, Angela," the face said, its lips moving, and she needed a moment to grasp that her own mouth had formed the words.

She backed away from the sink, the water still running, then turned and stumbled out of the bathroom. She banged her elbow on the doorframe; bright metallic pain jumped up her arm.

Hallucinating. She was hallucinating. Imagining things. Becoming paranoid, crazed. The childhood memories had caused it. She had opened a floodgate in her mind and now she was drowning in old fears, stale terrors.

Dr. Reiss. She had to call Dr. Reiss.

She took a step toward the phone on the end table, and then suddenly she was not in her living room, she was in a dark, smoky lair striped with moving spotlights and growling with atonal music, a place like some large sullen animal, fetid and restless and nocturnal.

She blinked and her apartment was back.

This was bad. This was so bad. This was how it felt to go insane.

"Help me," Angela whimpered. "Help me, somebody, please."

She lifted the phone. Tried to remember Reiss's number. Oh, God, think, *think*. It came back to her. She punched in three digits ... four ...

"My alchemy transmutes death into new life," she heard herself whisper. "Moveless you embrace me, lips like petals flower-soft on my breast ..."

The phone dropped from her hand.

Poetry. That was some kind of warped poetry. Had she written it? She almost remembered her hand moving, the pen tracing jagged script across a sheet of yellow paper—

You could never have written it, you stupid bitch. You could never be what I am.

Terror jerked a gasp out of her. She staggered away from the end table, her arms flailing blindly.

The voice had been her own. Yet not hers, not really. It was the voice of the apparition in the mirror. Somehow she knew that.

Look at you, cowering in terror. What a sad, helpless child you are. Did you honestly imagine that a worm like you could satisfy Robert Card in bed? Did you ever satisfy our father?

She clapped her hands to her ears, trying wildly to shut out the words, knowing the effort was useless because the voice came from within.

You were unworthy of his love. You rejected him, ran from him. I was faithful. He was my father, not yours.

"Shut up!"

You fear the truth. You try to hide from it, as you've always hidden from life. I despise you.

"My God, stop it, stop it, *stop it!*"

That's right, Angela, go on screaming. I like to hear you scream.

She staggered to the futon, fell on it, beat her fists against the floor.

Who are you? she thought wildly. Who the hell are you?

My name is Dominique.

The name shocked her, because it was familiar, like the name of an imaginary friend from early childhood, long forgotten but never fully erased from memory.

I know you, Angela answered slowly. When I was little . . . when my father came in . . . when I hid inside myself . . .

Then I emerged. Yes, dear Angela. While you cowered in your dark place, I enjoyed the gift of love—

I won't listen to this. You're not real, you don't exist. You're just . . . something I imagined. Some kind of defense mechanism that's gone out of control.

A defense mechanism? A silvery giggle. *Is that all I am? And how do you know that I did not imagine you, darling? Perhaps you're part of my dream, not the other way around.*

Go away. I want you to go away!

Oh, it's far too late for that. I have no intention of leaving now. I've accomplished so much already, and there's still a great deal left for me to do.

Accomplished? What have you accomplished?

The children, Angela. If you've seen this much, then surely you know about the children. It was not that many years ago when we had our first.

Our first . . . what?

We were thirteen. Don't you remember?

And suddenly she did remember. She did.

A low moan rose in the room like the cry of a tortured animal.

The memories were clear and sharp as glass. Her father, drunk and reeling, scared into savage anger, smashing the television set, shattering china, blaming it on her. Whore, he called her; slut; rutting bitch dog. He smacked her, beat her. It was her fault because it was her body.

Finally he was calm. Her mother said they would have to get it fixed. Her father nodded. But not in Tucson. Word might get out. Phoenix was safer. They could go there tomorrow. Take the old highway, Route 89. The interstate would be too crowded; someone who knew them might happen to be on the road, catch sight of their car, wonder where they were headed.

The drive seemed very long. Her parents sat up front, and she was curled in the backseat, crying. As they reached the outskirts of Phoenix, her father started coaching her. The people at the clinic would ask questions; she had to have the right answers. She had to say that her boyfriend had knocked her up.

Say anything different, he had warned, and I'll kill you.

Other girls sat in the waiting room, looking blankly at their folded hands. Her father paid in cash—three hundred dollars. A nurse took her blood pressure, did a urine test, drew some blood. A counselor interviewed her; she said what her father had told her to say. She signed a consent form. Half an hour later her name was called.

Then she was on the examining table, its flat surface so cold and hard. She remembered the doctor's gloved hands exploring her. Her cervix dilating, the tube sliding in, the sudden suction.

The trip back to Tucson was slow and silent, like a long fall in a dream.

Her father never visited her bedroom again. Angela tried not to think about what had happened. After a while she forgot that part of her life entirely.

But I never forgot, Dominique said quietly. *I was always conscious of the child inside me, my father's gift. And I knew that I had not lost it and never would. The baby would always be part of me—not its physical being, which was nothing but blood and tissue anyway, easily soiled and corrupted—but its spirit, its essence, which would remain pure and innocent forever. Its spirit, which would cleanse my soul and inspire my art.*

Angela barely heard her. Eyes shut, she whispered, "Were there other children?"

One other, so far. Jamie Frisch.

The name burst in her mind like a popping flashcube, illuminating a string of scenes in its pale strobe light.

A little boy in a park. The same child, blue and dead, breath-fogged plastic pasted to his face. His small body rolling into dark waters, vanishing with a secret splash.

"What have you made me do?" Angela breathed. She lifted her head from the futon, cheeks shiny with tears. "My God, *what have you made me do?*"

It was another purification. Another holy union. A new child for me. I drew his spirit into my body and renewed myself.

I murdered him. I . . . I murdered . . .

You had nothing to do with it. It was my achieve-

*ment, my masterpiece. The child is mine, not yours.
And the next one will be mine, as well.*

"The . . . next?"

Then the last of her amnesia melted away, and
she saw Mike Card asleep in bed, the dachshund
curled beside him, and she gasped.

"No."

Oh, yes, dear. Yes.

"Not Mike." She was crying. "Please, not him,
not him."

I will take the child tonight.

"I won't let you!"

*You are no match for me. I can suppress you at will.
This body obeys me now.*

This body, Angela thought. She looked at her
hands, touched her face. This body.

She knew what she had to do.

A lamp stood on the end table beside the futon.
She reached for it, switched it on, tore off the shade.
Unscrewed the light bulb with trembling fingers.

You little fool—sudden panic jumped in Dominique's voice—*what do you think you're doing?*

The bulb fell to the floor. She knelt on the futon,
leaning over the lamp. The socket loomed before
her like the barrel of a gun.

Two fingers. Use two fingers.

Her world was blurred, sight dissolving in an
eyewash of tears. She raised her right hand, index
and middle fingers extended together.

One thrust was all it would take. One moment
of courage, and she could save Mike. Mike and all
the others who would come after him if the crazi-
ness inside her were not stopped.

Was the voltage high enough to be lethal? She didn't know. She prayed it was.

Don't think. Just do it. Do it now.

She lowered her hand toward the socket, and then her body began to shake.

It was not fear. It was Dominique. Fighting her, trying to seize control.

Her hand wavered, inches from the lamp.

"No, you won't," Angela gasped. "You won't, you won't, you won't—"

Blinding pain.

She tumbled off the futon and collapsed on the floor. Pain filled her head like air swelling a balloon. Her brain was on fire, sizzling; a hissing crackle rose in her ears.

For a wild triumphant moment she thought she had managed it somehow, had stuck her fingers in the socket, had electrocuted herself.

Then she realized that the pain was Dominique's weapon, her way of immobilizing the body they shared.

"No." Her voice was a thin, strangled whisper. "No. No. No."

A vise of agony tightened around her skull. She couldn't fight the pain, couldn't stand it. Her thoughts broke up into static. She ground her palms into the carpet, twisted her legs together.

"No," she said again, but she no longer knew what she was protesting.

She curled into a fetal ball and lay still.

A stretch of silence. The scene in the room, a frozen tableau.

Then, eyelid twitchings. Subtle movements of the fingers. An arm unwrapped itself from her body and stretched languidly across the floor. The other arm dropped limply. Her legs unbent and extended, and her head lifted, neck arching, as she rolled onto her back.

Her eyes fluttered open, and Dominique groaned. That had been close. Too close.

It was her own fault for failing to cover up the evidence of Gregory's bedroom game. After he left in the middle of the night, she had tried without success to wipe off the smeared makeup on the pillowcase. In desperation she had changed the sheets, stuffing the soiled ones in the hamper with the pillowcase turned inside out. She had gambled that the bitch would not notice. But she had, and now she knew everything.

Amazingly she had proved to be a fighter. She had battled hard to keep Dominique submerged, beating her down like a woman struggling to drown a cat. Though she had lost, she had delayed Dominique's emergence nearly long enough to destroy them both.

The bitch was dangerous. She could not be allowed to emerge again. Ever.

The date with Card was still essential to the plan. It would be necessary to impersonate Angela tonight. Well, that shouldn't be too hard. Dominique had observed her alter ego for years; she knew every inflection of Angela's voice, every mannerism, every careless gesture.

"I can do it," she whispered. "Of course I can. I've never needed that little cunt. Now, at last, I'm free of her."

Dominique laughed, confidence growing in her.

"You got your wish, Angela dear. You're dead. Do you hear me, darling? You're *dead*."

49

Card got home at seven-fifteen and found Mike helping Consuelo fix dinner in the kitchen. His assistance consisted mainly of pouring glasses of milk for the two of them; *leche,* he called it, having learned the word from her. He didn't spill too much.

"Hey, sport," Card said.

"Dad!"

Card lifted his son in his arms and found himself once again surprised at how big the boy was getting.

"Consuelo says you're going out with Angela tonight."

"Uh-huh."

"Why doesn't she come here like last time?"

"She and I decided to see a show instead. Dating is like that. You do different things to keep it interesting."

"Is it interesting?"

"Very," Card said with a smile, and Consuelo laughed.

"Can you play Chinese checkers with me before you go?"

Card teased the boy's hair. "I really don't have time right now. But I'll tell you what. Tomorrow I'll give you two games. Okay?"

"You're on!"

Card showered and changed. A picnic and an evening outdoors required casual clothes; he settled on corduroy pants, a plaid shirt, and a faded blue denim jacket. As always, he wore both the ankle gun and the shoulder holster. Some of the parking lots around the Hollywood Bowl could be dangerous at night. He caught himself half hoping that some punk would cause trouble, so he could impress Angela with his cool response.

Once dressed, he brushed his teeth and fooled with a comb, worrying about the part in his hair. He wondered if romance made all men vain.

At seven-thirty he was ready to go. He found Mike and Consuelo having dinner in the living room, trays balanced in their laps, while an episode of a syndicated sitcom played on the tube. Willy stood on his hind legs, forepaws drawn up against his chest, begging for scraps. He seemed to sense that the effort was hopeless; his small wrinkled face looked both puzzled and pained.

"You look nice, Mr. Card," Consuelo said. *"Muy guapo."*

"Thanks, Connie. I should be home by midnight." He frowned, reconsidering. Suppose Angela invited him back to her place after the show. "Well, maybe later. Anyway, go to bed whenever you feel like it. I'll let myself in."

"Yes, Mr. Card."

"Remember to walk Willy before bedtime. And—"

"Sí, sí. I know everything to do." She waved a fleshy hand at him. "Go meet your pretty *señorita."*

"Right." He kissed Mike on the forehead, then

on the cheek, while Mike squirmed, obviously too
old for that sort of thing. "So long, pal."

" 'Night, Dad."

Card headed for the door. Mike's voice stopped
him.

"Dad?"

He turned. "Uh-huh?"

"Say hi to Angela for me."

"You really like her, don't you?"

"I think she's neat."

"She feels the same way about you."

Mike blushed. "Nah."

"Yeah, she does. She told me so. She thinks
you're very special."

"Maybe she really will be my mom someday."

Card nearly uttered a reflexive denial, then
stopped himself. The same thought had been on his
mind. What was the point in pretending
otherwise?

"Well," he said carefully, "anything is possible.
But—"

"I know, I know. Don't count on it."

Card smiled, hearing the words he'd used the
other night.

"Still," Mike added, "she'd make a real good
mom for some little kid. Wouldn't she, Dad?"

He remembered Angela sitting on the edge of
Mike's bed, reading him a story. Slowly he nodded,
half to himself.

"Yes, Mike," he said softly. "Yes, I think she
would."

50

Dominique drove fast on her way to the Hollywood Bowl, humming tuneless songs to herself, riding on adrenaline.

It was lovely to be rid of Angela. Lovelier still to know that soon Mike would be hers.

After leaving her apartment, she had stopped at a market and gathered the ingredients for a picnic dinner, filling a wicker basket with bread, cheese, cold cuts, potato salad, and a bottle of wine, all the sorts of obvious, unimaginative items Angela would have chosen. The basket was beside her now, on the Pinto's passenger seat, rocking slightly as the car bounced, reminding her of a crib swayed by a mother's hand.

The drive to Hollywood passed with the effortless fluidity of a piece of music skillfully played. At seven o'clock Dominique found a space for her car in the crowded parking lot on the grounds of the Hollywood Bowl. Picnic tables were arrayed under the leafy branches of graffiti-scarred trees. She opened the basket and put out plates and napkins, still humming cheerily, then waited, contemplating the fiery sunset, while long minutes drifted past.

"Angela."

She looked up and saw Card striding toward her, handsome in a jean jacket and corduroys.

"Hello, Robert." The bitch had called him that.
He leaned across the table. They shared a kiss.

"God, you look great," he said.

Dominique smiled. She thought she looked absurd in Angela's borrowed outfit, a cute summer dress with a flower-print pattern. Still, the dress did reveal a good deal of cleavage and legs, didn't it? She was conscious of the bulge of her breasts against the thin cotton, the smooth skin of her bare shoulders, the graceful line of her neck.

Card kissed her again. As he drew back, his denim jacket flapped open, revealing the strap of a shoulder holster. A tremor of lust shivered through her, weakening her knees.

"Sorry I'm so late," Card said.

She glanced at her watch. Ten after eight. "Oh, the show won't start for twenty minutes."

"There was traffic—and then I had trouble finding a place to park—"

"It's fine, Robert. Everything's fine. Come on, now, dig in."

Dig in—now, there was a witless turn of phrase, perfect for the girl she was impersonating.

Dominique sat across from him, rummaging through the basket and making gay chatter she scarcely heard. The wooden bench was hard, as hard as the stool on the spotlit stage. She would sit on that stool soon. Sit and recite to Mike.

A teasing breeze plucked at the corners of the paper napkins and played poltergeist games with the plastic utensils she set out. The Styrofoam plates briefly hovered like flying saucers before being loaded down with sandwiches and side dishes. Card uncorked the wine and filled two plastic cups.

"To us," he said with amusing solemnity.

"To us," she echoed, an empty smile printed on her face.

Their dinner together sped by in a flurry of meaningless words and loving glances. She had no trouble being Angela, none at all. She heard herself talking and laughing, acting like an utterly conventional woman on a date, and she knew she was playing the role to perfection. Card suspected nothing.

At eight-thirty they put the basket back in the car, then strolled up a hill past stands of bird-of-paradise and sweet-smelling eucalyptus trees. A tunnel led them into the amphitheater. Their seats were high up in Promenade 4, the R section, near the upper lip of the great semicircular sweep of laddered rows looking down on the white band shell.

The sky was a very pale blue like the water of a shallow pond, the sinking sun hidden behind the hunched backs of the enclosing hills. The musicians tuned their instruments in the dimming light, the scattered sounds they made rising weird and vaguely malevolent through the still air, like the croaks and hisses of a swamp.

"Have you ever seen a Gershwin concert?" Dominique asked, just to have something to say.

"No. To tell you the truth, I'm usually not much for this kind of thing."

"I think you'll enjoy it." She consulted the program. "The performance starts with *Rhapsody in Blue.* Everybody likes that one."

Angela certainly did. Dominique, of course, had finer sensibilities. She did not care for any melodic compositions other than lullabies. Melody annoyed

her, as did rhyme and meter in poetry. She was
above all that.

Applause pattered through the amphitheater as
the conductor took the stage. At the podium he
lowered his baton, giving the downbeat, and then
Gershwin's *Rhapsody* began with the famous clari-
net glissando that ascended to a drunken wail.

Dominique swallowed a gasp.

She had never heard this music in this way before. To her ears the wild, whooping scalar run was
the cry of a terrified child. Its impact was electrifying, breath-stopping.

Impulsively she reached out and took Card's hand.

The piece became frantic, the orchestra blaring
out the nattering, madcap melodies that were
Gershwin's interpretation of New York. Her mind
wedded the music with images the composer had
not intended and would not have understood. The
hubbub of taxicabs and bustle of crowds became,
to her, the struggles of Jamie and, soon, of Mike.
The pianist pounding out a dramatic cadenza full
of exuberant key changes—it was the sound of
small hearts pumping, lungs straining, eyes growing huge with horror and helplessness. Then a
slower, more stately movement—the ponderous
lowing of the horns, the weeping of the strings—
grandeur and majesty, dignity and a sense of exal-
tation. Spiritual union. That was what it was. The
merging of the children's souls with her own.

She tightened her grip on Card's hand. The muscles of her body were iron-hard with tension. The
music throbbed inside her skull, starting sympa-
thetic vibrations that set her ears ringing.

The theme of grandeur rose in volume and intensity, erupting at last in a howl of horns and a furious clashing of cymbals and then the clang of a gong. She thought of orgasm. She thought of Card pointing his gun at her.

The gong tolled again.

Bang—the gun firing. Bang. Bang.

The last chords faded. The audience cheered.

Dominique stood up.

"Robert," she whispered, urgency in her voice, "come with me."

Already she was pushing her way toward the aisle as the applause went on. Card followed, apologizing in a soft undertone to the inconvenienced people around them.

She found the exit, then ran. Distantly she asked what the hell she was doing. Any unusual behavior tonight was dangerous; she had to be Angela, Angela, Angela.

But Angela was boring. Angela was what she had fought against all her life. Now in this penultimate moment, only hours before her greatest achievement, she could not be safe and stupid and dull, she could not sit in her seat like a good girl and let this irreplaceable moment pass by. Could not.

Loss of control, she thought dimly. Like in the apartment—when I nearly used the knife on Mike—total loss of control.

Something was happening to her. Something was allowing her emotions to master her thinking. Something was driving her to fits of wild irresponsibility.

But strangely she didn't care. If this was insanity, then she would embrace it, revel in it.

She remembered dancing naked after Angela's first date with Card. This was like that. Complete surrender to passion. To wildness. To the voice of blood and instinct. She was an artist. She could not be coldly rational all the time, could she? Could she?

Card caught up with her at the door to the ladies' room.

"What's the matter?" he asked breathlessly. "Are you feeling all right?"

"Yes, fine." She eased open the door of the rest room, peered inside. Empty. "Only, I need something."

"What?"

She turned. Grabbed his arm. Kissed him hard. "You."

"Jesus—*here*?"

Already she was pulling him into the rest room. "Come on."

"If somebody walks in—"

"Come *on!*"

The door banged shut behind them, and then she was guiding him to the stalls, passing under banks of overhead fluorescents glowing like tubes of molten steel. She hustled him inside the nearest compartment, then followed, the two of them pressed close together in the tight space, her hand fumbling at the door of the stall and pulling it shut, then sliding the latch into its socket.

"You're going to think I'm old-fashioned," Card was saying nervously, "but I've never—"

"Hush."

"I really don't know if . . ."

She smiled up at him in the harsh clinical light. Pulled down one strap of her dress, exposing a perfect breast. Cupped her breast in her hand, gently kneading the soft flesh. Heard herself moan.

"What were you going to say?" she asked teasingly. "Tell me, Robert." Seduction in the words. "Tell me."

The sudden clamp of his hands on her bare arms was almost painful. He pulled her to him. Their mouths met. Roughly he pushed her backward, wedging her between the commode and the steel wall, the smooth metal cold against her skin. He planted kisses on her neck, cleavage, breasts. Then his hands were under her dress, tugging at her panties, ripping them apart—her dress was up around her waist—she found his fly, unzipped it— he thrust himself inside her—she wrapped her legs around his thighs as he drove in deeper—she felt him coming, and the thought of his hot seed in her vagina, the doorway to her womb, made her want to scream in agonized pleasure. He clapped a hand over her mouth to muffle her cry, and she flashed on Gregory doing the same thing last night. The faces of the two men flickered interchangeably before her closed eyelids. She bit Card's palm, drawing blood, and in the same moment he gasped, climaxing, pumping himself into her, semen and blood, love and death, joy and pain, her own climaxes bursting inside her in a series of explosions that made her think once more of gunshots, bang-bang-bang.

She sagged in his arms. Gently he withdrew, then zipped up his fly as she smoothed her dress.

"God, Angela, you're crazy. You're insane."

He was merely speaking colloquially. He still suspected nothing. She was too smart for him. Too smart for all of them.

The orchestra was midway through Gershwin's *Concerto in F* when she and Card rejoined the crowd.

51

At eleven-fifteen Lindstrom pulled into the parking lot of West Valley General Hospital. The white squarish building glowed against a purple haze of ambient light.

She entered the lobby, brushing past silk ferns and plastic coffee tables, and leaned on the receptionist's desk.

"May I help you?" the nurse said with a pointless smile.

Lindstrom badged her. "I need to talk to somebody about an employee of the hospital."

"Oh. Yes. Certainly. Which employee would that be?"

"Gregory Almont. He's an orderly. Works the three-to-eleven shift."

"I know him. He's on the fifth floor. Usually assigned to the Cardiac Care Unit."

"May I talk to the supervisor of that ward?"

"Sure, but it won't be Greg's supervisor. She already left. We're on the eleven-to-seven shift now."

"I understand. I'd like to talk to whoever's on duty."

The receptionist called ahead, and by the time Lindstrom emerged from the elevator on the fifth floor, a heavyset, moon-faced nurse was waiting.

"I'm Mrs. Raleigh, charge nurse for the CCU. You wanted to speak with me?"

"About Gregory Almont, yes."

The charge nurse was already leading her toward a central desk in the cardiac ward. "What is it? What's happened to him?"

"Nothing's happened. Just a routine inquiry."

"Routine. Uh-huh." Her voice was brittle with skepticism. "Well, I hardly know him. It's Mrs. Lynwood you want to speak to, and she—"

"She already left. I know. So did Mr. Almont, I assume."

"No, he wasn't here today. Called in sick."

"He did?"

"That's what Mrs. Lynwood told me at shift change. She was complaining about how short-handed she'd been without Gregory. He had the flu or some damn thing."

"Was he in yesterday?"

"Oh, sure. Seemed healthy enough. But I'm not doubting him, you understand." Having reached her desk, Mrs. Raleigh seemed suddenly more at ease, as if she drew comfort from the small island of white Formica that symbolized her authority. "Flu comes on suddenly sometimes, especially that nasty twenty-four-hour bug. Had that myself just last month."

"Does Gregory call in sick often?"

"No, very rarely. He's one of our most dependable orderlies. Look, is that young man in some kind of trouble?"

Lindstrom ignored the question. "Has Gregory done anything else that might be at all unusual recently?"

"I haven't said calling in sick was unusual—not the way you mean." The nurse picked up a sheaf of papers and flipped through them idly, not looking at them, just keeping her hands busy. "But the answer is no, at least as far as I know. Of course, Mrs. Lynwood is the one you should ask."

"Yes, I gather that, but Mrs. Lynwood didn't mention anything to you?"

"Not a word."

"Well, is there anything that's happened in the hospital in the last few days that was out of the ordinary? I mean, anything at all, whether it was connected with Gregory or not."

A wordless moment, filled with the riffling of Xeroxed pages.

"There was the fire," Mrs. Raleigh said slowly. "On the third floor."

"Fire?"

"A little one. Fire extinguisher put it out. The coffeemaker had a frayed wire, I think. The fire set off the smoke detector but didn't do any damage beyond a scorched wall. Have to repaint that. Wish they'd repaint the whole building; these nursery-school greens and blues make me ill."

"When did the fire take place?"

"About five P.M." During Gregory's shift, Lindstrom thought. "I wasn't here then, but that's what people were saying. Oh, and there was another thing."

"What?"

Mrs. Raleigh hesitated, as if regretful of having spoken. "It probably doesn't matter."

"Tell me, please."

"Well, this is just something I heard. I'm not sure

I should be telling you at all. But I suppose it might have some significance. Though I doubt it. Probably just one of those things. Carelessness, you know. We run a tight ship here but even so, mistakes are made."

Lindstrom controlled her impatience. "What sort of carelessness?" she asked evenly. "What happened?"

"This afternoon the charge nurse on the third floor, Miss Payton, took inventory of the contents of the refrigerator. She discovered that a vial of medication was missing."

"You said this was the third floor? Where the fire was?"

"Yes. She said she thought her floor must be jinxed. Of course that's nonsense. I'm not superstitious myself. Are you?"

"What kind of medication was missing?"

"Succinylcholine. Ten cc's."

"I'm not familiar with that drug."

"It's also called synthetic curare, because it has the same general properties as curare. Succinylcholine brings on flaccid paralysis. Anesthesiologists use it to permit intubation of the patient, and we keep it on hand in the wards in case an emergency intubation is required. Sometimes an endotracheal tube has to be inserted during a Code Blue."

"Let me be sure I understand. This stuff, this . . ."

"Succinylcholine."

"It paralyzes a person?"

"Yes, all the skeletal muscles."

"Isn't it dangerous?"

"In a large enough dose it can be fatal. It paralyzes the diaphragm, and then the person can't breathe. Of course in surgery the patient would be on a respirator anyway."

"Is ten cc's enough to kill someone?"

"Yes, I'm sure it is, but ... What are you suggesting?"

"I'm not sure."

"The vial may have been misplaced," Mrs. Raleigh said nervously. "Probably was."

"Yes, probably."

"It happens from time to time." Her fidgety hands were shredding the edges of the pages she held. "No matter how many precautions you take, there's always—"

"May I use your phone, Mrs. Raleigh? To make a local call?"

"Well, yes, of course. But why—"

"How do I get an outside line?"

"Dial zero. Look, can't you tell me—"

Lindstrom was already turning away, seizing the phone, stabbing at the button marked zero, then punching in seven more digits.

Robert Card's home number.

52

Directly across the street from the apartment building where Robert Card lived, Gregory sat in his Mustang, watching the entrance, waiting.

He had been parked there for more than three hours, reviewing the plan, wringing his gloved hands, and occasionally removing the wadded dishrag from the inside pocket of his black leather jacket to moisten it with more chloroform.

Nothing could go wrong. Everything could go wrong. The plan would work. The plan was hopeless.

He almost regretted having skipped work today. His job at the hospital was boring but safe. What he would do tonight was reckless, suicidal.

No. Wrong. The element of risk was minimal. He and Dominique had worked out every detail. She had described the exact location and layout of Card's apartment. She had told him where to find the boy's bedroom and what time the boy went to bed. Most important, she had reported that the family dog was taken for a walk every night. With Card out on a date, Consuelo would have to perform that chore. Probably sometime around ten or eleven o'clock, Dominique had said.

Now it was eleven-twenty-five. At any moment

the housekeeper might appear, and then he would have to do it. Really do it. No fantasy this time. This was life and death. Yes. And death.

The lobby door swung open, and a heavyset Hispanic woman emerged, leashed to a chuffing dachshund.

Gregory felt his heart kick. Suddenly he was dizzy, trembling, his head filled with a sourceless rushing noise.

He felt an urgent desire to start the car, drive away, leave the city, never come back.

No.

He had spent his life preparing for this assignment. He would not fail. Would not.

With trembling fingers he removed the plastic sheath from the stolen hypodermic. Inserted the needle into the lid of the vial, puncturing the membrane. Drew ten cc's of succinylcholine into the syringe. The colorless liquid climbed swiftly up the scale markings.

The needle went in the side pocket of his black leather jacket. He stuffed a spray can inside the other pocket. Picked up a folded map. Drew a shallow, shaky breath. Then got out of the car.

The phone at the other end of the line rang once. Twice. Three times. Four.

Lindstrom waited tensely. Someone had to answer. Bobby was out, but Consuelo was there, and Mike too. Of course Mike would be asleep by now, and there was no extension in his room. Still, Consuelo, at least, could surely hear the phone.

Five rings. Six. Seven.

She bit her lip, wishing she had a cigarette. Something bad was going down. Something very damn bad.

A suspicious fire yesterday. A missing vial of poison today. Gregory, who'd looked perfectly fit last night, calling in sick today. Angela out with Card, leaving Mike alone with Consuelo. And Consuelo not answering the phone.

On the eleventh ring Lindstrom hung up. She considered dialing 911 and telling them to send a black-and-white to Card's address. But his place was only ten minutes from the hospital; if she broke a few laws she could make it in five. Faster than trying to explain the situation to a 911 dispatcher.

She ran for the elevator, brushing past Mrs. Raleigh.

"What is it?" the nurse asked in visible panic. "What's happened?"

"Nothing," Lindstrom said over her shoulder. "I hope."

But she was no longer sure.

Gregory crossed the street, glancing in all directions. Darkness loomed everywhere. The neighborhood seemed deserted except for the housekeeper, the dog, and him.

Consuelo stood near a power pole, under the orange umbrella of a streetlight's luminescence, waiting patiently while the dachshund lifted its leg. The clacking of Gregory's boot heels caught her attention as he approached. She turned, and he flashed a polite smile, the smile he had honed to perfection in countless encounters with nurses and patients at Westside General.

"Uh, excuse me, ma'am." He struggled to hide

the quaver in his voice. "I'm looking for an address, and I can't seem to find it."

She was watching him warily. "Yes?" Her thick accent rendered the word *Jays*.

He mounted the curb. "Yeah, it's the most frustrating thing. I've been driving around for twenty minutes. Frankly, I think I'm going out of my mind."

His manner disarmed her. She matched his smile with one of her own. "Is very, how you say, confusing—these streets."

"You can say that again."

The dog stared up at Gregory, small brown eyes glinting in the chancy light.

"What is the street you are try to find?"

"I've got it marked here." He unfolded the map and extended it to her, holding it in his left hand. The intersection of Moorpark Street and Colfax Avenue was circled in red. "Sure hope you can help me."

She lowered her head to study the map. Gregory casually slipped his right hand into his pocket. His fingers closed over the syringe.

"You wish to find Colfax," she said. "That is east of here."

"East?" The syringe slid out of his pocket like a snake gliding out of its hole. "Gee, I'm all turned around. Which way is that?"

"Is there." She looked away from him, pointing with the hand unencumbered by the leash. "You must take Ventura Boulevard—"

Gregory slammed the needle into her neck.

Consuelo's head snapped back. Her mouth twisted. She made a gagging sound—dropped the map and leash—clutched blindly at her throat, trying to tear the needle free.

Already the poison was coursing through her bloodstream via the carotid artery. She thrashed and sputtered, eyes rolling. Gregory shoved her against the utility pole. She tried to cry out but her mouth wouldn't work. Her eyelids blinked frantically, and her facial muscles twitched.

The dachshund growled, then started yapping, its smallness making the fearsome display seem comic. Gregory lashed out with his boot, landing a solid blow to the dog's head that sent the animal tumbling backward in a frenzy of yips. It twisted to its feet and flew at him, seizing his trouser leg with its teeth, shaking vigorously.

He hissed a curse and reached under the sleeve of his left arm, where the knife was strapped.

It was an Eikhorn survival knife, purchased at a sporting-goods store five years ago. The sales clerk had praised its German craftsmanship and keen blade. Gregory had lifted the knife out of the display case and balanced it on his palm, liking the heaviness of the steel blade and haft. He had hoped to draw blood with it someday.

He unsheathed the Eikhorn. Slashed viciously at the dog. The dachshund yelped once, then flopped on its side and lay there mewling softly. Its tongue lolled.

Gregory turned back to Consuelo. The facial fasciculations had stopped. Her eyelids were shut, and her features had the slack smoothness of a discarded rubber mask. She flailed her heavy arms wildly for a few seconds longer, her movements uncoordinated, her fingers already limp and flaccid, then sagged against the pole.

Gregory lowered her to the ground, jerked the hypodermic out of her neck, and pocketed it. He put his ear to her chest and listened for breath or a heartbeat. Heard nothing.

She was dead.

He shuddered once, pleasurably, then looked down at his pants and saw a spreading stain on the inside of his thigh.

"Oh, honey," he whispered, "I hope it was good for you too."

Hooking his arms under the woman's armpits, he dragged her across the sidewalk to a clump of palmettos outside Card's apartment building. Hastily he concealed her behind the plants, then hurried back and picked up the dog, still shivering fitfully and leaking bloody foam from its mouth. He tossed the dying animal on top of the corpse.

A search of the housekeeper's pockets yielded a key chain. He stuffed it in his pocket, then knelt by Consuelo and put the knife to her throat.

He almost hated to mar the beauty of his work with what he was about to do. But he had no choice. No one must suspect the use of any sort of drug in the killing. That suspicion would naturally lead to inquiries at all local hospitals; and if the theft of the succinylcholine had been discovered, someone might make the logical connection.

Carefully he dragged the knife from one side of Consuelo's neck to the other, eradicating the puncture wound.

Now the coroner would never think of running any toxicology tests. Even if he did, he would be unlikely to find succinylcholine, which was quickly hydrolized into choline and succinic acid by the body's own enzymes, rendering it nearly impossible to detect.

Gregory considered delivering a last blow to the dog, as well, in order to put it out of its misery. He decided not to. Better to let the loathsome little cur suffer.

His gloves were bloody, dripping. Oddly, in none of his fantasies had he ever visualized actually getting dirty. He cleaned himself off as best he could with a scrap of newspaper from a trash can.

Then he walked quickly up the front steps. Fished the key chain out of his pocket. Unlocked the security door. Entered the lobby. There was an elevator, but he took the stairs instead. Less chance of being seen.

Ellen Lindstrom guided her Mazda east on Ventura Boulevard, wishing she had a TV cop car so she could clip the Kojak light to the roof and crank up the siren. As it was, she was slicing through traffic, blasting the horn, her gaze ticking restlessly from the windshield to the dashboard clock.

Only four minutes since I left West Valley General and I'm nearly there. That's good, real good.

But was it good enough?

A slow-moving pickup truck blocked her way. She swerved into the opposing lane, flashing her high beams at oncoming cars to scare them onto the shoulder, and skidded back in front of the pickup.

Christine would be proud, she thought. *I'm driving nearly as crazy as she does.*

Card's place was only a few blocks away now. She put on extra speed, exceeding the legal limit by thirty miles an hour, not giving a damn. If a cop pulled her over, she'd badge him and take him along for the ride. Hell, she could use some backup.

Should have called for some—she was carrying her walkie-talkie in the inside pocket of her suit jacket—but there'd been no time.

It didn't matter. She could handle Gregory Almont by herself. Wimpy little runt. She'd choke his scrawny chicken neck barehanded if he'd done anything to Mike.

The thought pumped her full of fear and she laid her foot down harder on the gas pedal, flooring it, praying she wasn't too late.

Gregory's footsteps echoed on the metal treads as he hurried up two flights of stairs. On the third-floor landing he eased open the stairwell door and peered into the corridor. Empty.

Quickly he went down the hall to Card's apartment. His hand was shaking as he tried several keys in the keyhole before finding one that fit.

The door opened silently. He looked in. A living room, brightly lit. No sound, no hint of movement. He stepped inside. Shut the door. Crept toward the hallway that led to Mike's bedroom. The hall was dark, the bedroom door closed.

His gloved hand guided the door open a few inches. The boy was asleep, lying under the covers, snoring softly.

From the inside pocket of his jacket Gregory removed the dampened rag. Approached the bed, his footfalls swallowed by the pile carpet. Stood over Mike Card, watching his chest rise and fall, rise and fall, in time with his steady breathing. His eyelids ticked with dreams.

An innocent angel. Gregory smiled. No wonder Dominique wanted him so badly.

He clapped the rag over the boy's nose and mouth.

Six minutes after Lindstrom left West Valley General, her Mazda screamed to a stop in a red zone outside Card's apartment building. She leaped out of the car and took a quick look around. Her breath froze in her chest.

Across the street. Parked at the curb. The Mustang. Gregory's car.

It appeared to be empty. She walked toward it, unholstering her Beretta 9mm as she approached the driver's side. Careful, careful. The guy could be hunched below the dash with a gun or a knife or a syringe loaded with that succinctile-cholera shit. Whatever the hell it was called. Chemistry had never been her strong suit.

She reached the car and looked cautiously inside. Empty.

She scanned the area. He might be hiding in the bushes or behind a building. But more likely he was inside the apartment building.

Killing Consuelo, maybe. Or Mike. Injecting him with that garbage. Stopping his breath. Oh, Jesus.

She ran for the front steps.

The sudden cold wetness on his face shocked Mike awake. Gregory saw his eyes flash open, pupils rolling in confusion, while his legs kicked at the sheets and his arms thrashed. A heartbeat later he went limp again as the chloroform entered his lungs.

Gregory held the rag in place for several more breaths till he was sure the child was deeply unconscious. Then he tossed the cloth on the floor.

He had never touched it with his bare fingers; there would be no prints.

He pulled down the covers, lifted Mike in his arms. Blue pajamas with white stripes clothed the small body; the boy's feet were bare. Gregory draped Mike over his shoulder, grunting with the unexpected strain. The little bastard was heavy enough.

Wheezing slightly, he carried the child into the living room, then set him down on the floor and took out the spray can. He scrawled a few words across a blank stretch of wall. Satisfied, he pocketed the can, picked up Mike, and fumbled open the door.

At the landing Lindstrom came up against a security door. Goddammit. She could buzz the tenants till someone answered, identify herself as a police officer—

Wait a minute. Bobby had given her a set of keys.

She fumbled them out of her purse and found the right one, got the door open. In the lobby she banged her fist on the elevator call button, intending to run for the stairwell if the elevator didn't arrive immediately. But she was lucky. The doors opened at once.

She flung herself inside, pressed the button for the fifth floor. Tried to stop shaking so badly as the car rose with maddening slowness up the shaft.

The hall was still empty. Gregory shut the door of the apartment behind him, hearing the latch snick into place, then shouldered the boy to the stairwell. The elevator would be far easier, but he

was still afraid of being seen. There was no way
he could explain an unconscious seven-year-old
slung over his shoulder like a laundry sack.

As he reached for the metal handle of the stairwell door, the elevator pinged. It was stopping on
this floor.

He shoved the door open. Ducked inside. Huddled against the concrete wall, breathing hard.

The elevator doors hissed apart, and someone
hurried out. Fast footsteps diminishing down the
corridor. He caught a sense of urgency in their
rapid tattoo.

Was somebody on to him? No, impossible.

But the thought energized him with a jolt of fear,
and he started moving again.

The door to Card's apartment was locked. Lindstrom rapped on it, heard no response, and used
another borrowed key to get inside.

Two steps into the living room she stiffened,
staring at the wall.

"Christ."

The bastard had been here already. Might still
be here, hiding. Might have heard the knock and
taken cover.

Holding the Beretta in both hands she quickly
checked out every room of the apartment, balanc-
ing caution and urgency. She satisfied herself that
he was gone.

Gone, yes. And so was Mike. And Consuelo.

But the Mustang had been parked outside. Gregory couldn't have left without it.

She ran for the door.

                    *   *   *

Gregory hurried down the echoing stairs. Through the lobby. Outside.

The street was deserted, as before. He ran to his car, laid Mike on the hood, and got the rear door open. A desperate need for haste possessed him, he couldn't say why. Those quick footsteps in the hall had blown his cool. He had to be out of here. Had to be out right now.

Grunting with strain, he picked up Mike and deposited the boy in the backseat. Seconds later he was behind the wheel, jamming the key in the ignition, revving the engine, racing away.

Lindstrom emerged from the building. The Mustang was gone.

"Fuck, I just missed him. Goddammit to hell!"

She thought about jumping in her Mazda and taking off in pursuit. But the Mustang was nowhere in sight, could have gone in any direction, taken any intersecting street. Might be headed for Gregory's apartment, or Angela's, or the Sepulveda Dam Recreation Area, where Jamie's body was dumped. Or, more likely, some other place entirely, some location she couldn't even guess at.

"Jesus H. Christ, Ellen, you are a sorry excuse for a cop."

She'd screwed up, all right. She could see that now. She should have stayed by the Mustang till Gregory returned. Except that she'd been unwilling to loiter outside at the very moment when Mike might be getting killed in Card's apartment. All right, then, she should have slashed the fucking tires, removed the distributor cap, sabotaged the car somehow. But things like that took time and she hadn't thought she'd had any time. As it was, she must have missed running into the perp by only a few seconds.

He took the stairs, she realized. While I was riding up in the elevator, he was coming down the stairs. Oh, shit.

She shook her head. Recriminations later. Right now she had to get on the horn to the Van Nuys station—this was their territory—and put out an alert on a white Mustang with a license number she'd memorized last night.

"Maybe we'll find him yet," she said to herself as she dug the walkie-talkie out of her pocket. "Maybe it's not too late."

The drive to Mere Anarchy seemed endless. Gregory drove with painfully exaggerated caution, coming to a complete stop at every stop sign, refusing to race through yellow lights, maintaining the speed limit scrupulously. The slightest infraction of the traffic laws could get him pulled over.

By the time he pulled into the alley behind the bar, his teeth were chattering uncontrollably. He couldn't imagine how Dominique had coolly driven for hours with Jamie Frisch dead in her car.

He parked well away from the rear of the bar, so as not to be seen by Jonathan when he left. Then he slipped into the backseat beside Mike, still sleeping deeply, and got out a roll of white nylon cord. It was the same cord Dominique had used to lash Jamie's wrists and to tie the bag around his head; she had given it to him last night.

He turned Mike on his side, pulled his arms behind his back, and wound a coil of cord around his wrists till they were securely bound. The gloves made tying the knot difficult, but he managed.

As an extra precaution, he gagged the boy, using a wadded handkerchief and a strip of tape to hold it in place.

He admired his handiwork. Mike was utterly helpless now, as voiceless and immobile as a ventriloquist's dummy without its master.

There was one thing left to do. Gregory returned to the front seat and rummaged in the glove compartment till he found the makeup materials he had stashed there. He turned on the reading lights and adjusted the rearview mirror, then studied himself, frowning in concentration, as he applied black lipstick and silver eyelash glitter. With a marking pencil he extended each eyebrow in a saturnine arch. He powdered his face to emphasize the natural pallor of his skin.

As he finished, he heard Mike stir behind him. He turned in his seat and watched the boy twist his upper body and roll his head. His blinking eyes registered confusion, then panic, then horror.

"Hello, my young friend."

Mike's head jerked up. He stared at Gregory, who leaned between the two front seats, watching him with a cheerless smile. Fear blanched the boy's face. Grunting, choking sounds came from behind the gag.

"No use trying to talk or free yourself. You're quite helpless. Entirely at my mercy." The delicious words, which he had spoken to imaginary victims in so many masturbatory fantasies, tasted even more flavorful now, as he uttered them for the first time in real life. "I'm afraid you're in serious trouble. And nobody will be coming to your rescue."

Mike squirmed into a corner of the backseat. His blue eyes stared out from behind a spray of brown hair sticky with sweat.

"Nobody," Gregory repeated. "Not Consuelo— she's dead. I killed her only a few minutes ago. And not your little doggie either. I killed him too. Cut him up with a knife." Steel flashed. "This knife."

Tears glittered at the corners of Mike's eyes. Gregory passed the Eikhorn from one hand to another, back and forth, back and forth, the dance of the blade hypnotic like the swinging of a pendulum.

"So I guess that leaves only your father. Detective Robert Card. He'll save you, won't he, Mike? Won't he?"

Mike screwed his eyes tightly shut and averted his face.

"No, he won't. He doesn't know where you are. He has no way of finding out. He won't see you again for days. And when he does, he'll be looking at you in the morgue." Gregory ran his tongue along his teeth. "Do you know what the morgue is, little boy? It's a place for dead people. And that's what you're going to be. Dead."

He lunged with the knife. The blade ripped through the seat cushion inches from Mike's head. The boy whimpered and drew back still farther. Shivers racked his body.

"Dead and in hell!"

Mike was crying.

Gregory watched him and fingered the knife and hoped Dominique would come soon. Very soon.

Because he wasn't sure how long he could wait before he finished this job himself.

53

Dominique kept the smile fixed on her face. Her impatience was mounting. She had to get out of here, get to Mike.

Card leaned back in the booth at the rear of the Melrose Tavern, watching her with bleary eyes.

"You know," he said, "I'm beginning to see why Gershwin is so popular."

A joke. How droll. She laughed obediently.

"Not everybody reacts to *Rhapsody in Blue* quite as emotionally as I did tonight," she said in a cool voice.

"Good thing too. The concert halls of America would no longer be safe for decent people."

She detected a slight slur in his speech. He was drunk. Disgusting. And disappointing—she wanted him fully alert when he learned of his son's abduction.

"I hope I didn't shock you too much," she said in her prim Angela voice.

"I'm beyond being shocked by anything you do."

"That may or may not be a compliment, but I'll accept it as such."

"Please do. Things aren't coming out exactly the way I want them to. These drinks seem to have gone to my head."

"I noticed."

After the concert Card had suggested a nightcap at a bar he knew in Hollywood. The two of them had driven there in separate cars, meeting at the entrance, going inside together into a pleasant thrum of voices. She had ordered only one Bloody Mary, which she hadn't finished; Card, not ordinarily much of a drinker, had downed two Manhattans and was nursing a third. Now he seemed to be worrying that he'd overdone it.

"I haven't embarrassed myself, have I?" he asked.

"Not too much."

"You mean I have, a little?"

She shrugged. "Just a bit."

"How?"

"You played 'My Way' on the jukebox."

A shrug. "I like that song."

"You played it four times."

"Yes, well . . . there weren't any other selections that appealed to me."

He stared out the window at the traffic rushing past. After a long moment he spoke again.

"I took off my wedding ring. Did you notice that?"

"Yes."

"I thought it was time to . . . let go."

"I'm glad, Robert." She would say anything to humor him. This damn speakeasy had to shut its doors soon.

"I loved her, but . . ." He swallowed. "But you can't love a corpse."

Try it sometime, she thought with a cruel smile.

"What I'm saying is, I want to move on. I want to be with someone new. Oh, hell. I want to be with you, Angela. I . . . I care about you. I know we haven't known each other very long, but . . ."

She took his hand. His palm was moist, his knuckles hairy. She was reminded of her father's hands.

"I feel the same way, Robert," she whispered.

He stroked her hand, smiling, and she thought about Jamie Frisch.

At one-thirty they finally left the Melrose Tavern. Card walked her to the Pinto. She slid behind the wheel.

"Would you like to stop off at my place," he asked, "maybe have some coffee or something?"

She forced a laugh. "Or something. Euphemisms, after what went on in that ladies' room tonight? I'd like to, Robert, but I'm tired. It's been a long day. An eventful day—and a very good one."

He nodded. "For me too. Okay, look, I'll call you tomorrow."

She closed the car door, then rolled down the window and blew him a kiss. "Good night."

He leaned in through the window and kissed her hard on the mouth, then drew away.

" 'Night, Angela," he said with disarming casualness.

She pulled away from the curb, tooting the horn in cheery farewell.

Her smiling lies had made him happy tonight. That was good. Happiness was a precarious state, a vulnerable condition. From his peak of joy he would plunge into agony. A steep descent. A shattering crash when he hit bottom.

He was not a tough man. He was glass. Soon he would be broken. And Mike would be hers.

54

Card walked to his car, whistling, and got in. He drove east to the Hollywood Freeway, then joined the river of headlights rushing north. A fair amount of traffic even now, at this late hour. He listened to the hiss of his tires and the hum of his engine, watched the wide band of concrete splashed with the Sable's headlights and the vaporous glow of mercury-vapor lights, and thought that life had never felt so good.

She loved him. She had said so. Perhaps not quite in those words, but close enough. "I feel the same way," she had told him.

He made the transition from the Hollywood Freeway to the Ventura Freeway without the need for conscious thought. It was nearly two o'clock when he took the exit for Coldwater Canyon Avenue.

He sped a few blocks west, then turned the corner of his street.

Abruptly he jerked forward, staring at a carnival of flashing blue and red lights.

Squad cars lined the block. Crime-scene ribbon was strung along the sidewalk outside his apartment building. Uniforms and dark-suited plainclothes officers milled in the lobby and on the front steps. A reporter fussed with his microphone in front of a TV van, getting set to do a stand-up. Pale faces watched the show.

"Christ," Card breathed. "What the hell's going on?"

He put his foot on the brake. Jumped out of the car. Ran to the nearest uniform and flashed his badge.

"I live at this address. What's happened here?"

The young patrolman was nervous. "You're Detective Card? West Valley station?"

"Yes, goddammit."

"Sir, I . . . I don't know if . . ."

A familiar voice broke in. "I'll handle this, officer."

Card turned his head and saw Ed Jacobs striding toward him. He stiffened with a rabbit punch of fear.

This wasn't Jacobs's territory. Van Nuys Division covered this neighborhood. There was no reason for the captain to be here. Unless he had a personal motive for showing up.

"Ed, tell me what's happening." Card heard undignified panic in his voice, didn't care. "Is it Mike? Does it have something to do with Mike?"

"Robert, I want you to get hold of yourself—"

Card seized Jacobs by the shoulders and screamed in his face. *"What the hell happened to him?"*

"We're not sure yet. We—"

"What do you mean, you're not sure? Where is he?" Jacobs didn't answer. *"Where is he?"*

He was looking around frantically, scanning the

crowd. His gaze fell on a white-sheeted body in the bushes near the steps.

"Oh, shit." Terror lanced him. "*Mike* . . ."

"No," Jacobs said hastily, following Card's gaze, "that's not him."

"Who the fuck is it, then?"

"It . . . it's Consuelo."

"Jesus. *Jesus*."

Then Card was running toward the lobby, and Jacobs was shouting at him to stop, his words fading with distance like the cries of a shadow figure in a dream.

Card showed his badge indiscriminately as he muscled his way past the cops in the lobby. His fist banged the elevator call button, but the elevator wouldn't come, so he took the stairs, pounding up the metal treads, the echoes of his racing footsteps reverberating in the stairwell like the amplified beat of his heart. He reached the third floor and sprinted down the corridor to the open door of his apartment, gasping as he tried to call Mike's name.

A uniform stood outside, guarding the crime scene. He raised a hand as Card approached. "I'm sorry, sir, but you can't—"

Card elbowed past him. Stumbled through the foyer into the living room. Then stopped, staring ahead, his gaze locked on the scrawled spray-painted words that stretched across the white wall.

JAMIE WAS ONLY THE FIRST, DETECTIVE CARD.

A sound like a moan forced itself out of his throat. He ran for the bedroom.

An evidence technician was inside, lifting prints with a roll of Scotch tape. "This is a secure area," she said harshly, before she recognized him. He paid no attention. He was staring at the bed. The empty bed.

The bedspread and sheets lay in a jumbled pile. The impression of Mike's head was still faintly visible in the pillow.

Card took a step toward the bed, reaching for the pillow, wanting blindly to hold it, hug it. The technician restrained him, her voice gentle in his ear. "I'm sorry, Detective. You can't touch anything in this room till I'm finished here."

"Mike," Card whispered. "Mike . . ."

"He'll be all right," the woman said.

Card made no reply. Cruel images crowded his imagination. Mike bound and asphyxiated. Floating in the river. Picked at by scavenger birds.

His breath was coming fast and shallow, the room canting dangerously. He must be hyperventilating. He blinked, trying to steady himself, afraid he would pass out. Nausea rolled in his stomach. A sudden nightmarish feeling of unreality threatened to overwhelm him, the bizarre sense that he was trapped in a hallucination or that he had gone insane.

Yet distantly, past shock and horror and fear, he was aware that even now his eyes were dry. In that moment he was sure the tear ducts had been cut out of him when Jessie died; he would never cry again.

"Bobby. I'm sorry."

Lindstrom's voice. Card turned slowly, the room revolving around him in a way that seemed strange and unreal. His partner stood in the bedroom doorway, watching him.

"Mike's gone," Card said pointlessly.

"I know."

"He's just . . ." Card raised one hand, palm up-turned, then let his arm fall loosely against his side. "Just gone."

"We'll talk about it. But not here."

"No, not here." He was nodding in senseless agreement. "Not here. Mike's not here."

Lindstrom closed the gap between them and took Card's hand. "Let's go, Bobby."

Card shuffled out of the bedroom. Some part of himself was telling him to wake up, focus his mind, get to work and think of something. But the rest of him, the greater part, was numb and blank and empty.

As Lindstrom escorted him through the living room, Card noticed for the first time that the place was crowded with Valley Section SID personnel, bagging and tagging, supervised by Martin Payton; an electronics technician was hooking up a tape recorder to his phone. Their presence reminded him of Laura Frisch's house, the wait for the ransom demand that had never come.

"You're not—" His voice caught. "You're not really expecting a call, are you?"

"You never know."

"He's probably dead already."

"Don't say that."

"Jamie was killed almost immediately after his abduction."

"This won't work out that way."

"Sure." Card coughed. "Sure it won't."

They were at the door when Payton said, "Detective."

Card looked at the lean, bespectacled man, normally so cynical and brusque, and was mildly as-

tonished to see what might have been grief
swimming behind the lenses of his steel-rimmed
glasses.

"I just wanted to tell you," Payton said huskily,
"that we're going to do everything we can, everything possible, every fucking thing."

Card could not remember ever having heard the
evidence technician use that particular expletive
before.

"I know you will," he replied. "Thanks, Martin."

The landlord had allowed the police to comman-
deer a furnished apartment three doors down the
hall. Lindstrom led Card inside, past a patrol sergeant talking loudly and rapidly into a telephone.

"Place was just vacated," Lindstrom said as she
guided Card through the living room, among the
shifting blue uniforms and snatches of radio static.
"Phone was still hooked up. Lucky break for us."

"Yeah. Lucky." He blinked, awakening from his
trance by slow degrees. "I'd better give the Homicide squad a list of Mike's descriptors."

"Later." She was still pulling him forward
through the crowd.

"They'll need to know—"

"It can wait. Come on."

For the first time he caught the urgency in her
voice.

"Where are we going anyway?"

"The den. It's empty. We need privacy."

"Why?"

No answer.

She led him into the den and shut the door, then
turned to face him.

"Where's Angela?" she asked without preliminaries.

"What?"

"Angela Westmore. Where is she?"

"Home, I guess. We left separately." He stiffened with a flash of terror. "Christ, she's not in danger too?"

"No. She's not in any danger."

The angry irony in her voice startled him. He studied her warily.

"Ellen . . . what's going on?"

She paced. Fumbled a cigarette out of a pack and lit it. Spat out feathery streamers of smoke.

"Remember when she phoned you at work and I took the call?"

Card nodded, baffled. "Yeah."

"Her voice sounded familiar. It took me till that night to figure out why. I'd seen her before. At a bar on Sepulveda."

"Okay, so she was in a bar."

"She wasn't just another customer. She performs there."

A beat of silence as Card took this in.

"Look," he said slowly, "what are you trying to say?"

Lindstrom took a long drag on her cigarette, expelled twin jets of smoke from her nostrils, and let a rush of words spill out.

"She's a poet—recites verses on stage—wears makeup that turns her face into a skull—"

He raised his hands. "Hold it, hold it. What is this, some kind of fucking joke?"

"I'm serious, Bobby."

"It's got to be some other woman."

"It isn't. Same voice. Same face."

"Angela isn't anything like that."

"How well do you know her?"

"She works in a daycare center, for Christ's sake."

"You told me. But that only makes it worse."

"Worse how?"

"Daycare. Kids. Think about it."

Card blinked. Slow comprehension bloomed in his mind. "Wait a minute." The sudden huskiness of his voice gave it an alien sound. "You think Angela is . . . involved in what happened tonight?"

"Yes."

His fists clenched. "Are you *crazy*?"

"She killed Jamie. Now she's going to kill Mike. She's a psycho, Bobby. She's—"

He took a step toward her. *"Shut up!"*

Lindstrom stood her ground. "I know you love her. But she's been using you, playing games with you."

Card stared at his partner, rage roaring in his ears, and for a moment he experienced a blind, savage urge to lash out at Ellen Lindstrom, strike her, batter her with his fists. Then he jerked his head away, staring into the shadows in the corner of the room.

"No way," he muttered. "Impossible."

"I followed her last night. Staked out her apartment and tailed her to the bar. I eyeballed her on that stage. There's no mistake. And . . . and I saw her meet a guy there. Skinny little runt with a ponytail. They went home together."

"Stop it," Card whispered.

"I got the boyfriend's license number," she went

on relentlessly. "Found out where he works. At a hospital. West Valley General. Went there tonight. He'd called in sick. And yesterday there was a suspicious fire on the third floor—the kind of thing that would be sure to create a diversion—and a vial of medication was taken from a refrigerator. Some kind of shit that causes paralysis."

He could barely absorb what she was saying; it was all too much, too fast. "Paralysis?" he echoed weakly.

"It can be fatal."

"You're saying ... they might have used that drug on Mike?"

"Not on Mike. On Consuelo. Vince Neal has already examined her body. He says the killer tried to make it look like she died of a slashed throat, but there's not enough blood. Her carotids were cut after she was already dead. I told him to look for a puncture mark, the kind of thing that would be left by a hypodermic. He found one, or what was left of one. The asshole stabbed her in the neck with the needle, injected her with that crap, then ripped up her throat later to try to cover his tracks."

"Vince is sure the same drug was used?" Card asked, his voice oddly slow and thick, the words coming from far outside himself.

"No. He won't be sure till he runs the toxicological tests. Even then, it might be hard to find this stuff in the body, he says. But under the circumstances I think we can assume it was used."

"We can't assume anything. Least of all that Angela is a kidnapper and murderer."

"I'm afraid we can." Lindstrom lowered her head. "I'm sorry. I really am."

"You're more than sorry. You're wrong."

"No, Bobby, I'm not. I wish I were."

"Wait a minute." He tried to force his brain into focus, tried to find the flaw in his partner's reasoning, the crucial fact she had overlooked. "I met Angela in line in the supermarket. You're saying Jamie's killer just happened to be there that night? By sheer chance? Isn't that pushing coincidence a little too far?"

"Not coincidence. She must have planned that meeting. Followed you or something."

"She couldn't have. I wasn't even on my way home from work. I'd gone to that neighborhood-watch pep talk. . . ." His words trailed off.

Lindstrom nodded, making the same connection he had made. "It was announced in the paper, wasn't it? She could have read about it in advance and known you would be there."

"She wasn't in the audience."

"No. But outside. Waiting. Watching when you left."

He made a limp gesture of denial. "That's . . . paranoid." But he was no longer sure.

"Her poetry is all about children," Lindstrom said. "And death."

Card shuddered, his jaws clicking together once with a hard snap.

"Fuck. Oh, fuck." He groped for the wall, leaned against it, feeling weak and aged. "You've got to be mistaken about this, Ellen. Angela wouldn't hurt Mike. She . . . she loves him."

Lindstrom reached out to him and took his hand.

"I don't think this woman understands love the same way we do," she said softly.

55

Dominique recited snatches of her own poetry as she drove from Hollywood into the Valley. She could not recall ever having been so happy.

How soon would Card arrive home and discover his housekeeper dead, his son missing? She smiled, imagining the pain in his face, the tasty anguish in his eyes, the shock and sorrow aging him, draining him of life. . . .

Oh, this was good, so good. Infinitely better than Jamie Frisch.

The Pinto's dashboard clock read two-fifteen when she pulled into the alley behind Mere Anarchy. She eased to a stop behind the parked Mustang, then removed a flashlight from her glove compartment, switched it on, and got out.

"Gregory," she whispered. "I'm here."

The pale funnel of light played over the Mustang's interior. The car was empty. Gregory and Mike must already be inside the bar.

Returning to the Pinto, she lifted the hatchback lid. She removed an innocuous brown paper bag containing her makeup supplies and the black spandex outfit she wore at her recitals.

As she approached the rear of the bar, the beam

of her flashlight picked out the broken pieces of a padlock on the ground. The nearest door hung open.

She went through the doorway into darkness, the flashlight's glow preceding her. From somewhere close by came a muffled whimper and the sound of fast, scared breathing.

"Mike?"

A strangled cry answered her. A cry for help.

She waved the flash. The beam flitted over the room, briefly illuminating rows of tables. Mannequin faces jumped out of the blackness, then receded. The light came to rest on Mike, sitting at a table near the stage, tied to a chair with multiple loops of nylon cord.

Gregory was nowhere to be seen. Dominique thought she should be angry at him for leaving the boy unguarded. But happiness had put her in a tolerant mood. A playful mood.

Slowly she smiled.

"Don't be afraid, Mike. This is Angela. I've come to rescue you."

She set down the bag, crossed the room to Mike, and laid the flashlight on the table. Its beam washed them both in a yellow cone of light. Carefully she removed the tape that secured the gag, then tugged the wadded handkerchief out of his mouth. He coughed, shaking his head and blinking.

"Oh, jeez," he mumbled. "Oh, jeez, oh, jeez . . ."

"It's all right, Mike. Everything's all right now."

"Uh-uh. It isn't. He's still around. We gotta get out."

"Mike—"

"He's still around!"

"Who?"

"This crazy guy—he kidnapped me—he wears lipstick like a girl and he says he killed Consuelo—"

"Okay, okay." She slipped behind the chair and bent to examine the cord. "We'll go as soon as I can untie you."

"Hurry up!"

She pretended to fumble with the cord. "Just a few seconds. That's all it will take. Where did the man go, anyway?"

"To the bathroom, I think. I heard a toilet flush a few minutes ago. He still hasn't come back."

Dominique bit back a smile. She had a fair idea what Gregory was doing. The excitement of the night's proceedings must have brought on certain urges that demanded relief.

"How'd you find me anyway?" Mike whispered.

"Your father thought you might be here. He said another little boy was kidnapped and brought here not long ago."

"Why didn't he come?"

"He was checking out a different place."

"How come he didn't send some cops?"

"He wanted me to do it."

"That doesn't make any sense."

"I guess all the police officers were busy. People are looking everywhere for you."

"Can't you get me untied?"

"I'm trying." Her clever fingers tugged here and there at the cord without loosening the knots. "But it's harder than I thought."

"Have you got a knife? You could cut the rope. Or just pick up the chair and—"

This game was becoming tiresome. She interrupted the boy's whining with a question breathed in his ear.

"Have you heard of Jamie Frisch, Mike?"

He craned his neck to look at her, screwing up his face against the dazzle of the flashlight. "Huh?"

"Jamie Frisch." She made no further effort to pull at the knots. "He was a little boy, seven years old. Your age."

"That kid who got killed. My dad tried to find the murderer."

"Yes."

"Is this guy with the lipstick the same one who killed that kid?"

"No. He had nothing to do with it. Nothing at all."

Mike swallowed. "Why aren't you untying me, Angela? What's going on?"

She circled around the chair. Squatted before him. Cupped his face in her hands.

"Do you want to know who killed Jamie?"

"Angela ..."

"My name isn't Angela. It's Dominique. Angela is dead."

He blinked at her, his small mouth opening and closing.

"Angela is dead," she said again, tasting the words, finding them sweet. "She wanted to save you. She would have saved Jamie too, if I'd let her."

"Did you ... kill Jamie?" Mike whispered.

"Yes, dear. I killed him. I put a plastic bag over his head so he couldn't breathe. I watched him die. Just like I'm going to watch you."

He shook his head blindly in protest. The chair

teetered under him like a dancing animal, its stubby legs pounding a frenetic tattoo on the wooden floor.

"And after I've killed you," Dominique went on calmly, "I'll have your soul inside me forever. Won't that be nice? Our two spirits will blend and merge. You'll like being part of me, Mike. I know you will."

"Stop it. *Stop*."

"You lost your mother, but now you'll have a new mother. A better one. One who will never desert you."

Tears tracked down his face, glistening in the flashlight's beam. "Where's my dad? Where is he?"

"I lied about your father. He didn't send me here. He doesn't know where you are. And he'll never, ever know what I've done."

"He'll find out! He'll catch you and put you in the electric chair!"

"No, Mike, he won't suspect a thing. He loves me. Perhaps he'll even marry me someday. Then we'll lie together every night. The three of us."

Mike went on crying, his body racked with gulping, catch-and-gasp sobs.

"There, there," Dominique breathed tenderly. She stroked his hair, and he did not pull away. "Poor little Mike. Poor innocent child."

56

Card stood motionless for what seemed like a long moment, leaning on the wall of the den, feeling Ellen Lindstrom's hand stroke his knuckles slowly. He struggled to bring order and clarity to his thoughts.

Ellen had to be wrong. Just had to be.

But if she was not . . .

Then he had misinterpreted every moment of his time with Angela, her every smile, her every kiss. It had been a brilliant, masterful deception. But she hadn't carried it out unaided. His three years as a widower had left him more than willing to buy the fantasy she'd been selling. Loneliness had made him desperate for love, desperate to believe he'd found the perfect woman.

Desperate and blind. And now his blindness might have cost him Mike. Mike, who even now might be strangling in a plastic bag . . . while Angela watched . . .

A knock on the door.

"Come in," Lindstrom said sharply.

The door eased open. A man in a gray jacket entered. "Detective Card?"

Card nodded.

"Alan Lasser, Van Nuys Homicide. We need some information on Mike right away." He flipped open a legal pad. Distantly Card wondered if he put on the same air of businesslike indifference when working a case. Probably. "Just the basic descriptors for the bulletins we're sending countywide. Height?"

"Three-ten."

"Weight?"

"Forty-eight pounds."

"Hair?"

"Brown."

"Eyes?"

"Blue."

"Distinguishing marks?"

"None."

The words came with effort. Something in Card recoiled at the thought of reducing Mike to a set of physical characteristics, like an item inventoried for auction.

"We think he was taken from his bed," Lasser was saying. "Would he have been wearing p.j.'s?"

"Yes. Long sleeves, long pants. Blue with white stripes."

"We'll need a snapshot of him, if possible."

"There's a photo album in the bookcase, on the extreme right, top shelf, next to the dictionary."

"Right. Now, this woman, Angela Westmore."

"Caucasian, twenty-four years old, five-foot-two, a hundred pounds, brown hair, gray eyes, no distinguishing marks. I don't have a picture."

"Okay. Thank you for your help."

Lasser started to move away. Card grabbed his arm. The interrogation had jolted him at least partially out of his trancelike state of shock. He felt something like a cop again, a professional with a job to do, stratagems to recommend, lines of inquiry to explore.

"Jamie Frisch was dumped in the L.A. River near Sepulveda Dam," Card said. "You'd better have someone watch that location."

"Your partner already suggested that. Both Van Nuys and West Valley are on top of it. Patrol units are scouting the length of the river channel throughout this area."

"How about Laura Frisch's neighborhood? The park where Jamie was abducted?"

"We covered that too," Lindstrom answered. "We've got black-and-whites patrolling the neighborhood, and plainclothes officers staking out the park."

"The parks in this area are also being watched," Lasser added.

"I assume you're canvassing the block for eyewitnesses."

Lasser nodded. "Got twenty officers on the detail right now. Interviewing and reinterviewing. So far, nothing."

Card turned to Lindstrom. "Do you know what kind of car her . . . her boyfriend drives?" Saying that word was rough.

Lindstrom pretended not to notice. "White Mustang. I memorized the license number after I tailed it last night."

"We've put out an alert on that vehicle," Lasser said, "and the Pinto."

"And we've got cars staking out Angela's apartment, her boyfriend's place, and the bar where they hang out," Lindstrom added.

The bar. Card turned to his partner. "You said you saw her in this bar. Reciting poetry."

"Yeah."

"Her own stuff? I mean, she wrote it?"

"Definitely."

"Is there anything in what she said that might give us a clue to where Mike might have been taken?"

Lindstrom frowned. "Good question. Hell, I was focusing so much on just watching her, I barely noticed what she was talking about."

"Try to remember. You said the poems were about motherhood and death?"

"Yeah. That much was obvious. Oh, she said something about smothering. And blushing blue—it made me think of cyanosis."

"What else?" Card pressed.

"Transforming death into life. And blue mist. I remember she mentioned blue mist."

"Shit," Lasser said irritably, "none of that means—"

Lindstrom cut him off. "Yes, it does. Or it might."

"How?" Card asked.

"The spotlight on the stage in the bar—it's blue. With all the smoke in that shit-hole, there's a blue mist, all right."

"You think she was referring to the stage?"

"Might have been. Because there was something else." Lindstrom's eyes were shut in intense concentration. "Something about the audience. I almost remember. . . ."

"They wouldn't have an audience for a killing," Lasser said. "No matter how crazy they—"

"Mannequin eyes."

Both men looked at Lindstrom.

"Mannequin eyes," she repeated. "That's what she said. A drama is played out before an audience of mannequin eyes." She hitched in a breath. "There are mannequins in the bar."

"She might have been talking about her recital," Lasser said dubiously. "Maybe that was the drama she meant."

"Maybe." Card was thinking fast. "But maybe not. She might be planning to use the bar as the scene of the murder. To kill Mike on stage. Make it a fucking show."

"If so, she's screwed," Lasser said. "We've got a car watching the place."

"Where is it stationed?" Card asked.

"Directly across the street."

Card turned to Lindstrom. "Is there another way in?"

She nodded. "Back alley. I— Oh, *shit!*"

"What is it?" Card demanded.

"Angela and her boyfriend went into that alley last night after the bar was closed. Hung out there for a few minutes. I couldn't figure out what the hell they were up to. Thought they might be planning a four-five-nine." Her eyes were sparkling, feverish. "And I was right. Only the break-in they were planning was tonight."

"If they drove into that alley and entered the bar from the rear," Card asked her, "would the cops out front know about it?"

"No way. From where they're stationed, they can't see the entrance to the alley."

"They'd see lights go on inside," Lasser said.

"No, they wouldn't. The doorway to the lobby is screened with heavy black velour drapes that would conceal any lights in the inner room."

Lasser frowned. "Then those two could be in there right now, and our guys wouldn't have a clue."

"Tell them to check it out," Card said. "But instruct them not to enter unless they have to. We don't want to scare these assholes into doing something rash."

Lasser was already yanking his rover radio out of his pocket. "Right."

"We'll go there now. Tell your boys to request additional backup if they need it. But no sirens."

Lasser nodded, already speaking into the radio.

Card started running, Lindstrom close behind him. They sprinted through the swirl of uniforms in the living room, out into the hall. As they ran, Card was aware that he was praying—praying, though he did not believe in God—praying only to the void, the unhearing universe, the vast emptiness around him—praying for the life of his son.

57

Dominique rested her gloved hands on the rim of the sink, gazing into the rest-room mirror, admiring her work with greasepaint and lipstick. She had taken special care with her makeup tonight. The surreal redness of her lips made a grotesquely shocking contrast with the magnolia white of her skin. Her eyes swam in black pits.

She wished Jamie had seen her this way. She wished every child could meet her in death's guise.

Stepping away from the sink, she enjoyed the sight of herself in the spandex body stocking.

Beautiful, she thought.

Men had said that word to her. Gregory had said it, as had Robert Card. Yet she felt beautiful only with her face masked as a skull. The skull was death; she was death; through death she nurtured new life. No one else, not even Gregory, truly understood. But to her, the logic of her philosophy was radiant, luminous; it shone with a garish, febrile light.

She was smiling as she reached into her makeup kit and removed a small, folded slip of plastic. She unfolded it. A plastic bag. Soon it would cover Mike's head, and then he would be hers, forever.

A sudden humming in her ears. A wave of weakness rippling over her.

"You can't do it, Dominique," she heard herself say.

No. Not herself. Angela.

The bitch was not dead. She had struggled up from the depths, and now she was fighting to emerge.

"Give it up, darling," Dominique whispered in answer. "The boy is meant for me."

Her mouth twisted. "You're sick, you're evil." Her own voice lashed her.

"Keep silent," Dominique snapped. "You could never understand me.

"I'd never want to.

"No, you're too normal. That's what you pride yourself on, isn't it? Being *normal*?" She lobbed the word like an obscenity.

"Better than being a twisted fuck," Angela shot back.

"Twisted fuck, how creative. Admit it, dear. You hate me because you envy me. You wanted to be a creative writer, but you lacked talent. I am a genius with words. You wanted to be worthy of Daddy's love, but fear made you hide. I never hid.

"You're pathetic, Dominique. You're no great genius, just a victim of your own delusions. You didn't find love in your father's arms, only abuse. You can't tell the difference between talent and pretense, love and torture—

"You cheap little tart, how dare you insult me?

"I'll do worse than that. I'll shove you down, I'll take control—

"Not again, bitch. *Not ever again!*"

Silence.

Dominique opened her eyes. She found herself squatting on the floor, her arms wrapped around her knees. Her throat was sore and her head pounded.

She had beaten back the assault. Had submerged the bitch once more.

Christ, the damned little slut was persistent. She refused to die.

"You won't stop me," she told the room. Her voice bounced off the tile walls. "Once I absorb Mike, I'll be stronger than ever."

That was a good thought. She held on to it as she rose to her feet, took a last look in the mirror, and left the bathroom, still clutching the plastic bag.

"Nine-A-fourteen"—the dispatcher's voice crackled over the squad car's radio—"meet nine-W-twenty on tac six."

Lawton frowned. "Wonder what the hell's come up now."

Tillis switched to the tactical frequency and keyed the microphone. "Nine-A-fourteen to nine-W-twenty, come in."

"This is Lasser. Any activity across the street?"

"Negative. Place is dark. No visitors."

"We have information there's a rear entrance. Intruders may not be visible from your vantage point. Instructing you to take a closer look."

"Roger."

"Remember, suspects are dangerous and may have a hostage. Check out the scene but don't make any moves unless it's life-and-death. Two West Valley detectives are on their way to join you." A pause. "One of them is the kid's father."

"Shit," Lawton said quietly.

"Understood, Detective," Tillis answered.

He replaced the mike and looked at his partner. Lawton sighed.

"Man, I hate that fucking crypt." There was an edge of fear in Lawton's voice. "Ever since the last time . . ."

Tillis nodded. They had both felt bad vibes in the bar when they'd chased that drunken Mexican inside. Neither wanted to get near the place again.

"I know what you mean," Tillis said. "Wish we hadn't drawn this detail."

"But we did. So let's get moving."

They left the patrol car and crossed the street to Mere Anarchy.

The lobby was dark, but Dominique had never been daunted by darkness. She found her way easily to the velour curtain, swept it aside, and entered the main room.

Just inside the doorway she stopped, amazed and gratified. Gregory had set up everything perfectly.

Most of the room was unlighted, the corners sunk deep in gloom, the tables and chairs invisible. Here and there the blackness was broken by the flickering phosphorescence of a TV picture tube displaying one of the soundless video loops or by the pale funnel of a spotlight focused on a naked mannequin. Discordant music played softly through the speaker system.

The stage was lit in blue. Near the microphone and stool Gregory had placed a table. Mike lay on it supine, his wrists still bound, a sacrifice on an altar. Gregory leaned over him, sweeping the knife over the boy's head and whispering words inaudible at this distance. Mike was crying.

"Oh, darling," Dominique said. "It's just the way I wanted it."

Gregory flashed a pleased, boyish grin. "I knew it would be."

She glided through the room. Plastic rustled in her hand.

"Are you going to do it now?" Gregory asked eagerly from the stage floating in the darkness ahead.

"First I want Mike to hear the poem." She smiled. "I wrote it just for you, Mike. There aren't very many little boys lucky enough to have a great work of art created in their honor. You should be proud."

Mike emitted a whipped-dog noise, part whimper, part groan.

Dominique mounted the stage, stepping out of the darkness into the mist of blue light. She lowered her gaze to the child, wanting to see his reaction to her new face. But he disappointed her. His eyes were squeezed shut. As she watched, a single tear rolled out from under one eyelid and tracked slowly down his cheek.

"Have no fear, little one," Dominique said tenderly. "You lose nothing but your life."

The microphone picked up the words. A whispery echo hissed from the speakers.

Lawton tried the front door of the bar, rattling it softly. Locked. He cupped his hands to his face to screen out ambient light and peered through a glass portal in the door.

"Dark as the inside of my asshole in there," he whispered. "Nobody's home."

"Better check out the rear entrance."

"The alley. Yeah, I guess so."

Tillis took a step away. Lawton stopped him.

"Wait a minute."

"What?"

"You hear that?"

"Hear what?"

"Inside the bar. Real low. Like a whisper. Listen."

Tillis strained to hear. Faintly he made it out: a hiss of breathy words. A woman's voice.

"Christ," he murmured, "somebody's in there, after all."

"I love you, dear little Mike. I love you very much."

Dominique leaned over the child and bestowed a gentle kiss on his forehead, her lipstick leaving a crimson imprint.

"Open your eyes. Look at me."

A moan.

"Come on, now. Look."

Reluctantly Mike's eyelids slid open. He stared up at her. The white skull. The blood-red mouth.

His mouth worked voicelessly.

"Aren't I beautiful, Mike? Don't you have a beautiful mother?" She lowered her head again. "Now be a good boy, and give Mommy a kiss."

Her lips brushed his cheek, and Mike screamed.

From inside the bar, a banshee shriek, high-pitched, terrified, impossibly loud.

"Shit," Tillis hissed, "what the hell was that?"

"The kid." Lawton drew his Beretta. "They're killing the kid!"

He fired at the lock on the door. One round. Two.

The lock shattered. Tillis kicked the door open, and then both cops were inside, padding into the dark lobby, gripping their service pistols tight.

The microphone picked up the sound of Mike's voice and amplified it. A keening wail exploded from the speakers around the room and reverberated madly through the bar.

"Shut him up!" Dominique hissed.

Gregory slapped the boy. The speaker system spat out a stinging whip crack. Mike sniffled and fell silent.

"I should cut your throat for that," Gregory breathed, glaring down at the boy. The knife trembled in his hand, coruscating in the blue beam. "Rip out your fucking heart."

Dominique snatched the knife away from him. "No, you don't. He's mine."

Gregory opened his mouth to say something, and then a second crack of sound, louder than the first, ricocheted around the room.

Not from the speakers this time. From the lobby.

A gunshot.

"Kill the lights," Dominique breathed.

Gregory stood motionless.

A second shot. A reverberating slam as the door to the lobby was kicked open.

"Do it!"

Gregory nodded and scurried off the stage toward the bar, where the light switches were located.

In the lobby, soft footsteps.

Dominique lowered the knife to Mike's throat.

58

"I can't reach them," Card said.

He was holding Lindstrom's portable radio in one hand, trying to raise 9-Adam-14, getting no response.

Lindstrom tossed him a glance as she guided the Mazda down the dark streets at fifty miles an hour. "Maybe they're still checking it out."

"Shouldn't take this long."

"We'll be there in two minutes."

"You sure you know the fastest way to this place?"

"I've been there often enough."

"Right." He looked at Lindstrom, her face lit from below by the dashboard gauges. "What the hell is the name of the bar, anyway?"

"Mere Anarchy. Ever hear of it?"

"No. Yes. Vaguely. It caters to a, uh, an offbeat clientele."

A grunt of laughter. "You could say so."

"So what were you doing there?"

"Drinking. Being bored."

"Alone?"

"With a friend."

"Boyfriend?"

"No."

He didn't pursue that line of questioning. Instead he asked, "Why do they call it Mere Anarchy?"

"It's from a poem. By that Irishman. Yeats."

Card shut his eyes, a memory clicking into place like a tumbler in a lock.

"The rough beast," he breathed, his own voice hollow in his ears.

Lindstrom glanced at him. "What?"

"The beast slouching towards Bethlehem. Mere anarchy . . . loosed upon the world."

"Yeah. That's the one. I didn't know you were a poetry buff."

"I'm not. But I read that poem in college. It stuck with me. I never knew why." He hesitated, feeling a twinge of what might have been superstitious fear. "I was thinking about it when I left for work . . . the day Jamie Frisch was found."

Lindstrom kept silent.

The streets were nearly empty of traffic at this hour. Orange streetlights smeared the Mazda's windshield, blurring past. Traffic signals swung out of the thick darkness and glided overhead like phosphorescent deep-sea creatures swimming through the murk.

At Magnolia Boulevard, Lindstrom spun the wheel. The Mazda hooked west, engine revving throatily. Card watched his partner's face in profile against the night.

"After Jamie was found in the river," he said carefully, "I said a few things about the kind of people who hang out in places like Mere Anarchy. You remember?"

"The creeps. The weirdos. The leather punks and their boyfriends wearing dog collars." Card realized she was quoting him. "And the dykes. With their shaved skulls. And their swastika earrings."

He noticed the emphasis she put on the last part of the quotation. "You came down on me pretty hard for saying all that."

"Uh-huh."

"Maybe now I know why."

"Maybe you do."

"I'm sorry if I hurt you, Ellen."

A shrug. "Hey, I can take it. I'm a tough bitch. Right?"

"Not so tough."

The wheel blurred under her hands. Card clung to the door handle as the Mazda swerved north onto Sepulveda, running a red light.

"Christ, where did you learn to drive like this?"

"Friend of mine taught me by example. Same friend who likes to hang out at bars. She's a maniac." She accelerated to seventy-five and sped around a slower car. "I think you'd like her. Maybe the three of us can have dinner sometime."

"You've never introduced me to any of your friends before."

"Guess I'll start." She blasted her horn and powered through another stoplight without braking. "Got a problem with that?"

Despite the circumstances, despite everything, Card smiled. "No, Ellen. No problem at all."

He lifted the radio and tried once more to reach patrol unit 9-A-14, but still there was no answer.

Lawton parted the black curtains in the doorway to the main room and stepped inside. Tillis followed, breathing hard.

The room was utterly dark. Strange atonal music played from unseen speakers. Lawton squinted, his eyes adjusting to the darkness by degrees, and made out what seemed to be a human figure a few yards away. He was raising his gun when he realized it was one of those goddamn mannequins. He remembered them from last time.

"Can't see a thing in here," Tillis whispered. "Maybe I should use my flash."

"No. Makes us a target."

They crept forward, side by side.

"Might have run out the back way," Tillis breathed.

Lawton shook his head. "No. They're in here. Watching us. Can't you feel it?"

"Yeah. Guess I can."

Lawton bumped up against a table. It rattled. He stood motionless, knowing that the noise might have given away their position. Knees bent, body tensed, he prepared himself for a headlong dive onto the floor at the first hint of an attack.

He listened. His heart thumped in his ears. The weird music went on. And something else . . .

Softly, a tinkle of glass.

His head jerked sideways in the direction of the sound. He brushed Tillis's shoulder. His voice a sleepwalker's murmur: "Over there."

Then they were moving toward the source of the noise. The long mahogany counter of the bar slid out of the grainy blackness. Someone must be hiding behind the bar. Crouching low, out of sight. Maybe armed. Maybe holding the kid at gunpoint. Anything was possible. Careful, careful.

Lawton reached the bar first. Padded past the

row of stools, listening for another clink of glass that might pinpoint the suspect's location. He heard nothing.

At the end of the bar, he found the hinged gate that permitted access to the work area behind the counter.

"All right," Lawton whispered to Tillis, right behind him. "I'm going to take a look back there. Cover me."

Tillis nodded, his face a pale smear against the dark.

The gate eased open with a creak of hinges. Lawton stepped inside. Licked his lips and tasted salt.

He still could see nothing. Had to use his flash. Otherwise, in these close quarters, the guy could take a swipe at him with a knife and open his throat before he knew what was happening.

His hand moved to the flashlight holder on his belt, and then something rattler-quick closed over his left ankle and gave a sharp tug and he was falling forward, a yell yodeling out of his mouth—smack of his head on the hardwood floor—red spirals cartwheeling before his eyes—he was rolling on his back and someone was on top of him—glimpse of spangled eyelashes, black lipstick—flash of motion, shatter of glass—he screamed as stinging pain bit his face—glass shards—he'd been smashed in the face with a bottle, and it hurt, Jesus, it *hurt*!

He remembered his gun. Too late. Greedy fingers tugged the pistol out of his hand. The cold muzzle kissed his cheek inches below his right eye.

There was a single shot, but Lawton never knew it.

Tillis had seen his partner go down, but leaning

over the bar he could make out only a blur of frenzied action as two bodies writhed together on the floor. He couldn't shoot, not without a clearer target. He was drawing his flashlight when a gun boomed once.

He clicked on the flash. The beam bounced down to the floor and Tillis saw a blue uniform with a bloody ruin where his partner's head ought to be.

"Jesus," he hissed.

The flash swiveled to illuminate a ponytailed man on his knees by the body, holding Lawton's pistol and smiling.

Tillis squeezed off two shots, and the man was hit and knocked backward, but not before he fired in return.

The round caught Tillis in the chest. He wasn't wearing a vest, goddammit, and he felt the shuddering impact of the bullet as it drilled through muscle and bone. The room canted and spun, and then he was sprawled on the floor near an overturned bar stool, his gun sliding away from his open hand, his breath suddenly hot and painful and difficult. He coughed, and blood came up, and then he was diving down into buzzing darkness, wondering if this was how it felt to die.

59

Lindstrom floored the brake pedal. The Mazda skidded to a halt outside Mere Anarchy.

"Think we should check the alley first?" she asked Card.

He didn't answer. He was staring at the double doors to the lobby. "Lock's been shot off."

From inside, a gunshot.

"Shit." Lindstrom threw open the car door.

Card exited on the passenger side. As he ran for the entrance, he pressed the transmit button on the rover radio.

"Ten-W-fifteen, shots fired, officer needs help. Mere Anarchy bar, Sepulveda south of Parthenia."

He pocketed the radio. He and Lindstrom entered the bar. She guided him to a doorway draped with black velour curtains.

Card went through the doorway first, Lindstrom following. They scanned the room. A nest of shadows. Faint discordant music like the chittering of bats. From nearby, a low animal moan.

"Hear it?" Card whispered.

Lindstrom nodded.

Card advanced cautiously in the direction of the sound. He reached a fallen figure and dropped to his knees.

Blue uniform. Utility belt. Spreading bloodstain on the chest. Faint rasp of breath. Another shivery moan, wet with blood and mucus.

"Oh, God," Lindstrom whispered, kneeling beside him.

The mound before them gave a final shudder, than lay still.

Card listened for breathing and heard only silence.

Gregory was in pain. That damn cop had shot him twice. Once in the shoulder, once in the side. Warm stickiness was pasting his clothes to his skin.

He had always enjoyed pain. Had taken pleasure both in experiencing and inflicting it. But this was different. There was nothing erotic about the agonized shivers racking his body. Death was a turn-on for him, but not his own death, not when it was for real.

He wondered where Dominique was. Hiding somewhere else in the dark, he guessed. At least he'd had time to jump behind the bar and flip down the light switches before the two cops entered. The darkness had given him an advantage, and he'd used it well. Had taken out both of the bastards.

Smashing the bottle against the first one's face—then putting the gun to his head and pulling the trigger—oh, that had been good. Better than Consuelo. Better than anything.

The memory of pleasure revived him slightly. He focused his thoughts. He was wounded but not dead. If he could get away, he might recover. His car was parked out back. All he had to do was reach it. If he could walk . . .

Teeth clenched, eyes shut, he struggled half upright. Pain stabbed him but did not bring him down. He could make it. Sure he could.

"Is he dead?"

The voice was a woman's. But not Dominique's voice. He looked over the bar counter and saw two dim figures kneeling by the second cop he had shot.

"Yes," the other figure said. A man.

Gregory narrowed his eyes.

He had seen that man before. Had watched him in darkness, from behind a windbreak of fir trees.

Robert Card. Dominique's lover.

Old jealousy flared in him. He looked down and saw that his right hand was still fisted over the handle of the first cop's service pistol.

He had squeezed off only two shots. Plenty of bullets left.

Card and his companion had no idea he was there. He could open fire from behind the bar, cut them both down before they could react. Then escape into the night.

Do it. Do it now.

Gregory raised the gun.

Card, on his knees by the uniformed corpse, took a closer look at the lake of blood on the man's shirt.

A lot of blood. A big hole. Either the gunman had used very large-caliber ammo or the shot had been fired from close range.

He guessed the latter. But from where? Behind one of the tables? Or maybe . . . from behind the bar?

He studied the bar and his breath froze in his chest.

Somebody was there. A dark scarecrow shape, leaning across the countertop, with a gun gripped in both hands.

Card grabbed Lindstrom's arm and pulled her roughly to the floor, rolling sideways. An instant later the barroom roared with a rolling thunderclap. Another. Another. The killer was emptying his piece at them. Card fired back blindly. Blue muzzle flashes lit the darkness like stroboscopic bursts of lightning.

Then silence.

Over the ringing in his ears, Card heard the quiet discord of the music on the sound system. Nothing else.

"Think you got him, Bobby?" Lindstrom breathed.

"I don't know."

"Look. There."

A flicker of movement near the back of the room. A darting human form.

"Stop, police!" Lindstrom shouted.

The man kept going. She fired at him twice. A creak of hinges, then a clatter of footsteps on asphalt.

"He took the back door," Card snapped. "The alley."

"I'll get him. You stay here, find Mike."

Lindstrom ran in pursuit. A moment later she disappeared through the same door, and Card was left alone in the big shadowy room.

But not quite alone. He was sure of that.

"Angela?" he whispered, looking around slowly. "I know you're here. Come on. Show yourself. Let's talk."

No reply.

"Angela . . ."

In a corner, a flashlight snapped on. A skull face, lit from below, floated in the darkness like a nightmare. Card needed a moment to recognize the familiar features beneath the white greasepaint and crimson lipstick.

"Hello, Robert."

Angela smiled, her teeth brilliant in the harsh light of the flash.

"Oh, God," Card whispered, numb. "Angela."

"That's not who I am. Not anymore." Her lips parted in a thin red smile like a paper cut. "Call me Dominique."

The flashlight bobbed down, and suddenly Mike's face was impaled on its beam. His eyes were blank and staring, his jaw slack. For a bad moment Card thought he was dead. Then he realized the boy was in shock.

A gleam of silver drew his eyes to Mike's throat. The long steel blade of a knife hovered there, poised to strike.

Dominique lifted the flashlight to her own face again.

"So here we are," she whispered, her mouth smiling, eyes dead. "One big happy family."

60

Lindstrom emerged from the bar and saw the killer limping down the alley, obviously wounded. She pounded in pursuit, pointing the Beretta as she ran. The gun bounced wildly in her hand, and she knew an accurate shot would be impossible.

"Stop!" she yelled. "Goddammit, you're under arrest!"

She felt stupid even saying it. Waste of breath. Anyway, she didn't want him to stop and meekly surrender. She wanted to shoot him, kill him. Bloodlust was ringing in her ears like a high tuneless melody. Mike might be dead already, and this sick son of a bitch was responsible.

He reached the Mustang and pulled open the driver's-side door. As he leaped behind the wheel, she caught a glimpse of his face in the glow of the interior light. Black lipstick, spangled lashes. Gregory Almont. Of course.

The Mustang roared to life, the headlights snapping on.

Lindstrom stopped, pinned in the beams, abruptly aware of how vulnerable she was.

The care tore forward, directly at her. She fired at the windshield. It shattered into a sunburst of fragments. But the car didn't slow down.

She turned. Ran. The alley was narrow, with no alcoves or recesses, no place to take cover except the bar itself, and the door was too far away. The bastard could mow her down, print tread marks across her back.

She threw a frightened glance over her shoulder. The headlights were huge and growing. Dazzling brightness everywhere.

Ahead, a trash Dumpster. She arrowed toward it. The Mustang swerved to follow. She stuffed the gun in her pocket, then reached out with both hands and hoisted herself onto the lid. She had time to think she had made it, really made it, and then the Mustang plowed into the Dumpster at full speed.

The impact sent her rolling backward. She cart-wheeled off the Dumpster and slammed down on the hood of the car, a spread-eagled hunting trophy. The driver reversed, and she tumbled onto the pavement. She lay there groaning.

The car fishtailed to a stop twenty yards down the alley, then revved its engine as the driver prepared to speed forward and flatten her like road kill.

She shook her head and fumbled in her pocket, searching for the gun. It was gone. Must have fallen out.

With a scream of tires, the Mustang accelerated.

Lindstrom groped in darkness for the Beretta, her fingers finding only asphalt, as the headlights expanded before her.

Card moved slowly toward the woman with the painted face, closing the distance between them.

"Why did you do it?" he asked.

"For love. For art. For my soul."

"Let Mike go."

"No."

"It's over. Patrol cars are on their way right now. Ellen has probably already got your friend in custody."

"Don't be too sure. He's surprisingly resourceful, as I've only recently discovered."

From outside, a gunshot. The sound of a car engine racing in high gear.

Dominique smiled. "You see?"

"Let go of Mike. Please."

"No. He's mine. He's got to be mine."

Card raised the .38 a fraction of an inch.

"Don't," Dominique said sharply. "I'll kill him. I'll slash his throat."

Mike stared at nothing, his eyes like black holes.

"Put the gun down, Robert. On the floor." The knife trembled in her hand. "Do it."

Card hesitated. Never surrender your weapon— that was a lesson they drilled into you at the academy.

"Do it," Dominique said again.

The knife jerked. A gleaming jewel of blood slid down Mike's neck.

Card licked his lips. Slowly he bent and placed the revolver on the floor.

In the alley, an echoing cymbal crash, followed by a squeal of tires.

"Now the other one," Dominique said. "The one strapped to your ankle. You didn't think I'd forgotten about that, did you?"

"No." He tugged up his pants leg. "I didn't think you'd forgotten."

She was watching him intently. He knew he would have no chance to draw the snub-nosed Smith and fire before she opened Mike's throat. But if he gave up both weapons she could shoot him and Mike before the squad cars arrived.

"Come on, Robert." The knife point was testing Mike's skin again. "Do as I say. Or watch your son die."

He had no choice. He reached slowly for the gun.

"Handle it with two fingers only," Dominique whispered. "No surprises, please."

With thumb and forefinger he took hold of the Smith and lifted it from the holster. Bending down, he laid it on the floor next to his duty revolver, then slowly straightened up.

Dominique nodded. "Good. Very good. Now take a step back. I want you to watch me kill your son. I want—"

A flutter of eyelashes, a ripple of tics and twitches under the skin, and suddenly she was gazing at him with pleading eyes.

"Robert, do something, *stop her*."

Tears welled up. The knife shook, her grip on the handle loosening. Then abruptly her face hardened, compassion replaced by fury.

"Shut your mouth, you scheming bitch," she hissed.

She closed her eyes. Opened them. Love and terror bloomed in her face once more.

"She's insane, Robert. It wasn't me—please believe me—it wasn't my fault."

Another trembling transformation. Her mouth

tightened in a sneer. "Hush, dear Angela. You've interfered long enough. The boy is mine."

Two of them, Card thought numbly. Two in one body.

There was nothing but malice in her face now; but the tears—Angela's tears—still tracked down Dominique's cheeks.

The Mustang was nearly on top of her when Lindstrom's groping hand closed over the butt of her Beretta.

She swung around to a half crouch, bringing the gun up fast. Fired again and again. Her finger pumping the trigger, squeezing off twelve rounds, emptying the clip into the windshield. The horn blared and went on blaring as the Mustang swerved first left, then right, then left again. She snap-rolled clear of the shrieking tires, and the car careened past her, so close she could feel the heat from the exhaust pipe singe her face.

With an impact that shook the alley, the Mustang slammed into the rear wall of the bar.

"Angela," Card said slowly, "I have to talk to you."

"I told you, I'm Dominique."

She spoke with effort, her speech halting, beads of sweat shiny on her forehead. He knew she was struggling to maintain control over the other personality within her.

"Angela is in there somewhere." He looked into her eyes, searching for a flicker of sympathy, of kindness. "I saw her."

"You saw a ghost. Angela is dead." The knife

moved dangerously close to Mike's throat. "And now"—she showed her teeth—"this little one will join her."

No use. He couldn't reach Angela. This other woman stood in the way. He tensed his body, preparing to spring at her and wrestle the knife out of her grasp.

From outside, a volley of gunshots, a howl of skidding tires. The bar rocked with an explosion.

Dominique glanced in the direction of the noise, momentarily distracted, her concentration broken.

A click. Her jaws snapped shut.

"No, Dominique," Angela whispered through gritted teeth. "You won't have him."

For one instant she was frozen, her body held rigid by an inner conflict Card could barely comprehend.

He stooped. Grabbed the K-frame Smith. Pointed the revolver directly at her face at point-blank range.

"Drop the knife."

A jerk of her head, and Dominique was back. She stared down the gun barrel, hatred burning in her eyes.

"Drop it!" Card screamed.

She hesitated. Slowly, almost seductively, she smiled.

"No, Robert."

"I'll shoot you." He heard quavering panic in his voice. "I swear to Christ I will."

"I never doubted it." Calm, so calm.

"For God's sake, drop the fucking *knife!*"

"Bang," Dominique whispered, the smile fixed on her face.

"Don't make me do this."

He was thinking of Angela, lost in a maze of darkness. Angela, who had fought the other side of herself as well as she could. Angela, who didn't deserve to die.

"Bang," Dominique said again. "Bang. Bang. *Bang.*"

The knife flashed in her hand.

Card squeezed the trigger.

A blast of sound, like an echo of the crash outside. Her head snapped back. The knife fell from her splayed fingers. Dominique slumped against the wall, blood oozing from her left eye socket, her crimson lips still drawn up at the corners in a skull's cheerless grin.

Then her face relaxed, the smile fading, features smoothing out; and in death she was Angela again.

61

The blare of the Mustang's horn went on and on. Lindstrom got up slowly, snapped another clip into the Beretta, and peered cautiously into the smoking wreckage of the car.

Gregory Almont was draped over the steering wheel, his face in profile. A single bullet hole had been drilled in the center of his forehead, above the bridge of his nose.

"Shit," Lindstrom whispered, astonished. "Got the asshole right between the eyes."

The shot, of course, had been dumb luck, nothing more. She'd had no time to aim. But she figured it was hardly necessary to inform anyone else of that particular fact.

From inside Mere Anarchy, a gunshot.

She ran back into the bar. Scanned the room. Saw Card kneeling, head lowered, hugging a small motionless shape.

Mike. Oh, God. Was he . . . dead?

"Bobby? What's happened? Bobby?"

Card looked up. Lindstrom stood near the stage. Shame stabbed him. He had forgotten about his partner. Forgotten completely.

"Ellen—are you okay?"

"Still in one piece. The guy's dead."

"So is Angela." He kept his voice steady.

"How's Mike?"

Card looked at his son. A few drops of blood smeared his neck where the knife had nicked his skin, but the wound was superficial. His eyes still gazed without expression at something far away or deep inside himself.

"In shock, I think," he answered. "He won't talk."

"Get him horizontal. Give me the radio."

Card laid Mike flat on the floor and handed Lindstrom the walkie-talkie. She radioed Dispatch and requested paramedics. As she finished, tires squealed on the pavement out front.

"That's our backup," Lindstrom said. "I'd better tell them it's all over."

She jogged toward the doorway, then paused, looking back.

"Bobby—he'll be all right. Everything's going to be all right."

"That's what they always say."

"This time it's true."

She went through the curtains. Card looked down at Mike and brushed a stray hair from his forehead. He saw a red smear marring the smooth skin above one eyebrow. Blood? No, lipstick. He winced, hating the thought of Dominique's mouth against his son's face.

He wiped off the smudge. As he pulled his hand away, Mike blinked, the first sign of alertness flickering in his eyes.

"Hey, pal," Card whispered. "Can you hear me? Mike?"

A weak voice: "Dad?"

"I'm here. Right here."

Mike grabbed his hand, held on tight. "Watch out for Angela. She's crazy."

"I know. Don't be afraid." He squeezed Mike's hand in reassurance. "Angela can't hurt you now."

"She killed that kid, Jamie. She told me so."

"Yes."

"And she had on this makeup, like for Halloween."

"I saw her."

"You were right, I guess. She's not like Mom."

Card grimaced. "Yeah. I was right."

"And there was this crazy guy with her. Did you get him too?"

"Ellen did."

"He said you wouldn't save me. He said the next time you saw me, I'd be where the dead people are."

Card swallowed. He didn't know what to say.

"Hey, Dad?" Mike cocked his head quizzically. "What's a morgue?"

Something broke inside Card then. He took Mike in his arms, pressing his face to the boy's soft hair, smelling its fragrance, kissing his face.

In distant astonishment he realized he was crying, crying for the first time since Jessica died, the first time in three years.

62

The dream woke him well past midnight. Card lay amid the tangled sheets, staring into the dark.

After a while he rose and padded down the hall, past the den where Lois, the new housekeeper, was sleeping. He pushed open the door to Mike's bedroom and went in.

The boy lay on his side, head resting on the pillow. He no longer slept with his thumb in his mouth; he seemed to have outgrown that habit at last. Well, he was eight years old, not a baby anymore.

Next to him Willy was asleep also, snoring softly. Mike had insisted on naming the beagle pup after his first dog, and Card had not objected, though the name pained him sometimes, bringing up memories of the long brown dachshund wriggling happily on the carpet.

He adjusted the blankets—the nights were getting chilly now, in late October—then stepped back and watched Mike a few moments longer. He had worried that his son might suffer from sleeplessness and nightmares for months after his ordeal, but amazingly Mike had recovered almost at once.

It was Card whose nights were restless. It was to him that the dreams came.

He left the bedroom, shutting the door with a soft click, and went into the bathroom. He poured a glass of water and drank it in two long swallows. The glass made a solid thump as he set it down on the counter.

He looked at himself in the mirror and saw a man of forty staring back. He remembered that night in the coffee shop when he'd tried asking Lindstrom out on a date. "I'm not getting any younger," he had told her, hating the cliché but finding no better words to express what he felt.

The truth of that statement bit more sharply now, in autumn, with the days growing shorter and the trees shedding their leaves. Autumn had always depressed him. Perhaps the changing of the seasons, as much as anything else, explained the dream he'd had nearly every night.

In the dream he is driving home from the West Valley station on a warm windless evening, under a sky that is the very deep blue of encroaching night. He arrives at this building and rides the elevator, then lets himself into his apartment. Mike runs to greet him, Willy yipping at his heels— sometimes the new Willy, sometimes the old. And in the kitchen Angela is fixing him a drink.

She kisses him as he takes the glass from her hand. They sit together in the living room, talking quietly about nothing in particular, while Mike plays with Willy on the floor. After a while the housekeeper—it is always Consuelo—announces that dinner is ready. They eat at the table, Mike and Angela trading smiles and jokes. Card watches them, feeling at peace and at home.

Then he would awake. He would reach for Angela beside him. And he would remember Dominique.

Now Card put his hand to the silvered glass, touching his reflection. "What the hell is wrong with you?" he whispered. "You know what she was."

Yes. He knew. He had talked to her therapist, Dr. Reiss. He had interviewed the people at the bar. He had even visited the public library next door to the station house and checked out a few books on dissociative reaction and multiple personality disorder. He understood that Angela had been only one aspect of the woman he had dated, and that the other part of her, the secret, hidden part named Dominique, had been a kind of monster.

But he hadn't loved the monster. He had loved Angela.

In the bar she had told him that it wasn't her fault, that she was not to blame. He believed her. It was Dominique who had killed Jamie Frisch and who had arranged Consuelo's murder. Angela had been only another victim. The last victim.

Card returned to his bedroom and climbed back under the covers. He watched the darkness. Darkness all around.

Forty years old, he thought. The days growing shorter. The nights, cold.

A shiver moved through him, a tremor of fear and need. He had not known how closely those two emotions were linked until after Jessie died. Then he had understood why Mike slept with Willy in his bed. The universe was very big; it did not hear or care; and so it was good to have the comfort of another body snug and warm against you, a companion in the dark.

Love was no more than that, perhaps. A buffer against the cold.

Rolling onto his side, Card pressed his cheek to the pillow. For a moment its softness became her skin, her hair.

"Angela," he whispered. "Angela."

He went on saying her name, low under his breath, long into the night.

If you enjoyed *Shudder*,
don't miss Brian Harper's
thrilling new novel,
Shatter
available this fall.
Turn the page
for an exciting preview . . .

Something was wrong with the guy. She wasn't sure what His come-on was smooth enough, his grin friendly and un threatening, but there was a hint of strangeness about him an aura of not-quite-right.

Maybe it was his eyes. They burned with an intensity tha was more than carnal—a hot febrile light.

"I said, what kind of party did you have in mind?"

She realized he was asking the question for the secon time.

Come on, Wanda, pay attention. This is business.

"Whatever you're up for, baby," she answered sweetly "You party with me, you're getting the best."

The words were a formula learned on the street. She wa smart enough to despise the charade of romance she of fered, along with the men who believed in it. Real romanc was a beautiful thing, she was sure, but so far she had en countered it only in thrift-shop books.

Traffic blurred past on Corona Beach Boulevard, a rive of headlights and taillights throwing the john into shadow relief against the dark mass of his parked car. He leane forward into the streetlight's glow. A brief, tight smile spl his face.

"I like it when a girl goes down on me. My wife used t do that sometimes. She did it extremely well. How abou you, darling? Can you do me like that?"

He was squinting hard, his irises squeezed into slits. Th rest of his face was all right, but those eyes still made he nervous.

She almost told him to get lost. She was broke, though and he was the first action she'd seen all night. *Go for it.*

"Mister," she said with a practiced wink, "I swear I ca make you feel real good."

The wink was meant to be sultry, but her round face made it merely childish. She looked like a girl flirting at a school dance. Ten weeks on the street had not aged her very much. Some tricks still asked if she was a virgin before she showed what she could do.

"How good?" he pressed.

"I'll put in you heaven. In heaven with the rest of the angels."

He barked a sound that might have been laughter. His breath brushed her face and she smelled alcohol.

Drunk. That explained the shine in his eyes.

She relaxed a little. She had no problem dealing with drunks. They could get violent, but she knew how to handle herself. Attached to her fingernails were razor tips; she could slash and stab like a wildcat if a trick turned mean.

"So what's the price of admission to heaven these days?" he asked.

"For a hose job? Forty bucks. In advance."

"Twenty."

"Come on, don't waste my time."

"Thirty, then. Final offer."

"Hell . . . okay."

Thirty was pretty good money, actually. She would have done it for less.

He took out a wallet and removed a twenty and a ten. She stuffed the bills into the pocket of her blouse.

"You want I should do you in the car?" she asked him.

"No. Not in the car."

"Okay, there's a motel down the block. We can get a room for a half hour, but you gotta pay—"

"We're not going to a motel."

"Right. No motel, no car. So where *are* we going?"

"Police station." He flipped open the wallet to display a gold badge. "You're under arrest."

"Shit." The guy was a cop. A cop with liquor on his breath. That was a new one.

"Turn around," he ordered. "Hands behind your back."

She obeyed. He snapped on a pair of cuffs.

"In the car."

"Aren't you gonna read me my rights?"

"Later."

"Look, maybe we could work something out—"

"Just get in the car, sweetcakes."

She climbed into the backseat. He slid behind the wheel. The engine turned over and the sedan snaked into the ribbon of traffic.

Rows of darkened storefronts passed by. A bum lay curled on a bus-stop bench under a drift of ratty blankets. Kids in Raiders jackets loitered in a cone of glareless sodium-vapor light.

Corona Beach was a crummy town, she decided. Almost as bad as L.A. Worse, maybe. The L.A. cops didn't breathe kerosene in your face when they busted you. Didn't slap cuffs on a working girl either, unless she got wild.

But she'd known she would be hassled by the law no matter where she went. At least here she wouldn't have to worry about Jay Cee.

Jay Cee was a Hollywood pimp, a wiry black dude with straightened hair, and he'd been out to make Wanda his girl. "If you workin' my territory, pretty thing, you workin' for me," he'd said to her in his mushmouth drawl. "Anyways, you be needin' a man to keep you safe on these streets."

Keep her hooked on junk, was what he meant. She knew the routine. Make the mistake of being alone with him just once, and he would find a way to get the needle in your arm. One fix, and you couldn't live without the brown sugar. Then you were Jay Cee's slave, and he would be pimping you hard, taking your money, doling out skin pops till you were scrawny and blotchy and half dead. When you were no good to him anymore, he'd kick you loose and you'd die in an alley.

Wanda had seen it happen, had seen the results. Cinderella and Sugar used to whore for Jay Cee, and look at them now. Burnouts, only a few years older than she was and already limping like wounded animals toward death. The only way they could make any money was by pimping some younger, fresher girl, the way they'd pimped Wanda when she was new in town.

Well, not anymore. She was through working for Cindy and Sugar, and she wasn't going to work for Jay Cee or anyone else.

I'm an independent contractor, she thought.

She liked that term: independent contractor. She'd heard

t once on some TV show, and it had stuck with her, as her idea of a good thing to be.

To preserve her independence, she had fled Hollywood, taking an RTD bus, getting off a mile south of the airport in this seaside town wedged between El Segundo and Manhattan Beach.

There was no particular reason why she'd chosen to stop here, except that the town had looked tacky enough to provide her with business opportunities, yet small enough not to ruin her prospects with undue competition. She'd had high hopes about the tricks she could turn, the money she could pull in, the new freedom that would be hers.

And now, on only her second night, she'd been busted. Fantastic.

As the car continued north, the scenery improved. No more boarded-up windows; sheets of plate glass glowed like giant picture tubes, showing frozen images of the luxury on display inside. Pool halls and cheap motels gave way to boutiques and beauty parlors. Couples sipped drinks at outdoor cafes. A crowd of young people in stonewashed jeans milled around outside the entrance to a movie theater under a rippling banner of marquee lights.

The town was nicer than she'd realized. She hadn't seen this section before. Hadn't had any reason to see it. This neighborhood was too upscale for her. But just wait. Someday she would have money. A rich john would marry her, or she would open her own escort service—and, count on it, she would treat her girls better than Cindy and Sugar had treated her.

Anyway, something would happen, something good. She was still young, only seventeen. She had time to work out the details.

A complex of one-story white-brick buildings, bracketed by windmill palms, slid into view. In front was a lighted sign: CORONA BEACH CIVIC CENTER. As the car drove past, she saw a glass-walled lobby, a uniformed cop at a desk. The police station.

Slowly the station receded, passing out of sight.

"Think you missed your stop," she said politely. Her mom had raised her to be courteous, and the lesson had stuck.

The cop didn't answer, just kept driving.

Jeez, he must be tanked. But maybe that was okay. If he was obviously drunk, he couldn't charge her with soliciting, could he?

Of course he could. Cops could do añything. Cops were like God.

The car hooked west, coasted downhill a few blocks, and turned onto a two-lane road that ran along a high bluff overlooking the sea.

A cookout fire burned on the beach. Glittery screams of laughter rose over the crash and drag of the surf. In the distance a carousel flashed like a diamond on the long finger of the Corona Beach Pier, extending into the black waters of the bay.

Wanda watched the pier through the rear window till a bend in the road swept it from sight. Then there was nothing but the dark sea and the empty road and the moonless sky, and as the car rolled on, engine humming tunelessly, she began to be afraid.

"Hey, mister . . . you *are* a cop, right?"

"Sure I am."

There was an edge of malicious humor in his voice, and she wasn't sure if his answer was serious or not.

Now that she thought about it, she hadn't gotten much of a look at that badge. Could have been a fake. You could buy one in a novelty store for five dollars.

"You running me out of town?" she asked, almost hoping the answer would be yes. "It's okay with me if you are. Just drop me off at a bus station." Actually she would have to go back to her hotel for her things, but she wasn't about to admit that.

"Really. Get me on a bus, and I'm gone."

"Yeah." His soft chuckle frightened her. "You're gone all right."

"I . . . I wasn't looking for any trouble."

"Maybe I was, though. Ever think of that?"

A beating rhythm filled her head. It took her a moment to realize that she was hearing the sound of her heart in her ears.

She tried to figure out what this guy was after. If he wanted a freebie, all he had to do was ask. He could park on any side street and she would show him a good time right here in the backseat.

No, that couldn't be it. There was no need to drive this far from the center of town for that kind of action. Unless he had something else in mind. Something she might not want to go along with.

With her hands manacled behind her, she couldn't use her nails. Couldn't do anything.

She tugged at the handcuffs. The cold metal rings chewed her wrists like hungry mouths.

In Hollywood she'd heard stories of girls picked up on the street to be found, later, feeding flies in a Dumpster or an abandoned car. Working outcall had been safer, but there'd been no money in it. Cindy and Sugar had taken everything, including her cut.

The money seemed meaningless now. She wondered why it had ever been a consideration.

She thought there was a good chance this man meant to rape and kill her. The rape part wouldn't be so bad, not much worse than what she did on the job every damn night, but the dying would be tough. She wasn't ready for that.

If she died, if the police found her body, they would have to call her mom. How much would they tell her? Would they say she'd been a whore?

Her mom still thought Wanda had a regular job. If she found out the truth, she might slash her wrists again, and this time Wanda wouldn't be there to call 911, wouldn't be there to save her from bleeding to death on the kitchen floor.

She hoped the cops had enough sense to lie, to say she'd been hit by a bus or something.

A spin of the steering wheel, a hiss of brakes. The car pulled into a dark side road and slowed to a crawl.

She stared out the side windows, drawing quick shallow breaths. Dark humps of hills crowded the left side of the narrow road. On the right stretched an unfenced field. The dim outline of a building, large and featureless and functional, hovered in the far distance, blurred by mist.

Nobody around. No people, no traffic.

She pulled harder at the cuffs, knowing it was useless to try working her hands free, trying anyway.

Now the car was easing off the road onto a dirt shoulder edged by a gray waste of weeds. Motion stopped. The engine died. In the abrupt stillness she heard a faraway hum, a faint, steady throb, like an echo of her speeding pulse. It came from the building, a power-plant sound.

The driver's-side door creaked open. Crush of footsteps on dirt. Squeal of hinges, sigh of shocks: the rear door swinging wide.

The man leaned in, his face half-lit by the yellow ceiling bulb. She saw his eyes. They were glazed and dead now. No personality registered in their glassy emptiness. It was as if a switch had been flipped, shutting off the person he had been, leaving only a programmed machine.

A psycho—Christ, he's not just drunk, he's some kind of nut . . .

Cold rippled over her. Buzzing panic thrummed in her brain.

She shrank from him. His hand closed over her arm. Roughly he hauled her out of the car, threw her down on her knees. A jolt of pain slammed through her, and she heard herself whimper.

"Please, mister, please don't hurt me. Cut me a break, okay?"

No reply.

He popped the trunk lid, lifting out a duffel bag. Rummaged in it, found a pair of black leather gloves, and pulled them on. His actions unnaturally deliberate, the expressionless pantomime of a sleepwalker.

"Come on, talk to me. I don't like you being so quiet all of a sudden. Say something, will you, say something to me."

The trunk lid slammed shut. A bang like a gunshot.

She watched him, wishing she knew what to say.

He shrugged the duffel bag over his shoulders, then leaned down, reaching for her. She spun onto her back and kicked. He caught hold of her flailing feet and held on as she twisted and screamed.

She shook loose one foot, pistoned a kick at his midsection. He grunted, doubling over. She kicked again; he sidestepped the attack. Her shoe spun off and spiraled into the tall weeds beyond the car.

He spoke one word. *"Bitch."*

Red heat flushed his face. His nostrils dilated; he blew a snort of air. Clutching his stomach, he circled her, his mouth chewing soundless curses.

Two quick steps closed the distance between them. His

foot went up, smashed down, stomping on her collarbone. A hard, solid thud of impact, a wet snap, a sunburst of pain.

Static rose in her ears, and she went away.

Her next awareness was of a series of bumps and jolts and a cloud of choking dust. He was dragging her off the road into the field. Thorns and brambles caught at her clothes, sliced her skin.

He pulled her into a muddy ditch strewn with burst trash bags. Somebody had been dumping garbage here. Glass shards and rusted cans spilled through rents in the green plastic.

He let go of her, then lifted the duffel bag off his back and began pawing through it again.

She lay stunned, winded, waves of pain broadcast in widening circles from her collarbone. It occurred to her that she would never be rich now. Never be anything.

All wrong," she murmured as her eyelashes fluttered against a burning rush of tears. "Turned out all wrong."

She might as well have stayed in L.A., gone to work for Jay Cee, stuck the needle in her arm. Might as well have ended up like Cinderella, like Sugar, wearing makeup to cover the lines in her young-old face, aimlessly prowling the boulevards, a gaunt apparition in cast-off clothes.

From the bag the man removed a small limp thing. He thrust it in her face.

"See this?" His voice was flat, barely managing the lilt of a question. "See it?"

Red curls, sewn smile, floppy stuffed limbs. A Raggedy Ann doll.

She thought of her favorite stuffed animal, Penny the Penguin, the friend from her childhood who had made the great trip west with her, the trip ending tonight.

"This is you," he said. It seemed important to him that she understand. He repeated the words, enunciating clearly. "This is you."

"Me," she agreed. She had no strength to argue.

"You," he said, nodding, smiling, pleased to find her a quick study, and then he gripped the doll's head with both hands and wrenched it halfway off, a rush of cottony fibers spilling out, the doll's eyes staring wide and lidless, the fixed smile abruptly grotesque like the gape of a corpse.

He tore off the head and savaged the doll, stripping it o
arms and legs, pouring out clumps of stuffing, until onl
flaps of ripped fabric remained.

"You," he said again, holding up the remnant of the dol
like a scrap of some small animal's hide.

Tears watered her world like a hard downpour. Wanda
shut her eyes and went home, back to the two-bedroom
apartment where she had lived with her mom for the firs
sixteen years of her life. She found her mother in one o
her good moods, not blue, not crazy, and hugged her tight
so glad to see her again. She didn't let go even when the
pain started, even when she felt the excruciating pops o
broken bones in her face and chest.

There were screams but she didn't hear them. No one
heard them but the man with the badge and, at the Phae
thon Waste Disposal Facility a quarter-mile away, a security
guard who paused to listen to the faint, shrill cries, the
shrugged.

Wind must have shifted, he decided. You could hea
some drunken kids carrying on down at the beach.

The thought reminded him of a girls' volleyball game he'
watched in Manhattan Beach last weekend. As he patrolled
the incinerator complex, restlessly fingering his utility belt
he remembered the players' olive legs, their oiled backs
their buttocks so tight and firm.

When he listened again, a short while later, he heard no
sound but the dull, pulsing roar of the furnaces, ceaselessly
disposing of the city's vast waste.